Love's Joy

By

Emil Toth

ISBN: 978-1-970024-72-2

DEDICATION

This book is dedicated to everyone bringing joy to people they know intimately and casually by letting them know they love them. I've found it amazing how my day changes when someone shares the words, *I love you* with me or I with them. For those who have, I want to say thank you and bless you. Love and hugs to all of you.

ET

CONTRIBUTORS

The generous contributions from my dear friends and family have made the *LOVE* series become a reality. I hope the goodness and love in these novels matches what is in their hearts.

BELIEVERS

Barbara Gatto
Suzanne Gibbons
Kelley Kelsey
Peter & Ruth Toth
Peg Weed

CONCEIVERS

Margaret Carmen
Joseph Gatto & Yvonne Hering
Joyce Hug
Phillip Rice & Mona Johnson
Joseph Warner & Lindy Warner

ADVOCATES

Catherine Lanigan & Jed Nolan
Ron & Patti Sikorski
Karen Sommers
Sheryl Toth

SUSTAINERS

Fred Colantonio
Jessica Dieter
Lindsay Dieter
Linda Jacobs
Mary Gatto
Cindy Gast
Brian Gibbons
Kayla Gibbons
John & Linda Hardy
Sally & Bob Milewski
James Pauley
Sally Schreiber
Gus & Teresa Thanos
James & Michele Toth
Rosemarie Turner

ACKNOWLEDGMENTS

I wish to thank my muse, Suzanne Gibbons for her love, encouragement, ideas, criticisms and editing.

BOOKS BY EMIL TOTH

FORGIVENESS SERIES

Seven Souls on a Cross
Release from the Cross

LOVE SERIES

Love's Transformation
Love's Sacrifice
Love's Wisdom
Love's Ancients
Love's Courage
Love's Joy
Love's Beloved

BOOKS CAN BE PURCHASED AT

emiltoth.com
amazon.com
barnesandnoble.com
lulu.com

INTRODUCTION

LOVE'S JOY represents the sixth book in the dramatic, inspirational and spiritual *LOVE* series. The first five books focus on the stages of love: transformation, sacrifice, wisdom, enlightenment and courage. I have again expanded my understanding of *LOVE* to include *JOY.* In this book, I introduce people transforming lives by sharing their joy and demonstrating it in their lives.

For those to whom it may be of interest, while the *LOVE* series of books are works of fiction, the stated philosophy of the Talker Healers in each book is an expression of my belief system. Most of the emotional, physical and spiritual events in the books have been experienced, to a lesser or greater degree, by myself and a few friends and teachers.

Over the years, I have sat down at the computer thousands of times to share my thoughts and feelings going into my novels. My anticipation ran high each time. The novels have exceeded my expectations. I believe it happened because I was in the right spiritual energy. I wish to thank those in physical and non-physical form who helped keep me in that sacred energy all these years.

ET

CHAPTER ONE

"You are crazy saying all those things," screamed Brock. "The gods will surely strike you dead, if you continue being sacrilegious. Our council was insane to let you be High Priest and allow you to change everything to suit yourself. Our people were safe and content with Romir as High Priest. You will never match up to him. He was a true High Priest."

Brock's face was an angry red. Even his conspicuous ears were inflamed.

Kaathi gave Brock one of her most endearing smiles. "My dear Brock."

He angrily waved his arm. "Stop calling me dear."

"I am sorry. I have to say I hope I never match up to Romir. He was not as good as you have led yourself to believe. I would like to talk about your gods for a moment, Brock. According to Romir, when you behaved, the weather behaved and when the weather turned ugly he blamed it on some of you not doing what he or your religion desired. If someone was killed by a predator, he jumped on the opportunity to claim the person had not followed the precepts of their religion. It was his way of putting fear into your hearts and his way of controlling you."

"I do not believe you," Brock yelled.

"The weather and environment have always gone through cycles in its evolution. Some people have chosen to associate natural disasters with people's behavior or temperament. It is easy to see connections when there were correlations.

"If you have been listening, I have never spoken of Creator in those terms. I have always maintained the only thing Creator desires for you is to love yourself and others. In the loving, you will attain happiness."

"You are a crazy woman," Brock yelled back. "It is an impossible task. There are too many angry and deceitful people. Your philosophy is a Pollyanna one and cannot work."

"You are correct. My philosophy will never work for you, if you are fearful, angry and deceitful, however if you shed those qualities, you will be open to discover love and happiness. The Spiritual Awakening Services and the Relationship Sessions are designed to remove your prejudices and change your view of life and your opinions about Creator and how to conduct your relationships with family and friends.

Not knowing how to defend his position, Brock's voice turned vicious. "Mark my word Kaathi, you will be dead by the end of the rainy season."

During the rainy season, Brock and twenty men attended the services for the singular reason to disrupt the proceedings with their derogatory comments. Kaathi answered all their questions and ignored their derogatory remarks. The men grew discouraged because they could not upset her. Brock along with the other men who had been verbally abusive and disruptive stopped coming the moment the rainy season ended.

The gods had failed them.

Kaathi was still alive.

The High Priest, Kaathi, concluded the Spiritual Awareness Service and people were disbursing. Ashlee and Scarlet had contributed some of their knowledge via personal stories to the congregants. The two had been apprentices to the High Priest, Kaathi, since Kaathi came back from Sumati, where she had introduced the Relationship Sessions to the Sumatians. Ashlee's nature was introspective and she set her sights on the devotional path to Creator and rarely spoke during the services. Ashlee had suffered as a slave to the mutant, Ezra, and escaped after eighteen years. She fled and was found by Kaathi and saved from death. When she recovered her health and weight, people told her how beautiful she was, which surprised her because the mutants only criticized and cursed her. Her blonde hair stood out like a beacon among everyone. Setting her apart even more from other women was her breathtaking beauty. Women would have hated her had it not been she was oblivious of her looks. She treated everyone with kindness and love. For her it was a pleasure to be surrounded by non-mutants or Normals as the mutants called them.

Scarlet, on the other hand, was interested in serving people and was comfortable with the cause and effect path to Creator. Had Scarlet not been married to Jacob, every woman would be worried her man would chase after Scarlet. Her eyes were beckoning and drew men to her like ants to honey. She was sultry and sexy looking, though her personality was in direct contrast to those attributes. Even her voice caressed anyone she spoke to. Whenever Kaathi relinquished the floor to Scarlet, she thrived in sharing what she learned from Kaathi to everyone who came to the Spiritual Awakening Services.

Kaathi, Ashlee and Scarlet stood outside the meeting lodge after the service to hug people wanting to be embraced. Jacob had been closely watching Scarlet and Ashlee during the service. He was fortunate to be married to both women who were Kaathi's apprentices. His eyes shone with pride. Keri, his first wife, his son Zar and his daughter, Katiya, sat next to him and shared the same pride.

Jacob and Kaathi had been close friends since Kaathi became an apprentice to Batu, the Talker Healer. Jacob had served on the council as the Warrior Hunter for several years before Kaathi took over as the Talker Healer upon Batu's murder. Jacob was handsome and a half head taller than most men in the village. He was confident, strong, agile and had great reasoning powers without being arrogant or overbearing, thus he was extremely likable. His skill with the bow and arrow was legendary, as was his strength.

The services under Romir and Kiirt, the previous High Priests, was mandatory. Attendance to the Spiritual Awakening Service was not mandatory consequently only a few hundred were attending the services. Scarlet and Ashlee saw it had no effect on

Kaathi's enthusiasm, while she shared her message of love. The messages were little more than stories and suggestions on how the congregants could enrich their lives. The stories touched the hearts of the attendees and endeared them to her. She ended her service with a quiet moment of peace, which she stretched out each service. Those attending appreciated the lack of pressure and religious threats. In spite of people enjoying the new approach to religion those not coming were happy they were not forced into attending. The attendance grew by word of mouth. They came and willingly shared how good it felt to attend. Consequently, there were a dozen new members at each service. One of the contributing reasons those attending the services liked coming were the hugs they received from either, Kaathi, Scarlet or Ashlee before and after the service. Some of the congregation made certain to receive an embrace from all three. The lines to receive embraces from Kaathi were triple the size of her apprentices. Some attributed Kaathi's long lines to the fact she was a Kahali native and her apprentices were not. Others more cognizant of how her hugs made them feel always chose to hug Kaathi. As Kaathi embraced each person, she sincerely told them she loved them and she sent them her love. Over half the people said they loved her in return. The apprentices had not yet reached the point where they could honestly say they loved everyone they hugged and their love was not as encompassing as the mystic's. Ashlee had made it a point to watch Kaathi and noticed her eyes brimmed with tears as she shared her words of love.

Everyone was gone and Scarlet took the opportunity to remark to Kaathi, "The last five services where pleasant without Brock and his bunch."

Kaathi nodded, saying, "I agree, though I have a sense Brock, in his confusion, will come to us and challenge us in a more intimate setting."

Ashlee giggled. "I miss him. It was fun seeing his face get all red when he could not upset you."

Kaathi smiled warmly at her apprentices. "Would either of you like to join me at Taja's sacred spot?"

Both smiled and took her hands.

"So what did you think of the man's remark concerning the monsters of hell?"

Ashlee was only partially aware of Kaathi talking. She was sensing the love pulsating as she held the mystic's hand.

Scarlet, being the more mental one, eagerly answered, "I liked how you explained to him the devils and monsters of hell will exist as long as there are people contributing to their existence by believing in them. He seemed shocked to hear they were creations of our fear. How did you know it was so?"

"I discovered it during one of my visits to the Land of No Shadows. These four ghastly creatures appeared and were tormenting me for no reason. I was startled. Once I recovered, I told them I did not believe in them and they shriveled into themselves."

Scarlet knew her mentor's belief was effective only because the strength of her belief. They arrived at Taja's favorite meditation spot on the bank of the river, where he had been bludgeoned to death. Kaathi and Batu had detected what took place and returned to the spot dozens of times to cleanse the area of the negative energy and bring it back to its original purity.

The trio sat down to meditate. Ashlee could not keep her eyes off Kaathi. Her eyes were clouded by tears. She reveled in the love she felt emanating from her mentor. She felt the facade of Kaathi's individuality disappear. In its place she sensed the spirit of all the women in the world. Her heart swelled with love. . . A long while later the sensation passed and she sensed the spirit of the Divine Mother, the Creator of the universe. . . She was unable to contain the enormous love she felt and sobbed. She covered her face with her hands and continued sobbing as she experienced Divine Love. Ashlee's exaltation lasted a long time, accompanied by her sobs.

When the sobbing stopped, she removed her hands wiped the tears from her face and gazed at Kaathi. Seeing Kaathi smiling, she smiled. She knew she would never leave Kaathi's side and if asked would follow her to the ends of Mother Earth. She had never experienced such love and wanted to experience it again and again.

There was a sense of awe in Ashlee's voice. "I had a strong, loving connection with you early on in my meditation. I could not close my eyes. The tears kept trickling down my cheeks. I could not take my eyes off you. At some point, you disappeared and became every woman in the world. The sense of who you are expanded and you became the Divine Mother, Creator of the universe. I could not contain all the love pouring into me and I burst into sobs. What I felt as I sobbed can only be described by using the word AWE. I cannot use any other words to explain what I felt. What was it I felt?"

"My precious one, you were blessed. The AWE you felt was the Creator within me. Creator is present in you and Scarlet and everyone although not felt by many."

Nobody spoke for a long while. Forever the pragmatic, Scarlet's curiosity got the best of her. "Will Ashlee's experience add to the energy of this place?"

"It shall. Everything people do in any given area contributes to the energy balance be it positive experiences or negative ones."

"When you and Batu cleansed this area how did you go about it?"

"We started at the outer most limits where we initially felt negative energy. We meditated and prayed at the spot for days until it changed. When we felt the change we moved in closer to where he was bludgeoned. Once we felt the negativity we again meditated and prayed to cleanse the energy. We repeated the process and kept moving in closer and closer until we were upon the spot he was killed and cleansed the area as well."

"Did you spend a lot of time doing it?"

"It took us a complete cycle of the moon. When we were not tending to the ills and wounds of the villager's we spent the rest of every day praying until the environment was free of the negative taint."

"Did you eat your meals there?"

"No. When we were in the negative zone we maintained a prayerful presence."

"Could I sense what took place here, if I concentrated on it?"

"You could. It would benefit you more to keep your mind focused on Creator or on your ministry or on your new family and others you love."

CHAPTER TWO

Durga and Leah were strolling outside the village of Kahali. Durga was in his late teens when Leah first saw him on the savannah three years ago. His mutant tribe, the Wanderers, attacked Evette and Gene. Two days later they were about to do the same to Kaathi's party. The mystic had talked privately to Carch, the mutant leader, and evaded disaster.

Durga had matured physically and emotionally, in the last three years. He was comfortable living among the Normals of Kahali. Having a Normal mother and a mutant father, the mutations he bore were not as severe as they were on Leah. The most prominent mutations were his deeply slanted forehead, which contributed to his overhanging brow, his strange looking toes and the occasional, wild, sporadic patches of body hair. When Leah had first saw him with the mutant scouting party, he was sick and could not continue the march with the Wanderers. Consequently, he was left behind to be tended to by Kaathi. For a long time, Durga was hurt by the slurs of some people in the village. With Kaathi's guidance, he slowly learned how to handle adversity and overcome anger.

Leah was a full breed mutant, of the Searcher tribe, and her body was stouter than Durga's. Her arms and legs were thicker as was her torso and neck. Her head and body had more patches of hair than Durga and her facial features were more pronounced. Leah's eyes were intelligent and expressive and she was able to communicate telepathically and orally in three languages and could sign. She had a moderate sized lump on her back, and her right arm was in proportion to her body, while the other was thinner. Her toes bore signs of being broken or disfigured and her gait was not as fluid as Durga's, though in a sustained march she could best him.

Durga took her hand. "Have you given any more thought to us living together?"

"I have. I have also weighed what people would say about us living together and not being married."

"I do not care. These are not our people. They adopted us as we did them. They have said disparaging things about me before and I have withstood them."

"It is not how I want to start our relationship. We need to do things conventionally. We are fortunate we can claim this as our home. I would not want to jeopardize what inroads we have made by angering them. If we are to stay here, I want to be married by Kaathi. There was a time when Isaac and I thought we wanted to live with the Wanderers in spite of how barbaric they were. We were fortunate we met Kaathi and never had live to with the Wanderers"

"We have been put together. Neither my people nor yours ever had marriage ceremonies. In spite of it, I will do anything to make you happy, Leah. I will exchange vows with you anytime. When do you want to do it?"

"During the Kahali marriage ceremonies."

"So it shall be."

Durga leaned in to kiss Leah. She returned his kiss and he took her in his arms and held her while he kept kissing her. While he was kissing her, he was thinking how wonderful it was going to be to create a baby.

Their wait for the marriage ceremony was not long. It took place the next full moon. Kaathi performed the marriages for thirty-two Kahali native couples and Durga and Leah. It was the first time mutants took part in the marriage ceremony and there were many residents who were troubled and many unwilling to hide their displeasure. Leah and Durga were happy and did not pay any attention to the small heartedness of the narrow-minded.

Their relationship grew stronger and to Durga's delight, Leah was eager to procreate. She missed bleeding for the third cycle of the moon and elected not to share the good news until she was showing she was pregnant.

Kaathi and Leah were spending time together practicing telepathic communication and Kaathi projected a baby to Leah. The mutant opened her eyes and saw Kaathi had hers open as well.

"Do you prefer bringing a boy or girl into the world?"

Leah shook her head saying, "I knew I would not be able to hide the fact I was with child from you. I would like to have a boy first and then a girl."

Kaathi's eyes twinkled. "Their births shall be on the same day."

"I have never heard of children having the same birth day years apart."

Kaathi smiled. "Nor have I. They will not be in different years. You are carrying twins."

"What? Are you certain? No mutant has ever given birth to twins."

"You shall be the first."

"I wish they were Isaac's children," Leah reflected sadly.

"I am sorry he is dead. I agree it would have been fantastic for the two of you. He is deceased, and you have to be in the present moment. You have a great man in Durga. He dearly loves you and will be a wonderful father."

"I know but. . ."

"No buts Leah. You must live in the present and appreciate the gift you have in Durga."

Leah looked guilty. "You are right. I cannot make Isaac come back. Durga is my present and future.

"On my, I never thanked you for telling me we were going to have twins. Durga will be ecstatic over the news. I am going to ask him if we can name the girl after you."

"You honor me Leah."

"I would like to name the boy Isaac. The trouble is I am not sure how Durga would react."

"Might I suggest you let him name the boy? I think it would make your bond stronger."

Leah looked away for a short while and returned. "You are right. Thank you for bringing it to my attention."

Kaathi touched Leah's arm. She looked deep into Leah's eyes. "It is wonderful how I knew the moment we communicated using our minds we would be friends for all our lives. You have been a blessing to me, my dear."

They embraced and told each other of their love.

Leah eagerly walked home to tell Durga the good news.

CHAPTER THREE

The young woman called hesitantly at the entrance to the Talker Healer's hut. The pleasant looking woman wore her tightly curled hair extremely short. Her bulging eyes showed great concern. Kaathi appeared and ushered her inside and noticed the woman had a slight limp caused by her shorter left leg.

"My name is Shamar," she announced. "My man, Namandi, is having seizures."

"Does he have any other symptoms?"

"He vomited a few days ago, and his left arm has not worked right for several days."

"Mara would you stay here while Marie and I go with Shamar?"

"Of course."

Shamar led them to her house and introduced them to her husband, who was lying on his cot. Namandi said nothing. He had his head turned to one side and did not turn it with the introduction.

"Namandi, have you injured your neck?"

He slowly turned his head and answered, "No, my head. . . I was in a fight. . . after being hit,. . .I fell backward. . . and smacked my head on a rock."

"May I look at it?"

He sat up and Kaathi checked out the injury as Marie looked on. As he was about to recline, he was gripped by a seizure. Shamar fearfully cried out. Kaathi and Marie held him to prevent him from injuring himself. After it ended, he opened his eyes. "It happened again. . . did it not?"

"Yes. How long has this been going on?"

He looked at his wife for verification. "Fifteen days. . . What is wrong with me?"

"I think you have blood seeping into your head and it is causing pressure and seizures along with your arm problems and vomiting."

As Marie listened, she remembered a year ago three hunters were killed by rogue elephants. Kaathi had requested the men be brought to the healer's hut, where the families could pay their respects. After they did, Kaathi asked the families if she could examine the bodies to gain knowledge of how they functioned prior to burying them on the river. The families slowly acquiesced and Kaathi carefully examined the bodies. As she did, she conveyed to Marie what she was doing and what she discovered. Marie remember her mentor removed a leather bag from the top most shelf in the healing hut. Inside it was another oiled skin containing well-oiled tools she had never seen. Kaathi explained they were tools from the Era of Destruction and she used them in examinations. She showed them to her and named the drill and bits, pliers, chisel, hammer, saw, tongs and a variety of surgical knives and probes. All were constructed from the finest stainless steel, which resisted corrosion. Kaathi examined the deceased man's exposed brain. Using the tools, she removed the rest of the skull to reveal the brain. Marie had never seen a brain and did not know it had folds and it was contained in a sack-like membrane. Namadi's voice brought her back to the present.

"Bleeding inside my head?"

"Yes."

"Can I get well?

"I will have to remove the pressure."

"How?"

"I will have to drill a small hole where you bumped your head and let the blood seep out."

Namandi's eyes widened. "No, no, I will die."

"No, you will not," Kaathi assured him.

"It will surely hurt."

"No."

"I do not believe you can do it."

"I can only if you trust me. Do you trust me?"

"How can I? My head is killing me and this is the first time I have talked to you. You scare the hell out of me, talking about drilling a hole in my head. It is insane."

He looked at his wife for help.

She looked at Kaathi. "Give us a moment."

The healer motioned to her apprentices and they left.

Shamar took her husband's hand.

"I cannot think straight anymore. Help me."

"All I can tell you is I do not want to lose you."

"I know and I do not want to die. Can you believe the woman wants to put a hole in my head?"

"She says it will help."

"Easy for her to say. I am the one who will die."

Namandi looked at his wife skeptically. "Would you do it?"

"I do not know."

Shamar bent and kissed his forehead. Tears accumulated in her eyes. She stood upright, and he saw the tears.

"Shit, shit, shit! Hold me. I am scared."

She bent down, rested her head next to his, laid her breast on him and held his shoulders. Her tears wet the side of his face. He touched her cheek. "Tell her to come in."

"You decided?"

"Yes."

She called for them. The trio of healers appeared.

"If it were just me I would say go to hell, but I am not alone. Drill your hole, and do not botch this."

"You have no need to worry. I have done this procedure several times."

A bit of confidence returned to him. "Did they all live?"

"I did it on the men who were killed by the rogue elephants."

"What?!? That is not reassuring me."

"I have the utmost confidence in myself, and you shall do fine."

Namadi looked pleadingly at his wife for reassurance.

She closed her eyes and nodded.

"I do not seem to have a choice."

"If we do not release the pressure, you will continue to suffer, and it will likely kill you in a short while."

Namandi eyes widened again. "How soon will it take my life?"

"It can be tomorrow or in the next moon cycle."

"Once again, it seems I do not have a choice."

"I am sorry."

"If I do this. ..will I live?"

"Of course and your chances are good your problems will be gone."

"When do you want to do this?"

"Now."

The answer surprised Namandi. His eyes found his wife. *If I do nothing, I will suffer and have a short life. I am too young to die. I do not want to leave Shamar.*

"Very well."

"We need to go to my hut to perform the operation."

Shamar helped her man up and the healers helped him make the journey to their hut. On arriving, Kaathi nodded toward the door. "Shamar, will you wait outside?"

"If I must," she stammered and went to kiss and hug her husband. She exited and anxiously sat on the bench outside the hut.

Kaathi instructed Mara to take down the surgical instruments and spread them out on a table and boil water. Mara removed the bag and laid the instruments out. Kaathi selected a probe, two small bits and the hand drill and wiped them clean of oil and used the antiseptic myrrh to further cleanse the device and her hands. She took the drill, probe and bits and went out to the fire and set them in the water and told Mara, "Let the water boil a while and bring the bowl in and remove the tools with the tongs."

Back in the hut, she looked at Namadi. "While Marie shaves and cleans your head, I am going to have you meditate in order for you not to feel a thing. While you are meditating, I will make a small hole in your head and let the blood drain. Do you understand?"

"Yes."

"Good."

Kaathi had him shift so the bottom of his head was supported by the table and allow her access to the injury.

"I want you to close your eyes and focus your attention on my voice, and do exactly as I tell you."

She took her time and helped him achieve a deep state of meditation. She looked at the area Marie had shaved and cleaned with myrrh and approved it. Mara came into the hut with the bowl containing the tools. She removed them with the tongs she cleaned and set them on a clean cloth on the table.

"To know exactly where to drill we must go deep within ourselves and ask for the exact spot."

The three healers moved to a deeper center of consciousness and asked for the exact spot to make the hole. A while later they exited meditation with their answers. They conferred and had arrived at the same conclusion.

Marie and Mara watched as Kaathi drilled into the skull. The mystic was confident for she, Mara and Marie had practiced it many times on the skulls of the three men battered to death by the rogue elephants. She drilled part way through the bone and stopped.

"I am about halfway through the bone. Would you clean out the hole and the bit by irrigating them?"

Marie used the bulbous syringe and squirted boiled, cooled water into the hole until she was assured it was free of any bone fragments. Marie carefully cleaned the bit with the bulbous syringe. Kaathi continued drilling until she felt no resistance. She withdrew the bit.

"I have gone through the bone and am at the brain membrane. You can irrigate the hole again."

Marie did and stopped when she was certain all of the bone fragments were washed out of the hole.

"Now I am going to use the probe and gently cut through the membrane and let the blood drain out."

She felt a resistance and applied more pressure and felt the probe move through the tissue. Blood immediately flowed from the hole into a small bowl.

She breathed a sigh of relief and smiled at Marie and Mara. "The next time we do this you two are going to do it."

Long after the blood had drained, Kaathi picked up the slightly tapered ivory plug cleaned it with myrrh and set it upon the hole only to find it was a little too big. Using a small, sharp knife she skillfully scrapped some of the plug away. Rinsing the plug and her hand in the cooled boiled water, she used myrrh to further cleanse it. She set the plug to the hole and smoothly moved it in. It resisted going further at about the halfway point. She used the hammer and gently tapped it in to secure it and wiped a drop of myrrh onto the surgical area to cleanse it.

Marie and Mara carefully observed every movement their mentor made and felt confident, if called upon, they could replicate the procedure.

Kaathi brought Namandi out of meditation.

"How are you feeling?"

"Okay. It was strange, as I got into meditation your voice got further and further away. The next thing that occurred, I could not smell anything. Then I could not hear you at all. I never felt any pain."

"Good."

Marie called Shamar in and told her, "Everything went well. Take this vile of myrrh home and apply one drop of it to where we put the plug in his skull for the next ten days."

Kaathi squeezed Namandi's hand. "You are going to be fine."

"Thank you healer."

Shamar touched the mystic's arm. "Yes, thank you. How can we repay you?"

"Love each other and those you know. And we will take hugs from both of you."

CHAPTER FOUR

The deep shadows of dawn gave way to the Great Sun's rise. Streaks of sunlight broke through the forest foliage. Birds were singing and squawking to announce their intentions and mark their territories. Mara, Ashlee, Marie, Scarlet, Jacob and Sharika were seated in a semi-circle in front of Kaathi at Taja's meditation site. Marie had finished sharing how she had been severely injured by a cheetah and saved from death by a Kahali patrol party, which protected the village and rid the area of predators. She shared how she was administered to by Kaathi who knew she was a gifted healer and showed Marie how she could assist in healing her wounds. Remnants from the attack were the slightly raised keloid scars left behind by the cheetah. Shortly thereafter the incident Kaathi asked her to be her apprentice Talker Healer.

"I might add," said Kaathi, "Marie followed my instructions and healed herself. I know some of us have seen Mara do self-healing. Mara's experience with healing is different from people in other tribes. Mara, would you share how the Uchakwa clan taught you how to heal?"

The twenty-one year old diminutive, hairless woman smiled in response. The people in her clan were all physically similar. She was slender, round faced and dimpled on her right cheek. Her eyes were deep set and dark and her ears were tipped forward to better hear the sounds of the forest. Her hands were square and her feet wide. Her short stature gave most people the impression she was still a preteen. When she had first joined Kaathi, after her small band of warriors was killed, she was wary and timid. It was understandable since they had killed her friends and relatives. She was made welcome by Kaathi and quickly grew attached to the unpronounced leader of the group. Kaathi asked her to help Marie attend to the ill in Kahali. Mara lost her reserve personality quickly dealing with different people needing her help on a daily basis. Taking on those duties came about when Kaathi, Jacob, Evette and Gene accepted Chief Victor's invitation to share Kaathi's philosophy. They had left at the start of the sunny season and returned before the rainy season. Marie and Mara were left to attend to the ills of the villagers of Kahali. Evette and Gene had remained behind in Sumati to continue sharing the importance of relationships at the sessions and to further instruct Pico and Nan. In time the locals would take over instruction of the Sumatians.

There was no hesitation in Mara's voice. "Ever since I could remember things, I recall my parents and relatives healing their wounds and mine mentally. I was told to see wounds as being healed. As I grew up everyone around me tended to their own wounds, including broken bones, At times a family member or a relative would help younger children without being asked. It was as natural to help heal a friend as it was natural to help in the preparation of a meal."

"Was there any illness or injury your people could not heal?"

"None we could see or feel."

"How long did it take to mend a broken bone?"

"It depended upon the person. Some of us were better at it than others. I was one of the better ones and could heal a broken bone in the course of a few dozen breaths. Jacob broke my arm and Kaathi sensed I could heal the break and they watched as I did."

Sharika shook her head. "It is amazing. Since your people were such good healers, did they live longer than the people here in Kahali?"

"No."

"Why not?"

"I do not know," Mara truthfully answered. She looked to Kaathi for help.

"I believe her people died of internal illnesses before they knew how serious the illness was. Even the most gifted of healers and enlightened people are subject to die from an illness. There were ancient writings which indicated people lived for hundreds of years and yet they died. This would be a good time to remind you the length of your life is not as important as what you accomplish during your lifetime. Contributing to your happiness and others is essential. Your contribution to society and to yourself is important. Your spiritual growth is important. Your desire to be united with Creator is of utmost importance."

Kaathi looked at Ashlee. "You were captive for eighteen years by the mutants. You must have had many opportunities to witness how they tended to the sick."

"I did. They were conventional. They used poultices, oils and plants to combat wounds and illness. I never saw any of them work with energy as you, Mara and Marie do."

Kaathi addressed Sharika, "I know you and I have talked about how your people treated injuries and illnesses. Would you share it with the rest?"

"Of course. I wish I could tell you we are doing something exotic to heal each other. Unfortunately, I cannot contribute anything spectacular. We, like the mutants, are also conventional in our approach to healing. We had a shaman who treated the wounds of our hearts and minds."

Kaathi looked at Scarlet and waited for her to share.

"The Homarians were primitive in their approach to healing. King Edmund had a personal healer. Sadly I never heard how he treated any of Edmund's illnesses. The rest of the population was on their own, although there were a few people who were more cognizant of which plants were good for certain illnesses. When an illness would puzzle a family they would seek out someone more gifted to help them."

Kaathi looked at each one of her dear friends. "What is the one thing tying all of these healing methods together?"

"Belief. Without it no one would be healed," answered Ashlee. "When we see a plant eliminate an upset stomach or heal a rash enough times, it reinforces our understanding and it becomes a belief.

"Exactly, it is the same with our thoughts on healing. Belief is essential and prominent across a wide spectrum of our lives. It gives the universe, society and individuals order. We utilize a belief until we discover another more valid one and supplant it with the new one. In Mara's case she was indoctrinated by everyone around her to visualize the body as whole and healthy to eliminate whatever ailed her."

Jacob made a connection to what Kaathi was talking about and spoke, "Now I see why Taja insisted the children attend the Relationship Sessions. If you can reach a child's mind before it is tainted by everyone, they can be taught a loving way to relate to each other."

"Exactly," responded Kaathi enthusiastically, "although we are born into the world with some carry over or residual influences, from other lives, we are basically taught how to love or hate from everyone around us. We are also influenced by our body in good and bad ways. It is essential to nurture the proper qualities of character for a child. It should be engaged the moment the mother knows she is pregnant. If the nurturing is sufficient, it will overcome the other qualities and dominate the individual."

"Is there ever a time when it is not true?"

"Yes, our cells carry all of the elements to determine how we will look and properties for how our minds and bodies will function and react to challenges, people and events."

"Can you give us an example about how we will act?"

"Of course. What is contained in the cells of our bodies determines how we are able to comprehend and react to stimuli. It is different in each one of us. Most of us act in what we would call a normal way to most things we encounter. Yet others may have a propensity to be angry, short tempered, unable to concentrate or cannot manipulate the body as well as others. Some of us cannot understand certain things we are taught. Others may need a different way to be taught how to do numbers. We are all different from each other. The truth is we are a mixture or combination of what is in our mothers and fathers and it contributes to a variety of ways our mind and body functions. Most of the time the combination gives birth to something new, which can be refreshing or unfortunate for the child. Here again you might see how important it is to have relationship skills to combat the differences in people and thus reduce or eliminate prejudices and misunderstandings."

CHAPTER FIVE

Leah felt the contraction. She had given birth to her son seventeen years ago and was familiar with the sensations. Her son had died in a skirmish with the Homarians at the age of thirteen. He was forced to fight like a man for a third of his life. Her son died the same year they confronted Jacob and Kaathi. The two Normals quickly became friends and convinced them to live in their village. Isaac, the father of her deceased son, had given up his life to save her from the jaws of a lion, while on the journey to visit the Ancients. Her current husband, Durga, was left behind by the mutants to die. Kaathi took it upon herself to help him back to health and he became part of the group. Now, at the age of thirty-three she was about to give birth to twins.

Leah missed the intimate conversations she had with Isaac. Most of them were by looks, signing and mental images. Her conversations with Isaac were charged with intimacy. They were bound to be for they grew up together and knew everything about each other. Durga talked more than Isaac and rarely signed to communicate and was unable to master sending her images of what he wanted to say.

Leah never thought she would marry after losing Isaac. Durga was a half-breed, a combination of mutant and Normal. He was thirteen years her junior and not as fiercely protective as Isaac had been. The important thing was he loved her and treated her with respect. She would soon discover what kind of father Durga was going to be.

The contractions were closer together and stronger. She knew Durga had never assisted with a birth, consequently, she asked him to get Wahi, the birthing-mother. He returned shortly with Wahi. Durga went about heating water, while Wahi checked to see how close Leah was to giving birth. Wahi was short in stature and moved about with an efficiency of movement born from years of helping mothers give birth to their babies. She was a calming influence to mothers birthing their first child or the fourth. Much to her surprise the birth was imminent. She gave Leah instructions, which were unnecessary. Leah had been present at several births in her Searcher clan. Leah did not scream as most mothers did. She sweated, grimaced and pushed at the right times, with little coaxing from Wahi. The first twin appeared. It was a boy. It came out crying. Wahi showed Durga where to cut the umbilical cord, she tied it and cleaned the baby in the warm water and gave the naked child to the father. Leah birthed the baby girl a short while later. The baby needed encouragement to breathe and Wahi lightly smacked her tiny behind and got the baby to cry and breathe. She cut the cord, tied it and proceeded to clean the little girl baby, dry it and present it to the weeping mother.

"This has been the easiest birthing I have ever had the privilege of assisting," praised Wahi of Leah. "It was a marvelous experience. It is over and I feel elated and joyful. You should be proud. The babes look healthy."

The birthing-mother waited for the placenta to discharge. Leah's face twisted with pain. Her abdomen tightened. Wahi saw it and wondered what was happening. The whole village knew she was to birth twins and everything went as well as could be expected. What was possessing Leah's body? Leah was sweating from the pain. Wahi wished her mother was present to advise her. In all the years of helping women birth their children none of the mothers reacted like this after normal births.

Leah clamped her mouth shut to stay the scream. She felt a horrendous cramp and involuntarily pushed with all her strength.

Wahi was startled to see the diminutive discharge of a third baby. A blue baby. She caught it before it hit the floor. She immediately knew the baby was stillborn. Leah and Wahi stared at each other not believing a third child had appeared. It was so tiny it fit into one of Wahi's palms. She quickly cut the umbilical cord, wiped the child clean and laid it on Leah's chest. She took one of the other babies so Leah could hold the stillborn. Leah's emotions caught up with her and she wailed.

Durga had watched the joy and the agony of birth. He took his daughter from Wahi and let her wait for the placenta to discharge. He saw how small the last triplet was and instinctively knew there was no chance she would survive. The way Wahi shook her head it told him and Leah the child was stillborn.

The placenta came out, Wahi set it aside, cleaned Leah and the surrounding area up, wished the parents well and left. *This is the best job in the world except for when death claims a new born. Blyth should have been here to witness the joy and the sadness. It is not often she will see a stillborn, thank Creator.*

Wahi's daughter, Blyth, was eleven and next year she would be assisting her. Blyth would take over when she tired of birthing children.

It took a long time for Leah to look at Durga. "My heart is aching. Look how tiny she is." She wept silently for a short while. "Never in my wildest dreams did I think we had triplets. They are beautiful." She heaved a huge sigh. She was like all the Searcher mutant women. They were strong, practical and faced every setback philosophically. It was the way life was. Goodness sat next to sadness and they accepted it. Still, it was her child. She took a deep breath. She had grieved enough. The living needed her.

"I am thankful to Creator for giving us two beautiful babies. I am happy the twins are both well. This is one of the most joy filled days of my life."

Durga knew of this side of the mutants. He had seen it in the Wanderers time and again. The difference between the two mutant cultures was that the Searchers' expressed joy. Life went on and there was little time for grief.

He drew in a huge breath and asked, "Are you sticking with the names for them?"

"I am. Our daughter will be called Kati after Kaathi and our son's name will be Marcel after your father."

They heard Kaathi's voice call to them.

Durga pulled the drape aside and Kaathi entered. She gave him a quick hug and bent down to kiss Leah on the forehead and saw the stillborn cradled in her arm.

"I am so very sorry. I truly am. I did not have the heart to tell you."

"You told us we would have twins and you spoke the truth."

"Did you want to have the funeral tomorrow?"

"Yes."

"I shall let the others know."

"Thank you."

The mystic smiled. "I hope your joy overshadows your sadness."

"It does. . . It does. . . We mutants are taught to live in the moment. So I know my sadness will not last long. I cannot let it hold me hostage."

"Bless them for teaching it to you."

My, what darling children you have brought into the world. The birth of a child is always an auspicious and joyful day. I'm happy for both of you."

"Thank you for coming."

"The others are coming tomorrow. I will tell them of your triplet's death. They wanted to give you some rest before they fussed over you and the babies. May I hold my name sake?"

"Of course."

Kaathi reached down and gathered the precious little girl in her arms. She kissed the babe's cheeks. "I love how soft their skin is."

She showered the baby with love and soft words. "May I hold Marcel?"

Leah smiled and exchanged babies. Kaathi kissed tiny Marcel.

"Kaathi, would you bless them?"

"It would be my pleasure."

She laid Marcel in Leah's other arm. She rested her hands on the babies, sent them her love. "I thank you, Creator, for blessing Leah, Durga and the world with these two beautiful children. May these newborn twins give joy to their parents and they themselves know joy all through their lives. May they fulfill their destinies with love and gratitude. I shall pray for your stillborn until I fall asleep."

"Thank you."

Kaathi kissed the babies again, hugged Leah and Durga and happily left.

CHAPTER SIX

Mara and Marie worked alongside Kaathi non-stop from early morning until late afternoon tending to the injured and sick. A young man sat down on the bench outside the healer's hut and waited patiently for his turn to be received. Marie escorted a patient out of the hut and saw the man.

"Hello, I am Marie. Do you need help?"

"I am Yamen and I do. The small of my back has been giving me fits. I can barely do anything."

Marie knelt down behind Yamen.

"Do you mind if I set my hands on it."

"Why do you want to do it?"

"I am going to pray and send your back healing energy from Creator."

"I suppose you can do it."

"As I am doing it, I want you to concentrate on what you are feeling in your back and see if it will send you a message as to why it is hurting. Can you do it?"

"It seems stupid."

"It is not. Kaathi has found that the area bothering us can tell us why it is hurting if we listen."

"Is it true? Does it work?"

"It has in many cases."

"I will try anything to stop this pain."

"While I set my hands on you, I want you to feel the pain in your back and then stop thinking about it, still your mind and expectantly wait."

"That is it?"

"Yes."

Marie set her hands on his back, said her prayer, opened herself to Creator's healing energy and went into meditation. The young man had no problem feeling his pain. He did have trouble quieting his mind. When he did quiet it words tumbled into his mind and kept repeating themselves like rolling thunder. He was so eager to share what he heard he turned around and faced Marie, as she slowly came out of meditation.

"I am sorry, but I had to tell you. The words, 'I am not supported by my parents in whom I want to marry,' bounced around my head over and over."

"I am not surprised to hear you say it. The small of your back supports you as you stand tall. I am certain your backache is due to the lack of parental support."

"Are you sure?"

"As sure as the ache in your back. Once you accept their lack of support and strike out on your own it should disappear."

"I think it feels better already."

"It does not surprise me."

"Thank you, Marie."

"You are welcome."

"What do I owe you?"

"A hug now and a favor later."

Yamen smiled. "I can manage both."

A lull came and Kaathi sent Marie and Mara off to relax. They did not have to be told a second time. They hugged the mystic and scurried off to relax and cool themselves in the shallows of the river.

Coming up from ducking under the water, Marie turned to Mara. "I never asked if your people were ruled by a man."

"Our chief was a man."

"What was life like among the Uchakwa?" inquired Marie.

"As a child, I can remember my parents, grandparents, friends and neighbors all taking an interest in me and my education."

"Your education?"

"Yes, we learned through stories about animals, plants, history and our relations. In one way or another many of us were related. Our clan was small and every girl a few years older and younger was a playmate and friend. When I was old enough I was taken on trips through the jungle to learn which plant was good to eat and what the animals looked like and which ones to avoid or kill for food."

"Do you know why you are small?"

"My people never knew they were small until two adventurers entered our territory."

"Did your people question them about their size?"

"No. We killed them."

"Why?"

"Our forefathers saw them as invaders and a threat."

"Without talking to them how did they know?"

"They did not."

"Do you find it sad they did not talk to them?"

"I did. I think it was after their appearance my people questioned why we were small. They reasoned it was to blend into the jungle better. My ancestors told stories about people with hair on them like monkeys and apes. We thought it was a form of curse on them. The first time I saw the simian Stalkers was when we engaged Kaathi, Jacob and the Stalkers in our forest. The Stalkers frightened me the most. At the time I thought the stories about them fit well and assumed they were being punished for something they did. I thought they were ugly. All of them were killed in the skirmish except Gauri. As I got to know her, I was no longer terrified of her."

Mara stopped and smiled recalling something.

"What?"

"I remember telling Kaathi about those stories and she chuckled and said every tribe has stories glorifying themselves and vilifying other tribes."

"I can see people doing it," replied Marie.

Mara continued, "I also recall being terrified of you tall people. Your strength was twice mine and I was at a disadvantage in close quarter fighting. The only good thing about your size was you presented us with a larger target for our arrows. The advantage was nullified in dense jungle."

Marie raised her eyebrows saying, "I never heard how you came to stumble upon Kaathi and Gauri."

"Our scouts saw her party and reported back to our people. Our territory was being invaded by a party of three distinct hairy people. I was one of twenty-eight warriors to investigate their presence. When we came upon them, I tried to convince Ogus to find out if the group was peaceful and simply passing through or was warlike. He would not listen to me. Ogus thought because we outnumbered them we could destroy them. Ogus was a stupid leader. It went badly for us because we could not use our arrows to kill them. The forest was too thick to shoot arrows. Me and two others attacked Jacob and paid a heavy price. The other two were killed and I suffered a head wound and a broken arm, while he went injury free. I was knocked unconscious. When I revived, I was the only one left alive among the Uchakwa warriors. Isaac and Leah suffered wounds and four of the Stalkers were dead. Their lone survivor was their female leader, Gauri. The whole battle was senseless. Later I found out Kaathi and her people were passing through and had no intention to steal our land as Ogus thought."

"How terribly unfortunate Ogus did not listen to you. It would have been tremendously beneficial, if your people had the luxury of attending some Relationship Sessions," Marie pointed out.

"I agree. How will we ever know someone's intentions if we do not sit down and talk?"

"Were you ever married?" Marie asked.

"No, three men wanted me to be their woman. I never was stirred by any of them. If I had been, I likely would not have wanted to go with Kaathi on her adventure."

"Do the Uchakwa have to reach a certain age before they get married?"

"No, when a man loves a woman it does not make any difference what age she is."

"Do widows get married?"

"If a man sees she can fill a role in his life he will marry a widow."

"Have you seen any Kahali men you would want to marry?"

Mara chuckled. "Three men interested me. Only one was single."

"Well, if you make your intentions known, they might consider taking you as their second wife."

"Hmm, perhaps I should make an effort to talk to them."

"You should, Mara, you are an attractive woman."

"I am still an oddity to the Kahali."

Mara gave Marie's question some thought. The unmarried man she had thought about in terms of being with was Coloma. He was already in his twenties and should have already taken a wife. "Why is Coloma not married?"

Marie smiled. "Evidently, he was in love with Batu and has never gotten over her. Perhaps he is ready to find love again."

It was Mara's turn to smile.

"Why have you not married, Marie?"

"Hmm, I have been so busy learning how to heal people I have not given it much thought. You would think my mother would be concerned with me unmarried. She is not. I have questioned her about it and she says she wants me to enjoy my prestige as a healer. I think she keeps telling me to because she never felt appreciated as a woman. My father is still a traditionalist. I was young when Batu had revolutionized our village and set women free. It did not set well with my father. On occasion he still shows his prejudice. He is not as proud as my mother is about me being an apprentice Talker Healer.

"I take it you are proud you are a healer?"

"I am proud to serve people any way I can. The ability to help people regain their health through herbs, oils, gems, plants, affirmations, belief, love and prayer is fulfilling. I am comfortable with the healing side of being a Talker Healer. Those responsibilities have kept me from delving deeply into the talker side. I am acquainted with how to roam the Land of No Shadows.

The problem is I am not comfortable meeting the strange conglomeration of beings."

"Have you found any man interesting?"

"Of course. Taja comes to mind. His courage, character and devotion to Batu, Kaathi and Creator are reaching legendary proportions. Jacob is also interesting for different reasons. He is a protector whereas Taja was a dreamer and way-shower. As far as men whom I might marry, I have not met any. I am only sixteen and have not had a suitable man show interest in me. Until I meet a man having Taja and Jacob's characteristics, I am unexcited."

After their conversation, Mara was a regular at Coloma's teaching sessions. Originally, she attended because she wanted him to notice her. Slowly her desire to know more about the Kahali culture kept growing. His ability to make stories exciting was a rare gift and helped him engage children in his teaching sessions. At some point, she noticed how eagerly she looked forward to his sessions. He was easy on the eye. She was quickly attracted to how he interacted with the children. Even when she lived in Uchakwa, she was drawn to men who got along with children. The fact she attended the sessions did not go unnoticed by Coloma. Mara asked intelligent questions and caught Coloma's attention. She grew more comfortable being among the ones learning about Kahali traditions, laws, history and myths and decided to take the next step and talk to him after a session. The current session ended and the children and adults were scattering. She walked up to him.

"I am fascinated by your ability to recall so many stories. How in the world did you learn them?"

Coloma was pleased someone from another village had enough interest in what he was teaching to attend his sessions. Her lack of hair was disturbing at first. Over time he grew accustomed to it. With her repeated attendance, he noticed she was an attractive woman, with a great smile and an inquisitive mind. Her willingness to widen her intelligence was something he always admired. As they talked, he noticed her eyes sparkling. He wondered if it was due to her desire to acquire knowledge or her interest in him.

"When I was a boy attending the teaching sessions, Thomas, the previous Story Teller, felt I retained information well and was curious to know if I wanted to be his apprentice. He was married to Batu, whom you know, was vocal concerning women's rights. Sadly, he was bitten by a snake and died before he could teach me all of the stories. Fortunately, he had taught Batu those stories and even though she faced expulsion, she taught them to me."

"Expulsion? Why would they expel a member of their tribe?"

She sighed in recalling her own people expelled Kacy thinking she was possessed.

"Prior to Batu and Taja, creating the laws protecting women from expulsion, our tradition stated if a married woman lost her husband and did not have a child she would be expelled for lack of worth. Before the council could cast Batu from the village, she found she was pregnant and thus had worth. Tragically, her child died in childbirth and she was again vulnerable to expulsion. At the expulsion, Taja offered to marry her thus giving her worth. She refused thinking the council would connive to still eject her from the village. Batu gave a rousing, courageous speech, attacking the council and our traditions. In spite of her stirring speech, she was expelled. Taja conceived of a way to save her by making her his apprentice and thus gave her worth and saved her from banishment. He enlisted Jacob's help and they went after Batu and brought her back. Her speech impressed Jacob, and he became her strongest ally. Taja, Jacob and I made an alliance and we controlled the council. When Batu and Taja proposed the set of laws to protect women and give them rights equal to men, the council passed it four votes to one. By passing those laws, it was the second time I actually felt good about anything I voted on."

"Batu must have been a dynamic woman," offered Mara.

"She was and also courageous, and she did not care what anyone said about her or what she did. She was the trailblazer for all women."

"How do you compare her with Kaathi?"

"I cannot. They are different. If Batu felt there was an injustice, she was in your face about it. Kaathi sees something needing to be rectified and quietly goes about correcting it by praying or convincing you to help her change it."

"You are fortunate to have known history changers like Taja, Batu and Kaathi."

Coloma nodded in acknowledging his good fortune. He also felt good about talking to Mara.

Mara smiled sweetly. "Would you be interested in having an Uchakwa meal?"

Coloma smiled at her invitation. "I think I would." His heart still belonged to Batu, though this young woman stimulated something in him lying dormant since Batu's death. Since the village lost their first heroine, he had not considered roaming the seas of love. His mother worried he would never see goodness and love in another woman. For a long time she had dedicated her life to finding a suitable woman for him to marry. He had accepted several invitations over the years from available women, knowing they were hoping to capture his heart. He had thrown himself into his teaching children the laws, traditions, myths, mathematics and history, burying the pain in his heart. It had filled his life until Mara appeared. Suddenly the pain was not so severe.

"If you are free for the evening meal, I would love to have you come."

"I am free, and thank you for the invitation."

"Do you know where I live?"

"You live with Kacy behind Jacob's home."

"Correct." She impulsively gave him a hug and said goodbye.

He liked her warm embrace and watched her walk away. He noticed she walked with the confidence of someone knowing their body very well. Most people did not.

He smiled. *It is nice to be surprised.*

Mara saw Kacy lounging on the bench outside their home and walked toward her. She was thankful to have someone from her village living with her. It was comforting to have another person who looked like her in Kahali. Kacy's face was slightly broader than hers and was more introspective looking. She was slow to smile, when she did, it lit up her face and transformed her, seemingly making everyone around her happier. While she had a close circle of new friends, Kacy was a distant relative and a reminder of her life in Uchakwa. Kacy was a significant part of her past.

Kacy looked up and noticed something new in Mara's face and her aura was filled with crystalline pink color. She raised her eyebrows expectantly as Mara neared.

"There is a lot of love in your aura and you are filled with joy. What is going on?"

Mara smiled. "I have invited Coloma to our evening meal."

"You never told me you were interested in him."

"Marie and I were talking and she made me aware of my feelings for him."

"Do you want me to eat elsewhere?"

"No, I would like you there to see what his colors are as he is talking to me."

"Do you not have enough trust in yourself?"

"No. Yes. I do, but before I put my heart out there I would like to know if I should."

CHAPTER SEVEN

Mara took great care creating the sauce and kept tasting it. She used the sauce to baste the meat and potatoes and a handful of vegetables. It was a simple, tasty meal, as were most meals the Uchakwa prepared. She and Kacy kept up a steady chatter as she fussed over the meal and waited for Coloma.

Coloma arrived and peeked in the open entrance and called, "Mara?"

"Oh, Coloma, please come in. I think you have met Kacy."

"Yes I have. Actually it was on the first day Kaathi came back from her adventure from seeing the Ancients. Hello Kacy, it is good to see you."

A huge smile erupted from the early teen. "I am glad to see you again."

"It must be reassuring to have left your village with someone you know."

"I am thankful. Mara has made my transition to Kahali life much more pleasant," Kacy informed him. "If she and the others had not taken me with them I would have been dead long ago. The jungle is a dangerous place."

"I know. I am thankful I am the Story Teller and do not have to venture into the jungle and the plains to rid those places of predators. Is Kemp going to lose his arm? I cannot imagine how terrified he was confronting a leopard."

"It is a day to day thing," explained Mara. "Kaathi sees him twice a day to assess how his arm is doing. He was lucky Bork, Clive and Tabor were able to kill the leopard before it killed him.

"Why do leopards come close to our village?" Kacy wondered aloud.

Coloma answered from what he had learned from others, "If a leopard cannot find enough to eat in his old haunt, it keeps expanding its hunting territory. It is why we have many scouting parties in the forest and the savannah. We are the ones who have encroached on their territory. They do not know any better. Hunger drives them as much as it does us.

"Enough of this tragic talk." He directed his question to Mara, "Why did you choose to follow Kaathi?"

"I did not have a man I loved in my village. I am an adventuresome person and Kaathi's group of people intrigued me. I heard stories about the mutants, and I had never seen one. Leah and Isaac were nothing like I imagined mutants would be like. Gauri, the Stalker woman, was like looking into the past to see what we might have looked like before we lost our hair and grew in intelligence. Even so, I liked Gauri. She had fought for her independence and won and was going back to her clan on her terms with new understanding and intelligence. I hope she was able to present her ideas to her people.

"In the skirmish with the group, I was angry with Jacob at first. He personally killed two of my friends and broke my arm and put a gash in my head. When I got to know him, I saw how much integrity, courage and strength he had and he became my friend. Kaathi is another story. She inspires me to reach for the stars. Her love surpasses what I felt from my parents. I would follow her to Mother Earth's unknown."

"I find you an interesting person, Mara. Why are you attending my sessions?"

"I thought it was obvious," she smiled. "I want to learn more about you, Kahalis."

Coloma raised his left eyebrow, as if to question her answer.

Mara avoided what she thought would be his next question with one of her own, "Are you ready to eat?"

"I thought you would never ask."

Mara dished out the meal to each of them. Coloma tasted it gingerly. He liked it and dug in and ate all she put in front of him, which made Mara smile more.

"I have heard you were in love with Batu. Is it true?"

"I was. I even asked her to marry me and she refused."

"Why?"

"I think she was not inclined to marry anyone after the death of her husband. I also believe being Taja's apprentice was abundantly filling her life."

"Are you over loving her?" Kacy wanted to know.

He did not answer immediately instead he pondered the questioned in earnest. "I believe I have grieved her death long enough, and I am ready to go on with my life."

A good answer. I hope Mara felt his honesty.

"Life does present us with a constant barrage of challenges," remarked Mara.

"Indeed," Coloma agreed. "Was making this meal a challenge to your memory or do you make it often?"

"Often enough so it is not difficult to get the right taste."

"Well I found it delicious. Would the two of you like to taste my specialty some evening?"

"I would," hastily answered Kacy.

"It would be nice," chimed in Mara.

"Consider yourselves invited four days from now. It should be enough time for me to practice and make it edible," he said smiling.

They rose from the table and Mara took the liberty to hug him as she did the last time they were alone, which pleased him. Kacy seeing them embrace did the same and the women bid him goodbye.

"Well, what did you think of him and what colors did his aura contain?"

"His colors reflect a stable personality and his interest in you. There is some pink in it showing his growing love for you. As far as his physical appearance, I suppose he is good looking enough. He is courteous and has a distinguished position. Honestly, I want someone with more intensity."

"Well I do not. My concern is did he speak truthfully?"

"He was telling the truth, when he said he was over Batu. It was hard to concentrate on his aura when he was talking. The colors clash with the words he spoke." She smiled. "I can see you are romantically interested and it does not take someone able to see your aura."

"I did not think I could hide it from you. Do you think he sensed how I felt about him?"

"An elephant could feel it."

The next day Mara showed up at the story sessions. After the session, she walked up to Coloma, smiled in greeting. "I hope you had a good time yesterday."

"I did. The food was marvelous and the company was delightful."

"Kacy can be extremely interesting."

"I was not talking about Kacy. I find you extraordinarily interesting. At first, I did not know how I felt about your bald head. Now I find it adds to your beauty."

"My beauty?"

"I hope I am not too forward?"

"Not in the least, it has been far too long since a man has paid me much attention. I am glad the Uchakwa men did not interest me."

"Are you saying I interest you?"

"Yes I am. I think we fascinate each other."

Coloma laughed. "I think you are right. Shall we see where this fascination leads us?"

I am sorry he invited Kacy. Ah, there will be plenty of time I will be seeing him alone.

"Yes." She reached for him and they embraced for a long while.

The meal Coloma had prepared was not nearly as spicy and tasty as Mara's but well done. The evening was filled with questions, none of which touched on personal events. The third meal Coloma and Mara shared was in his home as well. Kacy was not present and they had a chance to ask the questions they failed to with Kacy present.

"Did the parents of your young women dictate who they should marry?"

"Yes," answered Coloma. "It was a trying time for our women."

"Did Batu spearheaded the change in Kahali?"

"She did."

"Why do you think no other women ever were courageous enough to complain?"

"In all honesty, I think they were beaten if they were too outspoken."

"And Batu's father did not beat her?"

"No, actually he encouraged her to be inquisitive and debate everything. She was a product of her father and mother and not of society."

"Did you approve of her?"

"At first I had my reservations. I always thought she was one of the most beautiful women in Kahali. For reasons unknown, she came down with a rash, covering her whole body. It itched terribly and she scratched it until it became infected and she nearly died. She recovered, although her face breast and thigh were scarred from the infection. The scars detracted from her beauty yet added something to her character. Her personality changed. There was depth to her beyond her defiance and need for justice and respect. I imagine a good deal was due to her friendship with Taja and what he shared with her. As my love for her grew, I cast my old doubts aside. I became fully committed to her, after listening to her expulsion speech."

"How do you feel about a man being able to be married to more than one woman?"

"I am not sure. Since it has not come to be my personal problem, I have not thought about it. It does seem to work for Jacob."

She threw another question at him, "How do you feel about a woman having two or more husbands?"

Coloma chuckled. "If Jacob is allowed to do it, a woman should be able to do the same."

"How do you feel about me?"

The question surprised him, and it took him a moment to gather himself and reply, "I have come to think you are a desirable and lovely woman."

Mara smiled. She moved off her chair and sat in his lap. She put her arms around him and kissed him. Her tongue made its way into his mouth to his delight. He found his passion rising and found his hands undoing her clothes. Her hands slipped his clothes from his body and they moved to his bed. They made love excitedly the first time and passionately the next.

He laid there in the dark beside the only woman he ever made love to. *It is a good thing none of my friends can see me. I cannot seem to stop smiling and I love it. I can attest to the fact I am now truly a man. I never thought anything could fill me with such joy. I am content and in love with this woman and want her to be mine for the rest of my life.*

CHAPTER EIGHT

Janos approached the mystic's home and saw Sharika sitting with the healer and walked a bit slower to behold the Hun. He was not keen on foreigners and never went out his way to meet her. Janos stopped in front of Kaathi's hut, where she sat with Sharika. "Hello, Kaathi, here is the box you requested. I hope it suits your needs."

"Thank you, Janos." She noticed he had carved her face on the lid. "It is sweet of you to carve my face on the lid. It is exquisite and unexpected. It delights me you thought enough of me to decorate it."

He appreciated her kind words and smiled saying, "You have done so much for my family, it hardly compares."

She stood and gave him a warm embrace. She released him and sat down to watch his reaction to Sharika.

He turned his attention from Kaathi to the newcomer and smiled. The smile he gave Sharika had made many hearts flutter. Janos was not a man any woman could easily ignore. He was of average height; it was the only thing average about him. He was one of the handsomest men in Kahali. His sienna colored skin was hairless, and his muscled body was chiseled to perfection. He was blue eyed, with dark reddish, black, tightly waved hair. His smile melted every mothers' heart, and a rich, hardy laugh to accompany his light hearted, good nature. He was a marvelous catch for any woman. The reality was he had not been caught.

Janos had the good fortune of having parents who loved each other and adored their only child. He never had trouble understanding the interconnection of the council, High Priest and people. He knew how to make children and people happy and had more friends than most children growing up. Ever since he could remember women of all ages dotted over him and gave him affection. He in turn made them happy with his time and attention. There was no young boy more suited to be an apprentice to The Friend of All council person, Logan. It never happened. He never speculated why but every woman sensed it was Logan's ego. His jealousy of Janos clouded his decision and he refrained from making Janos his apprentice. The young boy would steal his thunder with the women.

"I presume this beautiful creature next to you is Sharika. I am sorry I have not met you sooner. I am, Janos, a friend of Kaathi, Pauli and Jacob."

Sharika stuck out her hand to the young, handsome man with the fantastic smile. "You presume correctly, Janos."

"The whole village is talking about you and Ashlee," he remarked.

"I know," she unabashedly admitted. "Most every head turns as I pass them. I am not sure if it is because I am a foreigner or I am notorious."

"I will give you a third choice; you are a stunning woman. Is your mother beautiful?"

Sharika's mother was a fine looking woman and her father was handsome. The combination of the two provided the world with a beautiful child and she never lost her beauty as she grew older, unlike some of the other children. Sharika valued her intelligence more than her looks. It grew in its prominence the more she discussed life and philosophy with the Chief of the Huns.

Kaathi smiled at how easily she was forgotten in favor of the two flirting. "Would you excuse me?"

They did and Sharika replied to his compliment, "I am not sure the others in Kahali would agree with you."

"If they do not, it is because their eyes have grown weak."

She grinned. "You do know how to make a woman's ego take flight."

"I shall take your compliment. I do tell women of their other qualities as well. Of course, I do it when I know them."

"And here I thought you were without substance."

"Oh, I am also good at hearing sarcasm. Are you attempting to chase me off?"

"Not at all, I am trying to determine if you can withstand it?"

"Madam, I have withstood much worse than what you have targeted me with. I am used to friends jesting at my expense. I think my looks have brought this upon me."

"Well, it does not seem to have affected you."

"It would, if I did not know it was done mirthfully."

Sharika's mind quickly compared Janos to Chief Victor. While Victor had many qualities she liked, Janos' lightness was captivating and refreshing. Perhaps it was going to be easier to soothe her healing heart then she suspected.

"What do you do in Kahali?"

He flashed his best smile. "Most of my time is spent trying to find a woman like you."

Pleased, she smiled.

"I live with my parents as all single men do. I go on hunts most of the days with my friends. The days I do not, I help patrol our area to keep it free from predators. In my spare time I carve wood."

"I saw by your gift to Kaathi, you are an excellent one. I never would have taken you to be a carver."

"I am glad I could surprise you. The piece I did for Kaathi was for her next trip. She requested me to make it to keep her oils safe. A friend of mine made her a number of tiny jars to store the oils. The insides are a little larger than the size of my thumb. It took him a long time to make the first one and get the glaze right."

"What is she going to use as a lid for them?"

"Another person she has treated is making them out of cork."

"Cork? I have never heard of it."

"Cork is the bark of a particular oak tree. It is soft and makes a watertight stopper."

"Can you show me this tree?"

"Now?"

"Yes."

"I need to get my weapons."

"And I shall get mine."

After gathering their weapons, Janos led her out of the village to one of the larger woods bordering the river.

"Are you in demand as a carver?"

"There are enough requests to keep me from being bored."

"I cannot imagine you getting bored. I would think any number of women would seek you out to do some carving for them or something else."

Janos smiled at her inference. They penetrated the forest and he informed her, "We only have six of these trees fully grown. The younger trees' bark is not ready to be used. They were discovered several seasons ago by accident. Part of the bark was dislodged by an animal and he came across it on the ground and thought it looked strange. He brought it back with him and gave it to one of our carvers who found it was not good for carving. He did discover it made good stoppers for small openings."

"How did Kaathi think of making small jars?"

"When her mentor, Batu, returned from Sumati, after discovering what caused their epidemic, Victor sent his best clay potter to instruct our people in the art of pottery. Kaathi first saw the potential in making small pots or jars to house essential oils."

"Your Talker Healers have a great many skills in many areas," she pointed out.

"They do."

Janos found the trees with the cork bark. Sharika found a piece broken away from the tree and looked at it. "Can I take this with me?"

"Of course."

They took their time walking back to the village.

"Would you mind if I carved a bust of you?"

The unexpected request pleased Sharika. "It would take up a great deal of your time."

He smiled. "I do not mind. It would give me the chance to see you often."

"What would you do with it once you have completed it?"

"I would give it to you."

Sharika smiled and took his arm.

CHAPTER NINE

Janos, Pauli, Sandor, Sharika, two other women and fifteen Kahali men finished meditating and Jacob made sure he had the attention of all of them.

"Before every session we shall meditate. The reason for meditating is to calm your mind in order for you to be aware of the lag between thought and action. Without the calm you will never experience the lag."

The group before him was the first to take advantage of the open invitation to the villagers to learn how to recognize the phenomenon. Prior to today only the Warrior Hunters and their apprentices were privy to the knowledge.

Jacob was not surprised to see Sharika. She had peppered him with questions on how he used energy on the long journey home from Sumati.

Jacob needed a volunteer to receive smacks on his back from a small switch. One of the men eagerly jumped up and went to Jacob.

"I am going to place blows on Bidu's back at different intervals and see if he can anticipate when the blows are going to land. Bidu, I want you to say, 'Now,' if you think the blow is about to land."

He turned Bidu around with his back to the group. Jacob landed four blows before Bidu spoke.

He turned Bidu to face the class. "How did you know the blow was going to land?"

Bidu sheepishly said, "I guessed."

"So you did not read my thoughts to know when I was going to strike."

"I did not."

"Thank you for being honest. A good warrior is cognizant of everything around him or her. It is essential for a warrior to stay alive and this skill helps him accomplish it. Pauli and Sandor have been learning this skill for some time now. Some of you may be quicker to sense thoughts than others. There is no shame in being slower to sense it.

"You need to know Bidu, the strange thing about this process is I do not actively think about hitting you, even though my mind registers it.

"Once again I urge you to not be afraid to speak up if you hear yourself giving you a warning or sense anything. Eventually, you will hear or sense something. It takes repetition and more repetition.

"Let us try this again. Turn around. Let me know if you sense my thought."

Jacob placed fifteen blows on Bidu's back. He called out on half of them and none registered correctly.

"Bidu was using something which was not the ability to sense the lag. What was Bidu using?"

"Anticipation," called out Sharika.

"Exactly. There is nothing wrong with anticipating. Warriors use anticipation in battles. What you are learning is outside the realm of anticipation. You are learning to sense or read the thought or energy before the blow lands.

"I want all of you to pair up and move away at least ten steps from the others. It will help prevent interference of sound or thought. Begin to experiment as I did with Bidu. Make sure you vary the time interval between blows." He smiled. "And do not take pleasure in striking your partner. Remember you will have to go under the switch next."

Sharika immediately walked up to Jacob and paired up with him.

He raised his eyebrows. "I thought you would have paired up with Janos since the two of you are seeing each other."

She smiled. "I want to learn from the best."

He had sensed she would and was pleased his intuition served him.

"Pauli, Sandor I want you to move around and help each pair while I work with Sharika."

"Remember to clear your minds and let your partner know you are ready. If you hear anything in your mind or sense anything on your body, which can foretell the blow, speak up," Jacob advised everyone. "Learn to trust yourself."

Sharika took the switch and grinned mischievously. "I hope I can control myself."

Jacob grinned back. "Just remember I do you next."

The moment Jacob turned around Sharika let her first blow land. Jacob did not respond.

"Why did you not say something?"

"I was still concentrating on how mischievous you looked. Do it again."

She took a long time before she struck him. He spoke up simultaneously with the blow.

She sent another blow to him immediately and he detected it before the blow sounded on his back. She waited two breaths and directed another blow to his skin. He sensed it, while her hand was moving. She waited seven breaths and made sure she did not think about landing the blow. It did not make any difference, he sensed it again.

"I am done. I want to try it."

"Good. Remember clear your mind and let me know when you are ready. As you wait for my blow, check for any impression made on you, your body or mind."

Sharika nodded and turned. "Ready."

Jacob waited two breaths and struck her.

Jacob waited four breaths and struck her.

Jacob waited one breath and struck her.

He varied the routine and somewhere around mid-morning she raised her voice as the blow struck.

"Good. How did you know I was about to strike you?"

"I felt a twitch on my forehead. Before I could think about it I spoke automatically."

"Excellent. Let us continue and see if what happened is repeatable for you and learn to trust it."

Out of the next twenty blows she determined four of them. With each one he stopped and quizzed her if the twitch made her aware of the blow. Jacob noticed the sun was overhead and excused the class to eat and attend to other things.

Jacob, Pauli and Sandor stayed behind to discuss their students' progress. Jacob was not surprised when the tally showed Sharika had doubled the correct calls of her nearest classmate. Anyone brave enough to journey alone into the unknown, as she had done, might very well be better equipped to do so than others. He wondered if there was something innate in her clan allowing her to be uniquely gifted.

CHAPTER TEN

Brock lie in bed going over the disturbing dream filled with Kaathi's image. The dream recurred several times in the past dozen nights to his chagrin. They often awakened him, and he had trouble getting back to sleep. He did not mind having dreams of women, provided they were sexual. He enjoyed them. These were not enjoyable. The statement Kaathi had made of Romir, a previous High Priest, also disturbed him. He had asked one of his friends if what she told him was true. His friend said the Elder had told the villagers he suspected Romir had lied and poisoned people to get them to behave the way he wanted them to and also said Kiirt had killed Batu. *How did I forget what Caleb said? Was I busy talking to someone? If what the Elder said was true, Romir and Kiirt were terrible representatives of the position. And what is wrong with the gods? Romir always told us to rely on them. There were nearly two dozen of us pleading for the gods to take Kaathi's life. They failed us miserably. Now these damn dreams are plaguing me and seemingly urging me to talk to Kaathi. Crap, I have to get things straight in my head, or I will never have a decent night's sleep.*

Brock stood in front of the Talker Healer's hut for some moments, vacillating whether to call Kaathi's name. She unexpectedly appeared at the entrance, seeing Brock she warmly smiled.

"Brock, I am happy to see you."

He offered no greeting in return. "I need to talk to you. Are you free?"

"I am." She turned her head to announce to those inside, "I have someone wanting to talk to me." She turned back to Brock. "Where do you want to talk?"

"Under the trees by the river."

"Do you mind if I take your arm?"

His reply was sharp, "Yes I do."

His mind was racing with all he wanted to say to her and it now included her audacity to want to hold onto him. He was married and married men did not cling to another woman. He remained silent until they sat down.

"Did you think by taking hold of my arm you could throw me off guard?"

"No it is something I have become used to doing with people to set them at ease."

"Well, it would not set me at ease. The reason I wanted to talk with you is due to my dreams. You keep popping up in them, and they are disturbing me. Are you causing them?"

The brows on her child like face puckered together. "I would never think of doing something to influence your subconscious. Can I ask, am I threatening you in the dreams?"

"No. The fact is I do not like you and do not want you in my dreams."

"Why not?"

His voice was forceful as he answered, "I am a traditionalist, and you are usurping tradition and it aggravates me."

She nodded. "Ah, I see."

"If we discard tradition and laws we will become barbarians."

"I agree. We did away with only those traditions suppressing women. The same goes for our laws. We created new ones to make certain our women were equal to our men. I hope you saw long ago some of our men were barbaric."

"I find your words offensive," he stated.

"I am sorry. I am not sure if you know this. My mutant friend, Isaac, treated his wife with more respect than most of our men treated their wives."

"Bullshit, it is not true," he stammered.

"On the contrary, their tribe, the Searchers, saw how men and women complemented each other. They lived from day to day and counted on each other to stay alive. They respected each other for all the things they did for each other. They knew without the help of their mates they would not survive in the harsh environment amidst the volatile and prejudicial tribes continually hunting them."

"You cannot compare mutants to us. It is where your philosophy fails. Men are superior to women."

"In what way?"

"They cannot hunt, think properly and are weaker."

"I beg to differ. Sharika has been on hunts with Jacob and matches his prowess with the bow, where none of our men do. In addition, she is quickly learning his hunting skills. Do you know why the Huns are not good hunters? It is because they have domesticated animals and have little need to hunt and they raise crops. As far as intelligence is concerned, Batu disproved men were superior during all her discussions and debates, and her memory was legendary. While women are indeed weaker than men, can you show me one man willing to go through what a woman goes through to give birth?"

Even in his anger he had to admit her points were well made.

"Were you angry with Batu?"

"Of course, she initiated all this crap about injustice, equality and respect. The two of you have been cast from the same mold."

"I shall take your remark as a compliment. Batu always had my highest respect. Not only did she have the courage to break barriers for women, she also saved my life by sacrificing her own."

He had conveniently forgot the fact and dismissed her answer with a shrug.

"May I ask you a question, Brock?"

He nodded.

"Do you consider yourself better or superior to your wife?"

"Of course."

"There is an old adage which says, 'Do not judge anyone until you have walked in their moccasins.' Do you agree with it?"

"No."

She looked shocked. "Why not?"

"It is a stupid saying."

"What makes you think so?"

"It does not make sense."

"I disagree. I think it is very profound. It implies, if I want to know someone, I should step into their skin and experience all the trials, tribulations, victories and blessings of their life. I know of no better way to learn what drives a person's character, heart and mind. How else can I or you understand the injustice, inequality and suppression she may be suffering and enduring?"

Brock glared at her. Despite his anger, her wisdom somehow got through to him and stirred his heart. His glare softened as did his voice. "I have to confess, I heard from a friend, Romir and Kiirt were not fit to be High Priests. For Kiirt to kill Batu and want to do the same to you is reprehensible. I do not know what to think of them now. How did the position grow corrupt?"

"First let me say they, like most of us, were not completely good or bad. Do you feel you derived some good from them or their teachings?"

Brock thought a moment and answered, "Yes, they followed the precepts of our religion, which has as its foundation the gods. They guided me for much of my life."

"It is what I expected to hear. So, do you see how a person can do good and not be a good person?"

"Yes. What if I had known of their dark side?"

"A good question, which you should strive to answer for yourself."

"I have abandoned friends who were not as bad as they were. Had I known, I would have challenged them as I challenged you."

"You do realize, if you had protested too often, Romir might have taken you aside and poisoned you for your behavior? And, when you were sick he likely would have said he would pray for you and when the poison wore off, he would claim his prayers had worked."

"Honestly, what I have heard about him has sent me reeling."

"Let us look at the situation, where Kiirt almost killed Batu by choking her. In the incident, Romir was a witness and sided with Kiirt because he hated Batu. What if you had questioned Kiirt about the attempt, and he said he was innocent? What would you have done? Remember it was Batu's word against Kiirt and Romir's."

"I would have looked at the character of both sides and chosen to side with Kiirt."

"An honest answer. Why would you have chosen to believe him and Romir?"

"I would have backed the High Priests because they had fine reputations. Batu was a trouble maker and a destroyer of tradition."

"With the passage of time, I hope you can see which one hurt the tribe and which one helped the tribe?"

"I now am able to see where the High Priests were evil. I also see our village is still struggling with all the changes Batu, Taja and you have created. Whether the changes are good or not is yet to be determined."

"If you look closely, you will see the changes are for the good. If you talk to enough women, you will find many thankful for those changes, and some men are seeing the benefits as well. Over time the benefits will become more obvious to many disbelievers."

Brock ran his hand through his thinning hair and sighed. "It will take a long time for some men, including me, to admit it. I am shocked with all of this new information about the High Priests. I am still uncomfortable with the changes taking place. I am a traditionalist, and I am not sure how all of this is going to affect us."

"Do you think you could have challenged Romir or Kiirt as you did me?"

He shook his head. "Romir was an imposing man. Everyone except Batu and Taja were afraid of him and they paid for their displeasure of him with their lives. People did not question him. It was not his style to be questioned."

"Why have you questioned and challenged me?"

"You are not threatening and you are a woman."

Acknowledging his answer, she nodded. "Setting aside all you know of Romir, which one of us do you respect more?"

61

"You."

"Why?"

"You are not threatening and have openly answered any question I have thrown at you."

"I will share something with you. When you and your friends came to the services and harassed me, I knew you were looking for the truth. Well, Brock the truth is inside you. All you have to do is still yourself and wait for the truth to be revealed. I know this conversation is stimulating you and you are going to be one of our greatest proponents for the services. I would like to ask you to do one thing for me."

"What?"

"Come to the next Spiritual Awakening Service with a sense of expectation."

"Is there something I should expect to happen?"

"Yes."

"Like what?"

"The unexpected."

"Now you are talking in riddles."

"Come to the service in anticipation of something good happening."

"What am I to anticipate?"

"Expect something good to occur."

"We are going around in circles."

"Brock have faith and expect good to take place."

"What sort of good?"

"The anticipation will bring it to fruition."

He mulled her words over in his head. He did not fully understand what she was driving at.

"What will come to fruition?"

"An unexpected good. It can be in the form of almost anything. You, my dear, Brock, will know it. All you have to do is be open to it occurring."

He finally saw what she was driving at. He was excited. He was aware he was enthralled by her and the things she shared. He sensed an anticipation in the moment. He closed his eyes hesitant to show her how she affected him. Thoughts fled his mind. He sat in an expectant stillness, waiting for he knew not what.

The fruition was at hand.

He felt it.

He felt enveloped in love.

His mind grew active and he felt the love slip away.

He stopped thinking and felt the love again.

He accepted it.

He breathed it in.

He reveled in it.

He felt blessed.

He felt tears cascading down his cheeks.

His mind engaged again and the sensation of love lessened. He opened his eyes and looked at her.

"It happened."

"When you expect good to bless you, it is marvelously enriching."

He looked deep into her eyes. "What am I to call you?"

"Kaathi."

"No, you are more than your name. You truly are the High Priest we have needed."

She giggled saying, "Will you be coming to the services?"

He smiled good-naturedly. "I will be there expecting good to be bestowed on me."

She smiled. "I shall look forward to your sacred presence with anticipation and joy."

He marveled at the turn around in himself. He shook his head and returned her smile. Deep in his heart he knew he would praise her to his friends.

He suddenly yearned to receive the warmth, love and wisdom contained within her over and over again.

CHAPTER ELEVEN

The council was done with the regular business and asked those present if they wanted to speak. A man made a motion with his hand. "I am speaking for these other five men. We have a complaint. Keeyon is in our predator patrol group and has time and again not done his share of patrolling the territory to keep it free from predators. It is his only responsibility and he shirks it."

The other men with him nodded.

"Have any of you spoken to Keeyon about his laziness?"

All in the group said yes.

The Elder looked at Jacob. "Would you take care of this informally?"

"I can."

"Is there anything else anyone wants to discuss?" asked Elgar of the dozen villagers present.

None did and the Elder adjourned the meeting.

The healers, Kaathi, Marie and Mara walked out of the meeting together and were met in the village center by a young woman, whose face was filled with consternation.

Kaathi stopped in front of the woman. "Can we help you?"

"I need to talk to you," said the woman in a desperate, soft voice.

Kaathi sensed the woman's tension. "Very well." The healer led them to the Talker Healer hut. Inside she directed herself to the woman who was a half head taller than she with dark eyes. The woman's lips were full as were her brows. Her arms and legs were hairless. Her hair was tightly curled and short on her head. She looked slightly underweight and fragile. Her delicate nature was reflected in her thin face and high cheekbones. The way she carried herself and her long neck gave her an aura of elegance. "What is your name my dear?"

"Rana."

"I am Kaathi. This is Marie and she is Mara. Tell us your story."

"Do they need to be present?"

"Yes. They are my apprentices and this is the way they learn."

Rana deliberated and told her story, "I have been married six years. We have no children. A while ago I noticed a man stalking me. I discounted it even though the man gave me the creeps. Eighteen days ago I was restless and took a walk along the river. I had walked a long way deep in thought before I realized I had wandered too far from home. I turned around abruptly and saw the man not twenty feet from me."

"What did he look like?"

"He was around thirty, a hand taller than me, dark skinned, broad of face with a large nose and his ears stuck out. Oh, he had a large knot on his left collar bone as if it had been broken and healed badly.

"He startled me, and I muffled a scream. I asked him why he was following me. He came closer and said, 'I am fascinated by you... I am infatuated with you.'"

"I told him I was married and to leave me alone. 'I may never get you alone again,' he said. He rushed to me and grabbed at my skirt to pull it down. I yelled and fought... He hit me in the stomach and I doubled up. He pushed me to the ground. I fought... He was too strong. He forced my legs apart... I kept hitting him. It only fueled his desire. He was wild...crazed."

She broke down and sobbed. She could not go on. When she composed herself, Kaathi asked, "Did he rape you?"

Unable to speak she nodded.

"You do not have to say any more. What do you want to do?"

Rana's eyes were bloodshot. Her voice trembled. "I am afraid to tell my husband. He would kill the man... I am not sure how he would feel about me, if I told him. I am afraid he would blame me as well as the man... I do not know what to do... I am terrified the man might rape me again. If he did, I do not know if I could live with the shame."

Tears streamed from Rana's eyes. Her lips trembled.

"I am sorry. We all are. Since you did not use the man's name I presume you do not know him."

Rana nodded.

"I know you came here to unburden yourself. It is good you did. I think you also came to get my advice, and I will give it to you. You must gather your courage and protect yourself and all the other women he might rape.

"Do you have the strength to tell your husband?"

Rana shook her head.

"Do you want to prevent him from doing this again?"

"Yes. . . but I do not want to be exposed."

"I assure you it will not happen."

Rana's face showed a glint of hope.

"How?"

"You and I are going to tell Jacob what happened. He is going to sit with you in the square until the man appears. It does not matter if it takes the whole sunny season."

Rana interrupted the mystic. "What if my husband sees me with Jacob, or what if someone tells him I have been sitting with him?"

"Tell him part of the truth."

"What do you mean?"

"Tell him or whoever asks you are helping Jacob with an important project and cannot say anymore."

Rana understood.

"When you identify him, Jacob will take him aside and come here. We will collect the council and meet at Batu's tree. He will be told of his punishment before the council."

"He may blame me."

"Do not worry yourself. I have sensed no blame on your part. Marie, has she told the truth?"

"She has."

"Mara, has she told the truth?"

"Yes."

"Your testimony and ours will be proof of his guilt. We shall deal with him and protect you from having to reveal what happened to your husband. At some time in the future, if you gather your courage, you can share what happened to you with him. If the courage never comes, you can remain silent. Are you willing to proceed to identify him?"

Rana hesitated for a moment. "If he raped another woman, or god forbid, me, I could not live with myself."

"I shall speak to Jacob. You need to go to his house every day after your dawn meal. He shall sit with you in the square every day until you identify the man. Have faith justice will prevail. You did the right thing by coming to us."

Rana looked relieved and apprehensive.

The apprentice healers hugged her and bid her goodbye.

Kaathi embraced Rana. "Bless you for your courage."

Rana waited in front of Jacob's hut each morning as Kaathi had told her to do. She and Jacob sat in the village square for eight days and had gotten to know each other fairly well. On the ninth day, she saw the rapist.

"There he is."

She choked on the words.

"Your description of him was excellent."

"I shall never forget his face," she hissed.

"Stay here."

Jacob walked to intersect the man.

"Do you know me?"

"You are Jacob."

"Come with me."

"Why?"

"I shall explain at the appropriate time."

Jacob stopped at the Talker Healer hut and called for Kaathi. She emerged.

"I have the man. Bring the rest to the tree."

Kaathi turned and went inside, while Jacob led the man out onto the plains to Batu's favorite tree and waited for the rest.

"What the hell is going on?" demanded the rapist.

"All in due time. Sit."

Kaathi collected Rana, while Marie and Mara collected the rest of the council. They all discretely left the village and met Jacob. The rapist saw Rana and the council and apprentices approach. Sweat appeared on his forehead and trickled down his armpits.

The Elder, Elgar, recognized the accused and asked for the benefit of the others, "What is your name?"

"Dirdan."

"You are here because you have been charged with raping Rana. Do you have anything to say in your defense?"

"This is insane. I never raped her. She is lying. When does she say I did it?"

"Twenty-seven days ago."

"Hell, it was so many days ago I cannot remember what I did and said to anyone. I am innocent."

"Since neither of you can produce a witness, it remains for our Talker Healers to intuit the truth."

"Hold on!" shouted Dirdan. "They are all women. They will side with her all the time against me or any man."

"You are wrong," stated Elgar. "These three women are beyond reproach. Their integrity is stellar and they never tell falsehoods. We shall abide by what they tell us as to which one of you is speaking the truth.

"Kaathi, which of these two is speaking the truth?"

"Rana."

"Marie, who is speaking the truth?"

"Rana."

"What do you say Mara?"

"Rana."

"You are all crazy," Dirdan screamed.

"By law you have two choices, Dirdan," announced Elgar. "Leave now and take with you the weapons, Janos has brought. Or you can chose to remain in the village. If you do, you will be castrated the moment we return and you shall not tell anyone you raped Rana. If we hear you have spoken to anyone about the rape, you shall be cast out of the village. In addition, I shall announce to the people you raped a woman. If you leave and are seen afterward, you shall be hunted down and killed on sight. Do you understood what I have told you?"

Fear and hate coagulated in Dirdan's eyes. He glared at Rana.

"You bitch!" he screamed.

The Elder waved his hand to silence the man. "What is your decision?"

Dirdan's head was bursting. *How the hell am I to decide in this instant? I cannot think straight. I hate the bitch. I wish I had never set eyes on her. The other bitches did not squeal. She should have kept her mouth shut. Damn her. Damn her. I am not losing my testicles. I can go to Homar where there are still some men who are men. Damn all of you.*

"Your decision, Dirdan."

He walked over to Janos and grabbed the weapons and axe. He glared at them. "Damn all of you to hell."

He turned and left.

Rana was weeping but breathed a sigh of relief thankful she took action.

Kaathi watched Dirdan storm away, recited a brief prayer for him and wrapped him in love. She turned and was embraced my Rana.

"Thank you for everything, Kaathi."

"You can thank Batu. She thought of the law and how to keep the rape a secret, if it was what the victim wanted."

Kaathi hugged Rana. Sharika, Marie, Mara, Ashlee and Scarlet surrounded them and embraced them.

CHAPTER TWELVE

Janos was on the plains hunting with Jacob, Pauli and Sandor. With no game in sight, Jacob started a friendly banter.

"Janos, I noticed you have been seeing a lot of the old lady, Alice."

"You have?" responded Janos with a smile. "I thought only the old women noticed."

"No, I noticed as well."

Sandor chuckled. "Hmm it puts you in the same hen house with them."

"Hey, watch your mouth," retorted Jacob good naturedly.

"Well, Miss Jacob, I am having a nice time with Alice," Janos said humorously.

Jacob glared at him. "What the hell do you mean Miss?"

"Well if the skirt fits. . ." Janos let the sentence hang.

The others laughed.

"Ah, you guys are full of shit and no longer funny," Jacob said in mock anger.

"Wait a moment. . .are you interested in Alice? Are you looking for a fourth wife?"

"No, and do not go spreading it around the village."

"You know, I am taking a good look at you, and I can see you have aged a good ten years since you have taken Scarlet as a wife. You look a little used up and thin."

The men slapped each other's shoulders and laughed.

Janos smiled saying, "I have also notice you are looking at Pauli a little doe eyed. Are you thinking of taking a husband as well?"

Jacob jumped over Sandor and fell on top of Janos and rubbed his knuckles on his head, while the other men laughed their heads off.

When Jacob got off of him, Janos shared a story about his grandfather.

"Grandfather was never one to talk about his warrior excursions. He did love to talk about all the foot races he won. At our yearly Test of Strengths Festival he won the race for the twelve and under age group. When the fourteen and under group assembled, he squeezed into the group. If you recall the twelve and under distance was a thousand steps in length and there was not much time for him to recover and get into the next race. The fourteen and under men had to run two thousand steps. No twelve year-old had ever entered the race. He was the first and he received a lot of strange looks from the group.

"The way he tells the story, he hung back to preserve his strength. Near the three quarter point he stretched his stride and made his way up to the leader. The leader looked over at him astonished to see it was my grandfather and even more surprised when he left him and crossed the finish line first.

"By winning the race he caught the eye of several girls and women, which made him happy."

"So, have you caught the eyes of the women because you are a swift runner?"

Janos smiled saying, "No, the race for over twenty year olds is too long. I keep tripping over all the men passing out in the races."

"I would have thought it would have been bodies of women," snickered Pauli.

"They were. I do not like to say it was so," he retorted.

He received a punch on the arm for his remark.

On the bank of the river, the three Talker Healers were relaxing after their evening meal. They rested in the shade watching and enjoying several children frolicking in the bathing cove of the river. A woman approached them. She was short, thin, middle aged, dark skinned, gaunt faced, with large dominant lips, dark brown eyes and dark, fuzzy hair. "May I speak with you alone Kaathi?"

"I would prefer Mara and Marie to be present to learn from our engagement."

She looked at the other women and thought a long while about the request. "Very well. My name is Bani."

The healers rose to give her a hug, which she grudgingly accepted.

"Now, what can I help you with?"

"I missed my menses for two cycles. I think I am with child. . ."

"Is it a problem?"

"It is. My husband died during the rains and left me with four children we could barely feed. Without him things are even tougher. We have utilized the village food cache, but I have found there never seems to be enough to go around. None of us are eating enough. I am not sure my family can survive another child. We are struggling to exist."

Kaathi jumped on the problem. "I shall bring up the fact you do not have enough to eat with the council at our next meeting and the food cache shall be increased. What about your family, have they been of any assistance?"

"My family are all dead and only his mother is living."

"Is she helping you with food and the children?"

"She does what she can. It is still not enough."

"The council meets in three days and the cache will be immediately increased. As soon as we are done talking I want you to come with us. We will supply you with some food to tide you over."

"I appreciate your kindness."

A brief quiet ensued in which Kaathi connected with Bani at a deep level of consciousness. "I sense you have something else troubling you."

"There is. I do not want this baby. I am thirty-eight years old and do not want to endure the difficulties of carrying a child and childbirth."

Marie was curious. "What sort of difficulties have you experienced?"

"During each pregnancy, I threw up many mornings. In each of my childbirths I struggled to birth them. I nearly lost my life delivering my last daughter. Wahi, the birthing-mother, told me not to have any more children. She told me it might kill me."

Bani stopped talking and was struggling to go on. The healers waited for her to continue. Bani wringed her hands and finally spoke, "I do not want to birth this child. I do not want to die. I am afraid of what will happen to my children if I die. I want an abortion."

"I presume you have given this decision much thought?"

"Oh, my god yes. It has been on my mind since my man died. Hardly a moment goes by it does not enter my thoughts. With my man gone it has become increasingly hard to give quality attention to my children. Now I am pregnant, and I am tired all the time. Giving birth to another child would be another burden in my life. I do not have the energy to take care of an infant. It is too much. I am at my wits end. It is why I am here."

Kaathi reached out and took Bani's hand and sent her love. As she held it, she opened herself to Bani to determine her sincerity. She found no flaw in her and felt the deep conflict she bore in her heart. She spoke only after she was assured the connection gave her all the information she needed to make her decision.

"Bani, I sense the turmoil you are facing. I heard you say carrying and birthing your children were difficult. I have also sensed you will not die in childbirth. I have made a decision to help you not to abort your child. I encourage you to give it life, let another family adopt it and give it a good home."

"You are not hearing me. I do not want to keep carrying it, Kaathi."

"Did you love your husband?"

"Of course."

"Perhaps it would benefit you to see this is the last gift your man gave you."

Bani looked at the mystic and absorbed her words. "You call it a gift I call it a burden."

"It is all I can offer you. Your unborn child is not a threat to your health, and I cannot in good conscience abort your child."

"I do not want to be sick every day as I was with my other pregnancies."

"I have oils and herbs to help lessen the problems you are going through," countered Kaathi.

Bani's eyes were filled with tears. It took a while for her to speak, when she did, her voice was filled with emotion. "I do not know if I can do it. I am too weak."

"Marie, Mara and I will take turns and help you with your children and tasks. I do not want you to regret aborting your child the day after you do it or the next day or any day afterward. I want you to go home and think about it and return tomorrow and we can share our thoughts and feelings again. While you are arriving at your decision, I want you to know my position on taking a life. As the High Priest and Talker Healer, I am committed to the sacredness of life. My positions impress upon me to save lives not take them. I believe we learn through our interactions with each other, and if one life is removed, it is possible some of our understanding of life may not be fulfilled."

Bani listened in earnest and shook her head unable to respond. Tears clouded her vision.

Kaathi, Marie and Mara embraced Bani and she left.

Once Bani was gone, Mara asked, "Why did you not agree to do the abortion? She wanted it."

"As you know, my decision to help a woman abort is based upon the need to save the mother's life. If the mother is in no danger, I cannot help her abort her child. It is my obligation to convince her to carry the baby to term. After the baby is born, it is my obligation to find a suitable family to adopt the child."

Mara shook her head. "Please do not take this wrong. It seems you are taking the place of a god by making such decisions."

"You have brought up a valid point. To avoid it, I go through a procedure in each case. In Bani's case, I emptied myself and went to a deep part of my consciousness, in order to make a connection with Bani's consciousness before giving advice."

"Have you ever failed at convincing the mother of the correct action to take?"

"Yes. Twice. As a healer, you cannot be dictatorial. You must realize, all you can do is provide advice, which comes to you. The decision is always theirs to make. In those two cases, I provided the liquid to abort the child. I did it to prevent them from aborting it themselves and possibly injuring themselves and the baby."

The next morning Bani awoke and again went through the reasons why she wanted to abort her child. She needed the reassurance of her own reasoning and emotions. She was assailed with doubts and sobbed often. A long while later, she composed herself and went out into an early morning mist to the Talker Healer's hut. She found Kaathi, wearing an oiled leather poncho, relaxing on the bench outside. Kaathi rose, embraced her for a long time and released her only after telling her she loved her.

Bani's already red eyes filled with tears. They went inside and the apprentices embraced her and told her they loved her. Everyone took a seat. Fresh tears slipped down Bani's face.

Kaathi and her apprentices silently waited for Bani to speak, while sending her love.

"I have gone over this many times. I examined it a few ways. This is my decision. If you help me with food and help me care for my children and my morning sickness is not bad, I will carry the child and birth it. You have to promise me you will find a good family for my child."

Tears of happiness poured forth from the healers on hearing her decision. Bani was astounded. These women were not her friends and yet they wept. Life was intriguing.

CHAPTER THIRTEEN

Kacy dropped by to visit with Leah and hold the new born babies. She had been doing it every day for the last two cycles of the moon. She had a tremendous attraction to little Marcel and found herself holding him twice as much as Kati. There was something about Marcel. It drew her to him on a much deeper feeling of love. It did not disturb her; it interested her.

The moment she arrived at Leah's house she hugged her and reached for Marcel. Leah always welcomed Kacy. There were times when Leah could not get Marcel to stop crying and Kacy would pick him up and he would quiet down. Leah noticed the attachment and marveled at it. She did not have to be a genius to see how Kacy was drawn to Marcel. Kati was often left in her crib or in Leah's arms, while Kacy cooed and sung to Marcel.

The next day Leah left the babies with Kacy and went to the Talker Healer's hut. She found Kaathi inside.

"Can I talk to you?"

"Of course."

Kaathi took Leah's arm. "I need to cool off." She steered Leah to the avenue and they walked leisurely toward the bathing area. On their way they greeted many people, with some they chatted briefly. At the water, they sat down away from the others and cooled themselves.

"You have seen how much time Kacy spends with Marcel. Have you sensed anything between Kacy and my son?"

"Other than how much they love each other?"

"So you have felt it too? It does not seem normal. Have you seen anything like this happening with other children and adults?"

"Not as strong as what is taking place with them. Are you concerned?"

"I am and I am not. It is unusual and I would like your opinion on what you think is going on."

Kaathi stared off into the distance for a while before she turned her attention to Leah. "Do you recall me telling you you would have a son named Abraham, and he would influence the mutant Wanderer tribe?"

"I do. How is this tied to my son, Marcel? When you talked about Abraham nothing was mentioned about having twins and my son's name is Marcel."

"I am going to share some of what I see for the future. I am telling you this in strict confidence. I am not prone to speak of the future. I am doing this for your benefit. Marcel is Abraham," Kaathi assured her, "and he will be a huge influence among the Wanderers. The wonderful twist is Kacy will be by his side to provide more energy and power to what he desires to accomplish as a peacemaker."

"Are you certain?"

"As sure as we are sitting here."

"How will they ever be able to infiltrate the Wanderer village without being killed?"

"It is where Ashlee will contribute to their success."

"Is she going there with them?"

"It is what I am seeing at this moment."

"How in the world will she ever be able to do it after being abused for eighteen years?"

"It will not be easy for her and yet she will do it because she will have grown bold with her spirituality and love."

"I cannot understand why Ashlee would want to go. She would be in her mid-forties, and it would be a difficult trip for her."

"The main reason for the trip is for each village to ratify a peace agreement. The Wanderer people will remember Ashlee and it will give credence to the peace treaty. The trip will also be a test of her ability to forgive them for holding her as a slave for eighteen years."

"My little Marcel is going to be so deeply involved?"

"Yes. To maintain the certainty of what I saw, I need you to keep what I told you confidential."

"Of course, I understand."

Leah was already deep in thought visualizing her son contributing to the peace between clans and tribes.

CHAPTER FOURTEEN

The season of blue skies was coming to a close and four more men and one additional woman were taking the energy sensing classes conducted by Jacob. Sharika was outdistancing all the others including Janos, Pauli and Sandor. She was also receiving lessons from Jacob on the use of poles and running with Janos to build her stamina.

After the noon meal, she got together with Jacob to learn the art of pole fighting.

Before they started to engage, Jacob said, "I want to tell you I admire how well you have been doing sensing a person's action before it occurs. You have a real gift."

"Thank you. I am not so sure it is a gift. Prior to any function I go into an expectancy mode."

"What do you mean?"

"Kaathi told me before I attend any workshop to expect something marvelous will happen. I found it works every time. I am always anticipating something wonderful to take place at every class."

Jacob acknowledged Kaathi's gifts. "She has a knack for helping people in so many ways. I shall keep her suggestion in my mind the next time I attend a class presented by her. With that in mind let us see how you do today. We have been working at half speed with the poles, and you have done well reading the energy and anticipating the strikes. I think you are ready to go through the practice at a faster pace."

They picked up their respective poles, which were wrapped at the ends with a layer of chamois stuffed with white fluff, to soften the blows. Jacob took his time increasing the speed of the blows. He was proud to see Sharika was having no difficulty in parrying his blows. He quickened his movements and freely struck her leg, hand and arm. Suddenly, he felt the blow on his leg. It was unexpected. He stepped back and assessed her. He saw a different look in her eyes, one he had never seen before. They went at each other for a long time. His blows were quick and she parried many of them. Impressive. Very impressive. Kaleez, the giant warrior of Homar, would be proud of her ability. He took a blow to his arm for his thoughts. He stepped back and called an end to the exercise.

They sat side by side sweating.

"You are doing well. Our men would be in trouble fighting you with poles. You seem to have an aptitude for sensing energy. How were you sensing what I was going to do?"

Sharika thought a moment before replying, "The twitch on my forehead was fine for you striking my back. I soon learned, in combat, it was too slow. Where I am now is at a place of knowing. I know what you are going to do and I can prepare myself for the most of the blows."

"It is exactly the way I sense things as well. I cannot believe how quickly you are picking this up. It took me two years to be where you are. Whatever you have in your bloodline it is serving you extremely well.

"So let us move onto something different. I asked you to bring your weapon today so we could practice. I would love to shoot your bow if you would let me."

"Of course. I am not superstitious about others touching it. I am particular who shoots it. I must admit not too many have touched it."

"I am going to hang the target on a tree limb and challenge you from different distances before I shoot your bow."

He moved to the limb, hung the target and walked back.

"Jacob, can I challenge you to a test of swiftness before we do it?"

"You can. What do you have in mind?"

"Let us see who can fire off ten arrows the fastest and how often we hit the target."

"This is a new test for me."

"One you should have been acquainted with long ago. Are you ready?"

"I am."

They took their stances. "Fire," announced Sharika.

Her first arrow hit the target before his. He kept losing ground to her with each arrow. She had fired all ten of her arrows as he was drawing his ninth. He hit the target center with it and the last. Both of them buried all their arrows in the target. She had three in the center and he had three.

"Very impressive," he admitted.

"Thank you. You did better than any man I have ever challenged."

"Well, I had the luxury of taking my time with my last two arrows."

They collected their arrows and went back to the original shooting line.

Jacob waved at the targets. "Do you want to shoot first?"

She fit an arrow on the bow, took aim and fired. It hit the target on the top right corner. He positioned himself, aimed and fired his arrow. It penetrated the top left corner. They shot ten arrows each and each one hit the target. Seven were in the center circle, four of his and three of hers. They stepped back ten paces and shot another ten arrows. One of her arrows missed the target, two hit the center circle. Jacob had three in the center circle. They stepped back another ten paces and fired ten more arrows each. The difference in bows came into play. Jacob had two misses and one in the center circle. Sharika had no misses and four in the circle.

They collected their arrows and came back to the last firing spot. "Your bow is very impressive. You get better with distance. It goes against the norm."

"I have not practiced recently and I was a little rusty. I should have done better. The more I shoot the more I improve, which is typical for me."

"You still did excellent. May I try your bow now?"

"If I can try yours."

"Of course."

She handed him her bow and arrows. He took the bow and pulled back on the bowstring to test it and liked what he felt. He extracted an arrow from the quiver and set it in place, took aim and fired. The arrow struck slightly off center. He acclimated to the weapon and his next nine shots he placed three in the circle and two on the line. She tested his bow and found the bow too large for her comfort and did not do as well with it as with her own bow, hitting the center circle once.

"Your bow is a masterpiece," admitted Jacob. "It is surprising; it provides more accuracy at greater distances without having to strain to hold the string."

"I could never figure it out."

"Would you be willing to show our men how to construct your bow?"

"I can, if you have all the material."

"If we do not have it, we can find it. Thank you, Sharika."

"You are welcome."

They walked back to the village. He took the opportunity to ask, "Has Kaathi talked to you about making the journey next year to Homar and Nubilon?"

"She has."

"Are you inclined to go?"

"I am. She said she wants me to meet someone."

"Did she tell you who?"

"No. She is mysterious about it."

He smiled. "It does not surprise me. The thing I learned about Kaathi is if she asks you on an adventure there is a definite reason."

CHAPTER FIFTEEN

The heavy rains cooled the air, drenching and renewing the parched land. The grasses grew quickly on the plains and the roaming herds grazed contentedly and put on weight. With the onset of the sunny season, the foals would be scampering excitedly alongside of their mothers. For now the rains kept villagers with minor problems from coming to the Talker Healer's hut giving the apprentices ample time to question Kaathi.

Inside the healer' hut, Mara quizzed the mystic, "Why can Kacy see colors associated with numbers and words and I cannot?"

"My sense is her gift has something to do with her brain. It may be physically different from yours and it accounts for her extraordinary abilities."

"I recall the stories you have shared about meeting Leah and Isaac and how you communicated mentally before using your voices. Is this similar to Kacy's gift?"

"I do not believe so. I think we are all capable of mental communication. In order to accentuate it, we must use it, practice it and become accustomed to it."

"Why were the Searcher's good at mental communication and the Wanderer's not?"

"If I have to give you an answer, I would say it was a strong, latent ability of the Searchers. The ability attracted other mutants together with the same gift. I have said this before, to be proficient at something, you have to practice. I believe the Searchers practiced a great deal."

"When there is an offspring between mutants and Normals, like Durga, is the best of both races received by the half-breed?"

"I am not certain. There appears to be a combination or collection of qualities and features from each species taking place. Some can be considered good and others detrimental. Behind everything there are reasons for them being present. Anytime a blending of races occurs there is an amalgamation of their physical features. There can be a softening in the features, a change in eye color, muscle density and bone structure and it can also affect the voice. The loss of some qualities can also take place. In most cases the dominant features will take precedence except in the case of strength, where the half-breed has less than a mutant. It is similar to what has taken place with us Kahalis. We are now a mixture of all the colors of the races. A beautiful blend in my estimation. The Story Teller has a tale telling how all races came out of one land and migrated because of lack of food, drought, curiousness and other reasons and all sorts of changes occurred to those people."

Ashlee and Scarlet were alone in their home. Ashlee was going back over what Kaathi had told her days ago about contemplating a trip to Ashlee's home village. The mystic had asked her if she would like to be part of the group making the journey. She was thrilled at being asked. The more she thought over the trip the more she realized she could be jeopardizing her relationship with Scarlet and Keri, who had accepted her as a sister and as Jacob's third wife. She wanted to make the trip and also did not want to mess things up between the women.

Prior to her marriage she had been rescued from death by Kaathi and Jacob outside of Sumati. She recuperated and spent the sunny season in Sumati with them. She had fallen in love with Jacob, gotten married in Kahali and was happily living with his wives, son and daughter.

Kaathi had told Ashlee, Jacob would not be making the trip. She was worried about leaving her new family behind. More than once Jacob had told her the decision was hers to make. Even so she was torn between going and staying home. The terrible memory of her return to her home village weighed heavily on her. She was losing sleep worrying about how to resolve the dilemma.

She made up her mind to unburden herself to Scarlet, Jacob's second wife, from Homar. The family had eaten the sunrise meal and she asked Scarlet if they could talk somewhere other than in their home.

Scarlet hooked her elbow around Ashlee's, and they walked off. They headed toward the river and sat on its bank.

Ashlee explained her position, "Kaathi is planning a trip to Homar and Nubilon and asked if I wanted to go. I talked to Jacob about it, and he said the decision is mine to make."

"Is there a problem?"

"We have been married less than a year, and it does not seem right to leave him and the rest of you. I think he is hiding the fact he would like me to stay, and I am beginning to feel comfortable you and Keri have accepted me. I do not want to disturb things and jeopardize our friendship."

"It is true we feel like you are our sister and are no longer jealous of you."

Ashlee's voice was filled with conviction. "I knew it. I do not want to ruin things."

Scarlet looked at her quizzically. "So, what do you want from me?"

"I need your advice. I am torn between visiting my relatives and staying here. What would you do?"

"Honestly, I do not know. I am fortunate I am not in your predicament. I know the chance to go back to your home is a huge reason to go, and I also know you have found a home with us you did not have as a child. Even if you talked Kaathi into postponing the trip, you may be with child or already have one. I know you would not make the trip, if it was the case."

"You are right. I would not leave my child."

"It seems you have a lot of questions you need to ask Kaathi. I can give you advice, but it will never be as good as what Kaathi would give you. You need to talk to her."

"What if she tells me she insists I go? How can I refuse? I owe my life to her. I would have to go and chance everything with my family."

"Ashlee, you are not risking everything with us. Furthermore I do not think Kaathi would insist you go. You will have to depend on Kaathi giving you the best advice possible. You have seen her do it dozens and dozens of times in the past."

"You are right. Will you come with me?"

"Of course."

"Now."

"Now?"

"Now. I cannot wait another moment. There are far too many questions I want answered."

They rose and made their way to the Talker Healer's hut. They stopped a short distance from the hut and sat on a public bench in the village square. Ashlee looked at Scarlet. "What if she thinks I should have been able to answer the questions myself?"

"Stop doubting yourself. Center yourself and go in and ask your questions and explain your fears. You know she will tell you the right thing to do."

Ashlee took a few deep breaths to calm herself. Scarlet sat beside her and sent her love. A short while later Ashlee opened her eyes. "I felt wrapped in your love, Scarlet. Thank you."

"You would do the same for me. I will keep sending love to you, while you are with Kaathi."

Ashlee wrapped her arms around Scarlet, released her and walked to the hut. Scarlet saw her stop, heard her call Kaathi's name and go inside. After what seemed like a reasonable time for a question and answer conversation, Ashlee emerged. She drew near and Scarlet saw her face was wet with tears and her eyes had a dreamy look.

Ashlee sat down without speaking.

Scarlet waited a reasonable time before throwing her question out, "Well, what did she tell you?"

Ashlee looked dumbfounded and took a long time to answer. "Tell me? Tell me what?"

Scarlet peered at her curiously, wondering what was wrong with her.

"You had all these questions you wanted to ask Kaathi. What advice did she give you?"

"Advice?. . .Honestly the questions never entered my mind."

"What? It is why you came here. It is why I encouraged you, now you get back in there and ask your questions," insisted Scarlet.

Ashlee rose looking confused. Scarlet waved her hand to move her along and watched her walk back to the hut. Scarlet saw her enter the hut, without calling Kaathi's name. She sent Ashlee love once again to help keep her centered and ask her questions. A while later she saw Ashlee push back the entrance cloth and walk slowly to her. Scarlet saw Ashlee's face was wet with tears again. She wondered what all the tears were about. Ashlee sat down and it appeared to Scarlet as if her friend was barely aware of her presence.

"Well, what did she tell you?"

"What do you mean?"

"What advice did she give you?"

"Oh goodness the questions. I forgot all about them."

"What. This is ridiculous. You get back in there and ask those questions."

Scarlet watched Ashlee wipe the tears from her face. She was concerned about Ashlee. *What in the world is happening to her? I have never seen her like this. I wonder if I should go in with her and help her with her questions?. . .No. She has to do this on her own.* "You have to go back and ask your questions, Ashlee. If you do not, you will be upset with yourself."

Scarlet's words seem to prod Ashlee to move off the bench. She shuffled slowly toward the Talker Healer's hut. She went in the hut unannounced. She remained in the hut for a long time. When Ashlee finally appeared for the third time, Scarlet knew from the look on her face she did not ask her questions. Ashlee sat down beside her.

"What is going on?

Ashlee did not answer for a long while, when she did, her voice was soft and filled with mystery and awe.

"I felt your love as I walked to her hut, and every time I went in my intention was to ask my questions. Each time I sat down and looked into Kaathi's eyes the questions and fears vanished. I sobbed uncontrollably every time I looked into her eyes. When I did manage to speak, the only thing to come out of my mouth was, 'Mother I love you, mother I love you.' I repeated it over and over and wept and sobbed. I could do nothing else. . . I looked into her eyes and her love overwhelmed me. . . My mind stopped working. I could not control myself. All the questions I had in my mind were swallowed up in her love. I lost all thoughts except to say 'Mother I love you.' When I stopped babbling and sobbing, I felt Kaathi rest her hands on my head and bless me. At some point I must have gotten up and left. . . She is much younger than me. I do not know why I called her mother. . . I do know why. . . I felt compelled to call her mother."

Ashlee looked to Scarlet pleading for help. "What happened to me?"

Scarlet remembered a story Kaathi had told her about an experience she had, and it sounded similar to what happened to Ashlee. She embraced her. "You have had a huge spiritual experience. I think you also received the answers to your questions. How could you ever stay here with us after being so deeply blessed?"

Tears trickled down Ashlee's cheeks. "I cannot. Maybe it will do me good to see my uncle and aunt and my home village. Hopefully they are alive."

Scarlet smiled and hugged Ashlee saying, "Thank goodness you have your questions answered and you are clear on what to do."

"I am clear. I know I was in the presence of someone holy and I will never leave her."

CHAPTER SIXTEEN

Kaathi collected the plants, oils and salves she thought were necessary for the upcoming trip to Homar and Nubilon and placed them in the jars and leather sacks. She turned to her apprentices saying, "The two of you should replenish what I have taken before I leave. Ask Jacob to go with you into the jungle to make sure you are safe, while you collect the medicinal plants and flowers. Between the two of you, you should have no problem finding them."

"Do not worry about us," Marie reassured her. "We have been to the sites often enough with you, we should have no problems."

"My sentiments as well," Mara chimed in. "We can handle it. You just enjoy your adventure."

"Thank you. I was not worried. I was simply reassuring the two of you of your capabilities."

"We will miss you," announced Marie.

"Both of you will be in my prayers and heart until I arrive back home. I love you."

Kaathi opened her arms and Mara snuck in before Marie and got her loving embrace from her mentor. She always loved her embraces. Back home, the Uchakwas were not known for their show of affection. Her mother displayed affection to her as a child only to have it dry up in her teens. Reluctantly, she released Kaathi.

Marie embraced Kaathi. She was smaller than her teacher when she first became an apprentice. In just these few short years she had grown taller and had filled out as a women. She owed Kaathi a great deal. She had an honored skill, the villagers respected her and she got to be near the mystic every day. She owed it all to her mentor. She took a deep breath and relaxed in

Kaathi's arms. She held onto her as long as she could without it making Mara jealous.

"I have to visit with my parents for a while," Kaathi informed her apprentices. "I will not see you until we leave. If you need me you can find me there."

Kaathi walked out of the healing hut and the ladies felt the energy drop. It did not take long for her to reach her parents' home. She greeted and embraced them and informed them, "I wanted to have some time alone with you before I left."

Millie, Kaathi's mother responded, "I am happy you did, dear. I do not know where you get the courage to go to these faraway places. This will not be easy on you and Ashlee."

"You know very little about these people," advised her father. "Please be careful."

"I will be Father."

Her mother spoke in her defense. "You know she would never go if her life was in danger, dear,"

"Promise me you will return."

"I shall, Father."

"It is all I need to know."

Her mother sighed. "Good we can talk of pleasant things. How are Leah's twins doing."

"They are fine. Getting bigger every day."

"Are they larger than non-mutant children?"

"A little."

"Tell her I asked about her the next time you see her."

"I will."

"And how are you doing? Has everyone you wanted to go with you accepted your invitation?"

"They have."

"Do be careful dear."

"I will Mother."

Pauli and Sandor had been selected by Kaathi to accompany her and they were conferring with Jacob about their responsibilities on the adventure to Nubilon and Homar for the last time.

Jacob took a deep breath. "I cannot stress enough your main responsibility above anything and anyone is to keep Kaathi safe from harm. In my estimation she is the most important person in Kahali, so keep it in mind."

"You can count on us," Pauli assured him. "She will be our main concern."

Sandor nodded his head in confirmation.

Jacob helped Pauli, Sandor and Logan's apprentices stock the large dugout with as much supplies as it could safely hold. Kaathi and Sharika placed various medicines and spices for the trip in the canoe.

The morning meals were eaten and most of the villagers were gathered at the river's edge to send them off. Scarlet, the apprentice High Priest, was not going so she prayed for the safety of the adventurers. Many in the throng wished to embrace them one more time before they departed. The last to send them off were the families of the travelers.

Kaathi's father hugged and kissed her and told her to be careful. Millie, Kaathi's mother, whose hair was graying, held her daughter for a long time. She released her saying, "I know I say this to you every time you go away. I am your mother and you are still my baby. Be careful, none of us know much about the people of Nubilon. I shall pray for you every day. Remember I love you."

"Bless you for your kind thoughts, Mother. Danger and risk lies everywhere for the fearful. I am not one of them. I do appreciate your prayers and I love you."

"Goodbye my child."

Kaathi was the last to step into the dugout. Jacob pushed the canoe off the shore and the travelers were on their adventure. Jacob waved and felt strange to be left behind. He had been by the mystic's side on every trip she made in the past. Every trip he made with Kaathi, she had always promised his wife, Keri, he would not shed one drop of blood. He knew Pauli and Sandor's wives did not have a personal meeting with her and would never have had the chance to receive the promise. He watched them paddle away and mentally prayed for the travelers' safety.

Many men followed the dugout with their eyes on Sharika. It was understandable. She had caught the fancy of dozens of men since her arrival a year ago. Sharika was slightly shorter than most Kahali women. What set her apart from other women was her physical presence. Her musculature surpassed most men in Kahali and her carriage was graceful. She was in complete command of her physical assets. A person had to look closely to detect her ancestral background. Her eyes were piercing and revealed her no nonsense approach to life. Her ribbed abdominal muscles were the envy of every man in the village and her quickness was spoken of during conversations in the village square.

Back in the dugout, Sharika watched Janos' image grow smaller and smaller and vanish. *Oh my, how he has made my life interesting and pleasurable. If it were anyone except Kaathi wanting me to go back to Homar, I would decline. Thank Creator, Janos promised me he would wait for my return. I cannot imagine why Kaathi was so adamant I come with her to Homar. There was nothing appealing to me the first time I was there. At least I will have the opportunity to see Nubilon and Ashlee's reaction to seeing her home village.*

CHAPTER SEVENTEEN

The canoe made its way up the river. Ashley's eyes clouded with tears, as she watched Zar, Jacob, Keri and Scarlet waving to her on the shore. Doubt flickered in her mind and she had to face it yet again. Family was paramount in her life, mainly due to the fact she lost hers and had lived among the mutants as a slave. Being accepted by Jacob's family, she grew content with life. She had come to another crossroad, when Kaathi asked her to come with her on this trip. The opportunity to see her home village was enticing, although not enough to pull her away from her new family. Her loyalty to the mystic and her mystical experience with Kaathi were the deciding points of why she elected to go on the trip. She wanted dearly to keep having spiritual experiences; being near Kaathi would help her continue having the experiences.

The images on the shore disappeared and her thoughts gradually shifted to what little she could remember about her life in Nubilon. The only people, other than her mother and father, she recalled were her Aunt Yara and her Uncle Ravi. She had difficulty putting a face to Ravi, although she recalled there was something unique about him. She had no problem remembering Yara. Her aunt always showered her with hugs and kisses. She did not have children of her own, and it contributed immensely to her show of affection.

She had no trouble recalling her mother and father's faces. Her mother's golden hair was what she remembered the most. Oddly, the next was her voice, possibly due to how often she was singing to her and in the home. Her mother shared many stories and went to great length to explain everything she did in their home. She saw her mother's face in her mind and marveled at her beauty. While in captivity, the only faces she could compare hers too were the faces of the mutants she associated with terror and abuse. In the quiet darkness of night, she had recalled her mother's face and hoped she looked like her.

Memories of her father centered on his handsome full-bearded face and strength. She knew he provided the meat and shared in caring for the acre of planted vegetables for their meals which her mother cooked. The only thing in common with the two cultures was the cooking smells. The mutants used a variety of spices to enhance the taste of their meals as had her mother.

The faces of her Aunt Yara and Uncle Ravi popped into her mind, and she wondered if they were alive. She was twenty-nine and they were likely around their fiftieth year, which was the average length of life. She prayed they were still living. There was much she wanted to ask them.

Pauli did not have the luxury of looking back at his family for very long. He sat in the foremost position of the canoe and had to watch for trouble on the water. He and Sandor had practiced paddling against the river current for the past ten days and he was thankful they had. His body was better accustomed to the strain.

Pauli had missed out on the journey to Sumati. The birth of his son had prevented him from going. This journey would have to do. What made it extremely pleasing was having Ashlee a member of the group. The moment he first saw her, he knew she was the most stunningly beautiful woman on the face of Mother Earth. The Creator could not have created a woman more perfect in face or form. He recalled an old story not often told of a woman named, Helen, whose face launched a thousand ships. He was certain Ashlee would not have to bow to Helen. It was hard to keep his eyes off of her. He was both thankful and disappointed she was behind him in the dugout. Although she was his best friend's wife, it did not preclude him from taking pleasure in looking at her. She had a time honored, wholesome beauty about her, while Jacob's other wife, Scarlet, exuded sensuality. Jacob's first wife, Keri, was like his wife, she did not have any such distinctive qualities.

The other newcomer, Sharika, sat in front of Ashley and he found her immensely interesting. She was one of the few women learning about sensing the interval between thought and action and the best at detecting it. He had heard from Jacob of her accuracy with the bow. For his mentor to praise anyone meant she had extraordinary skills. It was good to know, for on any trip another archer was always beneficial. He did have a chance to take a long look at Sharika before they stepped into the dugout. She wore a top revealing her midriff and he was able to see the muscle structure of her back, which impressed him as much as her muscled abdomen. While her arms were smaller than his, they were well defined. He had been told one story of her having to combat baboons from Jacob and knew most of her scars were received from them.

He took a deep breath and concentrated on his paddling and kept his eyes looking up river for any debris coming down stream.

His thoughts settled on his lifelong friend and mentor, Jacob. He had always liked and admired Jacob. Since Batu's banishment speech and his involvement with Kaathi, he had changed. He became a champion of women and treated all of them with respect and consideration. He wondered if the change was what prompted Scarlet and Ashlee to fall in love with him. The whole thing was strange. He had difficulty getting a grasp on how more than one woman could fall for the same man and not scratch the other woman's eyes out. He wondered if Kaathi approved of Jacob having three wives? She had to have given him her blessing otherwise they would not be friends. He hoped this trip would give him a better insight to whom she was.

Sandor could not believe his good fortune to be going to distant lands. He loved adventure and felt he was one of the luckiest men on Mother Earth to be making this trip. He knew Homar was on friendly terms with Kahali, thanks to Kaathi's persuasive abilities. He would have given anything to be present, when she and King Edmund went off to talk. Edmund had been angry and wanted to kill everyone in Kahali. He did not care how many of his warriors were lost in the battle. He had heard she got the king's attention when she thought he might die if he did not come with her. Whatever she told Edmund, its impact saved thousands of lives.

He never imagined the mystic would select both him and Sandor for this adventure. Kaathi had always been a puzzle to him, and this trip would give him a chance to see her in action on the adventure and hopefully shed new light on her personality. This journey would provide him with the opportunity to witness the healer's abilities. He knew she had many spiritual experiences and had expanded the content of the Relationship Sessions and introduced the Spiritual Awakening Services, after accepting the position as High Priest.

Sandor's wife wanted a child and had already lost two. She was twenty-seven and would soon be too old to safely bear a child. He wanted a son and was not sure how he would feel, if he had a daughter. He would not know what to say or do with a girl. Perhaps being able to influence the sex of the baby was something he could discuss with Kaathi. He knew the sex of crocodiles was influenced by the temperature of the nest. Perhaps something similar was true for humans.

The one thing he knew without fail it was great to be on the adventure with Pauli. Pauli missed out on the last trip Kaathi had taken, as had he. To be on an adventure was one of his lifelong dreams and it was being realized.

He smiled. Life was good.

CHAPTER EIGHTEEN

Sharika felt comfortable with the men and asked if she could help paddle. It was the third day paddling for the men and they welcomed the help to ease their burden. Before Sharika grabbed a paddle, Kaathi rubbed salve on her hands to protect and strengthen them and put leather covers on her palms. Sharika remained in the seat behind Pauli and welcomed the chance to keep her muscles toned. She felt more comfortable doing her share and it gave her mind something to concentrate on other than fleeting thoughts. She remembered Kaathi saying concentrating on physical actions was a way to meditate.

Sharika noticed how out of shape she was at the end of the day. At times she allowed her mind to wander and recall people and events in her new home, Kahali, and her old home, Hun Nation. She found herself comparing Janos with the other men in her life and found all of them falling short. She had feelings for the others but Janos had captured her heart.

Sharika smiled to herself and was aware she had missed a couple of strokes with her paddle. It was clear Janos made her forget where she was and what she was doing. It was also clear she had fallen in love with the lovable scalawag.

CHAPTER NINETEEN

The heat and humidity were intense for the past four days and took a toll on the travelers, especially the paddlers. A good amount of daylight was left, when Pauli pointed to a spot. "The place on the right looks like a good spot to spend the night."

"It is too early to stop," Sharika pointed out.

"The heat is getting to me, and I need to rest."

Sandor, in the stern of the canoe, welcomed Pauli's suggestion and set his paddle in the water to turn for the spot, while Sharika and Pauli paddled to it.

Sharika felt uneasy about the docking sight. She exited the dugout, and her unease continued. She stole a glance at Kaathi to see if she was uneasy and detected nothing. The others got out and they pulled the canoe far onto the riverbank. The clearing was large enough for the campsite. It did little to comfort Sharika. "This place is unsettling me. I do not want to stay."

"I have a pulled muscle," remarked Pauli, "and I cannot continue. It needs rest. This is as good a place as any."

"No, it is not."

Her comment fell on deaf ears. Sharika was thankful Sandor wanted her to accompany him to gather firewood. She did not want to be close to Pauli. Ashlee and Pauli partnered and went in another direction to gather wood. Kaathi and Caleb remained at the campsite.

Sharika's unease grew the further they were from the campsite. She and Sandor found some wood and were about to gather it. She bent down to collect it and the hair on her arms stood up.

She was about to say to Sandor they should leave and look somewhere else, when the sky exploded. She saw the object fall from above and crush Sandor to the ground. The few pieces of wood tumbled from his arms. The object on Sandor was a huge python. The huge snake's first coil had Sandor's right arm pinned against his body preventing him from getting to his long blade. He screamed for help. She was startled to see how quickly the python had wrapped itself around Sandor twice before she reacted. She knew with each scream the python would squeeze tighter and his breath would be shallower.

She was ten steps from him. She ran to him pulling her long knife from its sheath on the way.

Sandor eyes were on her and were crazed with fear.

She had never seen anyone exhibit such fear.

Even if Sandor could have gotten to his knife the snake's head was behind him. He and the snake were on the ground and his free arm was pinned to the ground. Without worrying about whether she would hit Sandor, she brought her long knife down on the python's body just behind its head. Despite the snake's massive muscles the blade drove its way through its flesh and into the ground beyond.

She used the knife to shove the head aside. She dropped her weapon and grabbed the snake where its head was severed from its body and pulled at it to unwrap its body from Sandor. Despite the head being severed it took all her strength to remove the rest of the python from Sandor.

She dropped to her knees. Her arms shook with effort and fear. Sandor took a huge breath and managed to get to his knees and grabbed Sharika and hugged her. They remained locked in the embrace until they stopped shaking.

Their eyes were fixated on the dead python's head. Its mouth was still moving as if it wanted to swallow Sandor.

"My God, thank you Sharika. If we had gone our own way I would be dead. I owe my life to you."

"It could have been me it chose to eat. You would have done the same for me."

He leaned toward her and gave her another hug.

The rest of the group heard Sandor's scream and came running. They saw the dead snake and assumed it was Sandor who saved Sharika.

Sandor shook his head. "I screamed. The damn snake had me in its clutches. Were it not for Sharika, I would be in the Land of No Shadows with my ancestors. She rushed to my aid and killed the monster."

The jaws of the dead snake were still moving, seeking to swallow its prey. Sandor watched it and shivered. The terrifying experience still dominated his body.

Pauli looked at Sharika and realized why she did not want to camp at this sight. "I apologize for ignoring you."

Sharika narrowed her eyes. "Thankfully, you are safe."

Her sarcastic tone hurt Pauli. He diverted his eyes from her.

Paul and Sandor drug the carcass of the python to the river and dumped it. Sharika stuck her long blade in the snake's mouth and dropped it in the river.

The group had eaten, stoked the fire and was tucked into the trees for safety. Pauli, Sandor and Caleb were close to each other and talked in soft monotones. Sharika, Ashlee and Kaathi were in another tree clustered together.

Sharika could still make out Kaathi's eyes. "You are supposed to be the intuitive one. Why did you not say something in my support? And you Ashlee, why did you not say something?"

Kaathi's eyes were smiling as she spoke, "Ashlee sensed what you sensed and quizzed me with her eyes. I did not want her to say anything and I chose to not speak as well."

"Why?"

"I sensed what was to occur needed to take place. It will enhance your standing in our village."

"I do not need it."

"I know. Regardless, your courage will be talked about by Caleb and will affect many decisions."

"What decisions?"

"Let us leave the future unfold and enjoy the surprises."

"You can be a frustrating woman, Kaathi."

"So I have been told."

"Does it bother you?"

"Not in the least."

In the tree holding the men, Pauli whispered to Sandor, "I hope you know I or Caleb would have saved you."

He shook his head. "Yes, but it was Sharika – a woman saved me. Never in a million years would I have guessed it. After the initial shock, she charged to my rescue and slashed its head off. From the angle of the cut I am sure its head was not sticking out far from its body. She was sure handed and strong as hell. I shall sing her praises to anyone willing to listen back home."

Caleb patted him on the shoulder. "This was your lucky day, and you will not be the only one praising her."

CHAPTER TWENTY

The next day was hot and unremarkable. The team of paddlers took a longer midday break from the intense heat. Upon making camp, Sandor suggested Sharika join him to eat her evening meal with him away from the group. They walked to the riverbank and sat down.

Sandor rested his hand atop hers. "I want to thank you again, and I thought I owed it to you to tell you a little about myself."

Sharika rewarded him with her brightest smile. "How nice."

"Pauli, Jacob and I grew up near each other. Jacob was the oldest and I the youngest. Jacob always was the best at everything he did and caught the eye of the then current Warrior Hunter. He was asked to be his apprentice at an early age. When his mentor died, I was hoping he would ask me to be his apprentice. It did not happen. He selected Pauli who was more his age. It did not matter I was a better shot with the bow. Jacob was looking for loyalty more than skills. It is hard to describe how happy I was when every councilperson could select a second apprentice and I was chosen by Jacob."

"Do you have visions of ascending to the position of Warrior Hunter?"

"No. It would mean my friends would be dead. It is too high a price to pay for the position."

"Tell me about your wife."

"I have known, Terchee, ever since I could remember. We were seventeen when we married. The only thing missing in our lives is a child. She has had two miscarriages. We are hopeful she will carry our next child to the end."

"So, you are happy?"

"Yes. We actually fell in love long before we were married. I do not know why I waited an extra year before asking her to be my wife."

"Do you have married friends?"

"We do. Besides Jacob and Pauli and their wives, Terchee has three ladies she grew up with and they are now married and we see them as well."

"What do you do when you get together?"

"We usually share a meal, wine and talk and play guessing games afterward."

"Do your talks ever touch upon Creator?"

"Rarely."

"Why not?"

"I do not know. Maybe we want to relax and have fun. Creator is heavy talk."

"Did you always believe in Kaathi's Creator?"

"No. When I was young, Romir was High Priest. I did not like going to the religious services. The High Priest kept putting the fear of the gods into us. It was distasteful to me. When Romir died and Kiirt committed suicide, Kaathi became High Priest, and the sessions were no longer mandatory.

"I knew she had talked King Edmund out of making war, and she had us visualize seeing the fire turn on itself and saved the village. Those occurrences made me curious what kind of person could do those things. I succumbed and attended one service she conducted, and I was hooked. It was easy to see how she could convince the king not to go to war."

"What are your thoughts about Jacob having multiple wives?"

"I have mixed feelings about it. I would not consider taking another wife. I will say, since I have been attending the sessions and services conducted by Kaathi, I am opening up to a different way of looking at life and relationships. I imagine as my friendship with Kaathi continues my personal philosophy will keep changing."

"Are you looking forward to visiting Homar and Nubilon?"

"Indeed. This kind of opportunity does not come often. It came and I jumped on it. The Homarians were an abusive tribe. Thankfully, the king is taking action to change the men by giving them the chance to attend classes about relationships. I do not know anything about the Nubilons, and I am more anxious about them. They must be a decent clan since Ashlee lived there as a child."

"We shall find out soon enough."

CHAPTER TWENTY-ONE

The travelers approached an area of the river Kaathi remembered to be dangerous from her last adventure. Pauli was in the bow of the dugout. "Pauli be wary of this area coming up. I recall this part of the river is a crossing place for zebra and the crocodiles congregate here in anticipation of them crossing."

"Thank you for the warning."

Soon after Kaathi's warning, Pauli spotted the first croc lying on the bank of the river. Not long afterward he saw several others on the banks and in the water. Up ahead he saw a large one slip into the water and angle its way toward them.

"We have one coming right at us," he warned the others.

Sharika spotted him. "I will try to discourage him."

Fortunately, for Sharika the animal did not submerge. The tactic puzzled her, and she took advantage of its stupidity.

"Stop your rowing," she sternly commanded.

The croc came nearer at a steady and frightening pace.

Both men obeyed her and the boat slowed and stopped. Before it was caught by the river current Sharika took advantage of the lull in movement. She timed its approach and fired off her first arrow. The croc's reaction was proof of the arrow hitting its mark, which was its right eye. It snapped at the air. Its jaws a menacing sight to those in the dugout. The croc thrashed in the water and swam at them full speed. It opened its jaw wanting to snap at the canoe, and she sent another into its mouth. Its jaw clamped down on the dugout. Sharika and Kaathi were splattered with water from the monster croc's rush. They leaned away from the open jaws to avoid being grabbed. Out of the corner of her eye, Sharika saw a blur of action. Pauli's arm rushed past her with a hatchet. He drove it into the croc's good eye. The croc reacted to the blow by bringing its tail to action. Its tail rose out of the water and swiped at Pauli. It fell short and he drove his hatchet into the croc's eye again. This time the croc released the dugout and drove against the canoe with its snot. It rocked the dugout.

"Paddle," yelled Pauli.

Sharika grabbed hers and stuck it in on the opposite side and frantically paddled. Sandor quickly drove his paddle into the water. They left the sightless croc thrashing about in the water searching for them. Other crocs sensing the old one was in trouble circled it, waiting for the opportunity to strike a death blow.

They put every ounce of energy they had into their strokes to get away from the menacing crocs. The crocs did not pay much attention to them. They were more interested in the old croc bleeding and fighting for its life. Nervous sweat ran down the paddler's bodies as they rowed furiously to safety. They cleared the danger zone and resumed paddling normally.

Kaathi was the first to speak, "I think we need to take a break to rest and eat."

"I agree," said Pauli and found a suitable place to make temporary camp. They drove the dugout aground, got out and pulled it further ashore. No one spoke until they had consumed fruit and dried meat.

"Jacob told us you were an excellent shot," said Sandor. "Putting an arrow in a moving croc's eye is quite a feat. Thank goodness you and Pauli were able to hurt the huge croc enough for us to escape. We were fortunate we did not capsize. Those teeth marks on our dugout will verify our stories of our close call."

Sharika smiled. "I am glad I am a good shot. It has saved my life and the lives of friends during altercations with baboons."

"Were you afraid?"

"I would be lying, if I said no. What about you?"

Sandor grinned. "Let me check my shorts and I can tell you."

CHAPTER TWENTY-TWO

Days later Kaathi pointed to a clearing indicating she wanted to stop. They landed the canoe and pulled it ashore and unloaded what they needed for the stay. The men gathered firewood, returned and allowed Sharika to ignite the fire with her tools. They settled down and the inquisitive one, Ashlee, asked Kaathi, "The men usually choose where to stop. Why did you want us to camp here?"

"This is where Jacob and I had our encounter with Leah and Isaac."

As they busied themselves making camp, Ashlee approached Kaathi, "Were you excited or scared when you met them?"

"I was excited. It was my first encounter with a human, other than the Ancients, who could communicate mentally. I had to contain myself and not confuse or scare them."

"It had to have been staggering for Jacob to accept mutants were intelligent."

"He did have a hard time." Kaathi smiled as she remembered the event.

"Jacob was assigned to protect you, I cannot imagine what was going through his mind."

"Oh, he definitely had his defenses up. Even when they showed themselves he was distrustful. I could not blame him. Mutants and the Kahalis had been enemies for centuries. You have to remember these were Searchers not Wanderer mutants. We Normals, or non-mutants, never knew the difference between them. The Searchers never raided Kahali. They were a peaceful clan trying to survive the wars between the mutants and Normals. They kept being drawn into the fray because they were mutants. Isaac and Leah had recently lost their son in a battle and fled their homeland to seek a peaceful existence. They were the last of their tribe and knew they had to procreate to keep their clan alive.

"We were together for several days and became friends. After I heard their story, I asked them to live with us in Kahali. They were skeptical. My promise to stand by their side and protect them had little effect. I had them stay behind at the campsite, while we went on to Homar to bring Prince Zach back with us."

"Why did you not let Jacob fight Kaleez for the right to bring back the prince?"

"I had promised Keri, Jacob would not shed a drop of blood on the trip. I did get a scratch as I dropped the shield and dripped blood onto the ground."

"The story is Kaleez was a giant and could have easily killed you. How did you prevent him from killing you?"

"I was fortunate he was open to my love."

"All you did was love him?"

"It was."

The group had gathered around and had listened to the women. Sandor spoke, "I am curious, was your mother like you? Did anything significant happen in her life? Did she encourage you in your endeavors?"

Kaathi smiled. "She was similar to most of the girls and women in Kahali and was unlike me. She did give me free reign to wander my own path. It was my grandmother, Attar, who was out of the ordinary. Attar had quit going to the services the High Priests performed. Mother told me Attar's parents, sister and brothers were praying for her to come back to the services and salvation. Her sister, Angelina, was praying for her to realize God. To Angelina, it did not matter how Attar attained realization. Do you see the difference in the two prayers?"

"I think I do. The first prayer concerns peoples' limiting beliefs. The second frees her to realize God or Creator. What little I know of the High Priests, they did not offer any hope of realizing God."

"You are right.

Sandor's mind switched to the current. "We know Homar is at peace with us, hopefully, we will be received peacefully in Nubilon."

"It is uncharted area we are entering after we leave Homar. We will need to be cautious," advised Pauli. He stretched sleepily. "I suggest we all get to our berths in the trees and get some sleep for our next day's journey."

CHAPTER TWENTY-THREE

Days later Kaathi recognized some landmarks and knew they were near Homar. She looked forward to seeing Renee and catch up on pertinent news. She had brought Sharika along to re-introduce her to Prince Zach. After how well she and Janos were getting along, she was not sure what was going to happen at the meeting.

The lone drum announced their entrance into the patrolled area of Homar. The travelers showed their hands briefly and continued rowing. A short time later they came upon the throng awaiting them. The travelers drew near the crowd and recognized Renee and the other Kahali women and the lone man who left to marry a Homarian.

The moment King Edmund's warriors saw Kaathi they lowered their weapons. Some smiled and called her name, remembering she had saved their lives by talking to the king.

Kaathi was greeted warmly by King Edmund, Queen Monika, secondary Queen Angela and her son Prince Zach as well as all the other secondary queens and children. Prince Lawrence was noticeably absent.

"Kaathi, it is pleasant to see you again," pronounced King Edmund. "You remember my family and my military leaders. We on the other hand do not recognize anyone, except for Jacob's apprentice, whose name escapes me."

"Let me introduce my friends," suggested Kaathi. She walked Edmund, Monika, Angela, Zach and the other royal family past each member of her party and introduced each one. King Edmund was hard pressed to release Ashlee's hand, during the introductions. He had never seen any woman so breathtakingly lovely. He was sorry to hear she was Jacob's wife. Had she not been, he would have instantly wooed her. Edmund lingered in front of Ashlee and gave her his best smile.

Regaining his composure, he was again in front of Kaathi. He waved his servant, Edgar, over. "I presume you remember Edgar. He is now a free man and is a servant of mine."

"Of course I recall Edgar, he treated us with great respect."

Edgar smiled at the praise.

"Edgar, would you make the arrangements for a sumptuous meal for the family and our guests? We will be dining in the lodge."

"It shall be done royally, King Edmund."

Edgar left and the king took Kaathi's arm and led her to the meeting lodge where they could lounge and talk until the meal was prepared. He specifically selected the lodge so his subjects could see and hear what transpired. They arrived at the hall and Edmund directed the family to one side of the largest table and the Kahali party on the other side.

Caleb waited for the king's attention. "Edmund, I heard you also had a son, Lawrence. Is he on a trip?"

"He is on a forced trip. I banished him from my kingdom. He and four of my military leaders attempted a coup."

Caleb's mouth dropped open in astonishment. "Was anyone killed?"

"Thankfully, no one. My daughter, Viola, saw Lawrence conspiring with one of my lieutenants and felt something was wrong and talked to Zach who confirmed it, and he asked Kaathi to confirm the coup. Armed with this information I confronted Lawrence and the four leaders. They confessed and I banned them and offered their families the choice to go with their husbands or stay. All of them stayed."

"What prompted the coup?"

"The four leaders did not like the changes taking place due to the Relationship Sessions. Lawrence fancied himself as king after Zach and I were killed. Slavery was going to be reestablished upon my death, and the lieutenants were to get more land, wives and slaves."

Ashlee was curious. "How did you feel about your leaders and your son's betrayal?"

"Before my transformation, I would have been filled with rage and felt justified in having them whipped to death in the square for all to see. My feelings were much different. It broke my heart to know Lawrence was conspiring to kill me and Zach. It made me sad he and the others could not accept honoring women and give them justice, rights and equalities. They did not attend the sessions thus they did not know how to change. I am still trying to recover from the shock of it all. Having someone hate you to the point they want to kill you is sobering."

"I am glad to see you and the rest of your family are well and survived the coup," added Ashlee.

Edmund looked at Ashlee as she spoke and marveled at her beauty. It was a rarity to have a woman with her startling looks and ego free personality. There had to be a reason she had such concern and compassion.

He waved his hand as if warding off a fly and directed his words to Kaathi. "We have talked enough about the coup. Ashlee is a beautiful woman and I surely would have remembered her had I seen her in Kahali. I assume there is a story connected to why I did not?"

"You are correct. Ashlee escaped from the Wanderers two years ago. She had spent eighteen years there as a slave to a mutant named, Ezra. Jacob and I found her outside of Sumati near death."

A pang of shame hit Edmund. He easily imagined what the beastly mutants had done to her over the years. His heart went out to her. He wanted to smash Ezra's face to a pulp for the atrocities and humiliation he had inflicted on her. He recognized his feelings and wondered if he would have felt the same were she a gangly, old, wrinkled woman. He shook his head at himself, knowing the answer.

It was only a few years ago he had emancipated the slaves of Homar. All of his servants had been slaves. They had been relegated to slavery as a punishment for being the offspring of the combined dark and light races of Homar. Actually, he had to give the credit to Kaathi. She had transformed him, and he freed the slaves. He and the kings before him had caused much pain and grief, and he still felt guilty at times. He pushed the shame aside knowing he had taken the correct action.

Edmund was cognizant of what mutant slaves looked like. They were all filthy, skinny and disheveled. This woman cleaned up astoundingly well. He was certain he had never seen a vision as lovely as Ashlee. Knowing the mutants never took children under the age of seven he calculated her age to be close to thirty. A remarkable thirty for she looked in the prime of her life, which for most women was somewhere between twenty and twenty-five.

"Do you remember what village you came from?"

"I do. I lived in Nubilon with my parents. It is where our party is going after our stay with you."

"I hope you stay here long enough for us to get to know all of you," remarked Queen Monika.

"Well spoken my dear. We shall not let you run off until you tire of us," insisted Edmund.

Secondary Queen Angela's first sight of Ashlee had her hoping she was near twenty. She would be a magnificent wife for Zach. She cast her eyes toward her son and saw he was keenly aware of Ashlee's breathtaking beauty. Perhaps her age would not be a hindrance to their romance. The dagger was driven into her heart and her son's with Ashley's words.

"I almost did not come," she announced. "I am a recent bride of Jacob, our Warrior Hunter."

"What?" exclaimed the king. "The rascal already had a wife and she took Scarlet into their home. I was this moment thinking of him."

"It is true and he took her as his second wife."

The king laughed. "Well, we did exchange something. We have multiple wives, now you have multiple wives."

Edmund's eyes drifted over to Sharika. "I recall you stayed with us for a few days and you left in a hurry."

"I did."

"Neither I nor anyone I talked to knows why you left. Was there a good reason?"

"Yes, I found too many of your men boorish and lacked respect for women."

"I am sorry you had a bad experience. We are working on instructing our men how to respect women and treat them as equals."

"I understand, unfortunately, I found it difficult to contain my temper after experiencing their horrible behavior."

"Once again, I apologize. We have around nine hundred men attending our Relationship Sessions, and more are attending every day. At some point we hope all of them will be attending."

Edmund turned to his son, Zach, and smiled. "My son is one of two dozen instructors and he has always had the utmost respect for his mother, Angela, and women. It used to upset me he was what I considered unmanly. Since my conversion, I can see the goodness in him. Perhaps it would do you good to have a conversation with him and learn what we are trying to accomplish."

Sharika looked at the prince and smiled. "If he is willing, I would love to talk in length about it."

"Excellent, I shall leave the arrangement to the two of you."

Kaathi smiled, wondering if Sharika knew it was why she had asked her to be part of the adventurers.

CHAPTER TWENTY-FOUR

King Edmund insisted the travelers stay at his palace. None of them opposed him. The accommodations were a welcome change from the nights spent in treetops and around campfires. On the second night of the traveler's stay, Edmund came across Kaathi and he guided her to a corner of his great room and they sat.

"I must tell you there is no one so filled with joy as you. The moment you stepped out of the canoe and smiled at me I felt it. Others in this world are stars but you are the sun. It is a blessing to see you again, Kaathi. I miss your energy. I can talk to others intimately and never feel what I feel when I am talking to you."

She embraced him and smiled. "You are gracious, Edmund. Years ago you never would have felt it."

"Indeed, I would not have."

"I can see ejecting Lawrence has taken its toll on you. How do you feel about your son's betrayal?"

"Ah, I did not think I could fool you. I talked to him time and again about attending the session on relationships presented by his mother and Zach. He would not budge. He hated them and I know he hated me and would not talk to me because I changed. I was a huge disappointment to him, and he did not see the need for acknowledging women. I have always felt uneasy talking about expelling him to my wives."

"It might be you felt guilty."

"I am sure it was part of the reason. On one hand, I understood Lawrence and my officers' anger. On the other hand, I felt I had let them down. Banishing Lawrence and four of my men was extremely difficult. It ate at my gut for a long time and often comes up in my thoughts. How can I rid myself of this guilt?"

"Decisions which affect people's lives often cling to rulers. What you need to remember is decisions are made with current knowledge. Part of your problem is your old self never looked back at a decision. This new self has a tendency to judge what you have done, and it is a mistake. Second guessing yourself can drive you to ruin. You need to keep yourself from getting mired in confusion. Trust yourself to know what is right and what is wrong. If you are still in turmoil, quiet yourself and wait for an answer to come."

"Where will this answer come from?"

"From your intuitive self, your greater self, from the self in touch with Creator."

"This is new to me."

She smiled. "Perhaps it is time you got in touch with a deeper part of yourself. Perhaps it is time you came face to face with whom you truly are."

"And you think I can do it?"

"I do, otherwise I never would suggest it. Are you meditating?"

"Not as often as I should."

"The more you do the easier it is to pull answers from your deeper self."

"Thank you for your counsel. And what about you, Kaathi? What is happening?"

"More and more of me is falling away."

"If true, what is left?"

"Enough to communicate with you and enough to recognize emotions. These emotions come and leave me in less than a span of breath. Only love remains for me to revel in. I am grateful joy is present for a greater expanse of each day. It becomes increasingly more difficult to deal with day to day matters. I am thankful I have two healing apprentices and two High Priest apprentices."

"If what you say is true, why did you come on this adventure?"

"I organized it for those coming with me. Each one has a special role to play in this adventure."

"How do you see it evolving?"

"It is evolving so everyone, including you, can learn. Sweet Ashlee was defiled and abused as a slave. Underneath all of her pain a rich, beautiful, greater self was filtering through to give her hope and courage. She has a Pollyanna personality and chooses to see the goodness in all circumstances and people. She hated what the mutants did to her but never hated them.

"She is making this trip in hopes of finding some living relatives and see if other women in Nubilon are as blessed as she in body and mind. The adventure will reveal her beauty is a resident of her heart."

"Our Elder, Caleb, will face challenges on this trip and be tested beyond his imagination. He will have to marshal his wisdom."

"And what of the two warriors?"

"They will be why Caleb will be challenged. The Nubilons are entrenched in smothering and stifling women. Sandor and Pauli will be the catalysts for the change to take place in Nubilon."

"And what of the Hun woman, Sharika?"

"Ah, her challenge will be here in the form of your son, Zach. I brought her along specifically to get to know Zach. The decision to pursue her relationship with him is up to her. She has a man back in Kahali who loves her."

Edmund smiled. "And now I come to you. Why are you taking part in this adventure?"

"To love you and everyone I meet."

Edmund smiled.

CHAPTER TWENTY-FIVE

Kaathi and Ashlee were on one of the palace verandas refreshing themselves with a cup of coconut water. Edgar approached. "Can I get you anything?"

"No. Could you do something for me?"

"Anything for you, Kaathi."

"Would you ask Renee and Andre to come here?"

"I can."

Edgar left and Ashlee asked Kaathi, "Have you noticed the wonderful color of his skin?"

"I have. All of the interracial people have it, and they seem to have the best physical features of the dark and light races. They are not as deeply tanned as most of the Kahali. I had a chance to talk to Edgar, and according to him, there is a resurgence in their desire to know their god. It gave me the opportunity to talk to him about Creator. He seemed interested. I assured him someone would share the philosophy with the Homarians. He was happy to hear it."

"Do you think there is anyone in Homar who can conduct the services?"

"I was hoping to talk to Queen Angela and Prince Zach about it before we left," answered Kaathi.

They saw Edgar approaching with Renee and Andre. Introductions were made and embraces given and they settled down in the chairs.

"You look radiant, Renee."

"Thank you, Kaathi. It is because there is a new love in my life. Andre and I have a daughter."

"Oh my goodness. Congratulations. What is her name?"

"Kate, in your honor."

"How sweet of you. You will have to let us see her."

"We will."

"I can see how it has affected Renee," noted Ashlee. "How has it affected you, Andre?"

"She is a blessing and as cute as can be. Before I met Renee, I would have been angry my wife did not give me a son. I always wanted to teach my son to be brave and skilled. For the moment, those feelings and desires are gone. It was the old me. I am utterly happy Kate has come into my life. If we have a son, I can still teach him all I know. The pleasure will simply be postponed."

"Do you have a son with any of your other wives?"

"I do consequently I am not too disappointed."

Kaathi smiled and touched Ashlee's arm. "If you would have seen Andre before he met Renee, you would have been terrified by him. He epitomized the male in Homar. He was rough, brash, brazen, unbending and constantly looking for a fight."

Ashlee turned to Renee. "Well Renee, you did a marvelous job of influencing him to change."

"Oh, I cannot take the credit. All the credit goes to Kaathi. Andre was angry the war between our villages did not happen. He wanted to return with the spoils of war, namely women. He spotted me one day and told my father he was going to take me back with him to Homar. Neither my father nor I wanted it to happen. Since Kaathi challenged Edmund, for the right to take Edmund's son back with her, Andre challenged my father so he could take me back to Homar. Edmund heard of the challenge and there was a meeting to discuss the challenge. My father would have been no match for Andre. Jacob was there and stood in for my father and humiliated Andre in a contest. Andre was shunned by his friends after the bout, and he was hurt physically and mentally. Homar's medicine man was nowhere to be found to tend to Andre. Kaathi saw how hurt he was and took him to her hut, tended to him, talked to him lovingly and won his heart. He left her hut a changed man, found me and properly courted me. We were married in Kahali and here."

"What a grand story," bubbled Ashlee.

Kaathi reached out and touched Andre's arm. "How are you getting along with your fellow military leaders?"

"Good. Edmund questioned the remaining leaders after the failed coup for recommendations and two of the men I recommended are now leaders."

"And how are you doing helping Renee at the sessions?"

"I am still learning, and my presence is influencing some men to attend. At times, I contribute something worthwhile."

"I knew you would be helpful. How are you and Carver getting along?"

"Good." He chuckled. "Sometimes he drinks me under the table and sometimes I do it to him. It is the same with the contests we have at our campfire gatherings. The new leaders fit in well, and they have the good sense not to challenge either of us. Occasionally, Kaleez shows off and whips our ass. Oh, excuse my language."

Kaathi smiled. "I have heard worse from others and from you."

He returned the smile. "I guess you have."

There was a small lull in the conversation and Renee asked Ashlee, "How did you become friends with Kaathi?"

Ashlee spun her story about being a slave and seeing Kaathi in her dreams. She related how she escaped from the Wanderer village, how she was rescued by Kaathi and Jacob and nearly killed by Ezra. She went on to describe how she fell in love with Jacob and married him and was made an apprentice High Priest by Kaathi.

"Now you are up to the present moment," ended Ashlee.

Renee smiled sheepishly. "I am sure everyone says something about how lovely you are. Do you ever get tired of hearing it?"

Ashlee smiled. "I do not. I have been called many terrible things, and it is wonderful to have people say nice things to me. In time, they will get used to my looks and talk about other things. Some are already doing it."

It was Renee's turn to be curious. "Has your beauty caused you any problems?"

"A few times men have tried to take advantage of me. I had to correct their behavior."

"You did?"

"There were many times while I was among the mutants I had to fight for reasons I would rather not talk about."

"I am sorry I brought it up," apologized Renee.

"No need to be. It is all behind me. I do not like to dwell in the past unless it is enjoyable or serves a purpose."

A servant appeared at the room's entrance and announced, "A woman wants an audience with you, Kaathi."

Kaathi excused herself and followed the servant to the woman. She was slight of build, dark eyed with dark, curled hair haloing her head. Her hands and fingers were delicate as was her nose and ears. Sweat glistened on her upper lip and her exposed teeth were white and evenly spaced. The woman spoke, "I heard you were not staying long. My name is Charmane. I desperately need to talk with you. Do you have a moment?"

"I do." She took the woman's arm and led her outside to the bench in the shade of a large tree. She felt Charmane's nervousness. "How can I help you?"

"Over the years my husband has become angrier and angrier. For the past three years has struck me in anger. My husband needs to attend the Relationship Sessions. He needs to learn how to respect me."

"Have you talked to him about attending?"

"I tried. The mere mention of it makes him angry. I want to attend but am afraid to go lest he hurts me. I am at my wits end. How can I get him to change?"

"Other than ask him to attend the classes, I have nothing. Have you provoked him to cause him to get angry?"

Charmane gave Kaathi a bewildered look. "No, absolutely not. I have come to you, why would you ask such a question?"

"I asked you because the truth of any situation or event lies somewhere between your perception of what is happening in your marriage and the perception of what your husband thinks is taking place in your marriage. I am sure from your standpoint, you feel as if you did nothing to warrant being abused. From your husband's position, he may feel justified in the action he took to put you in your place because he felt you did not respect him or his judgement. As the abused person, you tend to amplify certain events, issues and words and see them through your feelings, whereas your husband would downplay what he said or did and blame you for provoking him and point out tradition is on his side."

Charmane grudgingly saw Kaathi's logic. "What you say might be true. I can only tell you my experience."

"I fully understand, Charmane. I wanted to make sure you saw your husband's viewpoint in all of this. Having said that, do you still feel he has abused you unjustifiably?"

"Yes I do."

"I agree with you, he should attend the sessions. I can unequivocally tell you, if he does not attended the sessions, he is not ready to change any portion of his personality."

"I was afraid you would say that. His anger is escalating." Fear showed on Charmane's face. "I am afraid he will start hitting me in the face."

"Do you love him?"

She hesitated for the briefest moment. "I am not sure any more."

"The solution is to leave him."

"It is not simple," countered the woman.

"At this moment, it is also difficult because there is nothing in place to safeguard you separating from him. I have heard you say you are afraid of your husband. There is another truth and it is you are afraid of what lies beyond married life. The unknown exists outside of your home and in my observation of women with similar troubles, most of you are unwilling to remove yourself from one terrible existence and place yourself in unknown situation. Am I correct?"

"No," she stated emphatically and slowly recanted, "Yes, I am fearful of what lies beyond me leaving my husband. I am not sure who will help me. If I left him, I am fearful of what he might do."

"I fully understand your worry. Many hang onto a bad marriage or relationship simply because they are uncertain what lies beyond it. My advice is to seek help from Renee or directly from Queen Angela. You need to insist they have something in place for women like yourself. Keep the pressure on them so they will take action to help you. When help is in place, do not hesitate to take advantage of it and flee from your marriage. Any time fear has its grip on you it limits what you are able to do. Fear constricts our mental wellbeing and our abilities to become whom we want to become or need to become."

"It leaves me in a precarious position right now. How do I handle it?"

"Again I am advising you to see Renee or the queen and see how they can help you. The more women approaching them with such problems the quicker the solution will appear. For the present, appease your man as best as you can, and stay out of harm's way. I apologize I cannot do more than give you advice and pray for you."

Charmane nodded. A forlorn look clung to her face. "I understand. At least you have told me where to seek help."

Charmane rose and Kaathi embraced her and told her she loved her.

CHAPTER TWENTY-SIX

Edmund arranged for a meeting with the Elder at the palace. Caleb arrived and they seated themselves after the cordialities.

"I wanted this time alone with you, Caleb, to talk ruler to ruler. I did not want anyone else around to influence what either of us might say."

"I was wondering what this meeting was about. What is it you want to discuss?"

"How is the Relationship Sessions going in Kahali?"

"They are going well for Kaathi. As far as what they are doing for me, they are disturbing my peace. The fact is they are a pain in my ass. My predecessor, Morgan, complained near the end of his life about all the problems laid in his lap. The greatest of these were caused by Batu and Romir the old High Priest. Batu was a revolutionary thinker and was always finding something to change in our tradition and laws. Romir, being a priest, was upholding religious laws and tradition. The two were always in conflict. Morgan was constantly in the middle of it all. He often told me he was sorry he accepted the Elder position. There are times I feel the same way about Kaathi and the sessions and services. People are always coming to me complaining about losing our gods. They say the new society we live in has little or no respect for old traditions."

Edmund shook his head. "Do they not realize the changes are for the better?"

"No. They are angry they have to contend with change and they do not like it. They want stability in their lives and many people are talking negatively about the sessions and services."

Edmund took a deep breath before saying, "Damn, the same thing is happening here. Even as a supreme ruler, I hear about all of these disturbances from my people. They never would have had the nerve to say anything to me, when I was a ruthless, dictatorial king. I think they are taking advantage of my new personality. In some ways, the old way I ruled was easier, my word was law and no one dared challenge me. The trouble is I have changed too much to be cruel and dictatorial; consequently, my people come to me and bitch about a host of things I could care less about. It takes all I have in me to control myself. There are days when my stomach is upset. I do not know how long I can keep up the good face and not scream at them."

Caleb's eyes drifted away from the king for a moment. "Have you ever thought of letting one or more of your leaders handle the complaints?"

"What if the one I ask does not feel comfortable doing it?"

"Do you feel comfortable doing it?"

"No."

"I would not worry too much. If you see it is getting to him, rotate the responsibility every year or two to another military leader."

"I could always sweeten the position by offering land and I know women who want to be married. Those women would be another reward."

"A marvelous idea, Edmund."

Edmund beamed. "I am glad we had this talk, Caleb."

"I am pleased I could help you. My suggestion sounds good and I think I am going to follow it myself. I am going to have one of my apprentices handle the complaints."

"Indeed. It is always good to release oneself of burdens. Perhaps," reflected Edmund, "when I do not have to listen to all the annoying prattle, joy will come into my life."

CHAPTER TWENTY-SEVEN

After the morning meal, Prince Zach cornered Sharika and had her accompany him onto one of the three palace verandas. The air was still comfortable as they settled into their chairs.

"I am sorry," apologized Zach, "we did not see much of each other the last time you were here."

"I was pulled in too many directions," offered Sharika.

"How long are you staying?"

"I honestly do not know. Most everything is determined by Kaathi."

Zach wanted to know where her head and heart were and mildly pointed out, "Sounds a little dictatorial."

"Coming from a prince, your words sound odd."

He smiled. "I suppose every group has to have a leader."

"Were you concerned she was a dictator, when she took you away from your father?"

"No. We had been in contact with each other via visions for some time, and I knew her character."

"Then why suggest she is a dictator?"

"Frankly, I wanted to know where you stood with her."

She eyed him and threw a question back at him to determine where he stood now about Kaathi. "I know you and she were aligned. What are your thoughts about her now?"

He smiled at how she challenged him right back. "In my current brief conversation with Kaathi, I found her energy clearer, brighter and more focused. I would follow her anywhere, if she asked."

"You are a prince and you would submit to her wish?"

"Yes, I believe she is nearing enlightenment, if not already there. It is rare when someone like Kaathi comes into a person's life.

"Why have you come back to Homar? You seemed so anxious to leave the first time you were here."

"I am here because Kaathi wanted me to come. She never gave me a reason."

"It seems to be her style. I remember her saying she did not want to reveal the future for it was more enjoyable to be spontaneously lived."

She nodded. "I too have heard her say it more than once."

"Did you leave Hun Nation for a specific reason?"

"I did for personal reasons I am not going to reveal."

He glanced at her arm and legs. "Can I ask how you got your wounds?"

"You can. They are remnants of conflicts with baboons invading our village."

"Were lives lost in those battles?"

"We did lose friends, but not before we dealt them severe blows."

They stopped talking and he took the time to look at the parts of her body not covered.

"Your body is marvelously sculptured. I have never seen a muscular woman."

Sharika became defensive. "Does it displease you?"

"No, no, not in the least. It is rare to see a woman's body finely muscled. I find it beautiful. Every time you walk it is poetry in motion. There is a sensual fluidity as your body moves."

"Nobody has described me in those terms." She smiled. "I suppose I should be pleased."

"You finally look like you are," he remarked. "Are all Hun women as muscular as you?"

"Most of them."

"Is it a trait or something you women work at?"

"We work at it. We must be strong to fight beside our men against the baboons. We exercise a great deal to keep our bodies in top physical shape.

"Let me ask you a question, prince."

"Please call me Zach."

She nodded and continued, "When Jacob and Kaathi took you away from your father did you ever feel you were a pawn?"

"A pawn?" His brow furrowed as he thought. "No and the reason being I had a sense of why I needed to go with her."

She wanted to know his version of the story. "Why did you need to go?"

"So my father would come after me."

"Did you have an inkling he would radically change after talking to her?"

"No. All I knew was Father coming after me was to be tremendously significant for the future of Homar. I did not know he would be transformed from a barbaric ruler to a benevolent king."

"Has he revealed what transpired during the meeting?"

"No, only of the effect it had on him."

"May I ask another personal question?"

"Of course."

"Do you know what prompted Prince Lawrence to try to overtake the throne?"

"I think it was greed, anger, jealousy, desire of power and lack of communication."

"Ah yes."

Both were quiet in their own thoughts and feelings.

For Kaathi to bring her to Homar, he knew Sharika was an important individual and he wanted to see if she understood her role. "I sense you had a significant position in your Hun village."

"Of sorts."

He lifted his eyebrows in question.

"Oh, very well. . .you are like Ashlee. She asks one question after another. My family lived next to our village chief. We often fought side by side against the baboons and I went on occasional hunts with him. As you know, or may not know, there is a lot of time to discuss things while waiting for game to come into your territory. It gave us ample time to have serious and lengthy discussions. From them, the chief discerned I thought like he did. He did not have a son and he wanted me to stay on and assume his position upon his abdication. I thought often about it and decided I did not want to stay."

"Were you afraid of the responsibility?"

"Not in the least. I had my own reasons for leaving and going on my personal adventure."

"Can I ask what those reasons were?"

"I would rather not talk about them."

An awkward moment of silence occurred before Zach spoke, "I am pleased you did not stay. I find you interesting and exciting."

"Most women would want you to say, 'I find you intoxicating and beautiful.'"

He shook his head. "I am not used to talking to women. I apologize."

She smiled. *You are different my prince. Most men would use the alluring words, not the ones you used.* Aloud she said, "Apology accepted. Please tell me a little about yourself."

"Father has told me I am fortunate my exiled brother did not kill me in my sleep in my youth. Before he had his transformation, Father wanted me out of the way so Lawrence could be the next king. He did not like me. I was too dreamy, too shy and did not want to rule. I preferred to be in the fields, meditating and praying. My mother, Angela, taught me forgiveness, serenity and love. I am not sure if I am going to make a good ruler. Father has helped me. Frankly, I need someone with a different viewpoint to guide me to rule properly and justly."

"I assume you are speaking of a woman."

"Yes."

"Apparently you have not found a woman with the correct qualities."

"Not yet." He smiled.

CHAPTER TWENTY-EIGHT

Kaathi had insisted Sharika stay behind in Hamor much to the Hun's objections, while the rest of the travelers left for Nubilon. Kaathi's reason for wanting Sharika to stay was for her to have plenty of interaction with Prince Zach. Two days after Kaathi's departure Sharika realized why she was left behind and sensed a feeling of obligation to the mystic. She fervently directed herself to getting to know Zach.

She had finished dining with the royal family and Zach suggested a walk to settle their stomachs.

"It is not often we see someone returning to Homar. Why have you come back?"

"To be honest, Kaathi talked me into returning."

"Did it take much convincing?"

"Yes it did."

"Why?"

"I was not impressed with the men in Homar. They were boorish brutes with no communicative skills and no respect for women."

"We are changing thanks to the Relationship Sessions and coming to grips with the fact women are essential to our welfare and of course are equals and are to be respected."

"I am afraid, when I was here, I had too many experiences with barbaric men. I should have stayed close to the palace and attended the sessions."

"Were there any men in your Hun village with primitive personalities?"

"A few, and they were reprimanded for their ill behavior."

"I know I asked you once before. Why did you leave your village?"

Sharika weighed whether she needed to answer him and decided she should. "I left due to the onset of inbreeding among my people. I want to infuse new blood into the Hun bloodline."

"And are you looking?"

"In a casual sense, I am."

"What do you mean?"

"I am first seeking a society honoring women. When women are honored I know the men are honorable."

"So you have been to Kahali, Sumati and here. What village do you find the most appealing?"

"Kahali appears to be the most like my home village."

"If you find the man are you returning to your home?"

"It was my original intention."

"I take it you are open to not going back home."

"It is a possibility."

"Are you going to return with Kaathi, or can I convince you to stay on with us?"

"Why would I want to stay here?"

Zach smiled. "To get to know my family and me."

Sharika returned his smile. "I have a feeling it is the reason Kaathi insisted I stay behind."

"I have found the best way to get to know someone is to ask questions. Did you leave someone behind in the Hun Nation you loved or liked?"

"The relationships never got serious."

"Are the parents involved in any way in selecting a mate, and how old does the man and woman have to be to be married?"

"The final decision is up to the woman, although she may be influenced by the parents. The men and women must be fourteen and have had their Rite of Passage."

"At what age does it take place?"

"At the age of twelve for both sexes."

Zach directed his question to a more personal level. "What qualities are you looking for in a man?"

"He must be a provider, seeker of truth, honest, respectful, kind," she stopped thought of Janos, smiled and added, "and have a sense of humor."

Zach nodded. "I can see why you left us. Not many of our single men meet your standard. When you marry, how many children are you hoping to have?"

"I would like a son and a daughter later not immediately."

"What are your feelings about our men having more than one wife?"

"I know you do not allow women the same privilege, thus I am against it. The law in Kahali is just and it is due to Kaathi's insistence. Both sexes can have more than one mate."

"Let me ask you in a more direct way, what do you think of Kaathi?"

"She is more loving and wiser than anyone I have ever met, and from the stories I have heard about her, she is fearless."

"I suppose you are referring to the story of her having combat with Kaleez?"

"Yes and a few others I have heard from Jacob. The most unusual one being the one where three growlers had stampeded a herd of wildebeests and having killed one had their fill and they headed toward the travelers. Jacob and the others fled to the safety of trees and Kaathi inexplicably stayed on the ground. One of the growlers slowly made for her in a casual manner. The beast came alongside her and laid down next to her, and to the bewilderment of all, she scratched him. Who on Mother Earth can do that?"

"No one except her."

"You have questioned me and I think it is my turn to do the same," she stated.

"Please do."

"I have heard you are nineteen and thus five years past marrying age. Why have you not married?"

"My life has been tumultuous. Mother protected me from Father. He hated me until he had his transformation. When I turned fourteen there were no women on the spiritual path I was on and I wanted a woman who could understand my spiritual feelings. Kaathi came for me and took me back to Kahali and I stayed there for a year. For the last two years things have changed here due to the Relationship Sessions. I have met a few women I thought could be potential princesses. So far nothing has happened."

"You have been cautious in selecting a princess, what if you find one, will you entertain the idea of having a second or third wife?"

"It is hard to find one. I cannot imagine finding two or three."

Sharika liked his answer. "I have heard other people's version of why Kaathi came after you. Why do you think she did?"

"For the longest time, I thought she came to rescue me from my father and I could live out my days with her. It was only part of the story. Taking me away from my father did not anger him to the point of revenge. He wanted to destroy Kaathi, Jacob and Kahali because he was made to look like a fool. To do it he put together a huge armada and set sail for Kahali. Much to his embarrassment, his army was at risk on the river to the Kahali archers on the banks. He had to agree to sit down to a peace talk, where he exploded and threatened to destroy the village. Fortunately for everyone, Kaathi talked him into leaving the meeting and go with her to talk. During her chat with him, my father had a life altering transformation. Once he had his experience and war was averted, I came to understand father needed to be transformed."

"So, your father is seeking to bring about new values and understanding to the people he rules via the Relationship Sessions?"

"He is. There is still tremendous resistance after nearly two years. Change is taking place slowly, and except for the attempted coup, it is happening reasonably and voluntarily."

"Is your father showing you how to rule?"

"He is. Every fifth day, he receives people in the Meeting Hall and listens to their grievances and suggestions to improve conditions, and I am there by his side. Often, he asks how I would handle a specific situation and if it differs from what he would do he explains why he is taking his approach."

"About the coup, do you think he handled their punishment properly?"

"I do. I know in the past my father would have beheaded all of them in the arena for his pleasure and the people's. Has your village ever had to deal with a coup?"

"We have not. If there are enough people grumbling about the chief's decisions, he can be displaced by a majority count and a new chief rules."

"Does it happen often?"

"I am not sure. It has never taken place in my lifetime or my parent's."

"Is everyone as knowledgeable on how the Hun Nation functions as you?"

"If I had to hazard a guess, I would say no. For one thing my family is the keeper of our history. The other thing is the chief lived next to us and I discussed many issues with him."

"It appears women are equal to men in your village."

"They are. I believe fighting by their men's side contributed to it. When you count on your woman to keep you alive it gives them a great deal of value."

"Did you agree with all of the chief's rulings?"

"It was rare when we disagreed and on those occasions we did, we would present our sides of the issue and come to an amicable understanding of our positions."

Zach was impressed with Sharika's position in her tribe and with her intelligence. She brought to the discussion a wealth of personal experience which none of the women of Homar did except for his mother. She would serve Homar well if she were his princess and eventual queen. The lull in the conversation continued and he took the opportunity to open himself to her and found he liked the energy she had. He wondered how much of it had to do with being with Kaathi. He was well aware of how the mystic changed people's personalities and energy.

CHAPTER TWENTY-NINE

The scenery along the river had not varied much the last ten days. Even so, Ashlee and Kaathi had sensed they were near Nubilon. The twenty-second day after having left Homar drums announced their presence in Nubilon territory. Ashlee spotted two men she assumed were lookouts following their progress. Four more men joined them as they made their way slowly toward the village. The bearded men were visible and only disappeared when the forest growth prevented them from hugging the river shore. Her anticipation kept rising. She was eager to know if her home villagers met or exceeded the image she had of them. It had been twenty years since she had been stolen from her home by the mutants. She dreamed of her home often and visualized it in her mind even more. After living and recuperating in Sumati briefly, she lived in Kahali for almost two years, before taking this trip to Nubilon. She imagined and desired her home village would be more utopian than Kahali.

Ashlee caught sight of the horde of people awaiting them on the riverbank. Her stomach knotted. She had mixed feelings. She was eager to land and see if her uncle and aunt were alive. Still, there was a nagging and unsettling feeling inside her. She could not identify what bothered her and told herself she would deal with it, when and if it surfaced.

The dugout drew nearer to the mass of people. Ashlee noticed the line of bearded men near the shore had their weapons in hand. She saw the men were lined up in front of the women and children and wondered if it was done to protect them. The lineup gave the smaller children and women a poor viewing point of their arrival.

Pauli directed them to show their palms, and she raised hers along with the others, indicating they came in peace. The paddlers angled the canoe to the shore. The crowd was unusually quiet.

In the crowd, Ravi spotted the lovely, blond-haired woman and could not believe his eyes. She was his sister incarnate, lovely, graceful and alive. The woman had to be his sister's daughter abducted some twenty years ago. There could be no other explanation for the similarity. The foreigners came ashore and introductions were made between the foreigners and the two councilmen and chief council and the two priests and their families, using the common language. He waited until all the formal greetings were over and saw his opportunity. He quickly moved to Ashlee and presented himself to her. He greeted her tentatively, "Ashlee, is it you?"

She was shocked to hear her name called by a Nubilon. She saw a much older version of her light-haired uncle.

"Is it you, Uncle Ravi?"

"It is me my child."

She threw herself on him weeping, while those around them stood shocked at them hugging. It was a long time before she released him.

Her voice shook. "I was hoping you would be alive. I did not know what happened to you and Aunt Yara."

"I do not have much time to talk to you now. Soon you and your party will be entertained and fed by our council and priests. The moment it is over I want you to come to stay with me. I shall be waiting for you outside the assembly hall. We have a lifetime to talk about and a thousand questions to ask and answer."

They hugged again and she left him.

At the formal dinner, Ashlee was still excited at seeing her uncle but never felt comfortable and wondered why. While the council and the priests were friendly. She noticed their wives and children seldom spoke. She was used to meals in Kahali, where everyone had something to say. As she thought it over, she felt she had discovered the reason why she felt unsettled. She made a note to herself to speak to Kaathi and see if she had a similar reaction.

At an appropriate time, Ashlee excused herself from the dinner group and explained why she was leaving. She looked for and found her uncle's face in the crowd surrounding the large assembly hut. His face had a strong resemblance to her mother's. They hugged again and walked to her uncle's hut, with her clinging to him. People gawked at her as they made their way through the village. She sat down with him in the privacy of his home and was eager to ask the dozens of questions darting around in her head.

She started the conversation. "I never thought I would ever see you again. When I was a slave, I tried to keep Mother and Father in my memory. Too often my memory would shift to the horror of the terrible day they were killed."

His eyes filled with compassion as he spoke, "It had to be a horrible burden to bear. My friend, Devra, told me your father was killed trying to protect you and your mother."

"Devra, the name sounds familiar."

"She lived next to you."

"She told me your mother and you were abducted."

"It is how I remember it."

"Do you know what happened to my beloved twin sister?"

"Oh my goodness, I forgot you and Mother were twins. No wonder you remind me of her. I do recall there were only a few light haired people among our tribe.

"Thank God you are alive. I have lived the horrific day over and over in my mind countless times. I remember them killing father and dragging us away. They carried us and still outran our men. After seeing them kill father I was terrified. Mother kept calling to me saying she loved me. It did not help me. The mutants traveled through the night. The next day they must have felt they had outdistanced our men, for our terror began anew. A mutant was about to assault me and mother hurled herself at him in an effort to save me. He threw her to the ground, pulled his machete and he beheaded her. Her head rolled from her body, and I screamed and screamed and cried and moaned until there was nothing left inside me."

She stopped to emotionally gather herself. She had told the story often and was surprised she still exhibited emotion relating the horrible event. She continued her story, "I screamed, kicked, bit and hit the mutant attacking me. It did nothing to deter his savagery. He ravaged me over and over again. I had lost my mind for I do not remember much afterwards. For the next three years what I remember the most is the lightning storms. I regained my mind after those years by having to take care of the mutant's newborn daughter."

"I am sorry you had to live through such horror and brutality, my dear."

"I am too."

"You do not have to share all of the horrible things you had to live through."

"I appreciate your consideration. I have shared my story many times and much of the terror is gone."

"Why did the mutant mother not take care of her child?"

"I am not sure. All I know is the child saved my mind."

"And you were a slave for eighteen years before you escaped?"

"Yes."

"My days in the mutant camp were a series of horrific nightmares from which I could not awaken." She stopped again to compose herself. "The only thing keeping me alive was the mutant child, Gwen. What little love I had, I gave to Gwen. I think what kept me alive was thinking of her, even as I was being raped repeatedly. I vowed I was not going to die a slave and be subject to barbaric behavior for the rest of my life. I planned my escape for a year, and, while I was, I was having dreams and visions of Kaathi."

"The Kaathi you came here with?"

"Yes."

"She sounds psychic."

"She is."

"Did you have any confrontations with predators during your escape?"

"I did. I had run out of water and I ran into some water buffalo and knew they liked water. I tried to circle them and ran into three lions. They spotted me and were in the act of attacking me... Miraculously, the buffalo chased them away and did not trample me. It took a long time to stop shaking and get to the water."

"You were indeed lucky. It is well known the buffalo and lions are enemies. Do you recall how many days you were on the savannah?"

"I am not sure. I do remember running out of water on the ninth day."

"It is utterly amazing you could survive alone on the plains."

"If it were not for Kaathi, I would not be talking to you. She knew where I fell down to die."

She shook her head. "Tell me everything you remember about Mother and Father. Do I look like Mother?"

"Yes. I could not believe my eyes. The moment I saw you I knew it had to be you. There are only a few women with blond hair in Nubilon."

"I always hoped I looked like her. Tell me what Mother and Father were like and what they did."

"Of course my child. Their roles were probably similar to people in any village. Your father did not have a prominent skill so he hunted to supply meat for the meals and your mother gathered fruits, nuts and vegetables from the communal farm. Our religion influenced everyone's lives. Like most every man your father dominated his home. Our women are given little respect. We are extremely jealous of our women and yet, we treat them as sex objects. I am puzzled how it is alright for us to fornicate with jezebels and treat our women like them. Yet a woman is forbidden to talk or look at a man. It is a senseless standard. If a married woman looks at another man, she is beaten. Many a woman has been caught innocently interacting with a man and been beaten viciously by her husband, brother or father. My sister, your mother, was a free spirit, and when your father was not around, she demonstrated it and taught it to you. Had your father known what your mother was teaching you, he would have been upset and beaten her.

"Had I been a more traditional man, I would have surely told him what your mother was doing. Thankfully, I was a great deal like your mother. If I remember correctly my mother was rebellious and father had a rough time controlling her, but he never treated her wrongly. Being twins and growing up, there were many things binding us together. I loved her a great deal and could not stand to see her hurt. I cannot tell you how many times I spoke to your father about his mistreatment of your mother."

Ashlee's eyes showed she was trying to search for some way to forgive her father for his mistreatment of her mother. Her whole concept of her parents was shattered.

"Why did my father and our people stumble and fall? How did our religion go wrong?"

"I am not sure. It might be, in the past, one of our priest's went crazy from something his wife did or one of them was influenced by some men. Heaven only knows my dear."

"Ever since Kaathi rescued me, she has reinforced what I always knew."

"What was it my dear?"

"I have worth and I am equal to any man."

Ravi nodded his head. "Kaathi must be an extraordinary woman."

"Uncle, she is the most gifted person I know."

"Gifted, in what way? Religiously?"

"She is not religious; she is spiritual and loving."

Her uncle scratched his beard concertedly. "I believe I know what you are saying. My friend, Amira, is spiritual. Your life and mine changed forever on the dark day the mutants raided our village. I never saw what happened to you and your parents. We lived too far away from each other. I can only tell you what happened to your aunt and me. The mutants struck unexpectedly. The mutants must have surprised our outer guards and killed them, for there was no warning of their attack. One moment I was asleep the next I heard screaming and shouting. They threw a torch at our house. Fortunately, it did not land on the roof; it came through our entrance. I grabbed it and threw it at a mutant. Your aunt was at my side with my long blade. I used my spear and wounded one of them. Three of them charged us. Your aunt had my long blade and was swinging it at them while I jabbed. We wounded two of them. We fought to save our lives. Though she resisted valiantly, the mutants were a relentless horde of hyenas. She paid for her resistance with her life. In defending her, I was struck several times. One of the blows severed my arm and another knocked me unconscious. They left me on the ground for dead."

He automatically grabbed the stump of his arm, which was severed above the elbow. The finger long scar on his head which rendered him unconscious was clearly visible.

"The mutants fled with many of our screaming women and children. Our men gave chase but could not keep up with them. Many days later I recovered consciousness and was told you and your mother were abducted and your father killed."

Ravi's eyes focused on the past and he grew silent.

"Amira, the widow of my good friend, lived next door. She found me lying in a pool of my own blood. She told me she tied my arm above where it was severed and stopped any further loss of blood. She dragged me into my house, lit a fire, heated a knife and cauterized my severed arm. She tended to the rest of my wounds, the most serious of those being the blow to my head, which had rendered me unconscious. I was delirious for nine days. The tenth day my fever broke, and I was on the road to recovery. Seeing your aunt killed broke me. Frankly, without Amira, I never would have been able to restore my mind and body.

"As my mind began working properly, I remembered pieces of my experiences. From what I recalled, I had meetings and conversations with someone in the afterlife. Every day of my recovery, I remembered more and more of those talks. They literally changed the way I viewed my life and my interactions with others. Before nearly dying, my attitude and character were shaped by my religious beliefs. I believed women were inferior to men on some levels before my experience, afterward, I came to have a different view of life based upon those talks.

"Every time I was able to focus for a moment or two, I saw Amira by my side. She lovingly attended to me. Like you, with Kaathi, I have Amira to thank for my life.

"At one of our long talks, she told me, the mutants had driven an axe into her husband's head. She was unable to accept the loss and spoke openly and often to God. Long after she asked her first question she had dialogs with someone without form, at least the female voice never represented herself in form. Her perspective of life changed well before mine. We spent many days together in heartfelt conversation and I learned a great deal from her. I came to respect her and all women far more than before the attack.

"I slowly sensed something else about Amira. She had an energy no one else had in Nubilon, at least no one I knew. In her presence, I felt comfortable and at peace. There were times we sat in each other's company and did not need to talk."

He thought a moment. "Have you had a similar experience with Kaathi?"

"There were many times we sat in silence or in a meditative state."

"I think Amira would like to meet Kaathi. I failed to mention there are two other women who have come into my life. The four of us get together to discuss things and sit in silent prayer. Do you think Kaathi would mind meeting them?"

"Not in the least."

"What was life like among the mutants?"

She had told the story dozens of times to help others faced with terror and brutality. She did not hesitate to relate her eighteen years of slavery among the mutants and of her escape and near recapture. She spoke of her time with Kaathi and the planed adventure to visit her home village.

CHAPTER THIRTY

The group from Kahali were conversing with the Nubilon council and priests. During the talk, Ashlee managed to convince Zafir, the head of the council, she and Kaathi were best hosted by her uncle. Caleb was hosted by Zafir, while Pauli stayed with one council member and Sandor the other. The informal meeting concluded and Ashlee and Kaathi excused themselves, saying they wanted to talk with Ashlee's uncle, Ravi. He was waiting for them, along with three women, outside his house.

Ashlee introduced Kaathi to her uncle.

"I am sure you do not remember these ladies. They are Amira, Devra and Nena, my dearest friends," announced Ravi to Ashlee. The women greeted each other with embraces, and he hugged them as well. They made their way to Ravi's home.

The moment they were settled, Ashlee spoke, "Uncle we convinced Zafir to let us stay with you."

"I am delighted. It is my pleasure to host you and to tell you how strange this is to be talking to all of you women. Before my near death, I never would have dreamed of sitting down and discussing anything with a woman. Primarily because it is frowned upon by our religion.

"I am fortunate I am an old man and I am widowed, otherwise I would not be allowed to talk to these wonderful women."

"We do thank you, uncle for hosting us." Ashlee looked at the ladies "I hope you do not mind me asking, why is it necessary you women cover your body, head and much of your face?"

Amira answered, "Our religion dictates it."

"It seems strange to be covered in this heat."

"I feel the same as you. Even so, I do not want to go against our religion and be beaten," responded Amira.

Unable to comprehend such strange restrictions, Ashlee shook her head.

Kaathi abruptly stood. "Amira, would you mind taking a walk with me?"

Amira looked at her friends as if to ask if it was acceptable to leave with the mystic. No one voiced an objection.

"I would love to walk with you."

Amira rose and the two left Ravi's house. Ashlee and the others watched them leave each wondering about the urgent need for Kaathi to be alone with Amir.

"I found your request unusual. We all just met you and you separated us from them. Why would you do it?"

"I wanted to talk to you alone and the day is so beautiful I did not want to be cooped up inside."

Amira half-heartedly accepted her explanation.

"Are there any married women interested in meeting with your group?" asked Kaathi.

"We have talked privately with some friends but they have some reservations. None of them want to upset their husbands and if they found out what we are discussing their men would beat them."

"Have you approached other widows?"

"We have. Three are leaning towards attending."

A lull in the conversation found Kaathi locking her arm with Amira's at the elbow. Amira smiled at the familiarity. A man in his fifties was walking their way and stopped the moment he saw them and watched angrily as they approached. His graying beard touched his chest and his hair was longer than most other men. His deeply tanned face was fissured and thin. He glared at them in open anger and blocked their way

"Why is your arm locked with this infidel?"

"What concern is it of yours?"

"Because she is dressed abominably and looks like a jezebel. Her arms are uncovered. She is exposing her legs and her belly."

He was so enraged spittle trickled out of his mouth. "She is indecent and openly asking to have intercourse with any and all men."

His eyes were red with anger. He pointed his finger at Kaathi and shouted at her, "It is evil women like you that cause men to go astray."

He waved his finger accusingly at her. "You are the devil incarnate and should be beaten to death. If I were younger, I would throttle you myself right here."

Throughout his tirade, Kaathi kept sending him love. She finally spoke, "My dear brother, it is not what the eye sees that is offensive; it is what the mind has been taught that is offensive."

Kaathi tugged at Amira's arm and they made their way around the enraged man.

Not recognizing the truth in the mystic's words, he spit after them. "You will burn in the fires of hell!"

Amira turned to take a last look at the raving man. "I apologize for his behavior."

"No need to, Amira."

They walked along in silence until Amira stopped and looked into the mystic's eyes. "You deliberately wanted to walk because of the conversation back at the house about how women must dress. Am I right?"

Kaathi smiled. "You are perceptive as well as beautiful."

"You knew the old man would be angry with you. Why subject yourself to his rage?"

"He needed to hear what I said to him. He will lie in his bed tonight and ponder my words. He will be one of the first men to join your select group. Please refrain from telling about this incident until I am no longer among you."

Neither woman spoke on the way back to Ravi's home. Amira kept running the scene and Kaathi's words over and over in her mind until they entered his home. They settled down and Kaathi joined in the conversation. "After Ashlee told me about you, I was eager to speak to all of you. I am not surprised to hear you speak of events changing the course of your lives. I have noticed this happening to people after having a dramatic event in their lives. We tend to lead our lives the same way day after day until we are dealt a great tragedy."

"I have found it true as well," offered Amira.

"And it makes me happy to hear the four of you are getting together to support each other," added Kaathi. "Ashlee tells me you pray as a group. Group prayer is powerful and effective, especially if you have a specific goal."

"On occasion we do have a goal," interjected Amira.

"Devra and Nena how did you come to be part of this group?"

Devra answered, "With the death of my husband, I questioned God and did not get any answers. I stumbled upon Nena after she lost her man and was drowning in a sea of questions. By good fortune we struck up a conversation with Amira and found she was having discussions with her neighbor, Ravi. We have been meeting every fifth day ever since.

"The wonderful thing about getting together is we do not restrict our questions. We can ask anything."

Kaathi smiled. "It is a blessing to have others to help you with your struggles. Do you pray and meditate at your meetings?"

"Not all the time," answered Nena.

"I would like to suggest you do it at every meeting. Would you mind if we did a silent prayer session now and focus on changing the attitude of men here toward women."

No one objected, and they quieted themselves. Kaathi quickly moved deep into an exalted state. Not long into their session, Ravi settled his mind, recited his prayer and was flooded by Kaathi's true nature. Unable to contain his emotion his eyes filled with tears. Her loving energy engulfed all of them and each felt it to their ability.

Kaathi opened her eyes first and watched as the others concluded their meditation. "Do you do healings?"

"We do not," replied Ravi.

"You can do absent healing by sending energy to someone at any time. It is always better if the person requests it, although it can be done without the person's knowledge, so long as your intentions are for the person's highest good. I have found the more you engage in healing the better the energy will be."

"How long does a healing last?" asked Devra.

"As you grow accomplished, you will have a sense when to stop."

"Can we do healings with the person present?"

"Of course, as long as you and they are comfortable with it. It should always be a pleasant and exhilarating experience."

"Do we place our hands on the person?"

"If the person is comfortable with it."

"Do I send the person my energy?"

"Under no circumstance; it will deplete you. I always ask for Creator's energy to heal someone."

They heard shouting and screaming coming from the direction of the village center. They exited the house and followed the shouting to the village center.

CHAPTER THIRTY-ONE

Pauli and Sandor left Caleb talking to the Nubilon council. Pauli convinced Sandor to walk through the village with him to observe the Nubilons to get a true picture of what the people were like. The first thing they noticed was the scarcity of women on the avenues. They entered the village square and it was true there as well.

Pauli looked around. "Why do you think there are so few women outside?"

"Not sure. I wonder if some are banned from being outside?"

"Should we ask one of the men or a woman?"

Sandor responded, "If there is some sort of repression, a man might not tell us the truth. He would give us his version. A woman would give her version."

"You go ask a man, Sandor, and I will ask a woman."

"On second thought, I do not think we should stick our noses where they do not belong."

"How else are we going to find out what these people are like?"

"I do not. . ." Sandor did not finish what he wanted to say. He shook his head and watched Pauli walk toward a lady making her way through the village square. Sandor made his way to a local man in hopes of talking to him.

Pauli headed for a spot where his path would intersect with the woman. As he drew near her, Pauli saw an air of despair and a sense of abandonment in her eyes. The woman noticed him looking at her. Panic possessed her eyes and she veered away. He halted in his tracks and watched her hurrying away. It could not be more obvious she did not want to have anything to do with him. She looked defeated and petrified. His mind went to his recent visit to Hamor. The only women he spoke with were the ones attending the Relationship Sessions. He wondered if the women not attending the sessions had the same look of defeat and panic on their faces as this woman.

He had been a traditionalist in Kahali and never thought of looking for despair in the women he knew. He had always thought his mother and his wife were treated well. Batu exploded onto the scene, and it was then he considered he had not held women in esteem and saw other men did not. Jacob raised his consciousness after he heard Batu's expulsion speech and started talking about Batu's courage and the rights of women. After his talks with Jacob, he slowly grew aware of how women had suffered and were continuing to suffer suppression in his own village.

Due to what he had seen on the woman's face walking swiftly away from him, he should have sensed she was representative of all women in this village. He abandoned his intuition and instead followed his urgency to speak to a Nubilon woman to discover the truth of how women were treated here. He looked around and saw a woman walking through the center with her head bent down not watching where she was going. *Why is this woman not looking up? Is it because she is as beaten as the other woman running from me? I have to talk to her and find out for myself how women are treated.* He waited until she was ten steps away and put himself in her direct path.

The young lady was upon him before she noticed him. Surprised, she stopped. The woman was in her twenties and before she could turn and walk away he spoke in the common language, "Hello, I am sorry, if I scared you. I want to ask you a few questions."

Her face turned to fear. "No, no."

"Why not?"

She did not answer. She veered away from him.

He took a step to follow her and a man yelled, "Jezebel, jezebel!"

He turned and saw four men running toward him. One of them screamed, "Defiler, defiler!" Another was yelling jezebel over and over.

Pauli saw the look in their eyes and knew he had stirred a hornet's nest. He turned and prepared to defend himself. Other men in the square were also yelling and running his way. The man kept yelling jezebel as he ran toward the woman. He caught up with her, slapped her, threw her to the ground and viciously kicked her. Pauli reacted, ran to her rescue, slammed his shoulder into the man and drove him to the ground. The other men reached the melee. Two men pulled Pauli off the first man and held him. A third man drove his fist into his stomach, doubling him up. He sensed the knee coming to smash his face and turned his head. The man intended to drive his coupled fists on the back of his head. Pauli brought his foot up into his crouch before the man's blow landed. The man moaned and fell to the ground. More men arrived and drove their fists to his body. One landed a hard blow to his kidney sending shards of pain through his body. He was thrown to the ground and they used their feet to kick Pauli. He scrambled away and got to his feet.

The woman screamed and wailed as her husband unmercifully beat her. She covered her face as he brutally kicked her head.

More men appeared. One man came up from behind Pauli and grabbed him around the neck and held on. Pauli tried to wrestle free and was ferociously pummeled. He could not defend himself. They forced him to the ground. There were men on all of his arms and legs as well as the man with a strangle hold on his neck. Another man jumped in the air and drove his feet into Pauli's stomach painfully knocking the breath out of him. Another man smashed his elbow to Pauli's temple knocking Pauli senseless. While Pauli was helpless, the man smashed his face again and again with his elbow. The group released Pauli. He did not move. It did not deter the men. One man kicked him using the heel of his foot. Other men joined him and mercilessly kicked Pauli on every part of his body.

Sandor was talking to the Nubilon man and heard the men shouting. He turned to see four men running toward his friend. Suddenly, the whole square erupted. He dashed to the melee and crashed into the men kicking Pauli. He tumbled to the ground, jumped up and sent his fist into one man's face. He buried his other fist in a man's stomach and was jumped by three men and driven to the ground. Two men pinned his arms as five men kicked his body. He lashed out with his feet at the men. They managed to grab his ankles and held them. Each kick drove his body to one side or another. A kick crashed into Sandor's throat, crushing his larynx. He stopped struggling. It made no difference, they kept on cursing and kicking him until they satisfied their hatred.

Caleb, was discussing the acceptance of Leah and Isaac into the Kahali village due to Kaathi's persuasiveness and assurances, when he and the three Nubilon assembly members heard the screams and shouts coming from the square. The council members left him sitting there. Caleb ran after them. They got to the village center and made their way through the gathering mob of shouting and swearing men. Caleb shoved men aside to get to the center of the mob. His heart sank, when he saw Sandor and Pauli unconscious in the midst of the crowd. Some men were still stomping on his friends.

Outraged, Caleb jumped in the middle of them and yelled, "What the hell are you doing? Get away from them."

If the Nubilon councilmen not been with him he would have received the same battering as his friends. Five men yelled at once describing what had transpired to Zafir and the councilmen in their native language. Caleb pushed men aside and dropped on his knees to examine his friends. He glanced at the woman and instinctively knew what happened. He also knew what was about to take place was not going to be any better.

Zafir directed himself to Caleb. "The men say one of your men breached our law." He pointed to an angry man. "He reprimanded his wife and his friends did the same to your men."

"Reprimanded?" yelled Caleb incredulously. "They brutally beat the hell out of my friends. What stupid law did they break?"

"The one which states a married woman cannot talk to any man except her husband and her relatives."

"None of them deserved to be beaten. What your men did is disgusting and insane. My men did not know anything about your law," shouted Caleb, "and they have beaten my men senseless. Their actions are reprehensible, intolerable and barbaric. Pauli and Sandor were councilmen and the best of my Warrior Hunters."

In spite of the immense blunder and how he felt, Zafir knew what the other assemblymen's feelings were. "Ignorance of the law is no excuse. The men punished them and now want your men thrown out of our village. I am afraid I will have to enforce the law and ask you to leave."

"They beat my men senseless and you want us to leave? What punishment are they to receive?"

"None," Zafir answered in a subdued voice.

"You people are insane," yelled Caleb. "You do not have to tell me twice. I want to leave as fast as I can. You have not heard the last of this," vowed Caleb.

It was what Zafir was afraid of hearing. He feared the incident was going to trigger a war.

Before Caleb had a chance to say anything more, Kaathi, Ashlee, her uncle Ravi and the ladies arrived. Ravi plowed through the noisy and agitated men, making a path for the ladies. Kaathi looked at her friends lying on the ground. Her eyes found Zafir and observed him for a long while. He saw her looking at him and sensed her disapproval. For some reason, he could not fathom why her eyes disturbed him.

Ashley saw Sandor, Pauli and the woman lying on the ground had been brutally beaten and was appalled. Instinctively, she knew what had happened. Memories of the physical, mental and sexual abuse she had lived through gripped her. She shook with fear, as her body remembered the countless beatings and torment she experienced. Tears welled up in her eyes, as she grappled with flashing images from her past. It was all too much. She doubled over and vomited.

Kaathi heard Ashlee retching as she administered to the stricken trio on the ground. She knew at some point she would have to talk privately with her about the emotions flaring up inside her. She noted Pauli's aura was gone, indicating he was dead, and she went to Sandor whose aura was quickly fading and checked for a pulse. He was barely alive.

Kaathi's presence and command of the situation quieted the Nubilon men. Here and there muffled voices rose among them.

Kaathi took command of the situation. "Ravi, we need two stretchers."

"Of course."

Ravi knew two men with stretchers and quickly walked away to get them.

The mystic healer checked the Nubilon woman. Her husband moved aside. She turned to Zafir. "Can you have your medicine man look after her?"

Zafir considered the request. He was surprised the husband was not protesting. "Yes." He wanted to amend what had happened.

Ravi returned with the stretchers.

Zafir did not want any more blood on his hands. "I want all of you gone tomorrow." He said the orders loudly to satisfy the villagers not his guests. He struggled with his emotions, as he watched the beaten men carried away. He was stricken with sadness. These people had come in peace and because of the stupid rigidity of the men in his village the Kahali were going home filled with anger and their dead. He scurried off to get away from the idiotic mob and pray to his God.

CHAPTER THIRTY-TWO

Amira helped carry the stretcher bearing Pauli. She noted he did not have a pulse in his neck. *Of course, his pulse could be very weak. For his sake, I hope so.* The small party of stretcher bearers arrived at Ravi's house. Their faces reflected the gravity of the situation. Caleb went with the others to Ravi's home.

"Put Sandor on the table," Kaathi instructed Ravi.

Ashlee looked around. "Where should we put Pauli?"

"Set him on the floor. He has expired."

Ashlee moaned. Tears filled her eyes. She had gotten to know both men well on the trip. She sucked in her breath to keep from moaning again.

The Nubilon women set him and the stretcher in a corner of the hut. Kaathi got her medicine bag and worked on Sandor as the others observed. He had three broken ribs on his right side and two on his left. One of the ribs on his right side had punctured his lung. His eyes were swollen shut, and blood was trickling from his right ear. His whole body seemed to be one huge wound. She was concerned about his crushed trachea. He made strange noises with each breath. She feared his trachea was closing and he would not see the great sun set. She wrapped his chest to restrict the movement of his ribs and was greatly concerned with fluid and blood accumulating in his chest. She checked his arms and legs and did not find any other broken bones. His face was bloated from the blows and she could not determine if his cheeks were broken. She assumed they were. She looked into his mouth and saw blood. She turned him over on his side to prevent him from choking on his own blood. She cleaned the scrapes on his face, legs and arms and put a film of healing salve on them. Her face revealed her worry. She heaved a sigh and sat down.

Kaathi gave everyone a quick look. "Sandor needs a lot of prayers and healing energy to survive. Anyone who wants to assist me and Ashlee in sending energy to him can do so."

Ravi went to stand next to the table with Sandor on it. His friends followed.

"Good. If you are comfortable with laying on your hands please hover them over his body or rest them gently on him. When you are so inclined you can end the healing."

Kaathi stood at Sandor's head and hovered her hands over his head and closed her eyes and asked Creator for the energy necessary to heal her friend. The others took up places at his feet and sides and did the same.

Kaathi was the first to end the healing, and Amira was the last to raise her hands from the unconscious Sandor and sit down.

The Great Sun had moved a quarter ways in the sky and Kaathi sensed Sandor's passing. She checked his neck and wrist for a pulse. She lifted her fingers and shook her head. With tears in her eyes she announced, "He has expired."

Caleb shook his head in grief. "What am I going to say to Sandor and Pauli's family, and Jacob? They were the best of our warriors, and they died senselessly. I know our people will want revenge and more will die needlessly on both sides. I do not want it to happen."

The Elder looked at Kaathi for help.

"Caleb, the Nubilons know how angry you are, and the death of our friends will haunt them. Many of their conversations will concern their fear we will retaliate. They know our population is greater than theirs and we can field more warriors than they. The best thing we can do is pray for them and for Pauli's and Sandor's families."

Caleb was doubtful prayers were going to help. His mind raced as the others turned inward for the second time and prayed. Upon conclusion of the prayers, Ravi asked, "Do you want to give them a Nubilon burial or your own?"

Kaathi looked at Ravi. "I believe they would want to be buried on the river in hope their bodies would reach Kahali ground."

Ravi knew it was a huge stretch. If Kaathi thought it was what the deceased would have wanted, he was not going to oppose it.

Ravi took a deep breath. "I understand an apology will not bring your friends back. On behalf of the ladies and myself, I want to apologize for the abominable behavior of the men of Nubilon."

"On behalf of Sandor and Pauli's family, relatives and friends, Caleb, Ashlee and myself, we thank you."

Ravi, Amira, Nena and Devra embraced Caleb, Ashlee and Kaathi and wept as they extended their condolences on the death of their friends.

Kaathi announced, "I need to assure you this horrendous event is the beginning of the end of male dominance in your village."

Devra, the most skeptical and practical of the four stared at Kaathi. "How can this be? You saw with your own eyes how filled with rage our men are toward us and anyone who dares to intervene."

"A malicious event is like a two edged sword," explained the mystic, "it has a good side and a bad one. You have seen the bad side, which is filled with anger and hatred. The good side will be revealed later.

"Since you have formed your group, you have been witness to love's power and goodness. Love knows no boundaries and no laws. Your men shall come to respect your women through your group's prayers and actions."

Devra shook her head. "Our men will never hold us in esteem."

Kaathi shook her head. "I saw what was in Zafir's eyes today. He was ashamed of what happened. You will find him to be an ally. He will help you spearhead others to join you in your search for truth and justice."

Amira eyes filled with tears. Choked with emotion she said, "I believe what you say to be true, for I know God has sent you to us. I have seen you in my dreams."

Ravi looked gravely at Amira. "You never told us."

"There are things I keep in my heart. This was one of them, my dear friend."

Ravi recognized the voice calling his name. He went to the entrance and saw Zafir. He stepped aside to let him in. Zafir looked uncomfortable. He addressed the small group in a reticent voice, "I am here to personally apologize for the behavior of our men, and let you know I do not condone what happened."

"Their behavior was an insane, hostile act," hissed Caleb. "My two councilmen are dead because of their actions. I am not sure what is going to happen, when I tell their widows and my people what happened."

"They are dead? My God, I am very sorry. You have my deepest sympathy. I hope you realize I had to say what I said back there. My hands are tied. I hope the action of those angry, hot-headed men does not ignite a war between our people. I do not want more blood on my conscience.

"I know the men who did this have no remorse. It is why my heart is heavy. I am sorry for what they did. I hope you believe me when I say I do not want any more lives to be lost. I do not know what more I can say to avert retaliation. I am at your mercy."

Caleb saw Zafir's remorse. Would it be enough to satisfy his tribe? They would likely want revenge. At the moment, he was unsure what he was going say to his people to ease their need to retaliate.

"Because your men harbor an immense anger, two of my councilmen are dead. I must say I never imagined you would apologize. Still I am at a loss for what to say to my people to appease them. All I can say is I shall do my best to avoid war."

"I can ask for nothing more. Thank you all for listening to me. Again I am profoundly sorry for the loss of your friends." He bowed and left.

CHAPTER THIRTY-THREE

Zafir rose early to bid the group from Kahali goodbye. He hoped his reaching out would show them how troubled he was. The sky was lessening its shroud of darkness. The air was still cool but his thoughts kept him from noticing.

At the entrance to Ravi's house, he called softly. Ravi appeared and he entered. He greeted everyone.

"I am sorry to intrude."

Kaathi touched Zafir's arm. "How is the woman who was beaten?"

"Netti's husband refused to take her to get help, so I personally took Netti to the medicine man's home and stayed long enough to know she will recover from her beating. She had fits of sobbing and is not doing well mentally and emotionally. She stated she did not want to sleep with her husband and was staying at the healer's home."

"I can understand," replied Kaathi.

"Thank you. It is an emotional time for me as well. I never imagined anything like this would happen to her and to Sandor and Pauli. I truly am sorry and I apologize again for the behavior of my men."

"God knows we did not expect to be going back home without two of our most respected men. I know all too well you cannot control what anyone does. We thank you for your apology."

"I am truly sorry for your loss."

The Elder saw the anguish in Zafir's eyes. "Would you care to join us in sending Sandor and Pauli to their last resting place?"

"I would be honored to join you."

"I sense we need to eulogize Pauli and Sandor here and not on the riverbank," warned Kaathi.

Her remark drew curious looks from everyone.

Not wanting to delay, Kaathi, acting as the High Priest, eulogized the two Warrior Hunters, "We have lost two brave and gentle men due to this nation's inflexible, outdated, irrational religious beliefs. Pauli and Sandor have unwittingly contributed to the beginning of the end of Nubilon's barbaric religion. Yet on a deeper level of consciousness they knew this was to take place and they complied to assist in changing Nubilon history. May they find peace and their loved ones in the Land of No Shadows."

Kaathi's words made Zafir reflect. His found his attitude toward women had changed with the death of his wife a few years ago. After her passing, he found it strange he never fully appreciated her, while she was alive. He had taken her for granted and regretted it. She had been there beside him day after day. He let his thoughts roam and came to the realization every person had a purpose in life. Some were cognizant of the reason, some had an inkling of it and others never gave it a thought. A year ago he had broached the subject of the worth of women to his fellow councilmen. At the time, they were not interested in discussing women's merits. He abandoned his efforts and contained his thoughts and feelings to himself. The current events forced him to examine the actions of the men he guided. All was not well with them or his leadership. Things needed to change before a repetition of what happened would befall them. At the center of the senseless deaths of the Kahali warriors was a woman. The horrific act begged for the need of reform in Nubilon. Unfortunately, he had no idea how to present his ideas to his people without being thrown off the assembly.

Zafir was aware his compassion brought him here, though he felt there was another reason for his presence. He let the thought slip from his mind and watched and wondered if any of his people would have attended the funeral had it taken place later in the morning. He was glad he thought of saying goodbye to them and to pay homage to their friends.

Kaathi ended her eulogy and spoke directly to the council head, "I do not want you to torture yourself with regret. This horrendous act of aggression heralds the beginning of the end of male abuse in Nubilon."

"I do not understand." Zafir looked confused.

"My dear, Zafir, you shall be the instrument of change here and the way it is to come about is through your participation in the group meetings in Ravi's home.

"I know of no such group."

"It consists of Ravi, Amira, Nena and Devra. I know your heart is tortured by the death of our friends. There is much you need to learn and these gentle souls are here to help you acquire the knowledge. What you learn will impact your men to respect your women and your women to acquire self-esteem."

Zafir directed his question to Ravi, "Is this true, Ravi? You are discussing such volatile subjects?"

"I shall let Amira answer for us."

Amira knew Ravi wanted to demonstrate to Zafir how much he respected women. "Thank you Ravi. We discuss everything involving each one of us and our people. We have been talking a great deal about women's rights and equality."

Zafir nodded. "It is well and good other men have not heard about this group. What you are doing is revolutionary. All of you took a great risk. Had the wrong men found out, you might have been killed. I must admit this is an extraordinary and ambitious adventure and possibly the only way to accommodate the necessary changes." He stroked his beard and continued, "Very well, I will attend a meeting. If it agrees with my philosophy, I will keep attending. If people find out, my presence will give credence to what you are doing."

"The changes you seek will not happen overnight, even with Zafir's example and help," Kaathi informed them. "It will take place in the same manner it does to build a house. Branches must be placed beside other branches to accomplish it. Make no mistake your love is the foundation of it all. The might of force does not alter history as beneficially as the power of love. It is taking place in Kahali, Homar and Sumati and it shall come to be here. Not everyone will comply. However, I am certain the change shall come about slowly and surely."

Kaathi's face changed abruptly. "We must hasten to bury our deceased."

The need for haste caught everyone unawares. They carried the stretchers and items the party needed to the dugout. Zafir walked silently alongside Caleb. They came to a small clearing with a few trees.

They stopped abruptly at the horrific sight of Netti.

She had a rope around her neck and it was attached to a tree branch. She had been deliberating her death. The moment she saw them she kicked the basket away she was standing on. She dropped a foot and hung in space. Her legs flailed the air.

Her neck had not broken.

The sight shocked everyone. They recovered and raced to her rescue. Caleb drew his short blade from its sheath, as he ran. Zafir and he arrived by Netti's side. Without saying a word, Zafir held her up, while Caleb slashed the rope. Zafir laid her down gently on the ground. Kaathi was by his side and quickly worked the knot loose around her neck and slipped it over her head. The woman was alive and gasping for air. Her body spasmodically jerked.

Ashlee was weeping and repeatedly saying, "Oh my God. Oh my God."

Waiting for Netti to recover, Kaathi rubbed the suffering woman's arm gently and sent her love.

Zafir mumbled half to himself and the others, "This madness has to end."

Ashlee's stomach knotted into a hard ball. Her breath came in short, terrified pants. The image of Netti's feet kicking out in her struggle to get a breath, her eyes bulging and her face turning blue, ravaged her mind. As a captive, she had witnessed a slave being strangled by a mutant. She remembered the desperation in the slave's fight for life, only to have it extinguished. The sight traumatized her for days. This was not how her dreams and imaginings portrayed her home village. The poor woman lying on the ground in front of her represented stark reality and the truth of what life was like in her home village. Netti was representative of how defeated the women were in this forsaken village. Ashlee abhorred the men who attacked Netti and killed her friends. She wanted nothing to do with them. The Nubilon men were a breath away from being as barbaric as the mutants she fled.

Ashlee recovered her runaway mind and took a deep breath. She got on her knees and set her hands on Netti's arm and sent her love and healing energy.

Amira knew Netti better than the others present. Her tears were a testament to her friendship with the horribly injured woman. She was thankful her man had never beaten her to the point where she would contemplate suicide. Looking at her crumpled friend, she wondered how many beatings Netti had received before getting so despondent she wanted to end her life. The damn, insufferable clothes covering women also covered a multitude of beatings and mistreatments. *What was Netti going to do, after she recovered from this near tragedy? For a woman to try to take her own life, she had to be steeped in desperation. There is something ugly going on in Netti's household. For her man to beat her openly in the square was insane and demonstrated how little he and all men thought of women. The problem remains, if Netti survives, she will have to return to the hell she calls home. It can be a death sentence. I have to talk to the others and see if they will support me in asking Zafir to allow battered women to seek the safety of shelter, which our group can provide. If they are afraid, I will provide it myself.*

Kaathi caught Zafir's eye. "What is Netti's fate?"

"She will have to go back to her husband."

Kaathi shook her head. "Has she no other recourse?"

"None. He has complete control over her life."

Amira took a deep breath and straightened her back. "We can give her refuge," announced Amira. "If the group will not, I will myself."

Zafir could not believe what he heard. "You are opening the gates to hell and an avalanche of persecution."

"Zafir is right," agreed Ravi. "It is too soon. Our group has to expand and strengthen and Zafir has to persuade the council to examine its misunderstanding of our religion before you could do it.

Kaathi nodded. "I also agree. For Netti to go back to her husband would be a death sentence. . . I will take her back with me."

Caleb's brows lifted in shock at what Kaathi suggested.

"You cannot," exclaimed Zafir, "when she is found missing, they will assume she left with you, and they will want to follow you and kill you."

"I cannot leave her here to die a day or ten days from now. She is coming with us," insisted the High Priest.

Zafir looked at Caleb hoping the Elder would side with him. He saw no support in his eyes. He found it strange Caleb would not intervene. It meant Kaathi's presence and influence was greater than the Elder's. He gazed at Netti, knowing he needed to tell the other council members she left with the Kahalis of her own accord. If he forced the issue and stated Netti had to stay, he knew in his heart she would attempt suicide again. He knew it would be hard to live with if it happened. He had to let her go and let the future decide their fates.

"Very well, you can take her. Do it quickly. I do not want anyone to see you."

Kaathi turned to Netti. "Have you understood everything we were talking about?"

Not trusting her voice, Netti gave one slow nod.

"Are you willing to come with us?"

Netti gave another nod.

"Good."

The bodies of Pauli and Sandor were forgotten during the emotional rush and they were attended to again. Ashlee stayed behind to be with Netti, while the funeral party picked up the stretchers, walked into the river and let the bodies slip into the stream. They all watched as the bodies receded and disappeared. Zafir filled with regret and shame watched along with them.

Everyone returned to Netti and Ashlee. Ashlee stood and embraced her uncle. "I am sorry our appearance caused all this turmoil, but I am thankful to have found you alive. I cannot tell you how much this meeting has meant to me. I love you uncle."

"I love you as well my dear. Seeing you has completed my life in a way I never imagined. Your parents would be proud you. It has thrilled me to see you and how strong and lovely you are.

"I am deeply saddened for your loss and by the fanatical behavior of my people. Be safe on your trip home."

Zafir and the others embraced Caleb, Kaathi and Ashlee.

"Again, I am sorry for what has happened. Safe journey." Zafir extended his hands. Caleb took them for one last time, turned and walked quickly to the waiting dugout. Kaathi and Ashlee were right behind him helping Netti navigate the short walk. They helped her into the canoe. Caleb pushed the dugout into the water and stepped in. He turned and waved once to group on the bank and turned his attention to the river.

Ashlee and Kaathi looked at their new friends on the shore and wished there was more they could have done to alter the mindset of the men of Nubilon. They would have to rely on those trusted few on shore to stimulate the changes necessary for women to achieve equality and sovereignty over themselves.

CHAPTER THIRTY-FOUR

Caleb saw the spot he was looking for and headed the canoe toward it. Everyone disembarked and he pulled the dugout halfway onto shore. He saw Kaathi was tending to Netti and he asked Ashlee to help him collect firewood. After gathering their first armful, he got the fire going and they went looking for more wood. On their hunt they came across a group of berry bushes. After they carried the wood back, she went back to gather the berries in the fold of a large leaf.

They ate their meals in virtual silence due to Netti's presence. Netti did not eat much except for the berries. Caleb took Netti to the site.

With Netti gone, Ashlee broke down and sobbed. Her sobs subsided and she wiped her tears. A woeful looked still captured her face.

"You seem to know everything, why did you not intercede and prevent the mob from killing Sandor and Pauli?"

Kaathi took a deep breath. "Abdu's anger ignited the anger of the men in the center. It overtook their reasoning and almost instantly they became a mob. The mob's anger exploded into lightening like action. There was nothing I could do."

Ashlee accepted her answer but questioned her mentor's behavior. "I know you knew Netti was going to commit suicide. Why did we not leave earlier? Had we, she would not have had to experience such shame."

"Had we left earlier the impact of her action would have alluded Zafir," explained Kaathi. "He had to see her dangling at the end of the rope attempting to take her life. He had to hold her up while Caleb cut her down. Had he not seen her struggling, he likely would not have allowed us to bring her with us. Her attempt at suicide is going to be the impetus he needs to approach the other members of the council to take action and promote a more positive atmosphere for the women of Nubilon. In affect, it was the hinge point in his life. He needed to expose his true values and strength."

She absorbed what her mentor told her. "This whole sordid affair is dredging up memories I would rather not look at. I have had my share of anguish and want pleasant things to take place in my life."

"My dear, as a High Priest's apprentice, you will hear many stories you would rather not. For the sake of those petitioning your help, you must not let it trap you in the past. You must remain in the present. You must be level headed and give the best console you can to those in need. And no matter how seamy the stories or people you must freely give them your love."

Ashlee shook her head stubbornly. "I shall do my best, though I do not understand why she wanted to take her life. She is years younger than I am. I suffered physically and emotionally every day I spent as a slave, and I never thought about taking my life."

"My dear what makes you think she was not a slave? Like you she had no value or worth in her society. She was not appreciated as a human and was not honored or truly loved. She suffered from hopelessness as you did. The difference between you and her was she did not have the strength of heart and character you did. You learned it from your mother and it was also inherent within you. You brought it over from other lifetimes and were able to incorporate it into your character."

Ashlee was forlorn and heaved a sigh. "I apologize for my lack of understanding and patience."

"It is important you learn from this and apply it to what might take place in the future."

CHAPTER THIRTY-FIVE

Zafir watched the Kahali travelers until they were out of sight. He walked dejectedly back to his home. Inside he sat down and wished for the hundredth time his wife was across from him and he could share his troubles. She had, on occasions, made suggestions to clarify problems he faced. What he missed was her willingness to listen to his ramblings. It helped him come to decisions. His clarity of mind was never the same after her death.

His mind wandered to what Netti's husband would say after he found out she had tried to commit suicide and left with the Kahalis. He was certain her attempted suicide would not perturb him as much as her fleeing with the Kahalis. The man was a great fool as were many of his countrymen.

He had to find the right words to tell his story to the rest of the council. Hopefully, they would not be as unreasonable as Netti's husband. Having served on the council for so long, he found he never could be assured of anything with anyone. He knew this was the case due to his change in character. With this latest incident, he had become more aware of the narrowness of his countrymen and their constricting religious' views.

He gathered his weapons, some food and headed for the plains to get away from Netti's idiotic husband and the questions his fellow councilmen would ask. After some peace and quiet and a night's sleep he would approach the other councilmen and discuss the horrendous events of the day.

Zafir awoke the next day, ate and made his way to councilman, Abir's, house. He stopped near the entrance and called his name. Abir appeared. "Where were you yesterday? We tried to find you. Netti is nowhere to be found."

"It is what I want to talk to you and Mirza about. Are you free to come with me to talk to him?"

"Of course. We do need to have Netti's husband in on the discussions."

"Must we?"

"Yes."

"Can we talk things over before we bring him in?"

"Zafir, you know it is not the way we run the council. Let me tell my wife where I am going, and I will be right with you."

Abir ducked inside and reappeared in a moment. Although Abir was curious, he knew enough not to ask what was going on. They reached Mirza's house. Zafir called his name and he appeared. Before he could ask questions Zafir said, "Can you come with us? We need to talk about Netti."

"Of course."

"We can pick up Abdu on the way."

Mirza did not feel it necessary to let his wife know he was leaving. They stopped by Netti's house to collect Abdu and found him home.

"We are going to discuss the outrageous incident in the square and Netti's disappearance. Abdu, you are welcome to be present and contribute. Do you want to come?"

"Damn right I do."

The foursome walked to Zafir's house. They sat and Mirza wanted to know why they were there. "What is this about, Zafir?"

"I assume everyone knows Netti is missing?"

The three answered as one, "Yes."

"She tried to commit suicide yesterday," Zafir announced.

Abdu reacted in anger. "The stupid bitch. She brings more shame upon me."

Mirza had a quizzical look on his face. "Tried? If she is alive, where is she?"

"She left with the Kahali."

"We have to get her and bring her back. I am going to beat her ass," spewed Abdu.

Mirza's face showed immediate concern and he ignored Abdu. "This is not good. I am assuming she left willingly. How do you know all this?"

"I was witness to her attempt. I was walking with the Kahali travelers to bury their dead. . ."

Zafir was cut short by Mirza. "Bury their dead? Which one died?"

"Both of the council warriors died from the beatings they received."

Mirza and Abir faces showed great concern.

"This is not good," announced Abir. "Please continue."

"We were making our way to the river to bury the warriors and we saw Netti dangling by her neck on a tree. We rushed to keep her from dying. I held her up, while Caleb cut her down. She did not die."

The other two councilmen showed concern upon hearing the news. Abdu's face showed anger and humiliation.

Zafir went on with his story. "Kaathi questioned me wanting to know what would become of her and I told her Netti would have to go back to Abdu. Kaathi realized it was a death sentence and indicated she would take her back to Kahali. Netti agreed to it, and I let her go."

"She is my wife," yelled Abdu. "What authority do you have to let her go?"

"It was clear she did not want to spend any more time with you, Abdu."

"I do not give a shit what she thinks nor you," screamed Abdu.

Zafir was fully irritated with Abdu and stared at the little man.

"You should have tried to talk her out of going," yelled Abir.

"I thought she made a good decision," countered Zafir.

"You made an irrational decision," observed Abir. "Yesterday Abdu was worried. Today he is mad, and I can understand why."

"You see," Abdu pointed out. "Even your council thinks you are in error."

Zafir glared at Abdu. "The milk has been spilt on the ground, Abdu. She is well on her way to Kahali."

"I do not care. I can enlist a dozen men and go after her. She cannot run away from me."

"And how do you intend to take her away from the Kahali?"

"I will kill them if need be."

"It is exactly what you will not do," warned Zafir.

"Do not tell me how to handle my affairs," hissed Abdu. He stood, bent over and stuck his face into Zafir's.

Zafir shoved Abdu back onto his seat. He was visibly shaking in his anger. "Do not ever do that again. I have never struck anyone, but you are a breath away from driving me to do it."

Abdu was forty pounds lighter and a half head shorter than Zafir. He saw the fury in the councilman's eyes and stayed seated despite Zafir being ten years his senior

"In talking to the Kahali and Netti, my main concern was preventing their anger from escalating and wanting revenge for what you and your stupid friends did. If we allow you to do what you want to do, you will cause a war between them and us. It took all of my skills to keep them from declaring they were coming back to avenge the death of their two Warrior Hunters. Do you realize you and your friends killed two of the most important people in Kahali? Those two men sat on their council. I talked my ass off so they would not form an army and mount an attack on us."

Zafir pointed his finger angrily at the smaller man. "Here is what you are going to do Abdu. You will go home and tell your friends your wife has fled with the Kahali, and it is for the best because you never cared much for her."

"I am not going to lie."

"You are going to lie until your face falls off. If you do not cooperate, I am going to make your life miserable and you will wish you were never born. Do you hear me?"

Abdu glared at Zafir. He knew Zafir wielded power and had many loyal friends willing to make his life a living hell.

"Am I making myself clear?"

"Yes."

"Now get your ass out of here and make sure I do not here you are telling stories and causing trouble."

Abdu left without another word.

Abir was the first to speak after Abdu left. He looked at the council head. "Where did all your anger come from?"

Zafir thought about the question for a moment and answered, "Part of it was from Abdu's stupidity and his lack of respect for me. His anger could jeopardize all of our lives and is unacceptable. The other part was from his lack of respect for his wife. He acted like a barbarian. He almost beat her to death and for what? I am sure she knew he was in the square, and she objected to the man talking to her. Having the mentality of a baboon, Abdu could care less. His macho, animalistic mentality nearly cost us our lives."

Zafir shook his head, "This madness has to cease. We have to separate ourselves from such barbaric thoughts and actions. What took place in the square has prompted me to reflect on our society.

"As the head of this council I believe it is my responsibility to initiate change."

Mirza peered quizzically at him. "What are you getting at?"

"I would like to talk to you of an idea I have concerning how we are interpreting our religion."

"Stop right there," cautioned Mirza. "Any discussion about our religion must include the rest of our people. Many have led us in prayer, and their views are important. We have to include everyone."

"I would rather present my ideas to you, and if there is a degree of acceptance, we can go to our people."

Abir looked at Mirza and realized he was dealing with a Zafir he had never seen before. He shrugged. "What can we lose?"

Abir sighed. "Very well."

"First, I think I have interpreted parts of the tablets erroneously and we need to reconsider the interpretation to make it more uniform for both men and women."

The "tablets" were a collection of thirty stone tablets written in cuneiform. They prescribed the way of life for their tribe and possibly all of humanity.

"We need to reinterpret each tablet in terms of its value for the present day."

Mirza shook his head. "Where did you come up with such a crazy notion?"

"After what I saw happen in the square and why it happened, I think we must look into the validity of our understanding of the words in the book."

"Why?"

"Why? Because I had to pacify Caleb, otherwise he would have come back with an army to retaliate. If not for Kaathi's help in turning his mind, we would be in deep trouble. Had Kaathi taken the opposite view, she could have enlisted King Edmund to amass an army to help them in their retaliation. Such an army could annihilate all of us. I am not ready to die. Are either of you?"

Neither councilman spoke.

"I thought so. We need to take steps to alter the mentality of our men."

"No, no, no," warned Abir. "We cannot jump into this now. Things are too volatile right now. Perhaps in a year or two we can look into this."

Zafir shook his head. "How many more women need to suffer, and how many need to die of abuse or shame?"

"We must proceed with caution."

"What? Abir, if your sister was one of those women being abused, how would you feel?"

"My sister has a good man."

"One good man in how many dozens?"

"From our point of view the Kahali were at fault," observed Mirza.

"Netti was trying to avoid the man according to her. Abdu should have come to the council and spoken to us before taking any action. Had he and his friends, none of this would have happened. We must install a law to prevent this from ever happening again. The men of Kahali were ignorant of our laws. We should have been more tolerant of their ignorance. We were not, and they are dead and she tried to take her own life because of all the shame and abuse she has had to suffer at the hands of her husband.

"Now, you tell me, does it sound like we are a mentally sound society?"

Abir was not about to answer the question criticizing his people, even if it was the truth. He saw how frustrated Zafir was and saw the only way to settle the argument was to take a vote to see if they should proceed with Zafir's perceived problem.

"I am willing to vote on whether we should go forward with what you see as a problem. While I am aware of the atrocious behavior of men, I am voting to do nothing. We need to approach this problem cautiously. What do you think about all of this, Mirza?"

"I see it like you do, Abir. I vote to do nothing."

Zafir shook his head in disgust. "I am not letting go of this. I shall bring it up and hound you until you see the value in what I am telling you."

Abir and Mirza left.

Zafir was thankful he did not get mad and offend his friends. He needed them for the reform he sought in the future. He would keep up his pursuit with the council and hope they would see the problems as he did. Until then he would have to rely on Ravi, Nena, Devra and Amir and himself to contact people to see if they were willing to become part of the group to improve the life of women in Nubilon. The process would be slow until more people got involved and the word would spread quicker. The time would eventually come when their numbers would be great enough and the council would not hesitate at reinterpreting the book for a clearer understanding of its meaning.

CHAPTER THIRTY-SIX

Netti and the Kahali travelers had left Nubilon nine days ago. Netti was testing her voice more and more the last four days. Up to this point, whenever she had to interact with anyone, she answered with an economy of words. She had been observing the Kahali closely hoping her initial judgement of them was correct. Of course it was not like she had several options in her home village to adjust to what happened. The more she was with her rescuers the more she knew she had made the right decision to leave. Surprisingly, she had come to like Caleb. His personality was steady and unshakable and he had come to the aid of his friends and had saved her life by cutting her down from the branch. He was a father figure and she felt safe in his presence. Ashlee was warm, considerate and beyond beautiful and surprisingly not filled with herself. She sensed Ashlee had suffered deeply in her life just as she had. She was certain, as certain can be, Kaathi's life was an epic one, and she wanted to be made aware of it at some point. She adored Kaathi. There was a presence in her she had never felt and was left wanting to describe. It went way past the compassion the healer expressed. It was in the realm of love. Kaathi exuded it and it enveloped her and blessed her each time they were engaged. The moment Kaathi looked into her eyes, she felt there was a sacred part of herself she needed to discover.

The group found a suitable spot to camp. Caleb and Ashlee were off hunting firewood and she was drawn to talk with the mystic.

Netti was teary eyed as she softly asked in the common language, "Why did you bother to whisk me away from Nubilon?"

Kaathi leaned forward to embrace her and share her love with the sorrowful woman. She released her and answered, "I saw no legitimate reason for you to stay. You did not love your husband nor he you. Had you stayed, he would have continued to make your life miserable. It is not a marriage; it is unjust imprisonment and likely a death sentence."

Netti shook her head. Tears cascaded down her checks. "You are right. Had I stayed, my life would have continued to be miserable. Hanging myself, I exposed myself to every wagging tongue and every malicious man in the village. You were correct saying I would not have lasted long. I would have tried again and made sure I was successful the next time.

"You have looked into my heart and seen my sorrow... Based upon what I saw in other marriages, I entered into marriage knowing it could be filled with misery and happiness. I had no idea it could be filled only with terror and horror. I did not realize there would be no happiness. My husband knows me only as someone who feeds him and gratifies his sexual pleasures. It did not take long for me to hate copulating."

Her voice filled with anger as she continued, "I felt insignificant living with him. I was nothing. I was lost... He never loved me. He never touched me compassionately or in love. He lusted after me. I loathed it when he touched me... If I resisted him, he beat me into submission. He showed me only anger. In return, I grew to hate him and everything he stood for and did. I was helpless. I could not turn to anyone for help... After years of such brutal treatment, I lost my hate and was left with depression. I was alone in a village of people."

She broke down and sobbed in her memories. Kaathi leaned over and embraced her again and held her until she stopped sobbing.

"I am so, so sorry you had to experience such terrible anger and abuse. The good thing is you are now free from him and the past."

Netti shook her head savagely. "You are forgetting I am still married. Because I am separated from my husband does not mean we are not married."

Netti wiped her face with her hands as Kaathi asked, "Do you know of any marriages remotely filled with happiness?"

Netti was not used to being questioned and this question caught her by surprise. She frowned and in time she answered, "I know of two reasonably good marriages."

"Why do you suspect there are so few?"

She peered at Kaathi. "I suspect you know the reason and are asking me to see the wisdom in leaving my man."

Kaathi smiled.

"I can only answer for myself. It is the total lack of respect I receive from my man."

"Respect covers a multitude of problems does it not?"

"Indeed. He has no appreciation for anything I do. Because he does not appreciate me, it tells me he does not value me or consider me worth anything."

She halted and grew emotional. Tears brimmed her eyes. She took a deep breath and continued, "He demeaned me. In many ways, I became hopeless. My life was filled with terror, desperation and stress."

Her face turned ugly as she confessed, "I was thankful I never conceived. I cannot imagine having a child grow up in a toxic, unloving atmosphere. The last beating and humiliation was the tipping point. I could not go on any longer. I honestly could not. The only way out of my living hell was for me to take my life. I almost succeeded... Why did you get involved?"

"In Kahali, I am a healer in addition to being the High Priest. I saw you suffering and I did what I am supposed to do."

Netti nodded slowly. "By doing what you did, you have put yourself and Kahali at risk."

"It is not the first time I have intervened in someone's life, and I am sure it will not be the last. The truth is what you attempted to do is going to inspire the chief council to take steps to heal your people." The mystic paused to smile. "You my dear can feel good about being part of the revolution in Nubilon."

Netti peered curiously at the mystic. "A strange thing to say after I committed to take my life. Are you certain of what you are saying?"

Kaathi smiled again.

Netti eyes left the delicate looking woman, having the strength of a warrior. She stared off into space, dwelling on what the mystic had told her. Netti reflected before she spoke, "How do you know these things?" She waited a moment. When she realized no answer was forthcoming, she continued, "If what you say is true, my suffering is going to bring about good. . . It makes me feel better." It was Netti's turn to smile. "It does, and astonishingly, my smile is proof."

"Whenever a smile appears on my patient, it tells me he or she is on the way to recovery."

"I have years of terrible memories haunting me to bury."

"I will share something with you. Memories are part of your past. The beautiful thing about life is each new day is a new beginning. If you think of all the things you can look forward to experiencing in life, your old memories will soon be pushed out by all the wonderful new ones. I will be by your side to help you celebrate them."

Netti mulled her remarks around. "I have not had any good things happen since I was a little girl. It is hard to imagine what they might be."

"Well, I can see you are young enough to bear children."

"I was with my husband for nine years, and I remain barren."

"You are not barren, Netti. All you need is a loving man in your life for you to bear a child."

"Are you certain?"

Kaathi smiled in answer.

"It cannot happen. I am married."

"You are bound by Nubilon conventions and laws. We have left there and you are free of those restrictions."

"How can you make such a statement, especially since you are a High Priest?"

"My dear we are talking about human conventions and creations. They are always subject to change. Love is never subject to change. Accept a loving man and dispense with traditions, laws and conventions. It is my recommendation. You have rejected your man and now you might want to consider rejecting the clothing you wear and wear something which comforts you."

Netti thought over what she said. Altering her attire would be easy. She shook her head. "You are nothing like anyone I have ever met. You shatter foundations men make and seem unafraid you have done it."

"Netti, I will reveal a secret to you. The moment you are centered in love and in Creator there is no need to fear anything or anyone."

"Wait, you used the word Creator. I have no understanding of the word."

"I have come to realize Creator is exactly what the name implies. Creator is in a process of creating everything you see in the universe and everything you do not see. Actually, Creator's process is love in action or motion."

Netti liked what she heard and pondered Kaathi's words. She reached out and touched the mystic's arm. "Can you tell me why we went astray and have these irrational religious beliefs?"

Kaathi released a sigh. "In the past, one or several men in your village, possibly while in a specific emotional state misinterpreted your writings and prevented women from their rightful place in your society. Misunderstanding often comes about as we are engrossed in an emotional state of mind."

"It seems so insane to treat women the way our men do."

"Belief is a culprit and a curse in your culture's religion. Belief is also a blessing to other people, presenting them with countless ways to initiate an experience with Creator. Free will gives us the chance to choose the way and means. I have chosen to make people aware of my preference, which is the path of love and devotion. It is simple and helps you love everyone."

"It seems so senseless to cause oneself or others harm."

"I agree. Beliefs can be useful and harmful."

CHAPTER THIRTY-SEVEN

Caleb was thankful they were flowing with the river. It made his task of rowing easier. Kaathi had offered to help paddle but he refused her offer. He did not want to tax her in any way. She had special gifts and he did not want to dampen them by having her get overtired. He looked at the unused paddles lying in the dugout and immediately missed the male companionship Pauli and Sandor had provided on the trip. Without them helping to row, his body trembled and tired from the exertion of being the only rower. He was cognizant he never would have been able to paddle upstream alone. He was not physically up to the task. Despite Kaathi wrapping his hands in skins and treating them, his hands were a mess. The blisters on his hands had broken open and she had applied a salve to them, wrapped them and they still hurt.

When Kaathi first suggested the trip, he thought of it as an adventure and looked forward to it. He had always wanted to take a trip to discover what life was like outside his village. If he had not gone on this trip, the next journey might have come about when he was too old to be adventuresome. Had he known two of his best warriors would not survive the trip, he never would have made the trip and not allowed them to make it. The part he was going to hate the most was telling their wives they were dead. It was not a desirable task nor an easy one.

He abandoned the thoughts of what he needed to do and settled his mind on Kaathi. After days of travel, he had come to see why Jacob was keen on the woman. Talking with Ashlee, and listening to her explain the timing of how they came upon Netti's attempted suicide, he came to appreciate Kaathi's gifts significantly more than he did prior to this trip. The trouble he had was the loss of two outstanding men. The first opportunity he had he was going to talk privately with the mystic and question the sanity of the trip.

Two days passed and Caleb got his chance to talk with Kaathi alone.

"Are the deaths of Pauli and Sandor troubling you?"

She did not answer immediately. She looked over to where Ashlee and Netti were sitting on the bank of river. "I intensely miss their physical presence. I loved them a great deal."

Her first statement was expected. He waited intent on what else she would say.

"I have spoken to both of them in the Land of No Shadows and thanked them for their sacrifice. We spoke at length about the effects their deaths were going to have on the Nubilons. They lost a good deal of their anger after my explanation."

Caleb interrupted her saying, "I need to hear your explanation, because I am having a rough time accepting their loss and why we had to make this trip."

She nodded slightly and started her recitation, "The secondary reason for this trip was to allow Ashlee to find her uncle and see what life was like in her village. The primary reason for this adventure made itself known to me upon our arrival in Nubilon. Zafir needed to witness the beating to death of our men and Netti's tragic attempted suicide. Zafir needed to see how desperate she had become and how out of control the men of Nubilon are. She was representative of how deplorably women were treated by their men. The death of Zafir's wife had softened him and witnessing Netti hanging by her neck, tipped the scales for him to spearhead a cultural revolution."

Caleb shook his head angrily. "I do not care about what may or may not take place in Nubilon. Answer me this. You took Jacob on your previous trips and you even fought Kaleez in his place. Why?"

"I needed Jacob with me because he was the best man suited for the journeys."

"I heard you promised his wife he would not shed a drop of blood on any of those trips. Did you make the same promise to the wives of Sandor and Pauli?"

"I did not."

"Why?"

"Because neither of their wives requested it of me."

"Would you have made the promise if they did?"

"No."

"Would you have made the trip without them?"

"Yes. There would have been any number of men willing to experience the adventure."

Caleb shook his head. He knew if they had not accepted the invitation there would have been several men eager to volunteer for the adventure.

"Did you have a premonition of their deaths, and is it why no promises were made?"

"The answer to both questions is yes."

"Why did you not warn them?"

"I did. I told them there were deaths on two of my adventures and this trip was dangerous."

"I find it reprehensible you did not specifically tell them of your premonition."

"It was my choice, Caleb, and I fully understand my responsibility."

"My concern is for the lives we lost. If you saw the future, why did you allow them to die?"

"I believe anyone sacrificing their life is a heroic deed. In this case, the sacrifice of our friend's lives were especially so, due to their chivalry and what is to come from the violence. I have had visions and dreams foreshadowing what is to take place.

"As you well know, during many wars, military leaders have had to sacrifice men for the overall beneficial outcome. On a deep level of consciousness everyone involved in what took place back there participated willingly to bring forth change."

Caleb waved her words aside. "Once again, all I care about is the loss of Pauli and Sandor. I was responsible for them."

"I also had a responsibility to allow the future to unfold. I did not want to interfere with its manifestation. I truly understand why you are upset, and I am sorry I could not be more specific about the dangers."

"I am at a loss to know how you know all of these events. If what you say is true, I still have trouble sacrificing two of my best friends to a Nubilon cause. What happens there is none of my business. Nor is it of yours."

"It is my business. I believe we are bound to make life better for all the people of Mother Earth."

He shook his head. "It may or may not be true. The trouble is I cannot give their widows any comfort with what you have told me."

"Dear Caleb, because you were deep into your feelings about losing our friends, you missed hearing Zafir's words. His intentions were constructive as well as sympathetic. Did you hear him say, 'This madness has to end.'?"

Caleb's eyes moved back and forth as he tried to recall hearing it. He shrugged his shoulders. "I cannot remember him saying it. I agree it is a significant statement."

"It is," she agreed. "It was representative of everything taking place. Trust me when I say he is going to talk to his council about the madness. I am sure the widows would receive some comfort knowing their husbands were instrumental in a cultural revolution."

"It is a crumb, and I shall offer it to them. I do believe they were heroes." responded the Elder. "I must admit I am displeased with you. You have lost some of the confidence I held you in."

"I can understand your displeasure, Caleb. Even so, I am glad you were courageous enough to speak to me. Perhaps with the passage of time and the progress of the cultural revolution you will look at what took place back there in a new light."

He shook his head. "I am not so sure."

"Here is something I want you to remember. If we allow any woman to be abused, it is an injustice to all women everywhere."

Her words echoed in his mind.

CHAPTER THIRTY-EIGHT

A nearby drum announced their presence in Homar territory. Another drummer picked up the message and relayed it to a more distant one.

Caleb was relieved. He would finally be out of the confinement of the canoe for longer than a night and be able to sleep in a bed and not a tree. The drums reported their progress until he saw the landing. Caleb was sure every mobile person in Homar was awaiting their arrival. Their appearance would be a reason to have a festival with music, dance, food and wine. He was ready for the diversion. Even knowing he lost two men, it would be nice to be swept up in the villagers' enthusiasm to frolic.

They were met by applause from the villagers, King Edmund and the royal court. Sharika stood cozily next to Prince Zach. She looked happy to see them until she noticed Sandor and Pauli were missing.

King Edmund greeted Caleb and the group. He saw the two Warrior Hunters were missing and the sorrow in the traveler's faces. Edmund instructed his servant, Edgar, to make arrangements to wine and dine the guests, royal family and his ten military leaders. He hustled the travelers to his palace where the adventurers could relate why Pauli and Sandor were missing in relative privacy. His royal subjects would have to wait to know why Sandor and Pauli were missing from the group.

Edgar had set small casks of wine on the table and poured wine into each goblet. King Edmund allowed everyone to get situated. "You are missing two men and you have brought back a new woman. What is the story, Caleb?"

"It is a sad one Edmund. Pauli and Sandor were beaten to death by an angry mob and Netti here was a near victim."

The Elder went on to explain how the men met their deaths and how Netti was beaten and almost took her own life.

"Those savages!" exclaimed Edmund. Hearing his remark, the king caught himself and thought it was not too long ago he would not have been shocked. "For what reason?"

"Pauli had spoken to Netti not knowing the law forbid them. Netti's husband saw it and beat his wife while a horde of men beat Pauli and Sandor to death."

Edmund's jaw dropped. "Good grief. Those people are more barbaric than we ever were. How utterly stupid and senseless. They do not have many skills on a battlefield, even so, I have to admit they fight with emotion as most hotheads do." He looked at each traveler. "It is a shame to lose good men. You have my condolences."

"Thank you, Edmund."

Edmund took a long drink from his goblet and let the ugly news settle in. "Are you seeking revenge? Do you need me to marshal men to help you annihilate them?"

"I appreciate your offer. I cannot tell you how much it means to me and to my people. The trouble with it is I believe it would be counterproductive. All sides would suffer the loss of more lives. I cannot live with such results.

"I have spoken to Kaathi and she has provided me with a different view of what took place. I shall let her tell you about it."

Kaathi explained her position, "I have come to see good will come from the loss of our two brave warriors. The Nubilon men are not far removed from how the Wanderer mutants treat their women and slaves. The good news is Zafir, the chief councilman, has become progressive in his thinking of the rights and privileges of women. He along with Ashlee's Uncle Ravi and three women will be responsible for the changes in Nubilon. In essence, Sandor and Pauli did not lose their lives in vain. They should be looked upon as heroes. Sacrificing their lives was instrumental in the reformation taking place in Nubilon."

The king shook his head saying, "Hopefully, what you say will come to pass. Not long ago, if this happened to a friend of mine, I would have been charging off seeking revenge and crushed the guilty party. Now, all I can do is raise my cup in salute to two brave men who lost their lives. You have my condolences."

Edmund lifted his goblet up and everyone present followed suit and drank.

"Now, I would like to take this moment to welcome our guest, Netti. If you are inclined we would welcome you to stay with us."

Netti was not used to such cordialness. She answered guardedly, "Thank you for the invitation. I have a friend in Kaathi, and she has already invited me to live with her."

"You are well friended," the king pointed out. "She has taken many a newcomer into her fold, and they have thrived from what Renee has told me. I have had my own experiences with Kaathi, and I can attest to how deeply she cares and loves people."

"I have found it out for myself, Edmund," replied Netti.

Edmund turned his attention to Caleb. "What are your plans?"

"We plan on leaving in the morning to let Pauli and Sandor's families know what happened. I am not sure what we will do later. Zafir apologized profusely for the actions of his people and hoped there would be no further bloodshed. It is all I have to take back to my people."

"Did you believe him?"

"I did. I saw how remorseful he was. He told us he was going to join the discussion group with Ashlee's uncle. Kaathi assured us it will be the focal point in the reformation of Nubilon."

"It is enough you have had to share your grief with me and my family and my leaders. There is no need for you to share it with my people. I shall do it after you leave. Right now I want you to eat and rest for your journey back home."

Edmund lifted his glass in toast. "I know you have traveled some distance and grieved on the way here. It is time to celebrate Pauli's and Sandor's lives. Let us toast them and tell good stories about them and other friends."

Everyone lifted their cups and drank. Indeed many stories were told. The more wine they consumed the more embellished the stories became.

Carver found Netti's story fascinating. He knew the women in Homar were not treated well even before Edmund's conversion. The men in Nubilon were barbaric compared to men in Homar. He was not sure whether he was emotionally or physically interested in her, all he knew was he wanted to get to know her better. He made a mental note to speak to her.

The king stood and pulled Kaathi aside to chat. Caleb made his way over to Zach and Sharika. They seemed to be a couple and his curiosity got the best of him. "So, what has been going on with the two of you? Are you solving our villages' problems?"

"To tell you the truth, it has not come up in our conversations. We have found out a great deal about each other and we like what we have heard."

"It is always an encouraging way to start a friendship," noted Caleb. "I truly could have used your strong body as an extra paddler, Sharika."

"It is good to hear someone misses and needs me." She smiled. "You will have me on the way back."

Zach was surprised to hear her say she was going back. She had not indicated one way or the other until now. He had hoped she would stay. He needed to talk with her about her decision.

On the other side of the room, Carver saw his opportunity and got to Netti before she made off with Ashlee.

"Would you mind if we talked for a bit?"

The chance to talk with men was rare for Netti. "I would welcome it."

They walked outside and sat under the shade of a giant yellow trunk acacia tree.

"Why are your men so cruel to their women?" asked Carver.

"They are following the precepts of our religion."

"Ah, if such is the case, we are fortunate we did not have any religion to guide us to such terrible behavior. Even so, there was a time we did not treat our women with respect. Some of us were worse than others and some are continuing to resist change. Edmund is trying to rectify it by presenting classes on responsible living. We call them Relationship Sessions. The classes help us understand how we should treat each other. It is mandatory for our children and voluntary for the adults."

"It sounds wonderful. Our people should have had something like it in place generations ago. It would have saved many women a great deal of trauma."

Carver had noticed she was buxom under her clothing, which covered three quarters of her arms and legs along with her torso.

"Why do you wear all those clothes? I would think you would be too hot."

"I have shortened the length covering my arms and legs and I have abandoned my head cover."

"You have?

"Our religion dictates what we wear, and we suffer the heat for our sins.

"Sins? What are sins?"

"It is something we are not supposed to do and we do it."

"Like talking to men?"

"Yes. My husband went crazy when Pauli talked to me and set all this in motion."

"His loss our gain." He realized how flippant it sounded. "I am sorry, I did not mean to minimize your suffering. Are there any women not following your religion?"

Netti thought of Amira and her friends. She chose to say nothing about them. "None. If women do not follow, they are beaten."

"Beaten by whom?"

"If she lived at home, by her father or brothers. If she was married, her husband would do it."

Carver had never beaten his wives or children and shook his head. "You have left your man, do you consider yourself wed?"

"Kaathi and I talked about it, and she has convinced me I am a free woman. I like the sound of it."

"Would you consider staying on so we could get to know each other?"

She looked a long while into his eyes. "I have just emerged from the fires of hell and I do not want to make another mistake. I thank you for your interest in me. It is flattering, and I have never been flattered since I was a girl. My husband flattered me, won me over and showed his true colors after we were married. He was a despot and an abuser. I shall not be easily deceived again. I am going home with Kaathi and see where my life goes with her. I like the idea of being free to do what I want and to choose the man I will be with."

"I am sorry you will not be staying. I wish you all the best in your life."

Netti thanked him and walked away to find Ashlee or Kaathi in the palace. Carver watched her and wondered whether he should pursue getting to know her better. Kaleez had seen them leave the room and had been watching them. The giant headed toward his friend and stopped in front of him.

"What were you doing?"

Carver dodged the question. "Chatting with her."

"Bullshit. What is going on between you two?"

"I wanted to test the water to see where she stood on men."

"I thought so," the giant said, approving of his instinct. "Why the hell would you do something so stupid?"

"What do you mean?"

"Do not play dumb with me. I know you all too well. She has immense breasts and you are drawn to them. You have got to realize she is coming out of a horrendous marriage and a terrible beating and she attempted suicide. I am sure she hated having intercourse with the jerk and it is what you are after. She does not know what she wants right now. She needs to adjust to life away from her husband and people. Let it rest."

Carver shrugged his shoulders. "I suppose you are right. She did say she liked the idea of being free from the tethers of her husband." He paused, smiled and added, "You have to admit she is a looker and does have nice breasts."

Kaleez returned his smile. "Yes she does."

The next day the travelers were saying their goodbyes to the royal family in readiness for their trip to Kahali. Zach and Sharika slipped onto a veranda to be alone.

"I do not want our time together to end, Sharika."

"Nor do I. It is sad our time has been cut short by the deaths of two good men."

"Will you consider staying?"

"Under the circumstances, no. I need to support the others."

"I have grown fond of you, and I want our relationship to continue. Please reconsider," pleaded Zach.

"I know where you want our relationship to go. My time with you has been enjoyable."

Enjoyable was not what Zach wanted to hear from her.

"I do not want to give you false hope. I met someone back in Kahali, and my heart is with him. I know it is not what you want to hear. I cannot lead you on. Being your princess and eventually your queen is tempting. I did not leave my home for temptation. I left it to find love and a father for my children. I am truly sorry it did not work out for us."

Zach sighed. "Not half as sorry as me."

She went to him and embraced him. "I do love you."

Zach interrupted her. "But I am not in love with you. Yes I know the phrase."

He held onto her a long time knowing full well what he was losing. He would feel the loss for a long time.

CHAPTER THIRTY-NINE

The adventurer's sudden departure from Homar allowed for little fanfare. The deaths of their friends contributed to the mood. They were on the river for the third day, stopped, made camp, eaten and were relaxing before they climbed the trees for the night. Ashlee had been struggling with what had taken place in her home village and could not hold her questions in any longer. She needed to discuss her troubles with Kaathi.

"I know I keep asking question after question and here is yet another one. Why did you take me to Nubilon? The whole affair was horrific. Had I known, I never would have chosen to come."

"It is exactly why you needed to go."

"What do you mean?"

"You survived living with the mutants because you had a fantasy of what your life was like and would have been, had you not been abducted."

"Exactly, why steal it from me?"

"You needed to see for yourself how submissive the women of Nubilon are and how tragically they live. You needed to face reality. You are no longer a slave and need to engage in reality all the time. It is by being in the present moment you can truly serve others and recommend changes. You are coming to grips with this system of duality, and you need to understand how to function within it parameters. Having succeeded, you can fashion a more productive and flexible reality to the demands placed upon you by everyone you serve."

Ashlee saw Kaathi's wisdom. Still, it was difficult to have a dream she had nurtured for so many years dashed to pieces. She reviewed her life and Netti's. Poor Netti's mother died when she was five and could not recall experiencing love. Ashlee had the luxury of her mother until she was nine. Later she was fortunate to have been saved by the birth of Gwen. If Netti had a child to take care of, she might have been able to feel loved and given love. Perhaps she might not have tried to commit suicide. She would have had a reason to live. Ashlee nodded in recognition of how fortunate she was even in the face of mutants terrorizing her life.

"As a slave I dreamed of my village often. In my Pollyanna personality, I felt sure my village was like Evette's utopia. I remember my mother and father as loving parents. It was the way I recalled my uncle and aunt. I assumed everyone in Nubilon were like them." Ashlee's voice held a childish quality. "Was it wrong to wish for my people to be wonderful and kind? Did my memory fail me? Where did I go wrong?"

"My sweet Ashlee, the environment among the slaves and the cruelty you were subjected to influenced your remembrance. You desperately wanted life to be as beautiful as your mental creation. As a child, you likely were not privy to the harsh reality of your community. You were a child and were not concerned with anything other than playing and learning. The adult religion, mores and ethics were not your concern. You likely would have become aware of them in a few years had you not been abducted. Dreaming of a wonderful, magical village you once lived in was your means of staying sane and keeping your hopes alive.

"Memory can be a blessing and a curse. You embellished yours and there is nothing wrong with having done it. Some people remember regretful incidences by editing it to their advantage or magnifying it to blame others. Had you known the truth of what life was like in your village, it would not have given you the hope you needed to stay alive. After your escape, you needed to discover the women in Nubilon were not treated much better than those in the Wanderer village.

"Now I would like to address your question of where did you go wrong. You did not go wrong. The world went wrong. Both villages lacked the essentials in decency toward women. Both knew nothing of justice or how desperately women needed to be recognized and respected for what they provided to the community and family. When a woman is held in poor regard and is seen as less than a man by her man, she loses self-esteem. She struggles and grasps for some way to garner self-worth. Most women fall into themselves and become ill-suited for life. Fortunate are those women whose character is strong and can withstand all the abuse thrown at them and know in their hearts they have worth and respect themselves. A splendid example of this was Batu. She benefited from her parents contributing to her character and was able to oppose the council and the High Priests and change things in Kahali."

Ashlee's lips puckered. "Would she have been powerful in character had her parents not encouraged and respected her?"

"It is hard to say for certain. Each of us brings to life certain gifts and challenges. If she had different parents, the path she would have traversed would have been greatly altered. Who she was and what she did, to attain greatness, was predicated on every person in her life and every situation she encountered. Take away one or more of them and she would have been a different person, possibly capable of accomplishing only some of what she did or none of it."

Ashlee had tears in her eyes. "The only thing I see going for my village is Uncle Ravi and his group. I hope you are right and see the future of Nubilon moving toward a more spiritual society."

"I could not be cruel and give you or them false hope. Life and societies are always in cycles of growing less warlike, wiser gentler and conversely slipping and growing harsher, inflexible and warlike. Society and villages react and go through cycles as does a pendulum. It swings full right and full left even for the most democratic society."

"Why?"

"It happens to allow various situations and circumstances of this magnificent play of Creator's to bring about the multitude of ways we can experience life and love. An uplifting tribe respects, appreciates and sustains self-reliance, independence, ethics, justice and equality. When the slide from its pinnacle begins, people become complacent, greed and entitlement sets in, people become lazy, ethics slip, prejudices appear and soon the democracy is shredded.

"The moment we commit to involvement in physical duality, it guarantees we shall experience all points of the emotional and physical spectrum to the nth degree. Good and bad, love and fear, beauty and beast, health and illness and a host of others opposites shall complicate and enrich our lives."

"There must be a better way to learn how to love?"

"If there is, I do not know it. It might help you to think of your lives as a progression in understanding the power of creative love."

"Do I progress from life to life?"

"First your lives are not led linearly. They are all going on at the same moment. Often what you accomplish in one life affects another life. The same is held true for mistakes. All your lives are gloriously intertwined like a spider's web, with you at the center."

Kaathi saw Ashlee's eyebrow crinkle in thought and the mystic added, "Another way to look at is in relationship to your breath. If you breathe clean air, it helps maintain your body's health. If you breathe in smoke or certain contaminants for too long, it affects your health and may cause death. The moment you notice your health diminishing, you can remove yourself from the harmful environment or habit and reclaim your health."

Ashlee spoke her mind. "Frankly, I do not understand this talk about living all those lives. I cannot remember any of them, consequently I find it hard to believe."

"I appreciate your hesitancy in acceptance. I know it is part of your belief system and the views I am expressing are part of my belief system. What I experience is my reality and it is the same for you. Somewhere yours and mine intertwine. The intertwining is the mystery of life, the mystery of existence. Part of the beauty of life is allowing the other person to entertain and have different beliefs.

"In the case of the Wanderers and the Nubilons their beliefs can easily be seen hurting people. Based upon our beliefs we hold theirs as primitive and barbaric. All belief systems are evaluated in the same way. As we grow we see the childishness in one and the maturity in another and accordingly adjust our beliefs."

Ashlee looked at her mentor. *In spite of what happened back in Nubilon, I like the way she explains herself. It is easy to see why so many call her a mystic.*

CHAPTER FORTY

The villagers of Kahali gathered on the bank of the river to welcome the adventurers. The drums had already warned them Pauli and Sandor were not among the canoers. Questions were in everyone's minds as they saw the dugout appear. In spite of the two apprentices being absent from the group, a thunderous welcome greeted them.

The first line of welcome was the council. The next line was the families of the adventurers. Caleb went directly to Sandor and Pauli's widows. He cupped his hand to their ears to be heard and asked them to come to his home to talk in private. Pauli's widow gave her child to her mother. The child's eyes followed his mother as she walked away. Jacob went with them to help keep inquisitive people from lingering too close to Caleb's house.

Before Caleb spoke, each woman knew what he was going to say. Tears were already forming in their eyes.

"I am so very, very sorry to tell you your husbands were killed by the Nubilons."

The women sobbed and moaned. Their faces were fraught with grief as their hearts were broken by the terrible news. Villagers passing near the Elder's home heard the women cry out and interpreted it to mean they had lost their husbands. They whispered the news from person to person. Some made their way to tell friends and relatives of the news. The news spread like wildfire.

Sandor's widow was the first able to ask, "Why did they kill him?"

"As you know we went there so Ashlee could see where she was born and find any living relatives. We knew little of the temperament of the people. From what we could piece together it appeared Pauli and Sandor wanted to get to know how women were treated and went alone into the village center. Pauli approached a married woman and attempted to talk with her, while Sandor spoke to a man about their customs. Pauli had no idea what he did was prohibited by law. The woman's husband was with a group of his friends and saw him talking to her. In his rage the husband attacked his wife, while his friends attacked Pauli. Sandor ran to his aid and jumped into the melee. The fight drew another dozen or more men into the heated fray. Your husbands had no chance to protect themselves.

"Zafir, the Chief Councilman of Nubilon and I heard the uproar. We rushed to the square and the moment we got close the mob screamed and heatedly told Zafir what happened. They wanted us out of their village. Zafir told me we had to be gone by the next day. We took your husbands to Ashlee's uncle's house. Kaathi said Pauli lost his life in the square. Sandor lost his later, as we were praying for his healing.

"At sunrise the next day, we were going to set Sandor and Pauli's bodies on the river, and Zafir showed up. He apologized for his people's barbaric behavior and was extremely concerned the brutal act was going to cause a war.

"We made our way to the river to set the bodies of our friends free and came upon Netti, the wife who was beaten by her husband, hanging on a branch. We cut her down and she survived her attempt at suicide. Kaathi talked her into coming with us. Zafir was there on the shore, when we bid farewell to your husbands. We agreed a war would cause more deaths and left."

Pauli's wife screamed at Caleb, "I want vengeance. I want them to pay for what they did. My son needs his father and I need my husband."

"I know both of you want retribution for the loss of your husbands. We feel the additional loss of lives would be senseless. I am going to call a special council meeting to discuss the violent act and hope they will agree with us."

"They took the life of my husband. I want to take their lives," sobbed Pauli's wife.

"I know you do," said Caleb softly. "It is in the hands of the council. You can make your plea to them."

Sharika listened intently to what Caleb told the widows and felt their misery. If she ever had the chance to rectify what happened she swore she would deal harshly with the man responsible.

CHAPTER FORTY-ONE

The council met the next day in the meeting lodge. The perimeter was packed with villagers wanting to know what direction it would take concerning the deaths of the Warrior Hunter apprentices.

Caleb raised his hands for quiet and waited for the crowd to stop talking.

"This meeting is the second looking at whether we are going to go to war. I was an apprentice to Morgan, during the last such meeting. King Edmund invaded us with his armada and wanted to destroy us. We avoided a war because Kaathi talked to Edmund. Had she not many of us would not be here.

"The assembly of Nubilon is not present to represent themselves. Nevertheless, we did have the opportunity to speak with Zafir, the chief of their assembly. He was apologetic and prayed we would not go to war over the tragic incidence.

"Kaathi told Zafir she saw he would be instrumental in changing the attitude of the men in his village. The change would come about by them gathering in small groups to discuss injustices their women were suffering. She saw the change slowly happening.

"Is this enough for us to forgive them for what they did? It is up to you to determine. Remember you are the voice of our people. You have to be discerning, insightful, discriminating and just. Nothing short of this will be acceptable."

Caleb went on to give his version of the violence and fall out. Kaathi reported her involvement and Ashlee told the council her version. Caleb opened the floor to the assembly members.

Jacob moved his hand and spoke, "I have never lost an apprentice in my lifetime. I cannot tell you how angry and sad I am. Pauli and Sandor were my friends and to think a tragic set of circumstances together with old and antiquated traditions and laws allowed the men of Nubilon to take their lives is unimaginable.

"My first reaction was to mobilize an army and retaliate. It took a long time for me to take control of my emotions and see by doing it we would lose a great many more lives and more of our women would become widows. I thought I would go to Nubilon and challenge each man, who took part in killing my friends, to a duel of their choice. I felt sure I would survive and come back victorious. The longer I thought of this solution the more I saw how stupid it was. They would not stand by and let their men die at my hands. They would attack me, overpower me and kill me. It would have been my wives grieving. It was something I could not live with.

"So there had to be a better solution and I gradually came to wonder how Kaathi would handle the situation. It took a while, before I saw she had already taken the right path. She saw the senseless killing of Sandor and Pauli was the beginning of the end of an era of religious and traditional suppression of women. The tragedy would highlight the need for women to be respected, held in esteem and given the same rights and privileges as men. If it all takes place in Nubilon, the loss of my friends must be looked at as a sacrifice to better a whole society. In essence they are heroes."

The crowd waited for Jacob to continue, when he did not they mildly applauded his speech.

Logan, the eldest on the council and now graying, spoke next. "I have talked to many of you standing outside the lodge. I know how thankful you were when Kaathi spoke to King Edmund and we averted a war with Homar. As we grow older we have a greater aversion to the tragedy of war. We see more of the gray and less of the black and white of circumstances and situations. Idealism runs through the blood of our young and the hearts of Pauli and Sandor's wives. Since I see more gray now, I am inclined to say what took place in Nubilon was a brutal act and the cause of it was outdated traditions and laws. I was opposed to Taja, Batu and Kaathi and the changes they sought to alter our own traditions. It took me a long time before I saw our traditions were antiquated. If the Nubilon are on the path to equality perhaps we should let time take its course and let them live with their consciences."

Logan shook his gray head. "Did any of you ever think you would live long enough to hear me say that? I guess I have heard so many of Kaathi's talks they have sunk into my consciousness."

The crowd applauded.

Coloma stood and addressed the council and throng outside the meeting lodge.

"Fellow Kahali, it was not long ago we were a little barbaric ourselves. As a teen, I saw how rigid our council and I were when we elected to eject Batu from our village. We felt she had no worth due to her having no husband or child and because she was a troublemaker. Thank goodness Taja went after her and made her worthy by making her his apprentice.

"Can any of you imagine where we would be as a people without Batu's fire and search for justice? Because of Batu, women now can claim their independence. Each and every freedom women can claim now is due to the courage and efforts of Batu. We have Batu to thank women are respected. We have another wise woman among us. Kaathi has picked up where Batu left off and continued to improve our philosophy and understanding of the religious life by introducing us to a loving Creator. All of us have not accepted this new society. It is a process. It will be the same for the people of Nubilon.

"If Kaathi says the men of Nubilon are on the path to release their women from suppression and present them with equality and justice. I believe her. We do not need to lose more lives to prove anything."

He sat down and received a thunderous ovation.

Elgar, Caleb's apprentice, rose to say his piece. His eyes settled on the widows and then the crowd.

"I want to take this moment to say how sorry I am for your loss. Sandor and Pauli were men I looked up to and we became friends. I was a bit envious of them and the others making the trip to Homar and Nubilon. I wanted to experience the excitement of traveling and seeing different places and people. If I had gone on the trip instead of Caleb, it may have been me not returning.

"With the death of Pauli and Sandor, I have come to see how tenuous life is. I shall not take life for granted any more. I know the loss of their lives has affected many of us. I do not want to cast ourselves into a war because of what happened.

"It was encouraging to hear Zafir was saddened by the tragedy, and he was sincerely apologetic. If the Nubilon men who committed this crime have any decency in them, they will regret what they have done.

"I think we would be better served if we pray our wounds heal quickly and Pauli and Sandor find peace in the afterlife."

The crowd applauded in appreciation of Elgar's words. The moment it died down Marka, Logan's second apprentice, stood.

"What I am going to say is due mainly to the Relationship Sessions and the Spiritual Awakening Services I have attended given by Kaathi and her wonderful group of instructors. I, like Logan and Burk, went among you to get a feel for how you felt about the senseless killing of Sandor and Pauli. It has offended many of you and you want an eye for an eye. What astonished me was the number of you whose philosophy has embraced forgiveness for the horrible action of the men of Nubilon. Years ago there would have been only a few handfuls of you willing to forgive them. We have changed much in a short time. It is amazing and speaks highly for the people directing us. We can be thankful we are not barbaric like the mutants and Nubilons. We have raised our consciousness and we can thank Taja, Batu and Kaathi for spearheading the movement.

"I hope and pray those of you demanding justice will ponder what we have talked about and use your hearts to forgive them. We may never forget what they have done to our men. We surely can forgive them."

The crowd responded well with their applause.

Caleb waited to see if another member of the assembly wanted to speak. No one did.

"Since no one else on the council wants to speak, we will take a vote on whether to go to war or not."

"What about listening to us?" yelled a man in the crowd.

Caleb recognized him as the younger brother of Sandor.

"My brother took over the responsibilities of our deceased father. He basically was my father, and he is gone. I did not tell him enough times how much I loved and admired him. I for one am ready to revenge his death and go to war. Take it into consideration when you vote."

Dozens in the crowd offered vocal support and applauded.

Caleb stood. His voice was filled with emotion. "We will. We know you and many families are suffering. The council has to decide what direction is the best for the village and what affect it will have on all of us."

"You damn right." yelled Sandor's brother. "You do not know how I am suffering. They killed a brave and wonderful man. Perhaps you have forgotten my brother and Pauli were Warrior Hunters. They went along with you to protect you and the others and they gave up their lives. Would you be complacent if it was your brother who was killed? Would all of you say we must forgive them? I suspect not. So, we should honor them by fighting for them."

Before Caleb had a chance to answer, Jacob stood and responded, "You are right most of us would respond differently. Had I been there, I would have responded with my emotion and likely would have killed several of them and lost my life in turn. I was not there, and it is why I am reacting differently. I am going to tell you right now, if I had a brother, I could not have been closer to him than I was to Pauli. We knew each other since we could walk and talk. I loved him as if he were my brother. My grief will be with me a long time. I can see what took place in Nubilon was not an act of war. It was an act perpetuated by stupid men believing in some stupid tradition or misunderstood religion. As I waited for sleep to come last night my thoughts were on what happened to my friends. I wanted to go there and have my revenge. After my emotions calmed I could see the error in my desire. If what Kaathi sees is to become a reality, the sacrifice of my two friend's lives was worth it. I shall grieve a long time for my friends and I shall never forget their friendship and love."

Jacob sat and received a generous round of applause.

Outside the lodge another man shouted, "Two of our High Priests were there. I want to know what their feelings are about this tragedy."

Kaathi looked at Ashlee and got a nod from her. Kaathi knew the man by name. She stood, spoke and slowly turned and directed her reply to everyone outside the lodge.

"Charles, I am not sure if I ever shared this with you. My feelings are different from yours most of the time. I am usually in a state of love. When I saw Pauli dead on the ground and Sandor nearly dead, I was shocked. This emotion passed quickly and sorrow engulfed me. It also quickly left me and I was again in a state of love and I tried to save their lives. The reason those other emotions do not linger with me is because I can see the good, which will come from tragedy. In the case of their deaths, I saw how greatly it affected Zafir and he would be part of the group Ashlee's uncle, Ravi, was in. The group is discussing many of the things we do in our Relationship Sessions and in our Spiritual Awakening Services. I see Zafir quickly expanding his consciousness and influencing others to be part of their group. The group will expand and divide into smaller and more intimate discussion groups. The assimilation of these new thoughts will gradually reach a point where more than half of the Nubilon village will have been influenced by the original group's emerging philosophy."

At this point, Kaathi stopped talking and walked closer to Charles and looked only at him and continued,

"I saw how entrenched they were in their outdated traditions and twisted religious beliefs and forgave them their insanity and embraced them in love. When our children do something they did not know was wrong, how can we blame or punish them? The men of Nubilon are like those children. It was not too long ago we were similarly influenced by our own traditions and religion. I know nothing is permanent. Everything changes. The Nubilons are not any different. It will be many years before they are at the point where we currently are in our philosophy.

"I cannot condemn them, for I see each and every one of them are aspects of the Creator. They are participating in this play of life as all of us are. We are in this play to learn how to love more fully and lovingly create the situations, circumstances and relationships to promote our understanding of love and life.

"Seeing the Nubilons as my younger brothers and sisters makes it much easier to forgive them and forget their actions for they are learning at a slower pace than we."

She bowed her head to Charles and sat down to rousing applause.

Ashlee rose and addressed Charles, "I have led a different life than you. I lived the horror of seeing my parents slaughtered and beheaded by the mutants, and I was made a slave by them. It took a long time to forgive them. I might never have forgiven them, had I not had Kaathi's help. I know what my resentment did to me and I wish I could have forgiven them sooner. Kaathi has shown me how anger and revenge serves no good; it only perpetuates the insanity.

"Before I arrived in Nubilon, I had envisioned them to be virtuous, grand and glorious. This dream kept me alive, as did the visions I had of Kaathi, when I was a slave. My dream of who the Nubilons were was dramatically shattered. What I did see was a glimmer of hope in my uncle's discussion group. Like Kaathi, I am choosing to see the small group as the salvation of Nubilon, and I am doing my best at sending them love.

"Going to war with them is not going to solve anything; it will only bring about more deaths and sorrow to us and to them."

Ashlee sat and was applauded. Caleb looked at the crowd. "If there are no more questions, I declare we take a vote on whether to retaliate the deaths of Sandor and Pauli by going to war with the Nubilons." He waited an appropriate time and continued, "It is for me to cast the first vote and I vote, no. Council how are you voting?"

Each assemblyperson cast their vote and Caleb instructed the apprentices to vote. The votes were cast and tabulated by Logan. The vote was overwhelmingly in favor of not going to war. The crowd outside the lodge applauded the outcome and disbursed.

CHAPTER FORTY-TWO

The possibility of going to war was averted, and the village of Kahali slowly took on its natural way of living. When he thought it appropriate, Janos paid a visit to Kaathi's home where Sharika was staying.

Sharika was sitting outside enjoying the early morning weather.

"I am glad I caught you."

"Hello, Janos."

"Hi, would you take a walk with me?"

"I would. Let me get my bow."

"We are not going far," he assured her. He smiled at her cautious nature and watched her gather her bow and quiver.

They walked out to the plains and continued to walk around the perimeter. He smiled. "I am happy you have returned. I heard you did not go on with the others to Nubilon."

"Actually, I wish I had gone. Had I, the dynamics of events might have been changed and we would not have had to lose Pauli and Sandor. They were good men."

"They were indeed. So, what kept you from going?"

Sharika teasingly smiled. "I had many suitors in Homar, and I could not pry myself away from them."

"I can half believe it."

"Only half? Have I lost so much of my beauty since you last saw me?"

He did not join her in her lightheartedness. "You seem to be ignoring my question. Why?"

She became serious. "If you must know, I stayed behind to get to know Prince Zach better."

"Prince Zach? He was the one Kaathi brought back from Homar and nearly caused a war."

"Is he going to cause a war between us?"

Janos made a face saying, "No. I can understand you wanting to check him out, if he had an interest in you. You must have been interested in him otherwise you would not have stayed back."

"What do you want me to say, Janos? I like him as a friend and it is why I came back to you. You are my love."

Janos beamed. "Really? It is what I wanted to hear. Now I am happy."

"It is good to see you smile. You are like a little boy easily content once he gets his honey."

"And you are my honey. It is a good thing you are behaving, because I was ready to put you over my lap and spank your bottom."

"It seems my being a problem for you would still give you much pleasure."

He smiled. "I win either way. All joking aside my dear, you give me great pleasure and joy."

"It is also why I left Zach, my love. You give me great joy as well."

He opened his arms. "Come here and give me some physical joy."

She stepped into his arms and kissed him resoundingly. She playfully forced her tongue past his lips. He immediately pulled back saying, "You are now being a temptress." He drew her to him. "And it gives me much happiness."

Sharika made a face. "It is the burden I have on my shoulders. I have so many men to make happy, it is tiresome."

"May I suggest you forget about all the rest and concentrate on me?"

She smiled coyly. "Perhaps you are right. This way I can devote myself to teasing you to tears."

Both of them caught the movement out of the corner of their eyes and looked at what it was. Two cheetahs had been hiding in the tall grass and were now standing eyeing them. Janos and Sharika looked at them without moving. The cheetahs initiated their crouching and stalking walk. Janos reached for an arrow in his quiver only to find it was not on his shoulder. He had not bothered to bring his weapon thinking a walk around the village would present no danger.

Sharika's reaction was as swift as Janos'. She withdrew an arrow and set it on her finger and bow and raised it to a firing position. She took steady aim at the cheetah on the left and let the arrow sing its song of flight. The arrow caught the animal mid-chest between its legs before it had a chance to race toward them. The cheetah dropped in mid stride and tumbled forward. Its sister was in full running pursuit and already had made up half the distance to its prey. Sharika did not wait to see if the first arrow had done its job. She pulled another arrow and set it on the bowstring and her finger. She let her breath out, followed the swift pace of the cheetah, automatically calculating how much she needed to lead the animal and released the second arrow. Its song was short and it drove itself into the shoulder of the sleek animal. It lost the use of its right front leg and crashed to the ground, tumbling head over tail. Sharika pulled another arrow from her quiver and was aiming at the tumbling cheetah. She waited until it attempted to rise and fired the third arrow. It did not sing. The distance was too short. The missile drove itself into the predator's rib cage. It jerked and snapped at the shaft only to find another arrow imbedded itself into its lungs. The damage was too great and the cheetah fell to the ground, gasping for air and succumbed.

Janos had his short blade in his hand in readiness to defend their lives. It was not needed. While he was looking at the second predator, Sharika sent a second arrow into the chest of the first cheetah to end its suffering. Jason looked at the two dead animals and marveled at the swiftness in which she had dispatched them. The whole event had taken less than three breaths.

He shook his head. "I do not understand this. Our lookouts should have spotted these renegades. If anyone else would have been out here instead of us, they would have been killed. This is unacceptable. We need to double our lookouts. We cannot have this happen again. I am going to talk to Jacob."

Sharika, breathing heavily, spoke in a shaky voice, "I agree. They are quick, I barely had time to get my second arrow in her. Had my arrow gone astray we would have been mauled and possibly killed."

"Thank goodness for your quick reaction."

He took her into his arms until both of them stopped shaking. Having recovered her nerves, she went to the animals and removed the arrows she could and wiped them clean. They looked at the dead predators.

He took hold of her arms. "I think I owe you my life. How can I ever repay you?"

Adrenaline was charging her body, and she needed to release all the pent up energy. "First let us get away from here, so you can make love to me."

Janos ran his hand through her hair. His voice grew husky. "It is a hard task you ask of me. I promise to do my best."

CHAPTER FORTY-THREE

Bani's time to conceive came in the middle of the night. She sent her oldest child to fetch Kaathi. Kaathi and the child stopped by to awaken Mara so she could get Wahi, the birthing-mother. Together they walked to Bani's house. Everything had been in place when daybreak arrived, but the child had not come into the world. Kaathi asked Mara to bring the adoption parents, Satori and Lashandra, to the house so they could watch the birth. Mara then took Bani's children to her home hoping they would fall back asleep until their brother or sister was born.

Bani's labor was lengthy. The delivery took place while the Great Sun was overhead. Bani's children were awake and Mara fed the children and took them to their home and played with them outside. The baby finally arrived, without any complications. Bani delivered a small and vocal daughter. She breathed and cried without having to be coaxed. Wahi washed the child and laid the baby in the mother's arms. Bani wept as she kissed her baby over and over again and looked lovingly at her.

Kaathi went outside. "Do you children want to see your baby sister?"

The children yelled gleefully and ran into the house. They were in awe of their tiny sister and let loose a barrage of questions Bani patiently answered. Each child got their turn at holding the baby and fussing over it. They had had enough and went outside to play. Bani held her child again singing softly and kissing it now and then.

Kaathi allowed Bani to bond with the baby before she asked, "Do you still want to give your baby to Lashandra and Satori?"

Bani took her time answering. "I do not want to but I know it is best for my baby and for me and my family."

Bani bestowed more kisses on her new born. Tears filled her eyes. She heaved a loud sigh and extended her arms with the baby to Lashandra. "Take good care of her."

Lashandra accepted the child. Joyful tears cascaded down her cheeks. "We will, and you can come by anytime to see her."

Lashandra and her mate, Satori, had been wed eight years and were unable to create a child. She could not believe their good fortune when the mystic approached them wanting to know if they were interested in adopting a baby. She had a hard time accepting the fact Bani would give them her baby and trust them to raise the child as their own. She had many restless nights wondering if at the last moment Bani would rescind on her promise to give them her child. The moment had arrived and miraculously Bani had placed her child in her arms. Lashandra's fears and worries vanished. *This is the most joyous moment in my life. My prayers to Creator have been heard and answered. I am so grateful to Bani and at the same time sorry she has had to give up her creation. I am sure Bani's tears do not reveal the heartache tormenting her at this moment. I feel so sorry for her, and yet so happy for me. Thank you Creator.*

"Bani, I cannot thank you enough for entrusting your baby with us. And thank you Kaathi for bringing us together to help each other in our time of need."

Tears were rolling down Bani's cheeks. "Take good care of her, or I will strangle you with my bare hands."

Lashandra did not know what to make of the threat and finally answered, "I promise you we will."

They left with the child. Bani burst into sobs. Between sobs she eked out, "I carried her for nine cycles of the moon. I feel unfulfilled and empty." She raised her hand. "I know, I know it is for the best. It was my decision; you do not have to remind me."

Kaathi sat down beside her and lovingly stroked her hair for a long time until she stopped crying and grew calm. Bani's eyes found Kaathi's. It was then the mystic broke the silence. "The only thing I was going to say is you are a very courageous woman to give up your child. I am sorry you have been placed in this position. You did the loving thing. I love you, bless you and admire you, Bani."

Sharika sat in the corner being as unobtrusive as possible. She watched attentively as Marie pricked Carla's finger with a tiny knife and drew blood. She squeezed the finger to make one drop of blood fall into Kaathi's palm, one into Mara's hand and the last in her own palm.

Carla had come in complaining her husband felt a lump in her breast. She answered the usual questions and all three healers probed her breast and determined they needed to test her blood to find out the true nature of the lump.

Kaathi cradled the drop of blood between both hands, and prayed to receive the correct answer to uncover what was going on in the woman's body and waited patiently for the symbol to materialize.

Marie quieted herself and waited for a sign indicating what had invaded the woman's body. It took a long while before she saw the crab in her mind. She thanked Creator for the sign and opened her eyes. She saw Kaathi had hers already open.

Mara was not as accustomed as the others at receiving information about a patient and it took a little longer before she saw the familiar tug-of-war struggle play out in her mind. She too thanked Creator for the sign and slowly opened her eyes.

Kaathi saw they all had their eyes open, went to Sharika and whispered in her ear she saw an invading army running across the plains and a man constantly turning away from a woman and told her what it represented. She stepped back and Marie went to Sharika and told her she saw a crab in her mind's eye and what ailment the patient suffered. Mara took the few steps over to whisper to Sharika she saw a human tug-of-war and it represented a specific illness.

Sharika, having received the information, spoke, "Each of you received different symbols for Carla's illness. Each of you reported cancer was invading her body."

Kaathi took Carla's hands. "Now we know what it is we can concentrate our prayers on dissolving the lump of invading cells. While we are praying, I need you to take long walks each day, eat more grains, fruits and vegetables and refrain from meats. Drink twice the water you normally do and it would benefit you to pray for your recovery and enlist everyone you know to pray as well."

Bani was grim-faced. "What are my chances of surviving?"

"Before we can talk about it, I want you to return tomorrow with your husband. The three of us need to talk."

The woman left curious to know what Kaathi wanted to talk about.

Sharika looked quizzically at Kaathi. "Why does she need to come back?"

"I saw the cause of her cancer was a lack of nurturing on her man's part. It is why we need to see both her and her husband. If the relationship is continually stressed the cancer may never disappear, or if a healing occurs, it may reappear in another form. For any illness to be cured, the root cause has to be dealt with."

Kaathi smiled. "Thank you for helping us, Sharika. Had you not been here, I would have been the one receiving and holding the information to be given."

"I appreciated you letting me participate. Is this what you do when you cannot determine visually what the ailment is?"

"It is."

"How did you discover getting symbols was a good way to make a diagnosis?"

"Several generations before Taja was the healer, one of the Talker Healers had visited a woman with a particularly interesting malady and requested his highly psychic apprentice to make a diagnosis prior to him seeing the patient a second time. The apprentice made the correct diagnosis. They discussed how the apprentice knew the malady. The apprentice described how he went into meditation and waited for a sign to tell him what it was. Signs came to him in a number of different ways. He received impressions, mental images, words came into his mind and feelings upon his body.

"The apprentice taught his skill to his mentor and the skill has been passed down through the chain of Talker Healers. I found holding a drop of blood was an excellent way to get in touch with any internal or unobservable problem. I taught Batu. She was already an astute psychic, and went on to teach Marie and Mara. We have been using the method ever since."

Sharika shook her head in disbelief. "How accurate is this method in identifying the illness?"

"If all three of us name the malady, it is extremely accurate. If each one of us has a symbol representing different illnesses, it may indicate there is more than one thing affecting the patient, or it could mean we are confused."

"What do you do if you have conflicting or confusing symbols?"

"We usually will go back into meditation and wait for another symbol to clarify our first symbols."

"And what is your cure rate?"

"It varies on how strong our belief is and how strong the patient's belief is at the time and how many people pray for the individual and how prevalent the ingredient of mystery is at the time."

"What do you mean by ingredient of mystery?"

"During the course of history, there have been many purported, great healers. In one major religion, magnificent cures was a criteria for sainthood. Those judging the position of sainthood had to have proof of two people given no hope of cure and yet they were cured, because they prayed to the specific saint.

"It has been reported on any day one person may walk away from a gifted healer healed. On the same day a dozen or more may walk away not being healed. The puzzle of why all were not healed is a mystery. The major factor for all these people is the ingredient of mystery. Why was the one healed and the dozen not? It comes down to it is all a mystery to us. Even if our belief is strong the illness may prevail because there is a higher purpose which in unknown to the person."

"Ah, I see what you are driving at," observed Sharika. "In my Hun Village, we were attacked by baboons and three of them attacked a man next to me and was killed and only one attack me. The mystery is: why did the three attack him and not me?"

"Exactly," responded Kaathi, "there may have been a reason unknown to both of you."

"I noticed you used the words healed and cured. Why?"

"In the case of saints I used the word cured, because there had to be no reoccurrence of their illness. The word heal means the person may leave the healer relieved of the malady only to have it reappear a short while later in the same form or another."

"Can I ask you a question about you healers?"

"Of course."

"Do your interpreting and healing skills improve with age?"

"It depends on the healer. Usually they do. If the healer's ego becomes inflated and he or she thinks they are the one doing the healing their ability may wane. Other factors are: if they become alcoholics, if they become ill, if anger takes over their personality, if their prayer life suffers, or if any negative aspect of their personality becomes dominant their healing skills suffer."

"All of this is fascinating," admitted Sharika. "Do you mind if I spend time with the three of you to observe?"

Kaathi smiled at the request. "I have no objections. It may well be a good way for you to improve your own sensitive scent skills. Now if you recall I wanted you to keep in mind what odor this patient cast out. Were you able to identify a specific odor coming from her?"

"There was. It smelled similar to sewage. I know there are many strange smelling sewages, and I am not sure I have ever smelled this one."

"If you associate a certain scent on a person, and you identify it with an emotion, is the emotional scent always the same on each person?"

"Most of the time, although there are factors which make it difficult such as illness."

"Do emotions such as fear and anger always smell the same on each person?"

"Yes, only because of the strength of the emotion."

"As you know there is a spectrum involved with emotions, can you identify each one from love to hate?

"It is much easier to identify the extremes. Anything in between is difficult unless I understand what is happening to the person emotionally. Generally, the pleasant scents correspond to positive emotions and the unpleasant scents correspond to negative emotions. If I know what is going on emotionally with a person and I detect a specific scent and I smell the same scent coming from the person in the future I know his or her emotional state at the moment."

"I would hope as you become acquainted with certain patient problems you will be able to equate the illness with a scent," proposed Kaathi.

"I certainly hope so," responded Sharika.

CHAPTER FORTY-FOUR

Jacob listened to Janos' account of Sharika killing two cheetahs. The Warrior Hunter listened with great interest to the story. Not long ago Caleb had recounted how Sharika had driven an arrow into a crocodile's eye in an effort to ward off its attack on their canoe. The shots she made were under great duress and they impressed him. He knew she was a great shot for they had on several occasions went target shooting. She bested him as much as he bested her, which was saying a great deal about her abilities for there was no better shot in Kahali than he.

The deaths of Pauli and Sandor made him think of whom he would chose to replace them. He had toyed with the idea of asking Janos for several days. With all the stories surfacing about Sharika's skill and bravery, he concluded she would be an excellent apprentice and decided to ask her as well. Before he did he needed to make sure Janos would accept his offer.

"Thank you for sharing, Janos. I had almost asked you to be my second apprentice. I chose Sandor instead. Would you be inclined to accept my offer to be my first apprentice?"

Janos smiled as he took a deep breath and responded, "It would be an honor to be your assistant. I have always admired your courage Jacob, and I have enjoyed learning how to use energy to my advantage."

"I am glad you accepted. You are going to make an excellent Warrior Hunter. I also have someone in mind to be my second apprentice who you know very well, Sharika."

Janos' eyebrows raised in surprise. "She is a Hun. There will be some angry men because of the decision."

"Janos, this is something you will have to learn. Your decisions are not going to please everyone. It is an impossible task. If you feel in your heart the decision is correct, you have to go with it. Enough talking, I am off to find her and ask if she wants the position. Goodbye my friend and thank you for accepting."

"The pleasure was mine."

Jacob found Sharika in the Talker Healer's hut.

"Good morning ladies."

He was greeted by a chorus of hellos.

"What brings you our way?" asked Kaathi.

"I was looking for Sharika. May I take you away from these ladies for a short while?"

"Of course." Sharika was always eager to have a conversation with him.

Once outside he guided her to Batu's favorite relaxation and meditating spot next to a large acacia tree. He kept the conversation light until they arrived and sat down.

"Kahali was placed in a terrible spot by the deaths of Pauli and Sandor. It was especially hard on their families and on me. Pauli was my friend since I was able to talk. The position is not always filled by the best shot or the strongest person. I looked for personal characteristics such as bravery, ethics and leadership. Pauli had all of those and more. Those qualities are what got him in trouble with the Nubilon men. He was searching out the truth. I have filled the first apprentice spot with Janos. He has Pauli's characteristics. I looked for another man to fill the other position and I found all those qualities in a woman. I would like you to be my second apprentice. Will you accept?"

Jacob's announcement came as a surprise to Sharika. She thought over his request. "I am honored you would consider me. I know it is going to rankle a great many men. I know they will complain because I am not a Kahali. Are you prepared to stand firm if I accept?"

"Yes. I am sure you saw your friend, the chief of your people, make decisions not well received by his people. It is inevitable and impossible to make everyone happy. I am selecting the best person for the position. Had you been a native I would have chosen you over Janos for the first apprentice position. . . Please keep what I have told you confidential."

"I understand."

"So, my dear Hun, what is your answer?"

"Knowing my acceptance is going to bring men my way to complain, I accept. I can deal with them as it occurs. The important thing is your trust and value of me. I deeply thank you for it."

"You have shown you deserve it. I want you to be present at the next council meeting, where I am going to announce my appointments."

CHAPTER FORTY-FIVE

The High Priest, Kaathi, was discussing elements of spirituality with her apprentices, Ashlee and Scarlet. She noticed the questioning look on Scarlet's face and patiently waited.

"I have heard the words happy and joyful mentioned in the Spiritual Awakening sessions. What is the difference?"

"The difference is significant, and it can be a little confusing. Many people use the words to describe the same event or feeling. Happiness usually comes from things outside of yourself. Joy comes from what you experience internally or from your spiritual life experiences.

"I like to think in terms of happiness coming about from being the best at something, whether it is a footrace or being excellent at baking. It can be felt with good health or good fortune or the birth of your child. It can also occur when you find something you lost years ago or when an estranged child comes home and mends their relationship with you.

"One of the problems in defining joy is how it overlaps with the understanding of happiness. The birth of a child can bring about happiness. It can also be a deep spiritual experience, which gives you joy. It can also apply when you and an estranged son finally bury all the reasons why you were separated and you acknowledge your love for each other. I prefer to use the word joy to describe my internal, emotional and spiritual moments, which often includes my interaction with another person or being."

A woman's voice outside the hut called for Kaathi. She went to welcome the woman in and showed her to a seat.

"I think you know us. What is your name?"

"Zelda."

"How can we help?"

"I have attended a few of your spiritual services. I was hoping I could talk to you and you could help me. I am twenty-four and all six of my relationships have ended disastrously. I am getting tired of trying to find the right man. What can I do?"

"I believe Scarlet has had some personal experiences in this area."

Scarlet smiled to put Zelda at ease. "I was born and lived in Homar until I settled here after King Edmund wanted to destroy Kahali. Homar was a male dominated society. Our fierce fighters devastated their opponents in contests to acquire more wives. My mate was not strong or good at fighting with poles and it was the way for men to claim more wives. Because of his ineptitude, I was his only wife. Our marriage was arranged by our parents and his parents were rich enough to have literally bought me. He was typically not appreciative of me, and I was not a happy woman. He wanted another wife who would like him. To acquire another woman he had to participate in the annual contests. He had erroneously misjudged his abilities and died from a blow he received in his first contest to acquire another wife.

"I was twenty at the time, and the next year I was going to be placed in the open market for the winners of the fighting contests. I was aghast I would be put there to be fought for like a prize. I was distraught and knew I had to do something to avoid it. Some deep part of myself told me to repeat an intention over and over. My intention was one sentence: I am deserving of marrying a man who appreciates and loves me."

"You are married to Jacob, right?"

"I am."

Zelda needed more information. "How long did you say the affirmation?"

"I recited it every moment of the day, when my mind was not occupied with other things. I said it with all the emotion I have in me. I kept saying it for nine full moons and Jacob came to Homar. I fell in love with him the first time I saw him and wanted him to take me back with him as a second wife or his lover. He did neither because he was already married."

"If I remember right, you were taken in by his wife, Keri, when the Homar Armada arrived."

"You are correct."

"By the way, I thought Keri was insane to do it. Getting back to me, what are you trying to tell me?"

"I am telling you you must change how you think and what you believe. It will also create a new future for you. By creating an affirmation you believe in, it will bring you the right man. Your affirmation must initiate with the words – I am."

Zelda's mind was whirling with different ways to form her affirmation.

"Your affirmation worked for you. Can I use it?"

"Of course. You must remember to have faith. It will change your attitude and life and it will bring you the right man. Remember you must say it with as much emotion as you can."

"And you say I need to say it continually when I am not otherwise occupied?"

"Yes."

"For how long?"

"As long as it takes, which might be ten days or ten cycles of the moon," answered Scarlet.

"I shall start as I am walking home," said Zelda, as she stood.

The High Priests hugged Zelda and sent her on her way with blessings.

Ashlee looked at her friends. "How long do you think it will take her to materialize her man?"

"She seemed earnest in her request for help," observed Kaathi. "She knows the older she gets the more difficult it gets to have a man seek her hand in marriage. I would not be surprised if she was among the happy or joyful prospective brides at the ceremony next year."

CHAPTER FORTY-SIX

The rain curtailed many outside activities in Kahali, and provided ample time for people to relax, be with family and share stories. Jacob, Gene and Janos were exchanging pleasantries. The energy in Gene's hut changed dramatically the moment Janos brought up the subject of Kaathi's anticipated trip to Nubilon, Homar, Ebiji and the Wanderer village.

Gene, a member of the Ebiji village, sat listening to the conversation. His people were descendants of the Watusi tribe and he had inherited their tall stature. Because of interracial marriage they were not as dark skinned as their forefathers but darker than the Kahali. He was handsome and very thin, which was due to the weight he lost after the abuse he suffered at the hands of the mutants and never gained back.

Gene interrupted Janos. "I am sure you know Kaathi has asked Evette and me to accompany her on the journey."

Jacob and Janos nodded.

"Since she informed me, I have had six horrible nightmares about the trip." Gene stopped and breathed deeply. "It has been more than fifteen years since the mutants brutalized us, and I still remember the terror of those few days, as if was yesterday."

Perspiration appeared on his forehead. He looked uncomfortable. "I would like to go on another adventure, but I do not want to see Carch. I enjoyed going on the last trip to Sumati with Scarlet and the others. I know Kaathi is going on this trip, but I cannot see the Wanderers."

He was having problems breathing. "I cannot talk to Carch and his monster mutants. I just cannot."

His hands were trembling. "Evette wants me to face my fears. I cannot. I am not as strong as she. The only reason I left my home was because of my love for her. I would have jumped off a cliff for her. She sensed who I was and understood me and never criticized me for being emotional. She accepted and loved me. I could not have married a better or more courageous woman."

Gene stood and paced the floor. His armpits were wet and rivulets of sweat trickled down from them. His eyes changed; he looked like a pained, caged animal desperate and full of fear.

His voice trembled as he recounted his ordeal, "I went with Evette to find her utopia. After a number of days out on the savannah, we saw humans in the distance. The moment we identified them as mutants, we knew we were in trouble. We started trotting to outdistance them. No matter how hard we ran they kept closing the gap. I knew what they would do to us, if they caught up with us. Me and my sweet, brave wife filled with so many ideals, were the hated Normals - their enemy. Fear drove us past our exhaustion point. They caught up with us and we could not put up any real resistance... I was terrified... They brutally beat us. At times, six of them battered me. They did horrific, unspeakable things to us."

He halted and covered his face to hide his tears.

"I do not want to be sodomized again!" he yelled. "I cannot go," he whispered and dropped in a heap on a chair.

He set his elbows on his legs and held his head. "I cannot go," he groaned. He burst into sobs and moaned over and over "I cannot go."

Jacob wanted to console him and say Kaathi would never ask him to go with her, if she did not believe him capable of handling the emotional stress. Perhaps she had misread his state of mind and emotion. Something prevented him from saying anything. He did what he saw women do to each other in such cases. He got down and wrapped his arms around his friend.

A long while later Jacob and Janos emerged from Gene's house and walked through the light shower to the meeting hall. Neither man uttered a word until they were seated.

"I have never seen any man break down so completely."

Jacob nodded in agreement. "Few men have gone through what he has. I was there. I did not think he or Evette would survive the abuse they absorbed. Their faces and bodies were a mass of swollen bruises and cuts from fighting the mutants. They fought for their lives and the preservation of their minds. When the mutants came upon us, I saw Evette and Gene were bleeding from their genitals and anuses. They were a breath away from death. I believe, if Kaathi had not tended to them mentally and physically, they would have perished. It was a sight I never want to see again."

Janos questioned his mentor, "What should we do?"

"I am at a loss for what to do. We gave him what little comfort we could; it is up to Kaathi to salvage his sanity. Do you want to come with me to talk to her?"

"Of course."

At the Talker Healer's hut, the men announced themselves and were greeted by Kaathi, Mara, Marie and Janos' wife Sharika. Jacob spoke freely knowing her policy of including her apprentices in any consultation. Jacob covered what transpired and looked at Janos. "I think you covered everything," said Janos.

"Thank you for coming. Mara and I will go to him now."

Kaathi rose and embraced the men and they left. The two healers walked unhurriedly in the rain and came to Gene's house.

"Gene, it is Kaathi and Mara. Can we enter?"

A long time passed before he answered, "Yes."

Both women saw how hard he was struggling to keep control of his emotions. Neither of them had seen him look so distraught since he and Evette were rescued from the mutants. They sat across from Gene. He sat with his head bent over and rocked without glancing up. Mara's eyes were filled with compassion as she looked at Kaathi and raised her eyebrows in question.

"Gene, Jacob told me how upset you are. I am sorry I did not properly word my invitation to join me on my trip to see the Wanderers. I thought I mentioned, when the skies were blue, you and Evette were welcome to come. I thought I was clear when I said either one of you could refuse and not come. All coming are doing it of their own volition. Do you want to talk about your reaction?"

Gene did not reply.

"Gene, I know you have been stuffing your feelings for a long time and not letting people know how much you are suffering. Every time I wanted to know if you needed help you refused. On the surface, you appeared to be handling the abuse well and were working at forgiving the mutants. I knew differently. I was waiting for you to exhibit the reservoir of agony you were holding inside you. Do you want to talk about it now?"

Without looking up, he slowly shook his head. He released the grip he had on his hands and saw them shaking. He put them back together. He knew he had to do something or face the fact he could explode again over something someone would say. He opened the emotional dam as tears collected in his eyes.

"All my life I have been told to act like a man." He shook his head again. "I did not know what it meant, and I still do not know. I never felt I knew how to act like a man. I went through the motions and hoped I did the right thing. Most of the time, it did not suit my father.

"When I met Evette, she never expected me to act any particular way. She accepted whatever I did. Even when she declared she was going to look for utopia I told her I did not want to go, and she accepted my decision. As her father started teaching her how to survive on the savannah, I knew she was committed. I could not lose the one person who loved me unconditionally. She is the only person to accept me and my strange emotions. How could I refuse her? The funny thing is I never believed we would find utopia.

"The world changed the moment the mutants caught up with us. I knew the stories about their brutality and barbarism. I fought them for her first and myself second. It made little difference. Our resistance seemed to enrage them. The brutal degradation and shame they put us through was horrific and is something I am not willing to relive by going there."

He stopped, whimpered and put his head in his hands.

"I realized you were much more sensitive than most men the moment we met," confessed Kaathi compassionately. "With some men the feminine aspect is almost overbearing and the reverse is true with women. I received confirmation after confirmation you were living more from your feminine side than your masculine since I have known you. I have often wondered when you would unravel.

"Your experience of being brutalized is difficult to conceal. You cannot keep such horror and terror hidden forever. I knew you buried your wounds deep inside you to keep from falling apart. The truth is Gene, you need to fall apart before you can put a better you together. It will not come quickly or easily. Mara and I will help you every step of the way."

He raised his head and looked at Kaathi and Mara. His voice trembled as he professed, "I am telling you right now, I am never going to visit the mutants."

Kaathi took his hand saying, "You do not have to do anything you do not want to, Gene. Consider the invitation withdrawn. Would you be willing to see me and Mara every fourth day to help you through this darkness? Our discussions would be held in strict confidence. We can meet at Batu's tree"

He mulled the question over.

"We will be out at the tree tomorrow after the dawn meal."

Kaathi rose followed by Mara. Gene did not get up. He watched them leave.

The village square was too filled with people and the two healers did not speak until they were in the Talker Healer's hut. Kaathi spoke first, "The next time we get together I am going to relinquish being the therapist and have you conduct the consultations. I believe he associates me with the devastation he suffered. It may be he will not tolerate me as well as you."

"Are you sure it is what you want?"

"It is. I will assist you if necessary."

"What did you mean he was not able to act like a man?"

"From what little he and Evette have shared and from what I have sensed in him, it appears he has struggled with his manhood his entire life. In the Talker Healer stories, there are accounts of men not comfortable in their bodies and women not comfortable in theirs. In each of us are cells identifying what sex we are. In many cases, the proper division of cells is not there to help establish and solidify the mental and emotional person with his or her body. Gene is one such case.

"In some cases the genitalia of both sexes is present to confuse and horrify the person even more."

Mara squinted at her mentor as if she could not believe what she had just told her. "I cannot imagine dealing with such confusion."

"It can be crippling. Gene has been confronting two battles. The first was to properly identify with emotionally being feminine and the second is what he was put through by the mutants."

"Which problem should I approach first?"

"I would let your conversation determine which direction you proceed. Ask him what he wants to talk about. If he does not know, I would ask him questions about his dreams, fears, anger, shame and desires."

The next day Mara and Kaathi arrived at the tree and waited for Gene a long while. He appeared at the tree and the sessions with Gene started. At times, Kaathi smiled at the height difference between Gene and Mara the tallest and shortest people in the village. They slowly gained his trust. After some of the sessions, Kaathi offered suggestions on how she could have approached his hesitancies, fears and issues to get him to reveal more of what was troubling him. Kaathi helped Mara in guiding Gene to deal with his shame and anger, after being abused by Carch and the mutants. Mara's confidence grew with each session. The fourth counseling session Mara acted as the lone therapist. Mara utilized Kaathi's advice throughout the session. Afterwards, she went over what transpired with her mentor. The progress Gene and Mara were making assured Kaathi she would be able to make the journey and not concern herself how Mara conducted her therapy.

CHAPTER FORTY-SEVEN

The season of blue skies heralded the journey for the peace keeping mission. Friends, relatives and well-wishers bade the contingent goodbye. The two dugouts moved upstream away from Kahali. The group would stop at the villages of Homar, Wanderer, Nubilon, Ebiji and Hun Nation. The trip arrangements were made more than a dozen years after the brutal deaths of Pauli and Sandor in Nubilon. The first canoe held Kaathi, Ashlee, Jacob and Elgar. The second contained Evette, Kacy, Sharika and Marcel.

Many days into the trip Jacob recognized some signs and knew they would be in Homar the next day. He saw an excellent campsite and they headed toward it. The men pulled the dugouts ashore, collected firewood, built a fire and relaxed while the women tended to the meal. They ate and selected which male and female would tend the fire in shifts and watch for predators.

Elgar had made the most recent trip to Sumati two years ago with Kaathi, Gene, Janos and a dozen other people. The trip was concerned with the exchange of ideas and commerce as well as having Chief Victor ratify the peace treaty. This trip would be another monumental one and he had insisted he be part of the group to persuade the leaders of the villages to ratify the treaty. He had taken over the responsibility as the Elder of Kahali eight years ago, upon the death of Caleb. His mentor had traveled to Nubilon and Homar on a previous trip over a decade ago and related many stories about the villages and its people to him. He was eager for this adventure to be successful. This trip, if it fulfilled its promise, would be a huge step toward insuring peace among the neighboring and far flung villages. He wished he had thought of suggesting it and not Kaathi. He shrugged his shoulders. *What did it matter? My name shall be in the stories telling of this adventure and how it changed the history of our villages.*

"You look deep in thought Elgar. Thinking of home?"

"A little, Jacob," Elgar admitted. "I was thinking how much this trip is going to impact each village and the future, if we are successful. I hope we are as successful on this trip as we were on the one to Sumati. Nothing like this has been attempted since the Age of Destruction."

"If it happens," said Jacob, "it is going to change a lot of people's lives. I feel better about why I am on this adventure than any I have been on. We are a day away from Homar. Sumati was a good sounding board to see how other tribes would react to the peace treaty. Even so it never insures complete success, especially with the mutants."

A silence came upon the men. Each was thinking of how much their trip would impact the world around them. Jacob's thoughts drifted back to the first time he and Kaathi had traveled to Homar. They were committed to bring back a young man she communicated with telepathically and turned out to be the prince. He was still remembering the journey, as he fell asleep.

The next afternoon the travelers pulled ashore in Homar. A throng awaited them on the bank of the river. Jacob knew their arrival in any of the villages would be similar. The dangers involved in any trip discouraged travel, consequently people arriving from a nearby village was always a big event and the whole population congregated in welcome. Everyone was eager to see adventurers and find out the nature of their expedition. The moment Jacob saw King Edmund, he was stunned by how much the king had aged. Edmund's military heads fared much better. The king made the introductions for his family and military heads, and Elgar made them for the Kahali group. People who were not dignitaries stepped forward and renewed old acquaintances.

The select group walked to the palace, where the king's favorite servant, Edgar, had arranged for the sumptuous meal and drinks. Jacob made sure he was seated next to Kaathi. They sat across from the king. Elgar sat on Kaathi's other side.

Edmund ended his chat with Kaathi and found Jacob's eyes. "I must say I was startled to be introduced to yet another of your wives some years ago. It is nice to see some of our traditions have set well with you. It is nice to see her again. I find Ashlee stunningly beautiful."

"I do as well."

"For her to have escaped is astonishing," remarked Edmund. "I find it fascinating you have surrounded yourself with a marvelous collection of strong, distinguished women. I congratulate you."

Jacob smiled. "I have been blessed and extremely fortunate, as have you."

"Indeed," exclaimed the king. "I have been fortunate to be married to some beautiful and wise women." He looked at Monika on his left and Angela on his right. "If you will permit me my dears? In my old age I feel I can say this without anyone getting upset. I must let Ashlee know she is the loveliest woman on the face of the earth."

Angela smiled at Ashlee seated next to Jacob saying, "I agree."

"How kind of you Edmund. I humbly accept your compliment."

Angela took the opportunity to ask Jacob, "How is Scarlet?"

"She is well," answered Jacob. "She did not make the journey because she is with child."

"Oh, how wonderful. Congratulations."

"Thank you. The child will be the second for her. Our first was a girl. We named her Kaath, in honor of Kaathi."

"You must be pleased, Kaathi."

"She is a treasure to visit her. How are the Relationship Sessions going?"

"Excellent, even though there are dozens of men still not attending the sessions. All in all, I would say the transformation, from our old traditional ways is coming along well."

"I am happy for you and your people."

The servants kept busy keeping the wine cups filled. Having eaten, the men rose and gathered in groups to talk. Andre, Kaleez, Carver and Jacob were in one such group.

Andre smiled at Jacob. "I can understand how Ashlee fell for you. Hell, you saved her life by killing the nasty mutant. I remember a time when I got a lot of crap from you over Renee. It is my turn to give you a ration of crap. You snake. You stole Scarlet from us. How was it different from what I was trying to get away with, when I wanted to take Renee away from her folks?"

Jacob smiled sheepishly. "I will tell you. Renee did not want anything to do with you until you changed. I was always a decent chap and it is why Scarlet wanted to be with me."

"Decent?" guffawed Andre. "I am sure you have killed your fair share of men and lusted after a few women."

Jacob's voice feigned severity. "My wives think I am a sterling man."

"You are not sterling." Kaleez told him in his booming voice. Everyone nearby looked at him. "You are tarnished like the rest of us."

The men laughed loudly.

"I will make a toast to you Jacob," announced Andre, "Here is to your ability to sweet talk women into becoming your wives."

The men laughed and eagerly drank to the toast.

Across the room Sharika, Prince Zach and his wife Princess Gita were standing, sipping wine and catching up on each other's lives.

Sharika was looking at the group of young royalty one of whom was Zach and Gita's son. "Your son is a handsome boy. He has your nose Zach and your chin. He does have Gita's beautiful eyes. Have you spoiled him?"

"Of course. Despite it, he is well behaved. For a five year old he is already a fine shot with bow and arrow. We had a bow made for him fashioned after your design."

Gita touched Sharika's arm. "Zach has told me a great deal about you, all of it is favorable. Are you married?"

"I am. Janos and I have been married fourteen years. He is caring for our two sons and one daughter back home. Their ages are ten, nine and seven. They are my source of joy and happiness."

"I am glad you found the right man and are content."

"Thank you."

"Why is he not here?" asked Gita.

"Since Jacob and I are here, he had to remain in Kahali. One Warrior Hunter must always be in the village."

Nearby Kaathi inquired about Edmund's health.

"As good as can be for a man of fifty-two. I have weathered a few illnesses and I have noticed I do not have the stamina I once had."

"If you would allow us women to do it, we could lay hands on you, sending you energy and pray for you."

It did not take Edmund long to decide. "I would welcome it the moment it seems proper to do so."

The king caught Elgar's eye. "Elgar, I cannot imagine you have made this trip without a purpose. Why have you come?"

"Actually the trip is a peace keeping mission. We hope to discuss the treaty and its terms at your convenience. If necessary, we are open to changes and we would like you to ratify it, and we can move on to the Wanderer mutants with it. The people we hope will agree are the Wanderers, Nubilons, Ebijis, Huns and you. The Kahali, and Sumati people have already agreed to it."

"Sounds intriguing. Let us talk about it tomorrow after the morning meal," proposed Edmund.

"Excellent," replied Elgar.

Everyone was conversing and drinking. The king thought it a good time to do the healing mentioned by Kaathi. He motioned to Kaathi and retired to his bedroom, with Kaathi, Ashlee, Sharika and Kacy in tow.

"What do you want me to do?"

"Lie on your bed and relax. If you have a prayer you like, repeat it until we are done. Are you comfortable with us setting our hands on you?"

"Yes."

Kaathi took a position by his head, Ashlee at his feet and Kacy and Sharika were on either side of him. They gently rested their hands on him, each saying silent prayers asking for Creator's energy to move through them blessing them and pass it on to the king and blessing him. A short while later Edmund felt the energy coursing through him and silently thanked the women and Creator for the blessing.

His thoughts strayed to how tired he had been of late. *Perhaps it is time I relinquished my position to Zach. All I need is the assurance Zach will not have to face a devastating situation like another military uprising or a raid from the mutants. A peace treaty is exactly what we need.*

His mind drifted and he noticed he was very relaxed. He concentrated on the energy they were sending him. It made him relax deeper and he fell asleep.

CHAPTER FORTY-EIGHT

The next morning the king assembled his military heads, queens and children together for the morning meal. The king saw everyone was finished eating and he stood. The room quieted. "Edgar please thank the cooks for doing a splendid job. We have gathered here to discuss an important peace proposal from our Kahali friends. I shall allow Elgar to tell you what it is."

Edmund sat and Elgar rose. "Thank you, Edmund. Our council has already approved it and have received approval from Chief Victor of Sumati. Allow me to go over the tenents of the treaty."

Elgar went over the proposal slowly and finished by stating, "Those are the general tenents and they are open to discussion, revision and addition."

"What if a village does not ratify and raids us?"

"A good question. We should add if any nation does not agree, and they take any aggressive action upon a nation agreeing to the treaty all of those nations shall rise up and take action upon the aggressor. The agreeing villages shall contribute one half of their able bodied men to this peace keeping force.

"The aggressor can send a delegate to the offended village to explain the action, in case the aggression was made by renegades from their tribe. If it is the case the renegades should be killed or cast out of the village with no weapons."

"I agree with the new proposal."

Kaleez stood. "Was Kaathi the brainchild of this treaty?"

Elgar answered, "She was. Had it not been for the Relationship Sessions, we would not have attempted to propose the treaty."

Kaathi jumped into the discussion. "We realize half of the villages have not had the advantages of having the sessions. We hope to propose they allow us to send a delegation to their villages to introduce the Relationship Sessions and later the Spiritual Awakening Sessions.

"Our understanding is the mutants have not made a raid for a few years. Ashlee has told us their population has decreased during the years she was held captive and we believe they are hesitant to lose good men in battle. Evette and Gene are originally from Ebiji, the home of the giants, and they informed us the last skirmish they had with anyone was when they were children. While we are not altogether certain, we are hopeful the Nubilons have muted their aggression since they took the lives of our two apprentice Warrior Hunters."

Edmund ran his hand over his beard. "Thank you, Kaathi. With this additional information we can make a more informative decision. Are there any questions from my family or leaders?"

"I have one." Kaleez's voice rumbled even in the large room. "I think half of the able bodied men from each village should be part of the combative force is excellent. However, I think we need to go further and add another tenent. What if there is an invading army outside of the collective villages. How big a force can we count on?"

Elgar nodded. "A good question and one we did not anticipate. I will let Jacob answer the question."

"I must say we never thought about such a contingency. If the force is a large one I would say each village needs to pledge eighty percent of their able bodied men. What are your thoughts Kaleez?"

"I agree with you, Jacob. In dealing with any invading foe, the show of unified front and force is strategic. It must be shown the opposition shall be dealt with swiftly and surely."

"I agree," said Andre. "The larger the force the greater the misgiving of entering into battle."

"I concur," said Jacob.

The king looked over the crowd. "Is there anyone else who wants to contribute their thoughts on the new tenents or the whole treaty?"

No one spoke.

"Is there anyone who opposes this treaty?"

No one responded.

"Consider the treaty ratified, and I wish you good fortune with the rest of the villages you visit."

Elgar heaved a sigh of relief. "Thank you, Edmund."

"I believe this is a good reason to have the festival we did not have upon your arrival." Edmund turned to his trusted servant. "Edgar would you immediately tell the horn blower to announce the festival and have a table in the square for us?"

"Indeed I shall."

A while later Edgar returned to tell the king the table was set and people were congregating in the village center. The group walked to the square and were welcomed with applause by hundreds of locals. The village center quickly filled. Edmund stood atop the table and told his drummers to announce him. The crowd quieted and Edmund called out to his people, "My friends it is my extreme pleasure to announce our friends from Kahali and I have ratified a peace agreement. They hope to have all the tribes, nations and villages surrounding us ratify it as well."

The crowd roared their approval.

"If all of the villages and nations approve the treaty, it will mean we will live out the rest of our lives in peace not fear."

The crowd enthusiastically yelled and applauded.

"This is an auspicious day in our history. Let us celebrate it in song and dance."

He stepped down to thunderous applause and shouts.

Before the military leaders had too much to drink, Jacob asked Kaleez and Andre for identifying landmarks on the river and the plains to the Wanderers' village. A little later Edmund made his way to the group and pulled Jacob aside and had him walk with him.

Jacob grabbed Edmund's arm stopping him. "Before I forget to tell you, Edmund, I am thankful and respectful of whom you have become."

"Thank you. It means a lot to me coming from you. Because of the cultural and spiritual revolution taking place in my kingdom, I would like to know what precipitated it in your tribe. I know Kaathi does not like to talk about herself. It is obvious she has had a great influence in your village. I also know your tribe was a patriarchal society for dozens upon dozens of generations. I have heard a little about the woman, Batu, and I am intrigued. Can you give me a brief history of her and Kaathi?"

"I would be happy to," Jacob replied, "since I was on the council during the changes and in the middle of it all. The revolution started with Taja, the old Talker Healer. He was Batu's mentor. Batu was a vocal advocate of women before she became a woman. She was a thorn in the council's side as well as the High Priest's. When it came time for her to marry, she challenged her father's choice and convinced him to choose Thomas, the Story Teller, a council position. It was a stormy marriage until Batu became ill with a skin disease. Taja talked to her and helped her change her attitude from being self-centered to self-empowered. Less than a year after her recovery her husband was bitten by a snake and died leaving her vulnerable to being expelled from the village because she had no worth. A month later Batu discovered Thomas had impregnated her and gave her worth. Unfortunately, the baby died at birth and she was again vulnerable to ejection. During her expulsion, she gave a scathing speech criticizing the council and High Priest. Taja tried to save her by offering to marry her. She refused. She left the village knowing her death was imminent at the mouths of any number of predators. Taja and I found her and he rescued her by offering her an apprenticeship. She accepted, creating history by becoming the first woman on the council.

"Two years later Victor arrived from Sumati seeking help from Taja. A disease was making hundreds sick and several of his people had died with no end in sight. Taja sent Batu to help them. He sensed, if she succeeded, it would be a turning point in having the village accept her. She found the source of the problem and came back a heroine to find Kaathi and Taja had become close friends. It took only a short time for Kaathi to win over Batu. The apprentice High Priest's wife approached Batu and told her she was being abused by her husband. Using this as the impetus, Batu and Taja authored a set of laws giving women rights and protection from men.

"This inflamed the High Priest and his apprentice. The two of them killed Taja because he helped Batu. She accused the High Priest of murdering Taja. He was furious at her insolence. In his rage, he had a heart attack and died. Before he died he had his apprentice vow to kill Batu and Kaathi. He did kill Batu, spared Kaathi and took his own life."

Jacob nodded his head and continued, "Something only a few people know is Kaathi is very human. It was a long while later Kaathi confessed to me she was in love with Batu. Batu's death must have devastated her. However, it was never apparent. It does not surprise me she fell in love with Batu. Batu had a deep passion to grow spiritually along with other qualities Kaathi admired. I am not sure if there was any man with those distinctive attributes except for Taja, and he was deceased. I believe only a person with such strengths could attract Kaathi. I do know, after Batu's death, Kaathi put much greater emphasis and attention to her spiritual life."

Edmund nodded, showing he understood her personality. "Why did the maniac High Priest spare her, Jacob?"

"She told him she loved him."

"She loved him?"

"She would not tell me the whole story, just as she has not told me the whole story of how you were transformed after talking to her."

"Since you and I have gone through so much, I suppose it is only right I share what it was she uncovered for me that helped me transform. One day I upset my father and he snapped. My tyrannical, sadistic father sodomized me over and over again that day. I hated him for what he did to me."

Edmund stopped as he recalled the terrible day and took a deep breath.

"Only my mother knew about it. She was never the same after that day. She aged terribly in a few days. She died shortly afterward. The event shattered me. It stole my innocence and hardened me. I swore I would never be sodomized again, so I became like him. I raged at everyone. My father complimented me on my new fierceness. I grew more and more brutal and hard. It pleased him and kept him at bay. I waited patiently to revenge my mother's death and for what he did to me. It came within a year after my mother's death. My father died by my hand. In the intervening years, I destroyed everything he had built. I wanted no memory of him."

Jacob understood why Kaathi chose not to share what happened when she and Edmund left the meeting. He was stunned Edmund took him into his confidence. It was easy to see why the king had been so filled with anger for so many years.

"I am sorry for the loss of your mother and your humiliation. I apologize if you felt pressured to tell me."

"I felt no pressure. I felt you were a sensitive, strong man who has become my friend. It needed to be told to a male friend who would see how hard I am trying to make amends for all the brutality I inflicted upon my people."

Jacob leaned over and hugged Edmund.

"Thank you for your trust and for considering me your friend."

"It would give me great pleasure if you and your family would consider living here in Homar. I consider you and Kaathi family. No need to commit. I just wanted you to know you have a home awaiting you if you choose to move. . . Please get back to your story."

"Thank you for the invitation, Edmund. . . Subsequent to everything that happened, Kaathi and I became good friends and she wanted me to go with her to find your son and take him back to Kahali."

"I know that part of her history well," noted Edmund.

"The trip brought us here, and we came across the Searcher mutants, Leah and Isaac. Kaathi made friends with them and we brought them back with your son. Our people were in an uproar because she brought two mutants back. She explained how they were not from the mutant tribe raiding villages and were not a threat and convinced them to a trial period.

"The reason for bringing your son with us was to stimulate you into following Kaathi and she could have the intimate conversation with you, which changed your personality. It also provided Renee the opportunity to instruct your people about the importance of proper relationships on all levels of society.

"Two years later Kaathi, Leah, Isaac and I made a journey to find Ancient Mother and Ancient Father. Kaathi had been communicating with the Ancients telepathically. They are part of the twelve Ancients living around the world praying for the good of Mother Earth and all her inhabitants. On this trip we met three distinct races. Mara was part of an Uchakwa scouting party. They attacked us because we were passing through their territory. She alone survived the attack. Kacy was expelled from the Uchakwa clan; we came across her later. Both of them came back with us.

"We also interacted with a clan of simians. I called them Stalkers because they tracked us for a half day before they revealed themselves. None of the Stalkers chose to remain with us. We also rescued Evette, from the Wanderer mutants. You have met her. Her husband, Gene, chose to remain in Kahali for personal reasons. When the mutants came across us, one of them was ill and they abandoned him to die. Kaathi was able to heal him. His son, Marcel, is part of the peace contingent.

"Sharika was a different story. We met her in Sumati. She confessed she was looking for a husband. Like everyone, she became instant friends with Kaathi and came back to Kahali with us.

"My wife, Ashley, was saved from death outside of Sumati by Kaathi. Ashley had been abducted by the Wanderer mutants and made a slave for eighteen years before her escape. She came back to Kahali with us.

"Every person associated with Kaathi has played a major role in Kahali and the education of the surrounding villages. One of her most significant accomplishments is the peace treaty. Second to the treaty would be the initiation of the Relationship Sessions and the change in our religious practice with the Spiritual Awakening Services."

"She is a truly amazing woman," admitted Edmund. "If my memory serves me, Sharika is your apprentice and Scarlet is not only your wife but is an apprentice High Priest along with Ashlee. I thought I recall Kaathi saying the Uchakwa woman, Mara, is her apprentice."

Jacob nodded in agreement. "You are correct."

"Have those appointments caused unrest in Kahali?"

"They have. Somehow Kaathi is able to explain why she chose them in such a way as to quiet most of the rumblings."

Edmund nodded. "She does have a way with words. No. I retract what I said. She has a confident, dynamic aura and it seems to calm people's fears."

A small group of people interrupted them and took Edmund with them.

CHAPTER FORTY-NINE

Edgar found Kaathi sitting on the veranda.

"Miss Kaathi the king requests your presence. Would you please follow me?"

The mystic took Edgar's arm and went with him to the main palace room and deposited her there and left.

"Ah, Kaathi thank you for coming." King Edmund pointed to a chair. "Please sit. I have a favor to ask. A man has been a thorn in my side for nearly a year with his complaints."

"Why is he displeased?"

"He is a holdout at attending the sessions. I do not mind it, but he is vocal about it and is a nuisance. Would you talk to him and see if you can silence him or change his mind?"

Her eyebrows went up as she smiled. "It seems since you are not a terror some in your flock are not afraid of you."

"Yes. It was much easier being a dictator king."

"You know I would do anything for you."

"Good." He called out, "Edgar."

The loyal servant appeared.

"Would you take Kaathi to Gar's house?"

"Of course."

"Thank you for your help, Kaathi."

"No need to thank me. I am happy to talk to your people."

Kaathi linked her arm through Edgar's. He led her out into the village center. She asked about his family as they walked. They followed an avenue for a short while and took a right onto another and came to Gar's house.

He called out, "Gar."

Gar appeared. He was powerfully built, dark-skinned, well-muscled, younger and taller than Andre. His tightly curled hair was cropped short as was his beard. A wide, long scar cut across his left cheek and disturbed his nose. His eyes were piercing, dark and brooding and detracted from his looks.

"The king has asked Kaathi to talk with you."

"I am getting tired of him sending people over to talk to me. Is he afraid to talk to me himself?"

"You need to ask him yourself."

Gar turned his attention to the woman. She had extraordinary and expressive eyes. He looked suspiciously at her. There was something he detected emanating from her. He could not put his finger on it and wanted to discover what it was. He relented disgustedly. "Very well come inside."

"Can we recline by the river?"

In a sarcastic tone, he said, "By all means I want you to be comfortable."

She did not lock her arm in Gar's as they walked. Edgar followed discreetly behind them. They walked without talking on their way to the water. Gar found a spot he liked and sat down. Kaathi sat opposite him. Edgar sat and leaned against a tree out of earshot.

Gar squinted at her. "What is this about?"

She smiled. "Evidently you are a concern to the king."

"Damn right I am." He slammed his fist into his palm. "He is always sending his lackeys to get me to attend the shit sessions, and it is not going to happen. You are the most recent in a long list of people, including the instructors, trying to convince me to go. I am not interested in attending, so have your say and get the hell out of here and leave me alone."

She sat unmoving.

He felt like he needed to put more emphasis on what he said. He thumped his broad, hairy chest. "Now that he has given us free will I am using it."

"Oh, I do not blame you."

He was taken aback by her comment. He expected her to back the king and criticize him.

"Go back and tell him to shove the sessions up his ass." He growled angrily, sounding like a prehistoric beast.

She giggled. "You know I will do no such thing. It would be disrespectful."

"Well, I do not respect him so tell him whatever you need to so he will leave me the hell alone."

"I am not done talking with you, so I do not know what I am going to say to Edmund."

"You can tell him to kiss my ass. That is how I feel about all this crap everyone is trying to shove down my throat."

He was sorry he did not shove her to emphasize his point. He wondered why he did not. Was it because she was from Kahali? Was it the enchantment he saw in her eyes? She was small, but she did not look frail. She would not break, if he did push her over. Hell he had done it dozens of times with dozens of women. Strangely, there was something about her keeping him from doing it. At the moment, he was uncertain what it was. He was sure he would figure it out before they separated.

He laughed derisively. "I never thought Edmund would send a woman from Kahali to talk to me. What has he got on you?"

"Got on me? Nothing. I am doing a friend a favor."

"Bullshit."

"Do you always use such foul language?"

"I do what the hell I want to and nobody can stop me."

"I have noticed. I need you to know the way you are talking to me is disrespectful."

"Why the hell should I respect you?"

"Because I deserve it."

He waved his hand at her as if he was shooing a fly away. "Deserve it my ass. You have not done anything to deserve it."

"In your estimation only."

"It is what counts," he snorted.

"No, your estimation is distorted."

"Distorted my ass," he hissed.

"Let me ask you a question. Is this the way you talked to your sister?"

What the hell? She speaks as if she knows my sister. It cannot be. She never could have met her. She has not been in the village long enough for it to happen. So why does she speak with such certainty?

"You do not know my sister so do not talk about her."

She raised her eyebrows, as if to say she did know her.

A moment of quiet passed before he relented and answered, "It is."

"Did you disrespect her at home?"

"Why do you want to know?"

"Because it is important for me to understand you and how you were raised."

His answer was slow in coming. "I would give her shit, when she made me mad."

"Why did you get mad?"

"She was older and would tease me."

"Did you know her teasing was the way she showed you she loved you?"

Gar's brow furrowed. He did not answer.

Her voice was gentle as she asked. "Are you afraid to answer me?"

"Hell, I am not afraid of you or any man alive and that includes Kaleez. I fought him and nearly kicked his ass. I probably can now."

"Then answer me."

His eyes bore into her and he could not get her to cower. Finally he answered, "I gave her what she deserved."

"And what about your mother?"

"The only thing I remember about her is she moaned and cried most of the time. I was five when she died and left my father to raise us."

"Was your father angry because she died?"

"Hell yes. Not only did he have to hunt for our meat, he had to raise crops and make our meals until my sister was old enough to do it."

"Did he ever thank her for making the meals?"

"Are you crazy? It was her job."

"Did you ever thank her?"

His answer was a sour look.

"Did you respect your father for doing what he did?"

He nodded.

"So you respected him for doing your mother's work but could not give your sister the same respect for doing her work?"

He made a guttural sound and glared at her.

"Did you ever thank him for doing it?"

He made a face. "It was his job. We did not go around gushing about what we were supposed to do."

"Gar, it appears your father never learned how to be respectful, compassionate and show love. It is why he did not share them with your mother and could not teach you those qualities."

He glared at her and said nothing.

"I can see you did learn distrust and disrespect from your father. I cannot blame you for being angry and not giving love to anyone. You learned to hate women and face disputes with anger from your father. Kindness, compassion and love are learned. Unfortunately, no one taught them to you. I am sure your mother gave you love and your sister did, in her own way. Sadly, you were too young and the memory of being loved got buried inside you."

The mystic's voice grew softer.

"Some people face the challenges of life completely defenseless. Your defense of life's hazards is anger. It does not have to remain your shield. The sessions are your resource for helping you understand why anger is dominating you and will provide coping alternatives to handle arguments without resorting to anger or violence. The more you attend the sessions the more you will be equipped to come to terms with your feelings. Your family should not have to suffer the brunt of your anger. You will learn there is a give and take in relationships. The sessions can help you establish a warm and loving relationship with your family and sister thus allowing them to delight in the modification and your love."

Gar glared at her, but her words penetrated his heart and unsettled him. His glare slowly vanished. Confusion took its place.

The mystic rose and smiled at him.

"It was a delight to chat with you, Gar. Do you want a hug?"

He was startled by her question. "No," he said in a soft voice.

"Then allow me to say I love you. Goodbye."

He watched her take Edgar's arm and walk away. He felt an emptiness in his stomach and chided himself for not accepting her invitation to be hugged. He continued watching her and inexplicably felt charged with excitement. The others Edmund sent to talk to him did not have the mystic's energy or wisdom. Her explanations made sense. If he took to heart what she said, it was a chance to benefit from renewal, a fresh approach to life he never would have imagined just yesterday. She said his life would be altered by the classes. He already felt remolded simply by her presence and wisdom. He breathed deeply and felt awakened to the nuances of the delicate balances present in relationships she spoke about.

Two days later King Edmund, his family, military leaders and his subjects bid the Kahali group goodbye. As Edmund watched them go, he decided, when they returned with the news the peace treaty was ratified by everyone, he was stepping aside and let Zach rule his kingdom.

CHAPTER FIFTY

Nine days after the peace group had left Homar they came to a sharp bend in the river. Jacob recognized it from the description Kaleez, the Giant of Homar, gave him. They beached the dugouts. From this point, they would head overland to the Wanderer village. As they traveled overland, the conversation was held to a minimum in order for them to concentrate on the dangers lurking nearby and in the distance.

They had not encountered any problems the first four days on the land trip. They made camp and the women were in a quiet discussion of their own. Evette tuned out. Her thoughts were on the mental scars from her horrible encounter with the mutants. She was a Tall One and did not have the curvaceous figure of the Kahali women. Her features were delicate, her cheekbones prominent. She carried herself well, though lacking the grace of smaller women. Her nose was not flared as those of many women in Kahali, and she wore her hair longer and pulled together at her neck. Her husband, Gene, and a few friends built a new hut to accommodate for their height a few days after their arrival.

The closer they drew to the mutant village the deeper in thought Evette went, remembering her horrid experience with the Wanderers. Her thoughts revolved around her two days with the Wanderer mutants. The memories were not pleasant, and she bore an unease she could not cast off. It had been roughly two decades since the experience. At times it seemed as if it took place yesterday. With Kaathi's gentle help she had recuperated her physical health, which was badly damaged by the mutants. The emotional stability came long afterward.

The strange and wonderful thing to come out of the experience was the strength of character she had acquired after her recovery.

Due to the experience, she was able to help the Sumatians, as an instructor of the Relationship Sessions. She and her husband Gene had shared their experiences, insights and understandings with the Sumatian adults and children for two years before returning to Kahali. It was now many years since she had left her home, and she considered it the most rewarding years of her life and the most joyful. She had Kaathi to thank for the experience.

The travelers had been walking the plains for six days when they spotted a lone lion tracking them. The lion decided to overtake them and made its way toward them. Everyone who could fire an arrow readied themselves for the inevitable encounter. The lion came close and they could see it was an old, mangy male on the verge of death. As it came within its attack range, it tried to sprint to them and could not. It ended up trotting toward them. Jacob, Sharika and Elgar were designated to release the first barrage of arrows. The second group consisted of Kacy and Marcel. Elgar's arrow missed its mark. Jacob and Sharika's arrows struck the lion in the shoulders and it tumbled forward in slow motion. As it struggled on the ground Kacy and Marcel fired the next arrows, which buried themselves in its flesh. They walked to the lion to recover their arrows and found the lion was already not breathing. Sharika and Jacob could not recover their arrows. They had broken as the lion tumbled forward.

On the seventh day they zigzagged the whole day looking for the village and finally saw their destination. They came upon the Wanderer village and saw the entire population was on the outskirt awaiting them. As they drew near, they saw there were three classes of humans living in the village. Ashlee had prepared them by telling them the majority of the people would be mutants with some Normals and some half breeds.

The mutants eyed the small band of foreigners. All of the males had their arrows set on their bows ready to fire on command. Everyone from Kahali had at least one hand up showing their palm signaling they came in peace. Carch was not about to be fooled in his old age and did not tell his men to put down their weapons.

The woman with blond hair caught his eye. It was not often he saw anyone with blond hair. His mind searched his memory to place when he last saw a blond haired woman. His eyebrows shot up.

Ezra's slave!

She resembled Ezra's slave. He motioned Gwen to his side.

"Is the blond woman the one who was slave to your father?"

Gwen was a woman when the slave fled their home and she fondly remembered the slave. The slave had given her more affection than either one of her parents. Back then, the slave was a dirty mess, now she was clean and her hair was combed. She easily detected the slave's body language was much different than when she lived with them.

"It is her, chief."

Though weary, Ashlee stood as erect as she could. She wanted her body language to tell all of the mutants she was in control of herself and her destiny. They approached with Ashlee in the lead. The others came to stand beside her. She spoke in the Wanderer language.

"Chief Carch, we come in peace. I see you remember me. My name is Ashlee. I am now a member of the Kahali village."

Carch nodded and was surprised she was the spokesperson for her party.

"It has been a long time since you fled Ezra's house. After being a slave for nearly two decades, I never thought you would be foolish and return." He paused a long while as he assessed her. "I sense you are not a fool, so why have you returned?"

Carch voiced his thoughts aloud, "Could you be a scouting party? No, I do not think your council would send five women and three men to evaluate our strengths and weaknesses. It must be something else. With all the strength remaining in this old body I cannot detect the reason you are here. I shall close my mouth and listen to you speak."

"Your evaluation is correct. We are not a scouting party. We are a peace party. Let me introduce the rest of my party before talking in depth of why we have come."

She went to Elgar and laid her hand on his shoulder. "This is Elgar, our Elder, and leader of the Kahali."

She walked behind Marcel and held his arm. "Marcel is the apprentice Elder of Kahali. He is the son of Durga. He is a half breed Wanderer and lived with you. Durga was part of your scouting party and you left him to die. He recovered from his illness and is in Kahali."

Carch saw Marcel's resemblance to Durga. He had often thought the woman, Kaathi, had made more of Durga's illness than it actually was. It was interesting Durga's son returned and not him.

"This woman is Sharika. She is from the Hun Nation and is now an apprentice Warrior Hunter to Jacob."

Ashlee moved to Kacy. "Kacy is Marcel's wife. She was originally an Uchakwa, who followed Kaathi.

Carch wondered if all the Uchakwas were hairless. He found the lack of hair disturbing, yet he found it hard to take his eyes off the diminutive woman.

Ashlee stood behind Evette and introduced her. "This is Evette she is from the Ebiji tribe."

Carch gasped. There was no mistaking the giant woman. He recalled catching up with Evette and a man. They were the Tall Ones they had raped and sodomized on the savannah years ago. *I was sure they were going to die from the abuse they received from me and my men. How could this Ashlee and Evette come back and face me and my people without wanting to kill us all? Neither one of them seems the least bit angry. I remember another woman named. . . Kaathi. Yes, she was the witch, who held me spellbound and conjured up the face of my mother on her face. She talked me into letting them go.*

Ashlee moved to the Warrior Hunter. "This is Jacob. He is a member of the Kahali council and is the Warrior Hunter of our village."

Kaathi stepped out from behind Jacob. Ashlee put her hand on the mystic. "I believe you know Kaathi our healer and High Priest."

Carch could not believe his eyes. It was indeed the healer, and she looked the same as when he had last seen her. She was the one he had to be cautious of for she had magical powers. He hoped his face did not give away his shock.

Carch nodded and informed her, "My wife has died." He placed his arm around a stout, rugged and rather ugly mutant and announced, "This is my son, Alex; he will inherit my title upon my death. This woman beside me is Gwen. Her father, Ezra, went out to bring you back, unfortunately, he never returned. Gwen's mother died four years ago.

Carch agitatedly waved his hand saying, "Everyone significant has been introduced. Let us sit by the fire and talk."

Chief Carch and his son led everyone to the village center, where a large fire was going. He would have preferred to talk with these people with only his son present. The occasion was extraordinary and he had no choice and committed to the public meeting.

There were only ninety-three of his people alive along with thirteen slaves and concubines and less than thirty half breeds. The half breeds had only half the strength of one mutant. It did not make sense for non-mutant mothers to give birth to create warriors of insufficient strength. Some of his men still wanted to raid a village and bring home new women. It was never going to happen as long as he was alive.

Years ago Ezra wanted him to send a raiding party to recover the woman named Ashlee and he did not capitulate to the request. Ezra went alone to bring her back and lost his life. They had not made a raid in over seven years for fear of losing good men. Times have changed and he wanted his people to survive. He did the best he could to instill this bit of wisdom in his son. His son was not an easy person to teach or read. All he could do was hope his brain was recording things.

Every Wanderer was seated and still able to see Carch and the party from Kahali. The slaves were situated behind them and had to strain to see well.

Carch raised his voice. "What is so important you risked your lives on the river and the plains and now risk your lives here?"

"We have come to negotiate peace," announced Ashlee. Kaathi had convinced Elgar, Ashlee needed to be the one talking for all of Kahali because of her knowledge of their language and society. Elgar was intelligent enough to see Kaathi's point and relinquished his role as spokesperson.

Carch thought over what she proposed. There had not been any raids or skirmishes with the Kahali or Homarians for years. A year ago they had a skirmish, with a Nubilon scouting party. They had killed nine of them and lost four men he could ill afford to lose. He took his time thinking about her proposal. A treaty would assure him he would not suffer additional loss of men. He liked the idea.

He nodded his head saying, "Before you continue I want to know how Ezra met his death?"

"He found me and wanted to take me back. Luckily, Kaathi was with me and offered to go in my place. She vowed to go if he could hold onto her hand. He was unable to and he was about to kill her. Jacob was nearby and drove two arrows into him."

"Interesting. Go back to him taking her hand. Why could he not hold onto her hand? It seems a simple task for someone with strength."

"He was shocked every time he grabbed her hand."

"Shocked? How did she manage it?"

"She has an internal energy; it repels evil."

Carch accepted her answer, recalling how the witch, Kaathi, magically manifested his mother's image on her face.

"Did he not see Jacob?"

"No. Jacob was honing his skill with bow and arrow and saw him from a distance and circled him and Ezra did not see him."

Carch nodded in acceptance of what took place.

"Kaathi has shared a great deal with me of her personal philosophy and I eventually forgave Ezra and all of you for having killed my parents and making me a sexual slave,"

"You did not have to come here."

"No I did not. I chose to come in order to help you forgive all of the Normals for killing your people."

"Are you crazy? Do you know how many of my people's blood was shed because of you Normals?"

"No."

"Of course not, it was thousands. THOUSANDS," he yelled!

His people repeatedly shouted, "Thousands, thousands."

The moment they quieted Ashley softly reminded him, "And our people's blood soaked the ground as well. Our number was greater than yours. Your raids and ours were based on anger and vengeance. Neither one of us can afford to let emotions control us any longer. You cannot because your numbers are dwindling and we cannot because our philosophy has changed under Kaathi's influence."

Carch let her words settle in. She was speaking the truth. Neither one of them knew the complete truth how the animosity came to be. They simply knew it existed and would continue until one of them died out or something or someone came along to change their attitudes. *Could this woman, Kaathi, be the change?*

"I am listening."

"If you do not mind, I shall step aside and Marcel can speak."

Even though I have a slight admiration for this woman for escaping from us, I want to hear if Durga's son has a brain. Carch turned his attention to the half breed.

Marcel honored Carch by bowing his head. His father had taught him the expression and he noticed Carch seemed pleased he knew the old Wanderer tradition of bowing to a superior. He spoke in the Wanderer language addressing the aged chief, which he learned from his father.

"My father related many stories about your strength and tactical skills. It is a pleasure to finally meet you. I shall reiterate what Ashlee told you. We come in peace and want to negotiate a peace treaty so no kingdom, tribe, clan, village or nation needs to worry about warring tribes we do not know or raids or skirmishes or broaching of borders. The treaty will insure all people shall be able to live in peace."

"You speak of other people. Who are they and do you speak for them?"

"The treaty has been approved by the Kahali, Homar and Sumati people, and we do speak for them. After talking with you, we will go to Nubilon, Ebiji and to the Hun Nation and talk to their rulers and seek agreement to the terms of the treaty."

"I do not care if you speak for the others. I want assurance you speak for the Nubilons as well. They attacked one of our scouting parties last year and killed four of our men. We cannot think about agreeing to a treaty without their compliance. We are done here. Go back to Kahali."

The mutants grew vocal in backing their chief.

Marcel raised his hand. "Please, hear me out, Carch. We are certain we can get their approval, especially, if you agree to the terms of the treaty. Nubilon is the original home of Ashlee."

"And what of the Uchakwa clan? I did not hear you speak of them being part of this treaty."

"We are not going to visit the Uchakwa clan. Kacy told us her people never leave the forest, and their numbers are less than yours."

"What she says must be true. We have never encountered the Uchakwas and it is true for the Ebiji. We came across Evette and her man from Ebiji because they had entered our territory. Above all else I need to be assured the Nubilons have agreed to this treaty you are talking about."

Many of the mutants assembled shouted their support of Carch.

"It is our next stop. We are contending with the rainy season and want to be back in Kahali before the torrential downpours. If the Nubilons do not agree to the terms, we will return and let you know. If they agree to it we will not come back. Are you comfortable with us not coming back?"

Carch scratched his hairy chest and thought about what Marcel said and spoke, "Yes. I need to know the terms of this treaty."

"The first term concerns territory. Each village, tribe, clan or nation shall claim as their territory the area within seven days travel from their village."

The term drew immediate shouts of anger from the mutants. They found it too restrictive.

"I cannot agree. We hunt and patrol ten days journey from our village."

Marcel realized the mutants did not travel the river and the restriction applied to travel by water. "Since you do not travel by water we will stipulate twelve days journey by land for your people. Are you in agreement?"

The mutants clapped and shouted their approval. Carch nodded his approval.

"May we offer the next term?" asked Marcel.

Carch waved his hand as if shooing a fly away.

"The second term concerns raids. It states there shall be no raids on any other kingdom, village, tribe, clan or nation. There shall be no abductions or stealing of people. This is punishable by death. No goods are to be taken from any village. The act will be considered a heinous infraction of the treaty. Each village will supply half of its available fighting men and wage war on the guilty village."

Carch saw the retaliation would be devastating and nodded his approval. "What if the infraction is made by an individual?"

"It is the next tenent. If the individual is caught braking this treaty, he shall be contained and face judgment by a three man tribunal from his own village provided by the ruler of the village. His village shall not be held responsible for his actions."

"Hmm. Very well," responded Carch.

"The next term is significant. If a village experiences a natural disaster or an epidemic it can call upon any or all of the other villages to assist them. The other villages are charged to help if they have the resources."

The mutants spoke excitedly about the term. Everyone including Carch saw the advantages of the term.

Marcel, seeing the reaction among the mutants, was thankful Kaathi had the good sense to insist this term be part of the treaty.

"And who shall deem if the resources are available?"

"A good question, which I will answer. If you need help and you come to Kahali for assistance the assembly shall make the decision with your delegate present. In Homar, it shall be King Edmund and Prince Zach. In Sumati, it shall be Chief Victor and his sister. There is a three man council in Nubilon and a nine man council in Ebiji. In the Hun Nation, a chief will preside."

"Are there other articles of the treaty?"

"Yes." Marcel went on to describe how each tribe would send men to contend with an outside waring force.

Carch turned to his son, Alex, and whispered in his ear, "What are your thoughts on this treaty?"

"If we were what we were a few generations ago, I would tell them to stand in quicksand. We are not what we were. I say agree to the treaty."

Carch nodded his head. His son had voiced his own thoughts. Times change and he would be a fool to ignore what has taken place.

He looked at Marcel saying, "I agree to the terms of the treaty."

The Kahali party broke into smiles. Most of the Wanderers did as well. The mutants, like their leader, were cognizant of their stagnant numbers and the growth of the other tribes.

CHAPTER FIFTY-ONE

Joanne's heart raced as she saw her grandson. He looked every bit like his father, Durga. The tears in her eyes could not hide the fact the years had been good to Marcel. The years were not kind to Joanne. Her owner had died eight years ago and his brother and his wife inherited her and the widow. She now had to be servient to two females and a male mutant. It was not an easy life, it was an ugly one in every respect.

Since the arrival of the travelers, she spent every free moment she had hunting down her grandson and wait for the chance to rush to him and cling to him. Her eyes were moist during the moments she trailed after him. When the opportunity came, she moved quickly up behind him and called out in a trembling voice, "Marcel."

Marcel turned to see an old, haggard Normal. He looked at her a long time wondering who she was.

"I am, Joanne, your grandmother!" she cried out.

The news startled him. They moved to each other and hugged and openly wept. It took many moments before he stepped back and looked at her again. His heart ached at the sight of her. Her dirty, wrinkled face was evidence of the maltreatment she had suffered. Joanne had been abducted at the age of thirteen and lost all remnants of her childhood, being terribly abused physically and sexually before they reached the mutants' village.

"Father told me about you. I never thought you would be alive. I remember father telling me how cruelly you were treated and how difficult your life was. I am sorry for all the suffering you had to endure. I cannot tell you how good it is to see you, Grandmother."

The old woman stared at him. "Oh my goodness, I dreamt of Durga so often. At times, it was the only thing keeping me alive. When I heard the news he took ill and was near death I never imagined I would see him again let alone his son. The gods have answered my prayers. Is Durga alive?"

"Father died last year in the arms of Mother."

Sadness fell upon her face. Joanne was used to death and suffering, and the emotion quickly faded. "Did he marry?"

"A woman from the Searcher tribe, Leah."

"I thought they were all dead."

"Mother was the last to survive."

"I can die happy he lived long enough to sire a son."

She affectionately rested her hand on his face.

"Do not talk about dying, Grandmother. You are going to live a long time. I am not leaving here without you."

"Oh, do not try my dear. It will cause trouble and I do not want it for you. One of us escaped and it is enough."

"It is not. I am taking you with me. I promise you will be with me, when I leave."

"Do not make promises you cannot keep."

"I shall keep this one, Grandmother. I am going to talk with Kaathi about you. She will find a way for it to happen."

"Marcel, I have to leave. If I am gone too long they hunt me down and beat me or keep food from me."

"Please stay longer."

"I cannot."

He embraced his grandmother for a long time. He felt how thin and frail she was and his heart ached. He had to get her out of this miserable environment.

Joanne joyfully whispered to her grandson, "I love you. I love you. Never forget it my son."

Both wept as she walked away. He was filled with hope; she was filled with doubt and worry.

Marcel found his opportunity to talk to Kaathi alone and related how his grandmother found him, and he desired to take her back with him to Kahali.

Tears filled Kaathi's eyes as he unfolded his story. She felt his desire and love as well as Joanne's love for him and his grandmother's desire not to cause trouble. Marcel watched the mystic's eyes and tried to sense why she was crying. He finally asked, "Are your tears of sadness or joy?"

She embraced him. "They are both. I am sad your grandmother has had to suffer as a slave for all those years. I cry for her frailty and abuse and for the years she had to endure without having Durga by her side.

"I know her heart is filled with joy for having seen and held you. I am grateful you have found her alive and have been able to share your love for each other. I am thankful you have the desire and courage to take her away from here.

"My dear Marcel, my heart is also filled with sorrow knowing you will not be able to take her away."

"Why not?"

"There is nothing you can give the people subjecting your grandmother to slavery in exchange for her freedom, except yourself. Do you understand?"

Stunned, Marcel answered, "Yes."

"You have a life changing decision to make. Do not make it rashly. Go into meditation and pray to arrive at the right answer. Do you wish me to meditate with you?"

His eyes roamed the environment before he spoke, "Yes. Please."

"Very well, let us take a walk and remove ourselves from everyone. Once you have come to a decision, we can contemplate what our next step will be."

They were far outside the village and Kaathi roamed the area until she found the energy conducive to meditate and sat down.

"Are you clear on what to do in meditation?"

"I am."

"Good. Let us surround ourselves in love while we meditate."

She closed her eyes and created a field of love around them. Marcel went into a meditative state and posed the question to Creator and requested guidance. A long while later he opened his eyes and cleared his throat to let the mystic know he was done. He had to do it a second and third time before she started to breathe deeply as she exited.

"Have you arrived at an answer?"

"I have. I am going to ask Carch what I need to do to take my grandmother home."

"Very well. Let us find him."

They found him in front of his hut. He looked at them without speaking.

"I have found my grandmother," announced Marcel. "Her name is Joanne and she is a slave."

Carch nodded. "I know her."

"I want to take her back with me."

"Has her owner given you permission?"

"No."

"You will need it. I doubt they will give it unless they are compensated for their loss."

"What if I offer myself in return for her release?"

Carch eyes widened in surprise. "I know Samu well. He would likely agree to it, and you would be positioning yourself to be repeatedly raped."

Marcel was stunned. He never gave the possibility a thought. He steadied himself mentally before saying, "If he is willing to accept all I have with me, I want to take my grandmother home. If he does not want anything I own, I am willing to exchange myself."

Carch thought, *Marcel you are stupider than I thought. The last time I saw your grandmother she looked as if she was not going to see the sun rise, but it is up to you.* Aloud he said, "Just in case he does accept what you own, you will have to bring it all with you. Get your things and come back here."

Marcel left and Carch looked at Kaathi, "Was this your idea?"

"No."

"Did you encourage him?"

"No."

They waited in silence for Marcel to return. His hands and arms were full with weapons.

"Very well, let us walk over to Samu's."

The walk was short. After announcing himself Carch and the rest entered the hut. Samu, his two wives and Joanne were present. Samu looked puzzled. Protocol called for Carch to do all the talking.

"We have a situation," announced Carch. "Joanne there is Marcel's grandmother. He wants to take her back to Kahali. He is willing to give you all his possessions in exchange. What say you?"

Samu was uncertain what to say. To his knowledge Carch had never presided over any type of exchange.

He directed himself to his leader, "What has he got to exchange?"

Carch nodded to Marcel.

"I will give you my bow, arrows, quiver, spear, machete, long and short knives and my extra set of clothing."

Samu noticed the bow the moment he walked in. It was shaped like no other bow he had ever seen. He had fashioned it after Sharika's. It had a flat center to hold the bow and two near half circles in place of a near half circle.

"How did you come by the bow?"

"The design is one the Huns use. Sharika introduced it to us."

Marcel handed it to Samu. He hefted it and pulled the string. Samu appraised it in a variety of ways. Marcel's hopes rose. Samu gave the bow back.

"If Carch agrees to the peace treaty, I will have no need for this fine a weapon. I do not agree. Add a woman and I shall agree."

"There is no woman. Marcel has one last offer to make," announced Carch. "He will exchange himself for his grandmother."

Joanne screamed softly into her hands. *No my son, you cannot do this. I will not let you.*

Samu was genuinely surprised at the offer. *This is a startling turn of events. The old hag is hardly any good at copulation and the young buck would be a definite change. He is young and strong and can help me a lot more than the hag.*

"I accept the offer."

Joanne rushed to Carch and pleaded, "I do not want to go to Kahali. I do not want to put my grandson in harm's way. Please do not sanction this exchange. I implore you."

Carch saw the tears in Joanne's eyes. Something deep inside him stirred. He remembered what it was. Her eyes reminded him of his mother's eyes when she pleaded with his father to take her life. She had been suffering with an open sore on her stomach. The pain made her moan miserably for several days and nights. Her only reprieve was sleep, which was fitful at best and short. He remembered his father waited until she was asleep one night and he drove his knife into her heart to end her misery. At the time he thought his father a brute. Later he saw the wisdom in the act. From what seemed a distant place, he heard Marcel make his plea to let him replace his grandmother. If he approved the exchange, the young man would not be an asset. He would protest, moan and groan about everything he confronted and was told to do. It was not worth the trouble. He took a deep breath to bring him fully into the present. "I am taking this into my own hands. I decree Joanne shall remain here and you, Marcel, go back to Kahali."

Disappointment blackened Samu's face. He wanted the strong healthy male.

Carch turned and walked out of the hut. Kaathi followed him, leaving Marcel to say goodbye to his grandmother.

"I am sorry Grandmother. I tried."

"I know you did. I love you all the more for it. Go now and know I shall love you beyond my death."

She embraced him and clung to him a long time, unwilling to let go of him. She backed up enough to kiss his cheeks again and again with all the love and tenderness she could give him. She tasted the salt of his tears on his cheeks and kept professing her love as he did to her.

Samu and his wives watched not fully understanding such tenderness and display of affection. When they finally parted a tiny part of them felt a twinge of what the grandmother and grandson were experiencing.

CHAPTER FIFTY-TWO

The mutants set aside their animosity toward the Normals and were kind enough to share their evening meal. Evette suggested each one of them be paired off with a family able to speak the common language to provide an exchange of feelings and thoughts. Carch found it a good idea. He and his son were teamed with Evette and Ashlee was paired with Gwen and her husband. These were the most significant arrangements because of past experiences.

Carch and Alex were not in the least uncomfortable sharing a meal with Evette. She on the other hand dealt with recurring flashbacks to the horrible time she and Gene had spent with Carch and his warriors. She had done a great deal of work on forgiveness, during the intervening years. She had expressed to Kaathi on different occasions she had forgiven the mutants for the atrocities they had committed. She recalled Kaathi smiling and giving her words of encouragement though never confirming the tragic event was now past her. In the midst of the mutants, her forgiveness was being challenged over and over again. She shuddered and rubbed her arms.

Carch saw her reaction and remarked, "You did not seem uncomfortable when you first arrived. I see and feel it from you now."

"You are right. I am not with my friends." Her voice turned raspy. "I am being flooded by images and memories of the abuse you put me and my husband through."

She watched Carch shrug his shoulders in reply, as if it was what he and his men did to them was as natural as breathing. Clearly, he and his men had no sense of propriety, decency or morals.

"The two of you never should have been out there," he pointed out nonchalantly.

Her voice rose in defense. "You sound as if it was our fault and our presence gave you the right to do those atrocities to us.

"It is what we do," he said in a matter of fact tone.

"I left my village of Ebiji and my family because of male domination. Thankfully, there were no atrocities committed to the women." Her voice shook with emotion as she continued, "We are civilized and not barbaric like you."

"Do not talk to me about barbaric acts," he hissed at her. "Our stories are filled with barbaric acts you Normals inflicted upon us. We retaliated whenever we had the chance."

Evette was shocked to hear the venom in Carch's voice. Everyone in Kahali spoke vengefully about the mutants. Only Kaathi presented alternate possibilities of why they clashed so often. She wondered which side initiated the first attack or raid. "Do your stories tell which village was the first to attack?"

The leader of the Wanderers looked at Evette and was surprised she would voice the question. Usually the Normals were prejudiced toward them. It took a long while before he decided to answer her question. "Our oldest story tells of a small band of mutants being attacked as they drew near a village. The village was not named." He stopped and reflected a moment. "Why do you think they attacked them?"

The answer jumped into Evette's mind. "Fear. When my husband and I saw you closing in on us, we were filled with fear by the stories we heard. Once you were clearly visible we were scared a second time by how frightening you look. The terror, abuse, humiliation and shame you put us through was close to unforgivable."

Carch's eyes narrowed and he growled. "You Normals are our ancestors and you did this to us. The Normals placed greed above everything else and poisoned Mother Earth and created us. What we did to you is nothing to what we have to bear everyday of our lives because of you Normals."

She hung her head in shame.

"You are right," he continued, "we cast fear in the hearts of all who see us. All except the one you call Kaathi. I am sure she fears not man nor beast. The oldest tale we have speaks of your fear. The last words of the story goes, 'The last thing I heard as I fled was the Normals hated the sight of us.' I am sure they feared someday they would look like us."

"Have you created any stories about your encounter with Kaathi?"

"I have created one and I think some of my men have as well."

"Have you spoken well of her?"

"Yes, I spoke of her courage and wisdom."

Evette nodded.

Her voice was strained. "Did you ever think the reason you were stealing our women was because you craved beautiful women?"

Carch starred at her, while he thought of her question.

"It is something we rarely talk about, but I am sure it is part of why we kept making raids. Everyone prefers to look at something beautiful."

He turned to his son, saying, "No offense to your mother, Alex. You know I never took a slave to be my concubine."

Alex did not speak.

No one spoke for a long time. Carch reran the story of the Normals hating the sight of his people in his mind. Carch and Evette struggled with the anger boiling inside them.

Evette kept returning to the last lines of the mutant story. She recalled a story Kaathi shared of a country divided by a civil war. It took place because the two nationalities occupying the land brought up bitter memories of what took place four hundred years in the past. It was easy to see how one generation would instill hate filled stories into the next generation as they sat around the evening fires. The mutants were no different than the Normals. She saw if she and Gene would have escaped from the mutants and went back to Ebiji and told what happened to them an even greater hatred for the mutants would have developed. It did not take place. Instead she was healed and saved by a woman filled with love who helped her navigate the forgiveness road. She was now facing a crossroads where she had to make a decision. Was she going to continue hating the mutants or was she going to forgive them and go on with her life and attain peace?

Evette looked at Carch and his son. Truly she would have to classify them as ugly and frightening. It was easy to see why the Normals feared these people. The mutants were brutish and fearsome looking, yet here she was having a meal with them and discussing life altering issues. She wondered what Kaathi would say, if she were here now. The answer came as a lightening flash. *She would send her love to Carch.* She accepted the answer and stared at him. She floundered at sending him her love. She found his eyes and countenance disturbing and closed her eyes to concentrate on sending him love. It took some time to feel the flow of love. The moment the flow was present she opened her eyes and gazed into his. He easily saw the change in her eyes. His own changed as he grew aware of her love. She saw his eyes soften as he felt her love. Moments passed and she saw his eyes fill with tears. A great burden lifted from her heart, seeing him weep. Her own eyes filled with tears and cascaded down her cheeks.

She reached her hands out to Carch. He looked at them and took a long time to comprehend what she wanted. Eventually, his hands encircled hers. Because of her tall stature, hers were large and delicate looking in his hairy, broad, thick fingered hand. For them, the animosity and hatred they bore for each other stopped.

A huge divide had been crossed.

The bridge was love.

CHAPTER FIFTY-THREE

Gwen's hut looked like all the others. Ashlee remembered they were all dilapidated. Nothing seemed to have changed. The last time she walked these avenues she was twenty-seven. She was now forty-five and the memories of her life as a slave flooded her sending her into the past.

Gwen had been the only mutant in the village to show her any compassion and empathy. She had basically raised and loved the child after Gwen's mother showed no interest in taking care of her daughter.

Inside her home, Gwen turned and self-consciously touched Ashlee's arm in front of her husband. Gwen had never revealed how much Ashlee had meant to her as she grew up. She was afraid her father would find out and beat her.

Gwen pointed to a chair. "Sit. The years have been good to you. You do not look anything like you did when you were tending me and a slave. You are. . .oh what is the word? Beautiful."

"Thank you. The truth is I try not to judge a person on looks. I look for how well they treat and love me and others."

"You have changed. Your words are much different. You have learned much since you escaped. I do not have the chance to say a woman is comely or beautiful. None of us can be considered beautiful. Perhaps it is why we rarely hear such compliments. Like you, I try to sense if a person is nice or not. I have not come across many in our tribe who are. I learned to value how nice a person is from you."

"If it is of interest to you, Marcel's mother, Leah, is a Searcher and her grandmother is Joanne the slave. Leah told us all of her people were loving and kind. Kaathi and Jacob, our Warrior Hunter, made friends with her and her husband, Isaac, and

289

brought them back to Kahali. They were the lone survivors of their tribe."

"Is this true?"

"I would not lie to you."

"I wondered why they were able to display those qualities."

"They had to have learned them at some point," explained Ashlee.

Gwen thought about Ashlee's statement briefly and went back to the topic of her father. "I have often wondered if my father went after you because he considered you beautiful. I think mother felt it from him and it is why she beat you as often as she did. Did you know Ezra left twice to bring you back?"

"No."

"When he did not come back the second time I knew my father was dead. Mother grieved for him and cursed you. I grieved for you. You were the only person except my husband to give me love." She glanced at her husband, smiled and continued, "I never thought I would see you alive. Tell me all about what has happened to you."

Ashlee was touched by Gwen's show of affection. She told her story from the beginning. "After the mutants killed my parents and Ezra brutalized me, I went into shock. I could not feel anything until you were born three years later. You saved my life. Being a proxy mother for you, allowed me to give you all the love I could muster at the time. After Gadu attempted to rape me, I knew I had to escape. At night I would sneak out and watch the sentries posted outside the village. It took me a year to gain the courage to escape. I did not count on how hard it is to stay alive on the plains. After many days I collapsed and would have died had Kaathi and Jacob not found me. I do not know how Kaathi knew where to look for me. Kaathi is the medicine woman of the Kahalis. She saved my life. She has shared her love and understanding of the spiritual life with me. She has helped villages understand how to respect and honor women. She took over the responsibilities of High Priest and made me her apprentice. She suggested I was ready to make this journey to heal old wounds and help people understand why we need the treaty."

"You used a word which I do not know anything about. What does spiritual mean?"

"The spiritual life is how you relate to yourself to others and to Creator."

"Who is this Creator?"

"Creator is the energy creating everything you see and do not see."

"This energy sounds a great deal like our gods."

"Similar yet different. Your gods can be resentful, angry, perpetuate fear and a whole lot of other negative things and are figments of imagination. Creator is always loving and creating and is the giver of life."

Gwen was still unsure who or what Creator was and dropped the subject. She was curious about Ashlee. "Are you married? Have you a child?"

"I am married to Jacob. He has two other wives and we have two children and we are expecting a third. I do not have a child. We have made love sparingly because of what I suffered while as a slave."

Gwen knew of her suffering and chose not to talk about it.

"You say he has two other wives. Are they slaves?"

"No they are not. We have all freely accepted his invitation to be his wife. He is kind and strong and handsome. He is on our council and is the tribe's Warrior Hunter." She anticipated Gwen's question and continued, "As the Warrior Hunter, he has been designated as the best warrior and the best hunter among the Kahali. He learned from his mentor how to use energy to his advantage in contests and battles and is teaching others how to use it."

"As an apprentice High Priest, what do you do?"

"I am learning the responsibilities of being a High Priest from Kaathi. She is instructing me on the nuances of spirituality. She is sharing with me all she knows about her personal philosophy and Creator."

"Tell me more about this spirituality," pleaded Gwen.

"The basic component is love. Love is what Creator is, and since we are aspects of the Creator, we are love as well. She is teaching us all about love. I remember Kaathi telling us about a wise man of an old culture instructing people. He proclaimed they should do everything in moderation so they would not harm others and themselves. She said it was appropriate for everything except love. She said we should exquisitely love Creator, others and ourselves as deeply as we can."

Gwen shook her head. "I can point out a lot of unloving people."

"I know. It appears so and I will leave it alone for it is complicated. I am supposed to ask Carch if he and his people would be interested in learning how to love and treat everyone with respect."

It brought a chuckle out of Gwen as if it was the last thing Carch would do. She looked over at her man and he was smiling at Ashlee's remark. "Good luck with attempting that."

"I fully understand how difficult it is going to be, and I hope I am up to the challenge.

"So, what has been happening in your life, Gwen?"

Gwen's face turned sad as she reported, "One day is the same as the next, boring. Had our child lived our lives would have been different. Four years ago we lost our baby. He only lived a few weeks. We have been trying hard to have another. For some reason our people are having trouble having children. We have been married nine years and he was our only child. It was hard losing him. I do not know what would have become of me were it not for my husband."

"I am sorry. I did not mean to dredge up old wounds."

"Ah, you did not know."

"Do you mind if I pray for you to have a child?"

"What is pray?"

"Prayer is a petition to my Creator for help. In this case I will pray for you to conceive."

Gwen looked at Ashlee. *How can this woman pray for my benefit after all the horrible things my family and people have done to her? She is far beyond my understanding. I do not recognize her anymore. I wonder if it was all her own doing or did she have help from the mysterious young woman?*

"It would please me."

CHAPTER FIFTY-FOUR

Gadu kept staring at the blond haired Normal. Something about her looked familiar. Suddenly, it came to him. It had been well over a dozen years ago the slave escaped. Even so he was certain the woman before him was the same one. The only difference was she was cleaned up. He had never forgiven her and Ezra for the beating he got. She ran away and the fool Ezra, in his need to have her, went out to bring her back and died for his efforts. He wanted to kill Ezra for humiliating him in front of everyone. It did not matter now. The gods took care of Ezra for him, and now they delivered the slave to him.

Gadu spied on her, making sure he kept behind people. He did not want to be recognized by the Normal. Through the day, wherever she went, he shadowed her. He had to bide his time and wait for his opportunity. Dusk was approaching and the blonde slave separated herself from her companion and walked toward Gwen's home. He waited patiently for his opportunity for the avenue to empty. The moment it did he swiftly and silently crept up behind her and clamped his hand over her mouth and picked her up with the other.

Gadu was torn where to take her. His wife was dead, which made his hut available. He decided it would not due because someone could easily hear her. He decided to take her away from the village to a nearby, small grove of trees. Her muffled cries beneath his hand were barely audible. He easily carried her and within moments he was out of the village and making his way to the clump of trees far away from everyone. If she did cry out, she would not be heard.

The stars were appearing in the sky. Soon everyone would be asleep and he could take her as often as he liked, even if she screamed. He looked back and he could still make out the outlines of the village. They reached the trees and he let her slip from his grasp.

The moment he released her she kicked him in the testicles. He yelped in pain. Angrily he reached out and grabbed her arm to keep her from darting away and struck her in the head with his other hand.

"You bitching slave," he growled and struck her in the stomach. The wind rushed out of her and she doubled over unable to protect herself from the next blow, which landed on the back of her head creating an avalanche of stars.

Kaathi had finished her meal with Carch. She sensed something was wrong. She closed her eyes much to Carch's surprise. He himself was sensitive enough to know to keep quiet. She opened herself to the universal energy. She sensed Ashlee was in trouble. "Ashlee is in danger. Someone is carrying her away."

Carch eyes reacted to the claim.

"Who would be so vile?"

Gadu's face popped into Carch's mind. He recalled the reason why Ezra and Gadu fought was the blonde slave. He did not need this, especially since the treaty was ratified.

"Gadu!"

"Would he take her to his hut?"

The leader of the mutants shook his head. "If I were him, I would take her out of the village." He remembered the small clump of tree. "I think I know where he might be taking her.

He rushed out and she followed close behind. The moment they were outside he started running. Kaathi was only a couple of steps behind.

Gadu had Ashlee by the throat and was ripping her clothes off. Unable to bite his fingers, she grabbed at them trying to get a hold on one to bend it back. She managed to get a hold on his little finger and bent it backward.

"Argh, you bitch."

He let go of her clothes, smacked her across the face and ripped his finger free. He bent her hand back. She screamed.

Carch and Kaathi heard her cry out. They were fifty paces from the trees.

"Ashlee!" screamed Kaathi.

Gadu heard Kaathi and stopped to listen. He detected two people running toward them. He cuffed the slave in his frustration and released her. He stood and turned to face whoever was coming to the slave's aid. A moment later he recognized Carch running alongside one of the women from Kahali.

Gadu reacted. "Shit."

Carch saw he was correct in his assumption. It was Gadu. He pulled to a stop.

"Take your friend and leave," he commanded Kaathi.

Gadu reached out to prevent Ashlee from leaving, thought better of it and pulled his hand back. Kaathi put her arm around Ashlee and silently walked away.

Carch took one step forward and struck Gadu with his open hand as hard as he could. The blow snapped Gadu's head aside. Gadu made no move to retaliate. Carch knew he would not. The darkness prevented the leader from seeing Gadu's hatred. He did not have to, he felt it. Carch had made an enemy for life with the blow.

"What the hell is wrong with you?" hissed Carch. "These people are here on a peace mission and you do something this stupid. I swear you have zebra shit for brains. What the hell I am going to do with you? We are short of men, otherwise I would kick your ass out of the village. Heed my warning, one more stupid move and I will do it. Now, get out of my sight before I beat you to death."

Gadu sulked away incensed Carch sided with the Normals. He had been humiliated by Ezra and now Carch. It was all he could take. Someday his turn would come, and he would squash the life from Carch.

Kaathi and Ashlee talked about the incident and mutually decided to not mention it to Jacob. They did not want it to interfere with what they had accomplished. Ashlee slept fitfully and dreamt about her abduction. The next morning Mara and Sharika tiring of trying to converse with Carch and several of his friends left the group to relax and cool off in the shade of the trees outside the Wanderer village. They saw two mutants emerging from the village. The mutants, seeing the women, veered toward them. Both women had their weapons nearby and were not overly concerned seeing them approach. The two males stopped several paces from the seated women.

The mutants stared at them without speaking.

Sharika being the bolder of the two used the common language to ask, "What do you want?"

The one on the right spoke, "You."

Sharika scowled at them. "If you were the last male on earth, I would say no. Get away from me."

The man laughed. "When I want someone, I do not ask. I take what I want."

"And I am used to being spoken to in a civil manner. Even then I refuse ninety-nine percent of those asking. You are not a one percenter."

"Huh, I am going to be all one hundred percent of them in a moment."

He lumbered one step forward and Sharika was on her feet with bow in hand and her other hand swiftly moving to extract an arrow from its quiver and placing it on her hand and aiming it at the brute. He was still three steps from her and he knew he could not charge her without the arrow burying itself in his gut.

Mara was up now and had her bow and arrow ready and aimed it at the other mutant. He was still five steps away, looking confused at the swift action of the Normals.

The mutant closest to them raised his hands and back-peddled. He smiled. It looked closer to a sneer. "Hey easy there. I was just talking. We are leaving."

They turned around and walked away.

Mara's hands shook as she replaced her arrow. Sharika chuckled. "It does not take much to discourage these mutants."

"I am not as confident about it as you," remarked Mara. "Are you going to tell Jacob about this?"

"No. Those males thought we were little flowers they could pluck. We handled them ourselves. Jacob might stir the hornet's nest and get the whole village mad. There are too many of them to make them upset. Let us keep this to ourselves."

CHAPTER FIFTY-FIVE

In the afternoon, Evette and Ashlee had a private meeting with Chief Carch in his hut. Prior to the arrival of the peace treaty group, Carch never had a private conversation with any woman except his wife. A decade ago he would not have allowed these Normals to set foot in his village. He would have been suspicious the party would assess the number of men he had and determine his weaknesses. He would never have committed such a blunder. Times have changed and the offer of a peace treaty intrigued him. He was unsure what was going to happen talking to these women. He started things off. "What is so important you have to have a private meeting with me?"

"Kaathi suggested we approach you," Evette began, "and ask if you and your people would be interested in learning how to attain a higher state of peace and understanding of relationships?"

"If everyone agrees to the treaty, peace is assured," he stated.

"The peace you speak of is tribal. I am talking about a personal peace."

"I do not know what you are talking about. If my people are happy, I am happy."

"Are they happy?"

Carch took a deep breath. "Of course."

"It is not what I sense. You are aging and do not seem healthy, and I saw only a handful of children. It tells me your women are having trouble reproducing. Your health has to be a huge concern and not being able to reproduce is disturbing everyone. I am sure some of your people are wondering whether the gods are angry with them and others are angry with them or no longer believe in the gods. Am I right?"

Something about Ashlee reminded him of Kaathi. It was as if she could look into him and see the problems he faced. He responded softly, "Yes. It is apparent you have learned a great deal since you escaped."

"Have you counseled your people?"

He looked at her as if she was insane.

"Of course I have. What little is in me. This problem is beyond my capacity to understand. I do not know if it is a curse from our enemies or our gods or from what happened to us during the Age of Chaos?"

He took a long look at her. "Do you know?"

"I do not. The sessions on relationships and spirituality will help everyone cope and come to terms with what is happening."

"Do you realize the only education my people have had is through family stories? We have learned what is important to survive on the plains. If one person makes a better bow, he teaches the others how to make it. If one woman discovers a plant to curtail an ailing stomach, she shares her knowledge with all of the women at an evening campfire. Some of the stories we share around the fires are entertaining others are historical and others are informational."

Ashlee nodded her head a few times in acknowledgement of what he shared, which was enormous, considering she was an outsider.

Carch paused debating with himself whether he wanted to share something secretive. Having decided, he plunged on. "I must tell you I have mixed emotions about you. I dislike you for having escaped from us long ago. You are the only man or woman to ever have done it. Grudgingly, I also have a certain admiration for you because you were able to escape. It took cunning and courage. Damnit, I was furious with Ezra and his family for letting you escape. I sent him after you and told him not to come back unless he had you or your head."

Ashlee was astonished Carch was honest and came forward with her own confession. "Thank you for being honest. I knew he would follow me until he died or caught up with me. I almost did not survive. Were it not for Kaathi, I would have died. I must confess I never heard any of your people speak intelligently until now. I was never privileged to sit among you when discussions took place. Ezra never spoke to Sig or Gwen as you are to me."

"Ezra had brains. He did not think much of women. Too bad he was ruled by his emotions. There are others still alive capable of intelligent discussions. Sadly, some of my men are lacking brains, and I always attributed it to them being mutant."

"If you detected intelligence in your men," Evette pointed out, "it is likely your women are similar."

"It cannot be."

"Why not?" countered Evette. "There is not much difference between the sexes. The problem has been your prejudice."

Carch thought about what she said. On occasion he and his wife had interesting conversations. He wondered if any of the other men had such discussions with their wives. He never revealed to anyone his wife was intelligent and could hold her own in their conversations. As a leader it tread on quicksand. "I never believed our women were so capable," admitted Carch.

"In the past, you and your people have done what was required to survive in a harsh environment. It was paramount in your thoughts. If everyone agrees to the treaty, you will not have to worry about scouting parties killing your people. You will have community peace and you can turn to enlightening yourselves by taking advantage of the relationship sessions and acquiring a deep personal peace. I think you will be pleasantly surprised how intelligent your women are. If you are pleased with the effects, we would like to introduce you and your people to Kaathi's views on spirituality and God."

"It seems, if we have community peace, it is all we need."

"I can see you are reaching the end of your time on Mother Earth," observed Ashlee. "Are you at peace with what takes place after you die? Do you have questions about the afterlife? Are you curious about the gods and about the energy I call Creator?"

Carch rubbed his hand over his beard as he contemplated her questions. At night, when he could not sleep, he went outside and looked at the stars and marveled at their number. He had given thought to many questions and had no assurance his answers were correct. He did a lot of introspection since the passing of his wife and compared himself to what he was like in his youth. He found he had become emotionally soft. Now this woman who had been a slave and lived among his people was suggesting ways for him to acquire peace. *Damn, this woman touches the places in me I do not want to look at. It is a shame our women do not have this understanding or knowledge – or do they?*

"As strange as it seems to me, you are making sense," he admitted. "You have an inner capacity similar to Kaathi. If you are to convince me my people need your help, I need to be assured. I shall ask you questions and I want you to answer them as you would if you were instructing me in one of your sessions. Agreed?"

Ashlee smiled. "Agreed."

He fondled his scraggly beard for a long while. "My first question is: Are you teaching how to improve all forms of relationships?"

"Yes. What applies to a relationship with your child applies to a friend, lover or wife. The first principle is respect and I suspect this is not given in most cases to your women and daughters. Is this true?"

Carch took his eyes off her for a moment. His eyes returned. "It is true."

"Did you realize the Searchers respected their women?"

"I did. I was informed it was because they hunted and fought by their men's side."

"Fighting beside their men was part of why they respected their women. In talking to Isaac, a Searcher mutant, he told me all the things his wife did for him and his son. It was why he respected her. Why do you and your men not give your women respect?"

"Because they do not scout and sacrifice their lives as did the Searchers."

"Your women give you children and feed you and comfort you at night and repair your huts. Is this true?"

"It is."

"Do those things have value or worth?"

"It is not the same as dying in battle with a man or beast."

"I agree. The sacrifice is greater for men. It should be apparent without women all those other things would not exist."

Carch took a moment to examine what she was driving at. He had never looked at what women did in Ashlee's light. It was the first time he saw they did a great deal to make a man comfortable. He looked at his son to see how he felt. His son raised his eyebrows as if to say answer the woman.

"Well, I suppose they do things for us," he grudgingly admitted. "Tell me another thing you will teach us."

"Has anyone in your village ever taken the time to thank their women for all they have done for them?"

"I do not know."

"Do you realize your women want to feel they have worth?"

"What do you mean?"

"When a man thanks a woman it validates what she has done is worthy of doing and thus gives her worth."

It seems to run parallel to how my men feel when I praise them for something they do well. I never thought of doing the same for my deceased wife.

"Go on. What else gives a woman worth?"

"You accepting her as your equal."

He furrowed his brow and shook his head. "Not going to happen."

"It is why there needs to be a dialog at each session to allow differences of opinions to be expressed in a civil manner. How are you ever going to know what goes on in anyone's mind or what is in their hearts, if they are afraid to speak? I am sure your women are afraid to talk about what is wrong in their lives to their men."

"A man does not want to hear drivel and crap, when he comes home from a twenty day scouting trip. He is tired, hungry and horny."

"I understand. Has any man asked his woman what she wants and needs or what makes her happy, when he is gone for a length of time?"

"Of course not, it has always been the role of a woman to please her man."

Ashlee jumped on his statement. "Have you ever thought of pleasing your woman?"

"No."

"If you asked the women what gives them pleasure, I think you would be surprised by their response."

"You are not picturing our men in a nice light," he informed her. "It is our role and what we have always done."

"And you have done it because you played your role for generations. The trouble is women were never asked how they felt about a multitude of things. Let me ask you a question. Are you impressed with our conversation?"

"What do you mean?"

"Do I sound intelligent? Do I bring up imposing questions? Have I made you see women in a different light?"

Carch's brow went up as he thought. "Somewhat."

"What makes you think your women would not be able to sit down with you as I have and intelligently discuss these same issues?"

"I do not know. I never thought of them as thinkers."

"Perhaps you should. Should we bring one of them into this discussion?"

It was the only way he was going to prove her wrong and get her off his back. "Very well, get one of our women."

"Thank you." She looked at Evette. "Can you get Gwen for me?"

"I can."

Evette walked as quickly as she could to Gwen's hut and called for her. She came out and, using the common language, she explained what was taking place in the chief's hut. It did not take her long to agree. They walked off together.

Gwen made eye contact with her leader and bowed her head. "Good day Carch."

He nodded.

After giving Gwen a quick smile, Ashlee directed her attention to Carch. "May I ask Gwen questions and can she answer them without getting into trouble with you?"

"Yes, yes, get on with it."

"Gwen do you feel respected by the men in your village?"

Gwen looked at Carch for approval to answer. He nodded his head and she hesitantly answered, "No. I barely feel it from my husband."

"Does your man ever thank you for what you do for him?"

"He did once when I forced him to do it."

"Do you feel you have worth?"

"No and my mother never felt it. I know you did a great deal around our house and you never received any thanks."

"Do you feel you are treated justly?"

"Our justice is tied to our men."

"Are you able to speak openly about any subject you please?"

She looked at Carch again. He made a face saying answer the damn question.

"No. Most of the time I am told to shut up, so I know to not make trouble."

Ashlee looked at Carch. "Do I need to go on?"

Carch's eyes had a distant look to them. "No. You have made your point."

"Thank you Gwen," Ashlee said in appreciation. "I will talk to you later."

Before Gwen could leave, Ashlee hugged her. Gwen hugged her in return.

Carch looked questioningly at Ashlee. "Is it something you Normals do?"

"It is something I learned from Kaathi. Do you want one?"

He glanced at his son, made his decision. "Yes. I want to see what it feels like. I noticed both of you put your arms around each other."

"Come, put your arms around me and hug me."

Carch stepped to Ashlee. She embraced him and he clumsily put his arms around her and squeezed.

"Gently, you are not trying to squeeze the air out of me. Embracing another person is your way of showing affection or love and should be sensitively done."

He relaxed and gently embraced her.

"Now relax and breathe and be aware of any sensations in your body or mind."

He was aware of the contours of her body and grew excited. She withdrew and made a face. "Embracing a friend is not a prelude to having sex. It is a display of friendship."

He gave her one of his rare smiles. "I am new at this."

"We got off track with the hugging. What are your thoughts on having the sessions?"

"I shall think about it. A question. How long will this instruction last?"

"It depends on how resistant your people are to new thoughts and guidance. The relationship sessions with our instructors may take one to three years. It depends a great deal on how resistant your people are and the scope of the problems. We hope someone among you will be able to conduct the sessions on an ongoing basis. At that time we can talk about introducing the spirituality sessions."

"Will you be presenting them?"

"I do not think so."

A sternness returned to his face. "Whether I accept your offer or not hinges on Nubilon's acceptance of the peace treaty. If they agree, you can return next year with people willing to instruct us in the art of relationships. If I do not like the way the sessions are going I will send them back to Kahali."

"It is your prerogative. I am certain Kaathi will be pleased you have accepted our offer."

They bid each other goodbye and he watched her walk away. If someone had told him years ago he would be having a conversation with a former slave, he would have thought the man crazy. Now, he was wondering if he was the one insane.

CHAPTER FIFTY-SIX

Kaathi and the others from Kahali waved to the Wanderers, turned and walked away from the village. Their stopover was for four days. All of them were pleasantly surprised by how guardedly hospitable the mutants were after the treaty proposal was introduced. None of the women spoke of the incidences with the mutants.

Ahead of them was a long stretch of plains. Everyone in the party was watchful of predators, consequently, they were relatively quiet while making their way through the savannah. They ate dried meat and fruits and drank their ration of water, during the noon meals without any significant discussion. On the sixth day away from the mutant village, Jacob located an excellent spot to camp overnight. They busied themselves with collecting dry wood, starting the fire and preparing the meal.

Kacy could not keep her thoughts quiet. "I have never seen so many mutants. Isaac and Leah were my first experience with mutants. They were much more social than the Wanderers. I had a difficult time keeping a conversation going with the people hosting me. I sensed a lot of aggression, and their auras displayed it. I was disappointed I had to stay with a man and wife who showed an aggressive nature. I also noticed they have a different body odor than Leah. They must not bathe often."

"Mother told me there is a reason for it," explained Marcel. "In the dark, they want to be able to identify themselves from others."

"It makes sense," observed Jacob.

"I think they responded to me because I am part mutant," added Marcel. "Their questions and mine kept the conversation going till darkness claimed the day. I am glad we stayed the extra day. It gave me the chance to talk to my grandmother a little more."

"Did they ask why your father did not remain with them?" asked Kacy.

"They did, and I told them his nature was not like theirs and I attributed it to his mother being a Normal. Father was much more at ease living with the Kahali. They were curious about you, and I told them we were married and enjoyed living there."

"Did they ask how Isaac and Leah came to live in Kahali?" asked Mara.

"They were surprisingly curious about them. I told them how quickly Kaathi accepted them as friends."

Jacob's eyebrows raised. "Was the family you stayed with curious about you having no hair Kacy?"

"They did ask a few questions about my physical makeup. Once the topic dried up they were done talking to me. How was your experience?"

"Like most of you, this was the first time I was in the midst of a number of mutants. Being the Warrior Hunter, I was especially interested in their archery skills. I looked over their bows and requested a demonstration. They let me shoot at their targets. I found their bow required a great deal of strength to use, and for some reason their arrows do not fly true. Only thirty percent of them hit the target. It is possible their eyesight might not be as good as ours. In the construction of arrows the eye has to be able to judge the straightness of the wood for an arrow to fly true. I was interested in how stout and muscular they were. They seemed to have twice the strength I have. I know they cannot run fast. I do know from stories I have heard, their endurance is phenomenal. They like us are exceptional trackers. They are well suited to survive the harshness of the plains."

"I would like to say something about them," announced Ashlee. "I am sure most of you noticed there are few children. I spoke to Carch about it and he was concerned. He was not sure what was causing the decline. I believe the decline is the reason they have not made any recent raids and why he is amiable and listened attentively to the treaty proposal."

Evette chimed in, saying, "I noticed the lack of children the moment we arrived. I attempted to talk about it with the people hosting me without success. It is possible they were not willing to discuss it because they were past the age of producing children.

"I did have a breakthrough with Carch. You all know he and his men brutalized Gene and me until Kaathi rescued us. We had a heated discussion about his brutality and he shrugged his shoulders as if it was what they did. His reaction showed me he and his men perceived experiences through their cultural values and I experienced them through mine. It helped me to have the knowledge in order for me to forgive the brutality he and his men did to us. I did realize something. Back in Kahali I thought I had done my forgiveness work on the mutants. Facing Carch and being in the mutant's presence, I realized I was not done." Her gaze found Kaathi and she continued, "I am sure you brought me on this journey to achieve complete forgiveness."

Evette had a strange look on her face. Kaathi noticed. "Is something wrong?"

"I was thinking about the mutants and their vile nature, lack of compassion and strange beliefs. It is hard to like them much less love them and yet you seem to be able to do it. How are you able to do it?"

"It is because I know they are aspects of Creator as I am. In other lives they are choosing to look like us and acquire beliefs like ours. If you met them in those lives you would understand and like them. It is likely there are many of your lives you would question why you are living them, from your current viewpoint. Only when you have an understanding of the totality of your life experiences, can you see them without prejudice and discontent."

CHAPTER FIFTY-SEVEN

The peace contingent from Kahali trekked back to the river without any predator incidence. Approaching the river they saw they did not come to the exact place, where they left their dugouts. They walked the riverbank until they found them. The mutants had informed them it was a twenty-five day march to Nubilon. Because the mutants had superstitions about the river they refrained from traveling on it. The group left the area and did not have any problems navigating the river until they came across a small group of hippos resting in a rather wide area of the river. They kept to the shallow, far bank and were chased by one large hippo, which they outdistanced. They reached the first Nubilon sentry eleven days later.

A great Nubilon congregation of thousands awaited them on the riverbank. They showed their palms, indicating they came in peace. Everyone in the canoes saw the men of Nubilon standing in front of the women and children in the place of distinction. Ashlee recognized her uncle, Ravi, Zafir and Amira. She was puzzled seeing Amira next to Zafir. Clearly, she had attained a distinguished position since she last saw her.

Abdu recognized some of the foreigners in the canoes. He had forgotten their names. Not so with their faces. They were etched in his memory. His anger rose as they made their way out of the dugouts. He broke through the crowd and stormed over to them.

"So, you have returned to rub salt into my wounds," he shouted at Kaathi. "I have not forgotten you stole my wife. You made my life a mess. My god is great. I have prayed I would get my revenge and god has delivered you to me."

Zafir and two stout followers quickly made their way in between Abdu and Kaathi. He motioned for the men to restrain Abdu.

"Your behavior is atrocious, Abdu. As Chief Councilmember, I cannot condone it." He spoke to the two men holding Abdu. "Take him to his home and see to it he stays there."

"This is not the last of this," Abdu screamed as he was removed. "You better keep your eyes open while you sleep."

"I apologize for Abdu's terrible behavior."

"Apology accepted. It seems he has not changed and still does not know the true value of women," Kaathi said to Zafir.

"Come let me introduce you to the council and its two new members who you know."

Zafir introduced the new members, Amira and Ravi. Their placement on the council meant there was enough support from the villagers to allow the new interpretation to the religious tablets to happen.

Devra left Nena to stand next to Ravi, who took Devra's hand and proudly introduced his wife to the Kahali travelers.

Kaathi embraced Devra. "I am so happy the two of you found love. It is easy to see you are very happy."

Devra smiled. "I had a hard time convincing him he loved me."

"You did and that is what matters."

Ashlee heard the news and embraced her Uncle Ravi. "I am glad you found love, uncle."

"Thank you my dear."

Ashlee gave her uncle a warm smile. "I am so proud of all of you. What you started here is having an impact. There are a dozen questions racing around in my head. They will have to wait for the appropriate time."

They were led to the meeting hall were people rushed to cram against its outer walls. Jars of wine, water and cups were placed on the tables in preparation for the conversation between the village leaders.

Zafir addressed the travelers loud enough for those outside the hut to hear, "It has been several years since your last visit. We did not expect you."

Elgar, the Elder, replied, "We have a specific mission, which we would like to present to your council and people."

"You have our complete attention," responded Zafir.

"We are on a peace mission. We are hopeful every village we are aware of will ratify the peace treaty we are about to describe to you, the council and your people."

"It sounds intriguing. Have you approached others, and did they ratify the treaty?"

"We have assurances from the Kahali, Homar, and Sumati villages they will honor the treaty. We have also talked to the Wanderers and they stated, if you ratify it, they shall as well."

"The Wanderers agreed? This is a great surprise. Something has had to change radically in them to agree."

"Their population is not growing, consequently, they cannot afford to lose any men and they were amicable."

"Is our tribe the last you will visit?"

"No, after we leave here, we are going on to the Ebiji tribe. The tall lady, Evette, is from there. We brought with us one member from each village to help with any language barriers. We will go through the treaty step by step and give you a chance to discuss it at length."

"Please speak loud enough so our people can hear you."

"Of course," responded Elgar. He went through the treaty step by step. While there were discussions on most of them the consensus was it was worthy and viable. A vote was taken by the council and they accepted the treaty. They put the vote to the people surrounding the hall and it was resoundingly accepted. There were only a few dissenters in the crowd.

"I am curious. How is our former citizen doing in Kahali?" asked Zafir.

"Netti is doing fine," reported Elgar. "She met a man, fell in love and they now have a two year old daughter."

"I am glad to hear she has a better life than the one she had here."

Elgar shook his head. "It is sad the hooligan, ex-husband, Abdu, is still out of control.'

"When we told him his wife left with Kaathi he was infuriated. I had to set him straight. It has been a long time since he has misbehaved. For a while, he was angry he could not marry again," answered Zafir. "He had no proof she was dead. He was doing a lot of complaining, but he is stuck with his faith."

The Elder smiled, "I am glad to hear it."

CHAPTER FIFTY-EIGHT

Sharika wanted to meet the man was who caused Netti to attempt suicide. She had to find a way to make it happen. The day after the Nubilons accepted the peace treaty Sharika found Ravi's hut and called for Ashlee. She came to the entrance and Sharika took her arm and guided her to a bench a short distance from the hut.

"Can you spend some time with me today? I want to find Netti's ex-husband. He started the mess here, which caused Pauli and Sandor's deaths."

The request was a strange one and Ashlee wanted to know more. "Why would you want to find him?"

"I questioned your uncle if the man or men who killed our friends were ever punished. He indicated they were not. It is obvious this clan has no laws about abuse. Ever since I saw Sandor and Pauli's widows and children weep for the loss of their husbands and fathers I swore, if I was given the chance, I would seek retribution for them."

"Oh, Sharika I do not think it is a good idea."

"Good or bad. It is what I need to do."

"You should talk to Kaathi."

"No. This is my decision. No one is going to talk me out of it. Will you walk the village square and the avenues with me? All I want is company until I see him."

Ashlee thought about the consequences of her involvement if Sharika did something drastic. At the time Pauli and Sandor lost their lives and Netti nearly took hers, she also sought retribution. The intervening years had softened her anger. It was obvious the Hun woman before her was not forgiving.

"Are you going to kill him?"

"No."

Ashlee felt better. "Very well. We can camp out on a bench until we see him."

Ashlee went back inside and got directions from Ravi, after she explained why she wanted to know. She and Sharika found a bench not far from the man's hut.

The morning was half gone when Abdu noticed the two foreign women a long distance away. He kept his eyes on them as he approached his home.

"There he is," Ashlee nodded to the man coming toward them.

"Stay here," Sharika commanded Ashlee.

She got up and intercepted Abdu. She evaluated him, as he approached her. He was not a tall man, hardly a finger taller than her. He was thin and not muscled. She was sure he was the type of man who made himself feel strong by abusing his wife, sister and mother. It would end today. He was not going to abuse her, and she would teach him a lesson.

"So you are the simian who rallied your men to kill my friends?"

"What are you talking about?"

"Your wife tried to take her own life because she was miserable with you."

"Get out of my way foreigner."

"You have lived many years and have not paid the price for killing my friends. I am going to make you pay for it."

His voice was a snarl. "No one is going to make me pay for anything, especially not you."

The harsh exchange of words drew a crowd of over a dozen people.

He spit toward her feet. She moved them before the spittle could land. Her quick reflex surprised him. In spite of her having a terrifically muscled body she was no threat to him. He had nothing to fear. He swung his arm to push her aside only to have it smacked away with such intensity his arm hurt. He noted her quick reaction time. This time he drove his hand forward to push her backward only to have his hand punched forcefully by her. He shook his hand to ease the stinging sensation. His anger quickly escalated, and he was eager to teach her a lesson. He opened his arms to grab her and throw her aside. She grabbed his right arm and used the momentum of his body to throw him over her shoulder. He landed on the ground with a thud. The air in his lungs rushed out. His head was jolted by the ground. Shaking his head, he scampered up and was enraged she had embarrassed him by throwing him. He thought for a moment how he could throw her off. He decided to fake a charge then kick her in the stomach.

The commotion brought more people. The crowd of over three dozen encircled them. He was vaguely aware of the crowd. He ignored them. He was facing more pressing things. He had to beat her ass and teach her a lesson.

He made his fake charge and kicked out at her. Sharika was not fooled. She grabbed his foot and heaved it high in the air. He crashed to the ground again knocking the wind out of his body. He was startled and his back ached. He recovered and was incensed she had put him down again.

Abdu was on his knees and had venom in his voice. "You bitch, you are going to regret what you did. I am going to kick your skinny ass."

People in the crowd were yelling for others to come out of their huts to witness the fight. The crowd quickly doubled in size. None of them had ever seen a woman fight a man.

Abdu got to his feet slowly and was puzzled how the woman was combating every move he made. He had to take a different approach. He stuck his left hand out as if he was going to grab her with it and moved toward her. With lightening swiftness, Sharika latched onto his outstretched hand and quickly bent it backward. Abdu screamed. He did something unexpected. He did a backward flip and landed on his feet. She could not hold onto his hand and watched in amazement.

The crowd yelled and applauded in appreciation of the trick. Ashlee was hoping the fight would end soon. Even though Sharika was doing well, she did not want her to get hurt.

More people gathered around them.

Sharika waited for the man's next move. She focused on her ability to sense the split second time gap between thought and action. Abdu gained confidence breaking out of her finger hold. He had to end this. He put his head down and rushed her. She dropped to the ground and used her feet to propel him high over her. He landed with a sickening thud. She bounced up and swiftly kicked him on the side of his head. The blow stunned him. She landed another heel kick to the side of his head and he squirmed away. She let him get to his feet and proceeded to drive her foot into the side of his knee snapping the ligaments. He fell to the ground screaming. She walked leisurely to him and drove a punishing kick to the side of his face knocking him momentarily unconscious. The crowd moaned. It was some time before he recovered. He struggled to get up. His left knee was useless and hurt like blazes. He stayed there on one knee trying to get his bearings. His eyes were not focusing, and more troubling he did not know where he was. He heard people talking as if in the distance.

Sharika took her time and smashed her foot into his ribs. He screamed as his ribs broke. He flopped back on the ground moaning and crying like a seven year old. The crowd groaned. She took one last look at him and walked toward Ashlee. She took her arm. "I have had my retribution."

Many of the woman, under cover of their hoods, smiled at the resounding beating Abdu received by the slightly clad, muscled foreign woman.

CHAPTER FIFTY-NINE

The village was abuzz with the news Abdu was beaten senseless by the foreign woman. The next day the Nubilon council was sitting and drinking in the meeting hall, talking casually with Elgar, Kaathi and the others celebrating the ratification of the peace treaty. A disturbed Abdu, being assisted by a friend, entered the hall swearing and cursing.

His eyes found Sharika, and he shouted and pointed his finger at her. "She broke my ribs, mangled my knee and kicked me in the head and knocked me unconscious."

Jacob smiled. "I did not know she could send her foot so high."

Abdu gave Jacob a nasty look. "She cannot. She kicked me while I was on the ground."

Jacob was still smiling. "How did she talk you into lying on the ground?"

"You stupid oaf. She did not talk me onto the ground; she flipped me."

Zafir knew the whole story but asked anyway. "What possessed her to do it?"

"The courtesan was pissed we killed her friends."

"Watch your mouth little man," cautioned Jacob.

Abdu was about to snap back and caught himself after a quick appraisal of the warrior.

Zafir questioned the snake of a man. "So how did Sharika come to confront you?"

"I was walking home and she blocked my way, saying crap about she was here to avenge the death of her friends. I thought she was all bluff. She was not. She attacked me."

Elgar held up his hand. "Stop right there. I think we need to hear from Sharika."

Everyone nodded except Abdu. Jacob left and brought Ashlee and Sharika back and they sat and waited for Zafir to speak.

"I think we need to start from the beginning," announced Zafir. "Abdu, I want to hear your version of what took place."

Abdu story exaggerated how Sharika attacked him. The moment he was done Zafir asked for Sharika's version.

Sharika calmly gave her story and waited.

Ashlee spoke up, "What she said is true. I think she kicked him to let him know how it felt to be kicked while being vulnerable."

"I suppose we can contact others who saw the confrontation. What do you want to do, Abdu?"

He made a face and shook his head.

"Since you made the first advance on this lady, I cannot chastise her. What I can do is congratulate her for her courage. No other woman would have or could have done what she did."

"Are you telling me you are not doing anything to her?" yelled Abdu.

"You are correct. When you and friends killed those two fine men, I was sad we did not have any laws in place to deal with all of you. I am going to recommend at our next meeting we put in place safeguards so it will never happen again. I am also going to draft laws to protect our women from brutes like you. . . Get out of here you disgust me."

Abdu glared at Zafir, turned and left with the help of his friend. His limp was more exaggerated than when he had entered.

The leader of the council looked admiringly at Sharika. "I suppose I should thank you for being the catalyst to bring these issues back out in the open after all these years."

A warm smile replaced the frown on her face. "I am happy I could be of service. It was a pleasure to finally have revenge for the widows and children as well as for Netti."

CHAPTER SIXTY

The peace contingent had accomplished their task among the Nubilons and they bid old and new friends goodbye. In spite of haunting, old memories, a sense of accomplishment buoyed their moods and traditional Kahali songs were sung through much of the first day on the river. Jacob spotted a desirable place for the travelers to spend the night. Wood was gathered for the fire, the meal was prepared and eaten. Kaathi and Sharika volunteered for the first watch to guard those sleeping. The fire was roaring and there was sufficient wood collected to stoke the fire through the night.

Sharika cocked her head. "Are you going to chastise me for what I did to Abdu?"

The mystic smiled. "I suppose I could get all philosophical but I believe it was the best way for the man to learn to respect women."

Sharika returned the smile and dropped the subject. "I have heard the Teller of Stories version of why the world fell apart. Do the Talker Healers have a story about the Age of Destruction?"

"We do," responded Kaathi, "and it is the reason I have put so much emphasis in changing the attitude and philosophy of our village and other villages. Everyone needs to see how important and significant it is to love and understand their neighbor and their family.

"Here is the Talker Healer's story: Religion, race, land, pollution, water and lack of understanding were the main causes of disputes and wars for all of recorded history. Prior to the impending disaster, the world's scientists warned every one of what was going to happen, if we did not take preventative action. On one hand, there were leaders of government and business tackling the problem. On the other, there were some placing greed over the welfare of the people. Others did not believe the scientists because the changes were not easily detectable and other leaders were skeptical of the data. By the time the skeptics were convinced, the problems had become insurmountable and chaos was already in progress.

"The large land mass nations producing most of the edible goods used chemicals in their production and the chemicals leeched into the ground water and the technology to counter act its harmfulness was not widely utilized. The supply for uncontaminated water for humans and livestock simply could not keep up with the demand. Riots for food and clean water were commonplace.

"The world could not sustain the population explosion. Much of the produce eaten was contaminated and adversely affected people, causing mutation among all the world races. The land was polluted and the seas were over fished and were also contaminated. Much of the fish humans ate came from fish farms. Even this measure could not keep up with the demand.

"The world's climate grew warmer. It changed for a number of reasons. The foremost cause was gases polluting the air from vehicles and power plants. Tied to this was the demand for wood products and the need for farmland, which depleted our forests. It was known the forests were a major source of harmful gas absorption. Sadly, greed overruled knowledge. With the forests shriveling, the rain patterns around the world changed, causing droughts over vast areas normally providing farm goods. The droughts caused a huge drop in farm production. World leaders admitted too late the World Ecosystem was complicated and tied to everything. The warmer weather caused the ice at the world's poles to melt and the sea levels rose and flooded many large coastal villages.

"Uprisings and riots occurred in virtually every large populated village in every nation. As the situation grew worse, people fought to keep their families alive and nations fought each other to preserve their food producing land and water supplies.

"In the later stages, Mother Earth rebelled. Volcanos erupted and blanketed much of the world with ash clouds for months, which curtailed our ability to raise crops due to the lack of sunlight. Famine and disease were rampant. Adding to humanity's problem, the weather changed and we faced an abbreviated Ice Age. The end result was only the hardiest of people survived. Much of mankind's survival was due to having a clean supply of spring water. As the chaos ran its course the survivors eventually congregated in social groups, which gave way to our villages."

Sharika shook her head. "Your story is much more descriptive than ours. Having heard it, I cannot fathom why all of the nations did not heed the scientist's warnings. It is sad the leaders were so stupid. Now I have a clearer picture of why you have worked so hard to help people learn the importance of relationships and why you initiated this peace mission. I hope we do not make the same mistakes our ancestors made."

"It is my hope as well," extoled Kaathi. "It can work, if we keep our minds open to what is happening around us, and we are able to express our concerns, fears, doubts, compassion and love with each other."

"I have noticed people not attending the sessions are still argumentative and disruptive about them."

"There is nothing wrong with having people voice their discontent, so long as the minority does not control the majority. At times, the loud and discontented minority are the voices heard by governing bodies."

"Why are they not learning how to get along?"

"You are observant and I am sure have noticed we are not created with the same skills and reasoning powers. Differences are prevalent in our physical bodies and in our temperaments. In addition, there are imperfections in our body composition making it difficult for some to control certain aspects of their personality."

"How unfortunate."

"Hmm. I like to look at the differences in us as what makes us unique. Those of us better able to control ourselves are the ones who should exhibit more compassion for those having trouble controlling themselves. These gifted people should be teaching those less knowledgeable and less emotionally even keeled."

A pensive look settled on Sharika's face. "I suppose you are right. I know several such people in my village who fit the category. I never could figure out why they were so different. A young man of nineteen suddenly started acting strange. He had huge emotional swings from excitement to deep depressions. His wife and he sought help from our medicine man and he had him try various ointments and even had him eat food he normally would not eat to see if anything helped him regain his normal behavior. Nothing seemed to work. I felt sorry for him and his family."

"His situation is an example how challenges can appear at any moment in our lives," added Kaathi. "It is why we must seek Creator when we have all of our faculties. Sadly, many people turn to Creator only when tragedy strikes."

CHAPTER SIXTY-ONE

The peace emissaries, floating on the river, were screeched at by a large gathering of monkeys in the trees on the banks of the river. It was the largest such family they had ever seen. A half day later they left the monkeys behind and welcomed the relative quiet. Evette remembered hearing stories of the massive number of monkeys, as a child. The advent of the monkeys told her she was nearing her home village. No one in the canoes was more anxious and eager to arrive than Evette. It had been nearly two decades since she and her husband, Gene, left Ebiji to find utopia.

She had left behind her husband, Gene, and their seven year old son and five year old daughter in Kahali. She thought of them every day and missed them, even though the urge to see her parents and her friend, Nia, pulled at her heart. She prayed they were all alive and well.

The group had been in the canoes for twenty days and beached the dugouts early to take time to eat and relax. They had eaten and all the preparations were set for the evening.

Evette sat next to Kaathi and directed her words to the mystic. "I am glad you had Sharika and I come, Kaathi. I have had the opportunity to observe you intimately for many days and have noticed what extraordinary people skills you have."

"Thank you. It is so because I have cultivated them. Most of us have seen many qualities displayed in each other and have been pleasantly surprised. Frankly, I think all of us are extraordinary. The level of awareness I operate at is what appears to set me apart from others. This awareness is within everyone, waiting to be cultivated in much the same way as any one of the other skills we utilize."

Jacob sat opposite them across the fire and shook his head. "I highly doubt it."

"It is true. One of the major problems is even before birth we are flooded with stimuli and it continues incessantly for much of our lives. Much of it is useful for survival, yet there is a great deal cluttering our ability to function efficiently."

Jacob tugged at his ear. "I am not sure I follow you."

"Prior to birth your consciousness contains information from other lives, other acquired beliefs, skills, remembered experiences and intelligence to name a few. While you are in your mother, you are collecting and processing new information, experiences and beliefs from your parents and everyone your mother comes in contact with. Upon birth you contend with learning how to function and manipulate a physical body, learn languages, accept new beliefs and acquire reasoning and a host of other important life skills, in a relatively short time. Learning how to exist in this maze of dualities is a challenge. For most of us, there are far too many things to distract us from reaching our potential."

"What is our potential?"

"It is to be aware of our origination and to be fully love oriented.

"While I think I know what you mean by being love oriented, I have no idea what you mean by being aware," admitted Jacob.

"A general description would be to be aware of yourself and what your source is. You are an expression of Creator and Creator is your source of being. You are subjected to and guided by your memory, but be aware your memory is not who you are. In essence, you are consciousness and are in a state of constant creativity. It involves you being aware of the various levels of consciousness comprising your essence. Your awareness is also the expression of cells in your bodies, their function and joy. Awareness connects you to Creator and all of creation."

Jacob was dumbfounded. "Are you saying you are aware of all of it?"

"I have experienced some of it and I have seen hints of it."

"I am going to have a hard time falling asleep thinking about all of this."

Indeed Jacob did spend a great deal of time thinking, while he awaited sleep. He recalled Ashlee telling a marvelous story of awareness. She and the group from Kahali and Zafir had come upon Netti struggling in her attempt at suicide. Ashlee had sensed Kaathi knew of the attempt beforehand and the mystic waited to marshal everyone until the last moment to rescue Netti. Kaathi explained why she held them back. It was so Zafir could see how horrible things have gotten in his village. She said Zafir needed to feel the true impact of Netti's desperation, otherwise he would not have been the spearhead of the reformation in Nubilon.

Jacob smiled. He was proud he had recalled the story and was able to marry it with Kaathi's description of awareness.

CHAPTER SIXTY-TWO

Ashlee was deep in thought and not conscious of her surroundings. She was remembering how happy she was to have seen her Uncle Ravi was married and to renew her friendship with Amira. She was pleased to have renewed her friendships with Devra and Nena and happy the peace treaty had been accepted. It was a testament to the unifying skills of Kaathi. In spite of how nice her visit was with her uncle, she had to admit there was still too much anger and negativity in Nubilon. She was happy to have left her birth village and on her way to Ebiji and then home.

There was a lull in the conversation in the dugout. She took advantage of it. "Kaathi, you have taken a few trips and while talking about them, you often use the word adventure. I know you use words purposefully and I was hoping you would share why you use the word so often."

"They were indeed adventures. The word adventure implies new and exciting events will take place. I wanted specific people to go with me because they needed to see me do things they thought were impossible to do. On my first adventure, Jacob needed to see love is more powerful than anger or might. We also needed to make contact with the mutants, Leah and Isaac and bring them back to Kahali to show our people not all mutants are hostile and they are only different from us in form and nothing else. We brought back Zach so King Edmund would come after him. By coming, Edmund discovered his true identity and went on to reform his kingdom. It also provided Scarlet the opportunity to come to Kahali and rekindle her love for Jacob. Keri saw how strong her love was for her husband and opened her heart and home to Scarlet. Keri and Scarlet were instrumental in bringing about the Kahali law allowing women to have more than one husband.

"The second adventure allowed us to come in contact with a simian race, Jacob named Stalkers. They were dominated by men. Because of our interaction with them, a simian woman, Gauri, was accepted as a teacher and a leader of their tribe. Her acceptance was a gigantic step for women in the clan. When Mara's people, the Uchakwa attacked us, we killed the warriors except for her. She saw the folly in the attack and did not blame us for their deaths. She wanted to learn about wisdom and spirituality and came with us, as did Kacy from the Uchakwas. On the adventure, we saved Evette and Gene from the mutant Wanderer tribe and they went on to teach the Sumati people the Relationship principles for two years. That same adventure to Sumati was significant because we saved you from death on the savannah. You my dear, heroic lady have shown everyone how powerful your need was to be free from tyranny and slavery.

"The adventure, which took you back home to Nubilon, was essential. Zafir needed to hold a suffocating Netti in his arms while Ravi cut the rope around her neck. Seeing her attempted suicide shook him and made him look at what men had been doing to their women for so many generations. He and your uncle's group are instrumental in the cultural change sweeping your home village to improve the life of women.

"On this peace treaty mission, we will stop in Ebiji. It will give Evette a chance to see what effect she had on her father with her talks about equality and justice for women. She will also find out if any other woman has taken up her banner to further justice in Ebiji. She will also discover how great or how little her family and friends have missed her.

"Lastly there is Sharika. She is the ideal for all women seeking to be physically equal to men. She has fought beside men in her village and has been acknowledged for her bravery and skills. Her adventure brought her to Kahali in search of a husband. She found him and so much more. She never dreamed her heart could lead her on such a magnificent adventure to discover her relationship to Creator. When we set foot in Hun Nation, it will present them with the opportunity to see a side of Sharika they had never seen. Hopefully, they will see she glows with a new light, the light of love and spirituality."

"How well did you see our interconnectedness?"

"Well enough to know we needed each other's friendship and help. In spite of it, I did not probe the depth of them for I wanted the pleasure of the pliable, exciting and suspenseful future."

CHAPTER SIXTY-THREE

Evette sensed she was nearing her old home. With it came a restlessness for she was uncertain what to expect after being away for so many years. The yearning to see her parents was distinctly prevalent. She prayed they were still alive and healthy. In spite of all the differences of opinion she had with her father, she had never wished him harm. They were the first people to love her and she them. Nothing could break the bond.

Her eyes closed as she went inward to think of her husband, Gene. No amount of talking and reassuring could convince him to come. She was certain he would have come on the mission, were it not for having to visit the mutants. She was aware he still had the recurring dream about the atrocities he and she suffered. He was able to function under normal circumstances in Kahali and Sumati, however his gentle character was unable to handle coming face to face with his horrific memories.

She was honestly surprised he had made the trek with her to find her utopia. Despite what he shared about why he accompanied her, she felt the driving force was how everyone in Ebiji would think him a coward. He was not strong enough to survive being shamed. His feminine nature was too powerful and drove his personality. She was well aware of him being trapped into being a male. His parents and society had cast his future and he was unable to proclaim his true identity. She loved him for his gentle nature and for standing bravely next to her as she voiced her proclamations. She was proud of him, and he would forever remain her hero, while fighting demons in his mind.

The dugouts ran aground and brought Evette out of her thoughts. She exited the canoe and helped unload the supplies and gave a hand in securing some of them in a small tree so animals could not get to them. She refrained from talking as she worked and was quiet while they ate. There were no large trees nearby so the men were gone a long time collecting sufficient wood for a large fire to dissuade predators from approaching during the night. While the men were away, Kaathi sat next to Evette.

"I have noticed you have hardly spoken today," observed Kaathi.

"I think the nearness of my home has made me introspective. I have been lost in thought about Gene and my parents. I was thinking how nice it would have been for him to see his parents and his sister. She was fourteen when we left and must have her own family by now."

Kaathi patted Evette's hand. "Unfortunately, Gene's past throws huge, haunting shadows on his life. His willingness to wrestle his memories and work with Mara will a big step in his recovery.

"After the attack by the mutants, Gene had been floundering. I was hoping teaching the Relationship Sessions in Sumati would give him a purpose in life. Perhaps he would be willing to go back to Ebiji to teach, if he knew you were going back to teach."

Evette perked up on hearing the news. "Do you think my village would be willing to accept us as teachers?"

"More shocking things have happened in this world. It is one of the reasons I have brought you along on this trip," Kaathi pointed out.

"I had a fleeting thought about you wanting me to teach again."

"Your intuition is working well. You were vital in establishing the sessions in Sumati. You went to the village center and questioned women whether they felt honored and respected. Your easy manner and probing questions together with being an oddity brought women to you."

Evette smiled. "Many a youngster came to us wanting to know how we grew so tall."

"I noticed they took a liking to both of you and it helped you as instructors. Are you eager or anxious about going back to you home village?"

Evette thought a moment. "A little of both. I was such a persistent protester, I am sure it is what people will remember about me. Fortunately, I was not always contentious at home. Thinking back I realize my father was patient with me. I am not so sure about the assembly. My father told me many times there was no one in Ebiji who gave the synod more grief than me. Anyway I will find out soon. I have felt we are close to my home."

"You are right, Evette. I have felt the same thing."

The men returned carrying armfuls of wood for the fire and Evette and Kaathi ended their conversation; it did not end the thoughts bouncing around in Evette's head. Kaathi was correct, she did feel a little nervous about returning home. She had left without apologizing to the synod and was certain they were not going to be thrilled about her returning. At least her father had prepared her for leaving by teaching her all he knew about survival. What he had not prepared her for was the utter brutality of the mutants. No one could have.

CHAPTER SIXTY-FOUR

Late the next day drums announced the traveler's presence in Ebiji territory. With the first striking of a drum, Evette caught Kaathi's eyes and smiled. A quarter day later they saw the villagers on the bank of the river. Evette's eyes darted around the crowd hoping to spot her parents. She found her father, Adama, in the midst of the synod. She waved. Adama had spotted the tall woman in the dugout and knew it was his child. Even so, his face showed his surprise at seeing her. The group beached the dugouts and a few Ebiji men helped pull them farther out of the water. The moment her feet touched the ground she ran to her father. He separated himself from the synod and walked to meet her. Everyone's eyes were on them as they embraced and cried. Evette's mother, Nyah, trudged slowly from the crowd. Evette watched her mother approach and was stunned at how old and shriveled she looked. Nyah threw herself on her daughter and husband, weeping with joy.

When they broke the hug, Evette's mother exclaimed, "Oh my god. I never thought these old eyes would see you again. Evette you look wonderful."

"It is so good to see you, Mother, and you as well Father."

She was pleased to see her father was smiling and weeping. He missed her!

The spontaneous group hug kept her from saying anything more. When they released her, her mother asked, "Where is Gene. Is he dead?"

"No, he stayed back in Kahali. I shall tell you everything when we are alone."

She saw Elgar patiently waiting for her to finish her reunion. "I have to go to help with the introductions. Come."

She grabbed her parent's arms and walked the short distance to the awaiting group. Disdaining protocol, she introduced her parents using the common language to her friends. Next she requested her father to introduce the synod. She did not see the head of the synod. Evette's father, Adama, surprised her by making the introductions of the nine member synod and their families, which meant he was the head of the synod. When she was a member of the village, the synod had always separated themselves from their families at any formal function. This was a huge departure from tradition. Elgar introduced the peace contingent and their responsibilities in Kahali.

"I know you have not come all this way just to bring my daughter back for a visit," announced Adama.

"You are correct," replied Elgar. "We are here to present you and your village with the opportunity to ratify a peace treaty."

Adama looked at each one of the Kahali group before he spoke, "Before we discuss anything so serious, the synod and I want to acquaint ourselves with you first. We need to know what kind of people we are dealing with. After we share a meal and talk we can discuss the treaty. . . if we approve of you."

"Fair enough. I love to eat and have a good conversation."

"Very well." Adama turned to one of the synod members behind him. "Could you arrange to have our wives prepare a meal for our guests?"

"I can." The man hurried off to make the arrangements.

While the food was being prepared, the visitors were inundated with people wanting to talk to them.

Evette recognized Gene's mother standing in line waiting her turn to talk to her. She stepped away from her friends and went to her.

"Lana, it is good to see you. Where is your husband?"

"He died three years ago."

"I am so sorry."

"It was for the better. He was sick and death was a blessing." Lana's lips quivered. "What about Gene? Is my son dead?"

"No, no. He is alive. He could not make the trip. This peace committee had to stop in the Wanderer village and he was not strong enough to do it."

"Why is he not strong? Is he sick?"

"When we left, we had run into the mutants. Our attempt at fleeing them failed. When they caught up with us, they did many unspeakable things to our bodies. He was not ready to face them again and relive the horror."

Tears filled Lana's eyes and cascaded down her face. "He was such a sweet boy. I was surprised when he went with you. It had to have taken great courage on his part to go."

"He is indeed sweet and showed his courage by trying to save us. He fought valiantly against five and six mutants at once. They beat us unmercifully. Both of us would have perished had it not been for Kaathi coming to our rescue."

"The woman rescued you from the mutants? How was it possible?"

"She is an extraordinary woman. When I have more time, we will sit and I shall tell you about her."

"Please. If it is possible I would like to thank her myself."

"I will try to arrange a meeting. I have to get back in the receiving line."

People were still lined up waiting to ask questions from the Kahali people. Shortly, Adama informed them the meal was ready.

The meal was set out in the synod meeting hall. There were three tables set. The Ebiji synod and their wives sat on one side of them and the Kahali contingent on the other.

Elgar seated across from Adama questioned the synod leader, "As we approached your village I noticed you are growing a number of different crops and men tending cattle. How long have you domesticated cattle?"

"It has been many generations. Some of the cattle is not butchered. We keep them alive and take the blood from them to consume it but not so much that it would kill the animal."

"Interesting. I do not know of any other village using cattle blood as you do. Does everyone have a parcel of land on which they grow their crops?"

"No everyone helps maintain the whole farm," answered Adama.

"We maintain individual plots. As yet we have not domesticated any animals except for dogs," responded Elgar. He abruptly changed the subject. "I have always been impressed by Evette's tallness."

"Our stories tell us we are direct descendants of the giants of the Watusi tribe. While the bloodline is not pure any longer because of the catastrophic events of the past, most everyone in Ebiji is tall. Can I ask you how Kacy, of the Uchakwa clan, came to be with you?"

Elgar shared the story of Kaathi's adventure to visit the Ancients and how she saved Kacy.

"I also saw the man named Marcel has some mutant heritage."

"Again, Kaathi brought Marcel's mother and her husband back from her first trip. They were the last two alive of the Searcher Trib. She rescued Marcel's father, Durga, a Wanderer half mutant from his leader, Carch."

"Kaathi seems to be an adventurous woman. What drives her?"

"With all the dangers present on any journey, frankly, Adama, I do not know. I know she has been on more adventures than anyone in Kahali."

"So others have become adventurers?"

"Some of the Kahali men have taken to exploring the country. None with the purpose she has in mind."

"And she is your High Priest and healer?"

"Yes."

"Those are two divergent positions. How on earth did she come by them?"

"It is an intriguing story. She was an apprentice Talker Healer and her mentor was killed by the High Priest."

"Killed by your High Priest? He must have been an evil man."

"He was. We assigned a man to be our temporary High Priest. He held the position for a year and felt inadequate in the position. He refused to permanently take the position. Kaathi accepted the duties because of her spiritual nature. Her teachings released us from a vengeful god and she introduced us to a loving one. It was also a significant decision for the council, for she was instrumental in creating the peace treaty proposal."

"She seems unassuming and yet is brave and more adventuresome than most men. She is an amazing woman," Adama said admiringly.

"Yes she is," agreed Elgar. "She also was instrumental in developing the Relationship Sessions in Homar and Sumati and the Spiritual Awareness Services."

"Can you tell me more about each one?"

Elgar went on to outline what both sessions were about. The conversations at the tables were spurred on by questions on either side. When everyone was ready to retire, the nine synod members opened their homes to the visitors. Evette went home with her mother and father.

Inside her old home, Evette raised her eyebrow. "Since when have the wives of the synod been able to sit at such an auspicious function as today?"

"The year after you left the head of the synod died and I was appointed the head. I insisted our wives sit with us at special functions and they have for the past twelve years."

Adama looked at his wife lovingly and continued, "I think you should know soon after you left, your mother became despondent and took ill and has never been the same. I knew the cause of her condition was due to you leaving. I thought a great deal about how a broken heart can affect a person. The change in your mother's personality clearly indicated the great loss she suffered."

Adama's eyes were teary as he went on with his explanation, "I saw how my stubbornness drove you away from us to seek utopia. I grew concerned my actions might have made you ill as well. I was heartsick. You were gone and your mother was sick all because I was stuck in my ways, the ways of our traditions. I thought of all the things you wanted to have changed. It took two years before I got up the courage to tell the men of the synod we needed to seriously look at giving honor and respect to our women. It took another three years of hounding them to see the first article of change to appear on our agenda. Within a year we had six articles securing rights and privileges for women. Basically, all of them were introduced to us by you. So, my dear, you have had a great influence upon me and the synod."

Her mother smiled at her. "I and all the Ebiji women are indebted to you."

Evette was weeping. Her mother gathered her in her arms and lovingly stroked her hair, saying, "It was all because of you. . . It was all because of you."

Evette stood back from her mother and smiled warmly saying, "It is gratifying to hear it has come to pass. Frankly, what is giving me joy is Father has come to realize your worth and mine and of all women. My heart is bursting with joy."

Evette turned to her father. "I am so proud of you Father."

"I have learned much from you, my child," confessed Adama.

"So, do we have any grandchildren? You need to keep our family genes alive."

"You do, Mother. Our son, Cirsum, is seven and our daughter, Katiya is five. They are wonderful, well behaved children. I left them in Gene's capable hands."

"I wish you could have brought them all with you," lamented her mother.

"It would have been hard on them."

"I am interested in what you were teaching and learning," said Adama.

Evette went on in detail about the years she and Gene spent in Sumati and everything they were learning from Kaathi into the darkening sky. Evette finished her tales and was ready to climb onto her sleeping pad and found her parents had never removed it from its original place. Even in the dark, mother, father and child could not stop asking questions and reminiscing. After her parents had fallen asleep, thoughts of her childhood and young womanhood flooded her. She smiled often in the dark.

CHAPTER SIXTY-FIVE

Two days later the nine man synod met in private with the peace group and by the end of the day agreed to ratify the treaty. The moment the meeting was concluded Evette told Kaathi about her mother's desire to talk with her. Kaathi did not have anything pressing and she walked arm in arm with Evette to her parents' home. Kaathi warmly embraced Nyah and Adama as introductions were made. Nyah fussed over Kaathi, sensing something special about the young woman. Kaathi was at Nyah's side as she made tea. She rubbed the older woman's back, asking about her health and praising her for the wonderful job she did raising Evette. The mystic made her feel appreciated and loved. Nyah spirits were buoyed with the presence of her daughter and Kaathi. She happily poured the tea for all of them and sat down.

"I am glad you wanted this private chat Nyah. I imagine you want to know about my relationship with your daughter. I will pass over the hard times and talk about the good times. Some years ago we came upon Evette and Gene and I asked them to accompany us to Kahali. Both of them were interested in expanding their understanding of life and came to our Relationship Sessions and the Spiritual Awareness Services. Mainly due to their experiences and interests in the sessions, I asked them to come with me on my visit to Sumati. I saw the Sumatians were in need of growing emotionally. It was easy to see Evette and Gene were perfect to teach the children and adults about the correct way to conduct relationships. It involved a lot of the principles Evette had brought before the synod. They did a fantastic job and were highly complemented by Chief Victor. They have also contributed many times to the Kahali Relationship Sessions."

Kaathi went on to explain some of the basics of respect, kindness and acceptance and other traits, which were introduced and stressed in the sessions by the instructors.

"Evette and Gene have impressed me with their sincerity to help people and their clarity of thought. They bring to the sessions life experiences vital and pertinent to the discussions.

"Evette and I have discussed a little about what I am going to present to you, Adama. With the synod's permission, and with Evette and Gene's acceptance I would like them to return next year and conduct the Relationship Sessions here and in time the Spiritual Awakening Services."

Evette waited for her parents' response.

Adama did not have to think long before he answered, "I think most of us in Ebiji would benefit from the instruction. It is a positive approach to enrich our lives. If Evette agrees, I can speak to the synod and have an answer whether they will accept your gracious help before you leave." He looked at his daughter. "What are your thoughts my dear?"

Evette found it hard to believe she heard her father saying what he did. They had engaged in many disputes over the very thing he was agreeing to now. He and the council were stuck in tradition the year she and Gene left her home in search of freedom. "I love the idea. I think Gene will jump at the chance to return and see his family."

She threw herself on Kaathi nearly knocking the smaller woman to the ground. She grabbed her in time and crushed her to her breast.

"Thank you, thank you."

"Seeing you happy gives me joy, Evette."

Evette kept weeping. "All our suffering and humiliation was for nothing. We should have stayed here."

Evette stopped crying and Kaathi took her hands and spoke lovingly to her. "It is true all you worked for and desired would have come to pass. The difference is in what you now have to offer because you left. Your courage and newfound strength, which is so much a part of you, would never have developed in your character had you remained here. You had to suffer to grow, so you could share what it taught you.

"Returning and sharing your experiences will give your people a much greater appreciation of you. They will respect you more than had you not left. You have gone places and done things the villagers have not. You are a woman of the world and will receive the accompanying respect."

Adama immediately saw what Kaathi said was true. "I cannot agree more. Your experience has made you a heroine and a teacher. We desperately need you my dear."

Nyah's eyes were shining with tears and her heart was swelling with joy and pride. Her heart had broken the moment Evette told her of her desire to leave home in search of utopia. The loneliness was over. Her child was coming home. All was well again. For Nyah this was utopia.

CHAPTER SIXTY-SIX

The travelers had left Ebiji days ago and the weather grew a bit cooler as they made their way farther north. Sharika knew it would not be long before she saw familiar signs along the river to tell her they were near her home village. She had left her home years ago and wandered off in search of a husband and new adventures. *It will be good to create new memories with mother and father and talk of the old ones.*

Evening arrived and Ashlee took advantage of the fact Sharika was resting and soaking her feet in the river. She sat next to her. "Are you happy you married Janos and not the prince?"

Sharika cocked her head and looked at the lovely woman next to her. "Upon first meeting you I would have told you you were getting far too personal with your question. You, Kaathi and others have taught me to not be so closed and reserved. I have discovered personal things in my life can also benefit others, if I am open and willing to share. I will answer by saying, while living next to the chief, I saw how often he was besieged by everyone. Being a queen would also present a great deal of similar responsibilities. I did not want it to be my life. As tempting as Zach's offer to be his princess was, I am happy with Janos. What about you, are you content being one of Jacob's three wives?"

Ashlee looked away briefly to gather her thoughts. "I had two fears about falling in love with Jacob. The first was his having two wives and the other was he would press me into making love. My first fear was dissolved in my first meeting with Keri and Scarlet. I saw reluctance and concern in their eyes at first. After I opened my heart and made myself vulnerable, I shared my story with them. They reciprocated and opened their hearts to me and I was accepted into the family. We are as close as.

"Going to my second fear, Jacob had reassured me several times he would not press me into making love. He assured me the decision was mine. I have to admit I did not believe him. I had eighteen years of being brutally abused and I did not trust men. It was only after we were married for nearly a year I truly believed him. I also learned from others Jacob's word is sacred to him. So, to give you an answer to your question, I am extremely content being married to him.

"I have another for you. Are there any men in Hun Nation you have strong feelings for even now?"

"Ah, I had a few such relationships. One man was especially hard to leave. I wept several evenings, thinking of him. Looking back on everything I have done, I have no regrets. I had good friendships with a handful of women back home rivaling those I have with you, Kaathi, Scarlet, Marie, Mara and Evette."

"What made the other relationships endearing?"

"We grew up playing together. We shared our fears, happiness, desires and love. We also fought by each others side and discovered we would die for each other. I have similar feelings with you and the others although I did not grow up with you. You are different then them because you have made me think in terms of my spiritual growth and of being aware of what I am doing and why I am doing it. I had some awareness back home; it was never in terms of how it might affect humanity."

"Kaathi does have an effect on nearly everyone she meets," admitted Ashlee. "Did you have anyone in your village like her?"

"No. As I look back on my life, there were several men and women who were, oh what is the term I want to use. . . they were introspective. And what about you. Were there any decent mutants?"

"Only Gwen. Everyone else was mean, aggressive and abusive. I think she was different because I gave her attention and love.

"Did Kaathi ever tell you the story of how important love is?"

Sharika shook her head.

"During the second of the horrible world wars a great many parents were killed and their babies and tiny children were orphaned. The children were kept in huge houses, where ladies taking care of them were too few in number. Nearly all of the babies died even though they were fed and sheltered. Someone did a study after the war and determined the deaths were due to a lack of sufficient touch and love. Kaathi explained to me many times how love and touch is more important than food."

CHAPTER SIXTY-SEVEN

The sky was crystalline blue and a pleasant breeze cooled the travelers. White, fluffy clouds dotted the sky. Sharika's excitement grew as she recognized sites from her past. She was certain today would be the day her people's drums would announce their presence. She was correct.

Jacob noticed the river was twice the width it was in Homar. He saw Sharika keenly searching the right riverbank all morning and was not surprised to hear the drums. At noon the dugouts approached the village of the Hun Nation and were greeted by the whole village.

The travelers showed their palms indicating they meant no harm. As they paddled toward the shore, where the mass of Huns were collected, the locals recognized Sharika and greeted her with applause. Sharika picked out her mother and father and waved to them. Next she saw Chief Atti and waved to him. A few local men helped beach the dugouts.

Jacob's eyes swept the people on shore. He took note all of the women looked fit, while maybe not as muscularly defined as Sharika, they were close to it. The whole community was a fighting force. While their male population was somewhat less than Kahali's, if the Hun women were part of their attack force, they would number one and a half times as many as Kahali.

Sharika dashed to her mother and threw her arms around her. They wept and kissed each other.

"I thought I would never see you again my child."

"I knew I would return. I did not know when, Mother. It is so good to see you and Father."

She turned to her father, embraced and kissed him.

"Thank the gods you have come home."

"I love you both so much," expressed Sharika.

She broke the embrace and went to Chief Atti and his wife Ilona and embraced them and kissed them.

"Have I surprised you with my return?"

"I never expected you to return," Chief Atti answered.

"A pleasant surprise," added Ilona.

Atti's eyes swept over the travelers. "So who are all these people?"

"Let me introduce you to everyone." Sharika waved to the peace group to approach and introduced everyone.

Atti's eyes widened with the introductions. Many surrounding them burst into excited conversation. Sharika caught snatches of the talk and the gist of it was they were surprised she had returned.

Atti glared at her. "Why have you returned?"

"I am part of the team hoping the Hun Nation will ratify a peace treaty."

Atti recognized the significance of the trip. "We must conduct business before pleasure." He spoke loudly to the throng, "These people have come to discuss ratification of a peace treaty. Miklos, Pater and I are going to meet with them in my home and we will announce the outcome after it is over."

Atti and Ilona started out for their home, with Miklos, Pater and the Kahali group in tow and most of the villagers as well. The Huns followed the travelers until they disappeared in Atti's home. They clogged the avenue and stood conversing in anticipation of the outcome.

Chief Atti's house was barely able to accommodate the large group. The moment everyone was settled he spoke, "Who is your spokesperson?"

Elgar, the Elder answered in the common language, "We have chosen Sharika to represent us because this was her home."

Atti raised a hand. "It will have no bearing on what we decide."

Elgar was not fazed. "It was not our intention."

"Very well. Let us proceed," announced Atti.

Sharika went through the articles of the treaty slowly and made certain Atti, Miklos and Pater understood each one. The only one to draw discussion was the boundary of the Hun Nation. After pointing out hundreds of years may pass before any border dispute might arise it was accepted. Atti told the group he saw the treaty making travel less dangerous and expected commerce to commence and people to travel for the sheer love of adventure. Elgar agreed and saw it growing through the years. The formal meeting ended and wine was served as Pater announced the outcome of the meeting to those waiting patiently outside. The good news was greeted with a roar and the villagers disbursed with the news.

A while later Atti and Sharika were huddled on a small bench outside away from the others. He spoke in a confidential voice. "What on earth possessed you to come back?"

Sharika was stunned by her old friend's question. "I thought you and everyone else would be happy to see me."

"You heard the reaction from those close enough to hear us when you told me. They did not appreciate you leaving the way you did. None of us wanted to hear you say we had a problem with inbreeding. It never set well with us, Huns. Be aware many of the villagers will cast disparaging remarks toward you"

"I had expected some would be hurt. I honestly never thought you would disapprove."

"What did you expect?" he snapped. "I told you you would succeed me. You had the world in your hand and you threw it away. I cannot understand you. All I can say is you are fortunate you are not making our village your home. It would take a long time for you to rekindle friendships."

Sharika's voice was filled with her exasperation, "Before I left, I told you I noticed some of our people had succumbed to physical deformities and mental deficiencies. You seemed to understand my concerns."

"I knew I could not change your mind so I was being kind."

"I had hoped I expressed my concerns well enough."

"Oh, you did my dear. It does not mean it did not hurt. These are my people and I thought yours. I wanted you to lead them. I was greatly deceived. You were looking out for yourself."

"Not true. I wanted to change the pattern. I wanted to add new blood to our old blood. I gave it a great deal of thought. It is evident I did not explain myself thoroughly to you."

"I heard what I heard," he interjected.

Trying to make her point she added, "In my travels to four tribes, I noticed the number of deformities are substantially lower than they are in ours except for the mutants. I still stand by what I did. I chose to leave and find a suitable husband to strengthen our bloodline."

"Did you have any intention of coming back and living here?"

"Yes."

"I hope you see it was poor judgment. My poor judgment was thinking you were going to stay amongst us. I was terribly wrong about you."

"I am sorry, Atti."

He dejectedly shook his head. "Ah, it is done now. All I can do is wonder what might have been had you stayed.

"Had I not left, I never would have met Kaathi. The moment I met her, I knew I would not leave her. I have come to love Kaathi and I am learning a great deal from her and have chosen to live wherever she is living."

"With your words I can see she means a great deal to you."

"Yes."

"What if your husband wanted to live away from her?"

"I would stay with her."

"Tell me what is so special about Kaathi."

Sharika did not hesitate with her reply. "She is helping me understand myself and other mysteries."

Atti appeared to forget about how he felt moments ago. "I thought you knew yourself."

"She is showing me a more joyful side of life."

"Were you not living life joyfully here?"

She cocked her head and peered at him. "Are you living joyfully?"

In answer, he made a face.

"Do I need to talk any more about why she means so much to me?"

"No."

Atti wanted to change the subject. "So tell me about this husband of yours."

"He has a marvelous sense of humor and is playful. He is an apprentice Warrior Hunter as am I."

"Why is he not part of this group?"

"The Kahali law states one of the Warrior Hunters has to remain in our village."

Atti saw Elgar was not engaged in conversation. He abruptly excused himself saying he needed to talk with Elgar. She watched him leave. She saw she did not correctly gauge the depth of his displeasure with her leaving and marrying outside the tribe.

Sharika ate the last meal of the day with the others and afterward went to her parent's home. They greeted and embraced each other and a steady salvo of questions came forth from her parents.

Her mother's first question was, "Do you have any children?"

Sharika smiled. "We have a girl, Mariska; she is six." Her smile faded. "And Vern is four."

"Is Vern a boy or girl?"

"We are not sure yet."

A quizzical look fell upon her mother's face. "What do you mean?"

"Vern was born with both genitalia, so we are letting Vern decide when the time is right to be either a boy or girl."

Her father was stunned. "How is it possible?"

"It happens more often than you think, Father. Most parents are confused and ashamed and do not talk about it. The child can be perplexed as well unless the parents, relatives and friends are supportive. They usually end up not getting married."

She ended her explanation and was glad she never mentioned Vern's uniqueness to Atti.

"Oh Sharika, I am so sorry you and your child have been burdened with this affliction. Can we do anything?"

"No. Kaathi has been counseling us and Vern. She is helping us understand how to accept this challenge. She has also brought this to the attention of the people attending our Relationship Sessions. This has helped immensely by acquainting the village to this natural event. Others have come forward and announced they or their children also have the same physical anomaly. Others have said even though they have a specific male or female body their emotional makeup is in opposition to it. With more and more people and children revealing their challenges it has helped others to come forward."

Sharika's father listened to his daughter and the irony of her leaving the tribe to enhance her bloodline did not go unnoticed. He kept his thoughts to himself, certain she had already discovered it herself.

The face of a young boy, living in the village, popped into Sharika's mother's mind. He always seemed uncomfortable in a group of boys. He was remarkably at ease playing with girls. She pushed the image out of her mind. "Why did you not bring them with you?"

"It is too impractical. Janos is taking care of them. We left Kahali the second day of the sunny season and we do not expect to be back much before the rains. It would be a grueling trip for children."

Her mother was concerned. "How does Janos' parents feel about Vern?"

"They were confused and we talked to them a great deal about Vern. They have come to accept the challenge."

Her father wanted to change the subject. "What are your duties as a Warrior Hunter?"

"On this trip I am a rower, a wood gatherer, a hunter and protector. Back in Kahali, I am a source for people to ask me anything about survival, hunting and weapons. In times of war we are the ones to give strategic advice. I am also learning, from my mentor, how to anticipate blows from an enemy."

"Can you tell us about the woman named, Kaathi?" asked her mother. "There is something intriguing about her."

"She is the one responsible for this trip. She is the one who envisioned bringing all of the tribes together in peace."

"How did she become a High Priest?" her mother wanted to know.

Sharika told the story of how she attained the role.

"I cannot believe those two High Priests were so evil."

"They were dead before I got to Kahali. I am glad I never met them."

Her father jumped in with his question. "Did your Elder say the tiny, hairless woman was a member of the Uchakwa tribe?"

"Yes. Their numbers are small. They live in the jungle."

"Why does she have no hair?"

"I honestly do not know."

"Why is she so small?"

"Again I do not know."

"Your group is a strange conglomeration of people," professed her father.

"Yes they are, and they are a magnificent group of people."

CHAPTER SIXTY-EIGHT

Sharika made her way to her old friend's house and saw her sitting on a bench outside repairing a woven basket. The moment Mia saw her she dropped the basket and they ran to each other. They hugged and wept briefly and walked back to the bench hand in hand.

"You have not changed. How are you able to stay so young looking?"

Mia laughed. "Thank you for the compliment. I still find it hard to believe we are old enough to have children. Of course you did not know I got married and had a child. She is three and asks a hundred questions a day."

Sharika smiled. "I know what you are talking about. Mine were the same."

"How many do you have?"

"Two, a boy Vern and daughter Mariska."

Mia burst into laughter. "Oh this is too good to be true."

"What?"

"Our daughter is named Mariska."

Sharika giggled. "Well we were closer than sisters and it is no surprise our daughters have the same names. Is she inside?"

"She is sleeping. Come."

They went into Mia's house and she picked up her sleeping child and gave her to Sharika, who kissed her repeatedly while cooing to her.

"She is beautiful."

"She is," agreed Mia.

The child fussed and Sharika laid her back on her bed. The women went back outside and sat down.

"Is your husband taking care of your children?"

"He is."

"What is he like?"

"Before we were married he was the darling of all the women. In spite of it, he is a dear and he is a marvelous father and has a wonderful sense of humor. What is your man like?"

"Laszlo was single for a long time. It was his choice."

"How did you manage to catch him?"

"I ignored him for the longest time. It made me different from all the rest of the women. I think he saw me as a challenge and took it upon himself to make me his. Anyway it has been a wonderfully happy union. With the addition of Mariska my life has been joyful."

"I am so happy for you."

Mia pointed up the avenue. "Speaking of my man, here he comes."

Laszlo's face broke into a wide smile upon seeing Sharika and he walked briskly to the women. He was as captivatingly handsome as he was when Sharika had left. He whisked his old friend in his arms saying, "Sharika, it is good to see you."

"It is good to see you. Has Mia put the gray in your hair or your baby?"

"Neither. It is having to bury so many older ladies I have made friends with."

His statement caught her by surprise. It took a moment for her to recover. "May I ask why you are so interested in them?"

"Mother passed away, when I was nine, and I think I never got enough of her love, so I found it in the older women. I found widows are lonely and they are not afraid to tell me they love me nor am I afraid to tell them I love them. It gives me pleasure to do odd jobs for them, tell them stories and be with them. They seem to like my company. Mia does not mind. If she did, I would sadly stop."

Mia literally beamed with love for Laszlo. The look did not go unnoticed by Sharika. Laszlo's open admission surprised Sharika. When she was young, she simply thought of him as a flirt. He had much more depth to him than she expected. She knew bringing happiness to the lonely to be a noble endeavor. Her admiration of him was something new for Sharika. She was grateful Mia and Laszlo found each other and were blessed with a lovely child.

"You seem to have a distinguished position among the Kahali," said Laszlo.

Sharika chuckled. "I think they were impressed I was standing side by side with Hun men killing baboons."

"So their women are not fighters?"

"No. The roles of men and women are still pretty defined by tradition."

"Did you receive curt comments after you were appointed as a Warrior Hunter?"

"It went on for a long time. Thankfully it gradually died down and it happens infrequently now."

"You have not changed physically since you left," observed Laszlo.

"There is a regime of exercise Jacob insists we do every day. I like it and I have some of my own I do."

"So, are you ever going to come back here to live?"

Sharika cocked her head. "I suppose the future will dictate whether I do."

CHAPTER SIXTY-NINE

The peace group left the Hun Nation six days after they arrived assured all of the tribes ratified the peace treaty. Sharika was the only person in the peace group facing negative emotions from the Huns. While the Warrior Hunter, Jacob, had been by her side, no one spoke harshly to her. Sharika never had any regret making the trip, but she left the village with mixed emotions due to Atti's harsh feelings toward her.

On the way back to Kahali, the group stopped to visit each village they had stopped at to acquire ratification. The only one they bypassed was the Wanderer tribe because it was not situated on the river. The mutants had agreed they did not have to revisit them to inform them the Nubilon people ratified the treaty.

The return trip was uneventful. Although the sky grew more filled with clouds each day. Fortunately, the rains had not come. The group was happy to hear the Kahali drums announce their return. They heard the excitement before they were within eyesight. They were greeted with thunderous applause. Elgar, got out of the canoe and waited for the others to exit. He stepped forward, raised his hands for silence and raised his voice to address the assembly, "Thank you for the wonderful welcome. I want all the council members to stand with us."

Elgar motioned to the council members to come forward. The Talker Healers, Kaathi, Marie and Mara together with the Warrior Hunters, Jacob, Janos, Sharika and the apprentice Elders, Manti and Waru, along with the Story Tellers, Coloma, Milo, and Faro and the Friends of All, Logan, Burk and Marka gathered alongside Elgar.

"We bring you good news."

The audience broke into spontaneous applause.

"Because of Kaathi's insistence, the council approved of her recommendation to create a group to represent us to establish peace among all the known people near us. As of this moment, the Wanderer clan, the Homar kingdom, the Sumati tribe, the Ebiji tribe and the Hun Nation and we, Kahali, have ratified the peace treaty."

The crowd applauded the news.

"For the first time in our orally recorded history we are not at war with any people. Except for the village of Sumati, we took representatives from each village to make certain the native language was spoken to clarify any misunderstandings. This was a tremendous asset in our discussions with each ruler. We anticipated having a difficult time discussing peace with the mutants. I am pleased to announce it was not the case. We saw they are experiencing trouble keeping their newborn alive and reproducing. We were surprised to see their numbers are less than two hundred including slaves."

Murmuring arose in the crowd upon hearing the news.

"With the assurance adventurers will not be killed, commerce between our tribes will be conducted without fear. This will also bring about an exchange of ideas such as the Relationship Sessions. In addition people will be able to travel for pleasure and enjoyment. "

The news was met with shouts and applause.

"I think it fitting I bring forward the author of the peace mission, Kaathi and let her say a few words."

The applause and shouting was thunderous.

Kaathi stepped forward smiling as the applause and cheers continued. She raised her hands to quiet the crowd.

"It is good to be home. We cannot take all the credit for the tribes seeing the benefit of peace. Each ruler, chief and king saw the advantages of signing the treaty. And everyone in our group helped bring about the complete ratification. Actually, I have to go back to Taja and Batu; they were instrumental in bringing an awareness into our minds and hearts of how every man, woman and child should be treated with dignity and respect. Through them it began on a personal level and grew to societal proportions. We have endeavored to carry it forward to other villages so their women and girls would be honored and respected as well. The sessions have also brought an awareness of how debilitating it is to hound and bully a person. Any journey toward peace begins on a personal level and expands outward into the village.

"I have been extremely fortunate to be part of a council recognizing the sovereignty and blessedness of each person. It is because of our rightminded council we are experiencing the growth in social and spiritual consciousness, which benefits our village and all of Mother Earth."

Many heads nodded and words of agreement were shouted.

"Every man and woman on the mission was an instrument of peace. I implore each and every one of you to make it your mission to be an instrument of peace as you conduct business in the future with our new friends. As you go about doing it, you will discover you will be more joyful and content."

CHAPTER SEVENTY

Kaathi, Ashlee and Scarlet settled into their normal routine and were discussing the upcoming topics of the Spiritual Awakening Service at Taja's meditation site. While Kaathi was away from the healing hut, a woman, Deshawn, in her late twenties came complaining of not feeling well. She had tripped on a gopher hole ten days ago and fallen upon some rocks. She told the healers she had started to feel sick soon afterward. Mara, Kacy and Marie listened to the woman's account. Mara agreed to be the recipient of the information the other two would gather from Deshawn.

Marie directed Deshawn to lie down on the examining table. Marie was competent in using her hands to sense injuries and obstructions in the auric energy field around the body. Marie told Deshawn, "I am going to check for any variation in your body temperature and energy using my hand. This will tell me something might be wrong in certain areas. Kacy is sight sensitive and will check for color variations out of the ordinary in your aura or energy body. We do not want you to volunteer anything."

"All right."

"I am going to be the first one to examine you. I will do it by running my hand over your body and I will report what I feel to Mara."

With her preamble out of the way, Marie started by placing her right hand four fingers above Deshawn's forehead and moved it slowly around her head and did the same with her left hand. Marie moved her hands to the woman's right shoulder and arm and detected nothing out of the ordinary. She went to the left shoulder and slowly slid her hands down her arm. At the elbow she sensed heat and again near the wrist. She went back over the arm starting at the hand and found the same temperature increase in both places. She went over the right hip and leg and to the other hip and leg. She next moved her hands over Deshawn's chest and stomach and did it several times verifying what she felt. With her examination complete she whispered her findings in Mara's ear.

Kacy stood on one side of the table and slowly scanned Deshawn's body from head to toe, went to the other side and did the same thing. She repeated the process. She went to Mara and whispered her findings in Mara's ear.

Mara approached Deshawn saying, "You can sit up now. Both Kacy and Marie agreed on what they felt and saw. They sensed your left elbow, hand, wrist and hip is where you hurt yourself when you fell. Are they correct?"

"Yes."

"Those areas are healing well. The swelling is gone and the coloration from the bruise is normal. Both healers were puzzled by what they sensed inside you and believe it is why you are not feeling well. They sensed it had nothing to do with your fall. They felt an activity aside from your own energy. I do believe you are pregnant. Congratulation."

The woman gasped. "What? Are you sure?"

"We are sure."

"I never gave it a thought. My blood flow is erratic, so I was not concerned I have not had one for the last two cycles. Well, this is a wonderful surprise. My husband will be happy to hear the news."

Kacy and Marie were all smiles as Mara reported their discovery.

"I am happy to say, Kacy saw the intermingled aura of you baby. She had to go around your body a few times to reassure herself of what she detected. It is pretty safe to say you are with child and it is doing well."

Deshawn smiled. "Oh my. This is our first child."

Marie gave the expectant mother a hug. "Congratulations. Babies are such a delight.

"Do you want something for the morning sickness?"

"My joy is so great I have forgotten. I suppose I could use something."

Marie went to the shelf and removed a small vile of oil and placed it in the woman's hand. "First thing in the morning dip the tip of your finger in and rub the oil on your tongue."

The woman smiled. "Thank you."

Marie accompanied the woman out and saw another woman sitting on the bench she faintly recognized. "I am sorry. I have forgotten your name."

"Agnes."

"Mine is Marie."

"Did you need to see us?"

"I do."

"Please come in."

The woman followed her in. She was introduced to Mara and Kacy, greeted and embraced.

"How can we help you?"

"My daughter, Tara, passed into the Land of No Shadows last year. She was only twelve when she was struck by the fever. She was alive and well and four days later she was dead."

Agnes shook her head sadly and was overcome with emotions. She collected herself. "Kaathi performed the funeral services. I have become frantic she no longer exists in spite of what our old and new religions said we do exist after physical death. I want assurance she still lives as a spirit."

"We have had other people come to us with the same concerns," Mara informed her, "and we have assured them their loved ones do exist."

"I want positive proof and I want Kaathi to be involved."

"I can go to the other side and find your daughter," Marie assured her.

"You do not have the reputation Kaathi does. I shall wait for her."

"I understand. She should be here in a little while. Would you wait outside in case someone else comes?"

"I can."

Agnes did not have to wait long. Kaathi appeared before any other patients arrived. Agnes stood and informed her why she was waiting. Kaathi guided her into the healer's hut. "How can we assure you Tara is alive?"

"Tara had a favorite name she called me. If you contact her ask her what the name was. If it is correct, I shall have the assurance I need."

Kaathi agreed to go to the Land of No Shadows and find her daughter. Kaathi took the time to explain the routine she would go through to place herself in the Land of No Shadows. Since Kacy had never been present for the event, Marie volunteered to sit outside to prevent any disturbance from prospective patients. Kaathi closed her eyes and started to breathe deeply. She quickly accessed the level of consciousness she needed and directed her mind to the Land of No Shadows. Assured she was there, she concentrated on Tara's name and was drawn to her. She recognized the daughter even though she represented herself as an adult.

Kaathi initiated the conversation, "Hello, I see you recognize me."

"I do, why are you here?"

"I have come on behalf of your mother."

Tara's face quickly changed to one of concern. "Is she ill?"

"No, she is fine physically. Her problem is she pines for you and wants to know if you exist."

The daughter smiled. "Well, you can tell I do."

"She wants a deeper assurance. She has requested me to ask what your favorite name was for her."

The daughter chuckled. "It is so like her. I remember giving her the name because she was always so overly concerned about me, just as she is now. I cannot tell you how many times I would respond to her concerns by saying, 'Oh Ma.' You can return and tell her I cried it out again, Oh Ma you worry too much."

"I hope you appreciated your mother being so concerned over you?"

"Trust me I was and still am."

She came to Kaathi and gave her an embrace.

"Would you give it to her? And tell her I love her."

"I will. Goodbye my dear. I love you."

Tara cocked her head. It was rare for her to hear someone tell her they loved her even here in the Land of No Shadows. "I love you too."

Kaathi broke the contact and withdrew from the afterlife level of consciousness and slowly opened her eyes to find the mother intently watching her.

"So, did you find her?"

"I did. She looked amazing and wanted me to give you this. Would you stand?"

She stepped over to the mother and warmly embraced her saying, "I love you." She did not release her until she felt the mother relax and truly accept the hug. They parted and stood near each other.

"Oh, by the way Tara told me how concerned you always were and she would say to you, 'Oh Ma.'"

An instant flood of tears poured from the mother's eyes. She clutched Kaathi and held on weeping. A long while passed and she gradually brought her emotions under control, she pulled away and wiped her face with her hands.

"Thank you, thank you. I cannot thank you enough. It is hard to put into words how much my Tara meant to me. She was the world to me, and I loved her more than life itself. I thought I had lost her and you have calmed my fears. Thank you again. You have put joy back into my heart."

CHAPTER SEVENTY-ONE

Kaathi, Scarlet and Ashlee concluded the Spiritual Awakening Service and bid goodbye to the last person who sought personal advice. They made their way to the convergence of ley lines where Taja had often meditated. It was early in the sunny sky season. The air held little moisture, and the river was still swollen from the rains. The river had not lost its volume.

The moment they reclined Ashlee spoke. "I am still struggling with the Hindu philosophy of the universe. Could you cover it again?"

"Of course. The Hindu's believed the universe is in a constant state of flux and it is cyclic in nature. They envisioned its construction, preservation and annihilation to be a natural process of Creator."

"Their belief sounds similar to the belief we live many lives to fulfil our desires as we come to understand the nature of desire, love and creation," responded Ashlee.

"It does have its similarities. It runs parallel to how Mother Earth has transformed through the ages. We can look at the moon and see how pock marked it is and easily come to the conclusion the world has suffered in a similar manner in its history. Life on Mother Earth has gone through many changes due to cataclysmic events, which drastically altered life on her face. Humans, animals and plant life came and went based upon the cataclysms."

"So, we humans were not the only instruments for change upon this world," declared Ashlee.

"You are correct. There are tales saying the gods came to Mother Earth and assisted our physical and mental transformation."

"Did the gods actually do it?"

"People called the beings coming to earth, gods because they did not have any other words to describe them. Much later the gods were called extraterrestrial travelers."

"Is this true?"

"I am not sure. It does not matter to me how we arrived at our intelligence or philosophy or when we inhabited humanoid bodies. The important thing is we, as conscious sentient beings, at some point, utilized the upright human form to creatively express ourselves.

"The world has altered itself due to disasters initiated by droughts, ice, objects crashing into the earth and volcanic eruptions. Within the universe, there is constant destruction. A better term would be change. You must understand destruction is the state of construction of something new and different. We as humans have a difficult time in comprehending the process."

"Why does it have to change?"

"There are only a few things in life guaranteed and change is one of them. It occurs at every level of creation and consciousness. For example, your body is a composition of cells. Each cell is conscious and knows its purpose within your body. However the cells do not live for long. Within a comparatively short length of time all of your cells will have died, which can be seen as destroyed, and they will have been replaced by new ones, which is the construction or creation process. The whole process should be looked at as a magnificent and marvelous example of the ebb and flow of creation. It is the same with the universe. The universes' cells are the stars, planets and galaxies. Their births and deaths contribute to the formation of new stars and earths. The stars gave birth to our physical bodies. The longevity of the glorious heavenly bodies is measured in greater lengths of time, however the principle is the same. The tiniest composition of cells are related to the galaxies and they all have their own consciousness. Some of these forms of consciousness have a better understanding of their relationship to their environment than you do to yours."

Scarlet's face showed her confusion. "It all seems so complex. Do I have to know how all of creation works?"

"Absolutely not," answered Kaathi. "It is far more important to love and serve those you come into contact with in this life. In some other life, the how and why of creation will be important to you thus you need not think about it in this one."

"Interesting. Can you guarantee it?"

"Of course not. All I can tell you is your interests and desires appear to create a series of lives allowing you to fulfill your dreams and wishes. I have said this before, and it bears repeating. Every thought you have creates a portion of reality. Every decision of opposites has its reality. If you choose to do something it creates your soul's reality and every decision to not do something creates your soul's reality as well. So every choice presents you with a number of paths. Each path has its own reality because you have thought of it. You focus on the path of your choice, while the others are going on merrily without you realizing it. If your awareness was more pronounced, you could focus your attention on one or more of the other paths."

Ashlee waited for Scarlet to ask another question, when she did not, she did, "I have heard you tell us how over a period of time we can grow spiritually. Is there a way to experience Creator quickly?"

"There are ways a person not on the spiritual path can experience Creator. A near death experience can propel you or the death of a loved one can do it or facing your own death on the plains can bring it about. Being graced by a transformative spiritual experience can induce it and it can happen to the most awful person in the world. There is a way you can induce an experience with Creator, if your love and desire is great enough. To achieve it, you must weep honestly and continuously for Creator for three full days. This is not easy. Our minds are prone to think of many things during the course of a day. To focus on Creator and weep because you are separated from Creator for one day is difficult. To do it for three days is extremely difficult."

Ashlee's brow furrowed. "When I was taken by the mutants and saw my parents killed, I cried for days. I remember there were times during the day I did not weep. To cry continuously seems almost unbelievable. It takes a lot of energy to weep for a long time. Do any of our stories tell of someone accomplishing it?"

"I have not heard of any. One of the most spiritual persons in our past made the statement, so I would imagine it is true. I do know Creator's love is always with us as is Creator's energy. It is you and I who need to open ourselves to Creator to experience Creator."

CHAPTER SEVENTY-TWO

The Spiritual Awakening Session concluded and those wanting hugs and to chat with Kaathi, Ashlee and Scarlet had left. One man remained seated cross legged with his eyes closed in the back of the prayer hut. Ashlee touched Kaathi's arm and nodded toward the man.

Kaathi looked at her apprentices. "The two of you can leave. I am going to see if he wants to talk."

Kaathi walked over to the wiry-built man and sat across from him, emptied herself and waited with her eyes closed. A short while later she heard him softly weeping and opened her eyes to see his hand covering his face. He finally stopped and wiped his face with his hands. The darkly tanned face she saw looked as if it had the weight of the world etched on it. His hair was prematurely gray and thin and his eyes were bloodshot. His eyebrows were bushy and part of his right ear was missing. A wide scar was present by it and sliced through his cheek running halfway up his forehead.

"Can I help?"

"I doubt it. You tried years ago. My wife came to you and told you she was having trouble controlling her body. She is far worse; she cannot walk any more. I have to carry her to the river to bathe her. The same is true when she needs to use the latrines. I have to clean her up after she empties her body. Her relatives and friends have helped now and then but the burden rests with me. She has a hard time giving our two girls hugs. They are nine and seven. Sometimes she cries uncontrollably. The list of things she cannot do goes on and on and has been going on for years and frankly I am getting worn out."

"Do her parents help?"

"Her mother did, unfortunately, she has been sick for the last two years. Her father comes less and less because of his wife. He has also grown tired. When he does come he is impatient with my wife. He cannot understand her because of her slurred speech."

"How are your girls taking it?"

"They are afraid it is going to happen to them and they stay away from her. They are afraid it is catching no matter how much I tell them it is not."

He shook his head violently. "I have come to the services for the last five years. I have listened and tried to tell her this is an opportunity for her to meditate and get closer to Creator. She will not do it. She just stares at the walls."

"It is her choice."

Irritated, he ran his hand roughly through his hair. "I know, it does me no good. Between hunting for meat, preparing the meals and taking care of her it is taking its toll on me. I am looking forward to the day she dies so I can get on with my life. . . Am I a monster?"

"No, it tells me you are tired. You are under a great deal of stress and looking to reduce it."

"I have been thinking of the women I might try to develop a relationship with once she dies. I feel guilty after I have those thoughts, and it makes me feel miserable."

"Once again you are looking to the future in order to give yourself some comfort. This is normal and you should not beat yourself up for the thoughts."

"I feel I am failing her, because of how I feel."

"Are you going to leave her before she dies?"

"No!" he said heatedly. "I am all she has. It would be inhumane."

"Are you mistreating her?"

"Absolutely not."

"From everything you have shared with me, you are doing the right thing and all the other things you have told me are ways for you to reduce the stress you are under. My recommendation would be to keep loving her and pray for her peaceful passing."

He shook his head again. "When we fell in love, I envisioned us as two zebras running free beside each other on the plains. Now I feel those zebras are wandering the plains in a drought, looking for a vanishing love to sustain them."

Kaathi sympathized with his frustration. "There are many reasons why people come and go in our lives. I believe you have made a pact to be there for her, and now the pact is trying your energy and patience. Your wife may be clinging to life because she fears what lies on the other side.

"You can tell her I recently went to the Land of No Shadows to find a mother's daughter who had died a year ago. I was told by the daughter of the name she used to call her mother and came back to the mother and dispelled her fears with the name.

"Whatever you do, do not stop coming to the services. Keep praying for her peaceful passing, and I shall do the same. If she is willing to speak with me, let me know."

They rose and Kaathi embraced him for a long time. While in her arms, he calmed down and slowly became aware of her love. He relished it. He ended the hug and she said, "I love you." He surprised himself by saying, "I love you as well."

She watched him walk away hopeful her words gave him some comfort.

CHAPTER SEVENTY-THREE

Elisa sat on the bench outside the Talker Healer's hut for a long while. She was struggling to gather the courage to meet with one of them. It drizzled the moment she sat down. She moved to stand and her knees and hips rebelled at having sat too long. At the entrance, she said, "Hello."

Mara jumped up from her seat and pulled aside the drape and greeted a woman, with the saddest look on her face she had ever seen. The woman looked to be in her late forties, extremely thin, with a shock of white hair. It was her most attractive attribute. She had a large mouth and lips to match and heavy ear rings had stretched her earlobes. Her lazy eye detracted from her less than attractive face, which was streaked with lines. The moment Elisa entered all of the healers felt her sadness and sent her love.

"You are soaked. Please come in." She went to a hanger and removed a woolen blanket, put it over her shoulders and guided her to a seat across from Kaathi.

"I do not recall ever meeting you. I am Kaathi, Mara showed you in and rearranging the shelves is Marie."

Marie stopped what she was doing and sat next to Mara. Their guest did not acknowledge them and chose to state her name, "I am Elisa."

"How can we help you?"

Elisa cast her eyes down. "I am tired of living." Her voice was soft, almost muffled, and emphasized her emotional state. "My life is filled with difficulties, sorrow and pain and has no value. I cannot rid myself of this sadness. It envelopes me day and night. I do not know how to improve my life. If you cannot help me, I do not see any reason to go on living."

Elisa's words struck Kaathi's heart and tears gathered in her eyes. She moved her seat closer, reached out and held Elisa's hands. "I feel your sadness. Go on."

"My mother died eleven years ago. I was around ten when she first suffered the illness, which crippled her joints."

Kaathi remembered the woman. She had come to her for help complaining the joints in her hands had swollen with arthritis. Later all of her joints were affected and the ailment affected the quality of her life. All she could do was give her cannabis oil to help with the pain.

Tears rimmed Elisa's eyes as she continued, "Father and I took care of her. He loved her so much he did not know what to do with himself after she died. I felt his sorrow and spent a great deal of time fixing his meals and talking to him much to my husband's displeasure. Father was always reminiscing about the times when he and my mother were happy and healthy. Even as he reminisced he cried. I do not think he had a happy day once my mother got sick. He wanted his old mate back. After my mother died, his heart was broken and unamendable. He grew terribly depressed. Nothing I said drew him out of it. I kept hoping he would recover. One day he told me he wanted to take a walk alone. He walked away from the village and never came back. It was six years ago. It took Jacob's search party seven days before they found my father's bones a day's journey from here. Thankfully the hyenas left enough of his bones they could identify him."

Elisa looked up through watery eyes, as she spoke, and found Kaathi's eyes filled with love and understanding.

"My husband was never a compassionate man. I knew it when I married him. During my mother's illness and my father's depression, my absence from our home angered him. He repeatedly said I loved my parents more than him and our son. I told him it was not true. My parents needed me by their side. He often spoke to me harshly in front of our son. My son's attitude toward me gradually changed.

"At the time, I felt my parents desperately needed me. I thought I could give my husband and son the attention they needed when my parents no longer needed me. I now see I was not thinking right."

Elisa gazed into the mystic's eyes looking for understanding. Tears trickled down Elisa's cheeks. She moaned mournfully, gathered herself and continued, "After my father's death, I fell into an emotional abyss. My heart was torn. I cannot tell you how hard I took their deaths. Father walked to his death near the end of the sunny season. I could not function the whole of the rainy season. I am sure the weather contributed to how I felt. Since my father's death, my hands have become more and more swollen and painful. For the last two years my husband has had to make our meals and complains about it every day in front of our son. I needed comfort and compassion and turned to my husband for consolation and got anger."

She heaved a sigh and wiped her face with her knobby hands. Marie gave her a soft cloth to dry her face.

"I cannot comprehend why my man is so mean. My son is no different. He is as alienated toward me as is his father. It breaks my heart to see him cringe when I hug him. My life is in a cesspool and I do not know how to escape it."

Mara was about to ask her why she did not seek help sooner. She thought better of it and remained silent.

Elisa continued her tale with downcast eyes, "This past year I started to have trouble standing up after being seated for a long while. It was not long before I felt pain in my hands and every joint in my body. I suffered thinking this is what my mother went through. It is horrible and debilitating. The worse thing is how little comfort and compassion I receive from my man and son."

She stopped to let the tears wash over her face. A sob shook her. She wiped her face with the cloth, breathed deeply and went on, "I suffered in silence and spent the days outdoors to let the warmth of the sun soothe my ache. It helped a little. The trouble was there was no remedy for the emotional turmoil eating at my heart. I loved and longed to be loved. It got me nowhere, for I did not receive it from those I loved. The more I reached out the harder it was to be rejected. I do not feel like a wife or mother any longer. I feel like I am an object they avoid contact with. They spend more and more time away from home. Home is now a place where they come to eat and sleep.

"Between the physical pain and my broken heart it is too much to bear. I have too many thoughts about walking out on the savannah and ending my life."

Elisa brought her eyes up and pleaded with them.

She whispered. "I am afraid. . . I need help."

"My dear Elisa, you are wise enough to know you are afraid because you think you will never regain the love from your son and husband. It is why you are besieged with thoughts of ending your life. I am truly sorry you are suffering so much. I want you to know all of us are here to help and love you."

Elisa's eyes were riveted on the floor.

"Your mother's life ended naturally. Your father ended his because he could not feel his wife's love after she died. What was his belief of the afterlife?"

"He thought there was no life after death."

"It explains why he could not feel his wife's love when she passed on. His belief obstructed her love."

"So you believe in an afterlife?"

"Indeed. It is why my title is Talker Healer. I talk to people in the afterlife, as have all my predecessors."

"Regretfully, I wish my father was not so stubborn and had come to see you."

"If it is any consolation to you, I feel your father and mother are here this moment with you, and I sense their love for you and they thank you for everything you did for them."

Kaathi's words did not register immediately on Elisa. When they did she was taken aback. Fresh tears streamed from her. They eventually stopped and Kaathi said softly, "From what you have shared with me, I can see your love drove you to do what you did.

You followed your heart and did what was necessary. Unfortunately, things do not always end up as we envisioned them.

"It was hard to be tugged in two different directions as you were. I do not want you to keep on blaming yourself for what you did. It is not a curse to follow your heart in such matters, in spite of it appearing to be. If your mate would have had a heart as big as yours, he would have been understanding. It may have been he had never been taught the goodness of understanding the broader sense of love. His lack and your abundance were in conflict."

Tears were again accumulating on her eyelids. "What can I do to remedy my life?"

"I want you, your husband and son to see me after your morning meal for the next ten days. During those sessions I will hopefully help all of you come to a clearer understanding of the dynamics of what has controlled your lives and actions. I especially want to dig into the last few years of your lives. What I am hoping to achieve is a reconciliation of your relationships and a clearer understanding for your man and son of the physical challenges you are going through."

"You would help us?"

"Yes, it is similar to what we are striving for in the Relationship Sessions for the whole village."

She gave a small nod and while gently rubbing her hands together said, "Can you give me some cannabis oil for my arthritis?"

"I can, and I can help you understand why you have chosen to be challenged by this illness."

"Now you are talking foolishness. I have not chosen to be sick."

"I am sorry to say you have. Come to the next Spiritual Awareness Service. I am going to talk in length about this. I believe it will benefit you immensely in understanding some of life's mysteries."

Elisa looked skeptical. Gradually, she softened to the idea. Marie gave her the oil. She rose and received embraces from all of the healers and their love. She thanked Kaathi and left thinking this was the best she felt mentally and emotionally in years.

CHAPTER SEVENTY-FOUR

The alarm drums announced the presence of a lone, unknown male paddling down the Kahali River and approaching its namesake village. He had left his village shortly after the rains ended filled with hope. He had traveled so many days the rains would soon drench the earth again. Somewhere in this village was the person filled with the wisdom he sought. The people of Hun Nation and Homar had both given him the same name. Moshe was excited.

Moshe heard the sound of the great crowd talking before he saw them. They were converged on the river bank with equal excitement to see what the stranger looked like. The volume from the crowd increased the nearer he got. The moment he could see them he stood in the dugout and raised his arms in salutation. Those on the shore saw the foreigner was able to lift his left arm half as high as his right.

Moshe sat and paddled for the landing, where two men beached the canoe. The vocal commotion was high as he alighted and greeted a middle-aged man.

Moshe spoke loudly to be heard by those surrounding him. "I come in peace. My name is Moshe. I am from the Delta Nation in the north."

Elgar watched the well-muscled, middle-aged man keenly. His skin was lightly tanned and his hair was stark white, short and lightly waved, all signs indicating he came from the north. His large, green eyes were clear and intelligent. As the foreigner came closer, Elgar saw the huge scar on his left shoulder, likely gotten in combat, thus explaining why he could not raise it very high.

Elgar spoke loudly as well. "Welcome Moshe. I am Elgar, the Elder, of the Kahalis. Allow me to introduce the council representing our people." He led Moshe down the row of council members. The traveler took the hand of each person and visually and energetically assessed each one. His body had been tingling well before he had stepped ashore and presumed it was due to the woman he had come to see. At being introduced to Kaathi, he took her hand and the rush of energy almost made him weep. He lingered holding her hand and was lost in her eyes. He had never seen anyone with eyes able to speak so eloquently of love. He had to control the flow of tears yearning to be released. He held her hand a long while before kissing it. The Elder was used to people having strange reactions to the mystic and had never seen anyone kiss her hand. He had to repeat the introduction to Marie. Moshe released Kaathi's hand and took Marie's. As the Elder introduced him to Mara, he had his second surprise. He had never seen a person so short and hairless. He came upon Ashlee and was stunned by her breathtaking beauty. His immediate thought was she was a goddess come to earth. He held her hand nearly as long as he did Kaathi's. Scarlet, standing next to Ashlee, smiled at his obvious adoration of Ashlee's beauty. As Scarlet was introduced, she received an appreciative warm smile from the newcomer. It made her happy to see her charms were also appreciated.

Moshe clasped the hand of the Warrior Hunter, Jacob, and was impressed by what he felt emanating from the tall, muscled, handsome man. He was taken aback Jacob had selected, the Hun, Sharika, as his apprentice. She must have demonstrated her ability time and again to be chosen as his apprentice. She was a fantastic physical specimen of a woman and worthy of being singled out as a leader.

The strange conglomeration of people from so many different races serving on a council struck Moshe as surprising and odd. There had to be a reason for it and he quickly realized it. Kaathi, was the only one with qualities to coalesce them and convinced the villagers it was philosophically and culturally correct.

The introductions concluded, and the excited locals surrounding them pushed forward and introduced themselves. He greeted over three hundred before Logan spoke into Elgar's ear informing him the meal was ready. Elgar had the bull horn announcer to blow it. The Elder shouted to the crowd letting them know the council and Moshe were heading for the meeting hut to eat. The group arrived at the hut and settled down to partake of the meal, while hundreds of curious people congregated and surrounded the hut.

Elgar sat to the right of Moshe and Jacob to his left, while Kaathi, Coloma and Logan sat across from them. The apprentices filled the rest of the seats. Four seats were also filled by people Logan selected for the honor.

Elgar threw out the first question. "We were uncertain if there were any more tribes located near us. Where exactly is the Delta Nation?"

"The great Nile River has created a vast fertile delta. It is home to a variety of millions of migratory and permanent birds. It is a rich land able to produce abundant crops. The delta empties into a great sea. Because of its riches we have been attacked by three different tribes in the last twenty years from our east. I have lived thirty-three years and fought in nine battles for my nation. At one time, we were a nation of forty thousand. We have lost six thousand men to the insanity we call war. I was so good at killing our enemy they gave me command of half of our fighting forces. In each bloody battle, I lost men I loved. I lost my father to war at the age of nine. Another battle claimed the life of my oldest brother. My other brother lost his life as he fought next to me. It unnerved me more than any other death I witnessed. It was extremely difficult to lose my whole family. I nearly lost my arm, in the same battle I lost my last brother, and would have bled to death were it not for quick action on the part of my lieutenant.

"As I was recovering from my wound, I found it hard to see the worth in fighting. The gore and horror overtook my dreams and terrified my nights. The more I thought about it the more I saw how insane it was to continue fighting and lose the best men I have ever known. Seeing men lying in pools of blood on the ground with their guts hanging out and their heads or arms chopped off was maddening. I had enough of the madness. I knew there had to be a better way to live.

"The moment I recovered sufficiently enough to walk, I went to the emperor and said I could not fight any more. I told my mother I was going to live by myself until I had answers to the questions tormenting me. I went away and lived alone three years and discovered many answers to my questions. Toward the end of my personal exile, I started to have dreams and visions of a woman who was to help me understand my relationship to the universe.

"I canoed south on the Nile and the Sengali river, the same one you call Kahali, and reached the Sengali village. I did not know the village existed. I talked to a group of elders inclined to think as my people thought. I stayed three days hoping to uncover a better way of interacting with people. I did not find it.

"I left and after many days I came to the Hun Nation. I was impressed they were warring only with the baboons. In my discussions with them, I realized they were isolated from other people and it helped them in developing a friendly culture. They are good people, but they were lacking something. They were not being challenged by others, consequently they never knew how an unfriendly episode with another people would test them.

"I left and came upon Homar. This society had changed. King Edmund admitted to me he had been a dictatorial tyrant and ruled with an iron fist. He told me he had been converted by a woman in Kahali named Kaathi. He initiated changes in his kingdom by having instructors teach his people how to interact with each other. They learned by attending something he called Relationship Sessions.

"Every bone in my body told me this was the woman of my dreams. I was intrigued and sat in on every session they conducted until I left. I saw the worthiness of the sessions and was excited to meet the woman responsible for their creation. It is what brought me here."

Moshe turned away from Elgar and looked at the mystic. He did not see the pride he expected to see on her face after he had praised her. What he saw was peace and contentment.

"Where do you go from here?"

Moshe never took his eyes off Kaathi. "Nowhere until I am satisfied I have in my grasp all there is to know."

"A commendable endeavor," replied Elgar. "And once you have acquired it, what happens?"

"I shall return to my home and share what I have learned. Do you mind if I attend the sessions?"

"I have no objections. Do you?"

Kaathi smiled. "I welcome your attendance."

Moshe turned to Jacob. "Would you show me around your village?"

Jacob thought the request strange. "I can."

Many villagers upon seeing Moshe stopped them to chat. Jacob had showed him less than half of the village and Moshe touched his arm. "Can we find a place quiet to talk?"

"Of course." Jacob led him outside the village to the high energy spot at Batu's tree. They reclined. Before Moshe could ask a question Jacob voiced one of his own, "You seem too young to have a full head of white hair. Is there a reason for it?"

"Indeed. When I witnessed the death of my second brother it shocked me. As the battle wore on, I had maimed and killed several men with my sword. My luck changed as a soldier confronted me. He swung his sword at my head. I whacked his weapon and it missed my head. He spun around like no warrior I had ever seen and struck my arm. My sword fell from my useless arm. I was defenseless. My lieutenant saved my life by killing him. I almost bled to death on the battlefield. While men fought for their lives around me, my lieutenant ripped a cloth from the warrior lying dead beside me and tied it over my arm to stem the blood flow. He put a piece of cloth over my wound and tied it down. The fighting moved away from where I lie. I fussed with the tourniquet until the wound clotted. I kept thinking my name had been called and I was to appear before death's reaper. The death of my brother and my near death struck at the core of something in me. Fear shook me. The strength of my fear shocked me. I fell asleep quaking with fear. I woke the next day and my lieutenant came by to see if I had lived through the night. He was the first to see my hair had changed overnight and told me my hair had turned white. Such are the horrors of war."

Jacob shook his head.

"Enough about me. What can you tell me about Kaathi and be comfortable?"

"Anything you want to know. She is very open about herself."

Moshe nodded. "Was she the first woman on your council?"

"No. Her mentor, Batu, was the first. Batu was a trailblazer and reformed many concepts about women. Kaathi stepped into her position and furthered her ideals."

"I noticed she is also your High Priest. I find it remarkable and unusual to attain such a prestigious position and to also hold the position as healer."

"You have to understand she is an unusual woman with many gifts."

"Such as?"

"Hmmm. She is undoubtedly the best healer we have ever had and we have had some marvelous ones. Batu in particular was renowned. Batu went to Sumati to help them during an epidemic and discovered the cause and saved hundreds if not thousands of lives. Since you have talked to Edmund, you already know Kaathi's skills of persuasion. She assumed the role of High Priest and transformed our religion from fear based to a love based one by initiating the Spiritual Awareness Services. In addition, she convinced our people to accept a mutant couple into our society."

"Astonishing. How did it come about?"

Jacob told the story how he and Kaathi made the journey to Homar and came across the last of the Searcher tribe, Leah and Isaac and convinced them to return with them.

"And what is the story about Mara? I have never seen anyone like her."

Jacob told him of the journey to visit the Ancients and how they fought for their lives with the Uchakwa and Mara was the sole survivor of the attacking warriors."

"I find it incredible Kaathi initiated all of these adventures."

"She has been remarkable since she was a child."

"You mentioned Ancients. Who are they?"

Jacob shared his experiences with Ancient Mother and Ancient Father and told him Kaathi was in telepathic communication with them.

"The more I hear of Kaathi the more remarkable she appears to be. Can I ask a personal question?"

"You can."

Moshe raised his eyebrows. "Elgar introduced Scarlet and Ashlee as your wives."

Jacob smiled. "He did not introduce my first wife because she is not on our council. When I married Keri we were allowed only one wife."

"Whoa, I think your wife Keri should also be by your side. All the other wives and husbands should be present when important introductions are made."

Jacob smiled. "You are here only a day and you already see how we can improve. Excellent idea, Moshe."

"How did it come about you could have more than one mate?"

Jacob related the events leading up to how he came to know and marry Scarlet and Ashlee.

Jacob picked up the story about Kaathi. "Perhaps the largest jewel in her crown is having all the neighboring villages ratify a peace agreement." He went on to describe the reaction of each tribe.

Moshe nodded saying, "I agree. An endeavor to bring so many tribes to understand the benefits of peace is a huge accomplishment. She seems so young to have accomplished so much."

"She has been tireless."

"Tell me, Jacob. Are you able to sense energy?"

"I can."

"Are you aware of the energy emanating from Kaathi?"

"I am."

"I am as well. I have had this ability ever since I can remember, and I have never felt anyone so filled with energy."

Jacob smiled.

"I am eager to have a conversation with her and get to know her.

CHAPTER SEVENTY-FIVE

Moshe was staying in Elgar's home. He awoke hearing Elgar's wife preparing the first meal. He ate heartily with the family, thanked them and excused himself saying he wanted to talk to Kaathi. He asked about the announcement protocol, got directions from the Elder and easily found the Talker Healer's hut located on the periphery of the village center.

Outside her hut he tentatively called her name. She appeared.

"Moshe, it is nice to see you. What can I do for you?"

"Can we talk?"

"I would love to."

She wrapped her arm around his and led him to an opening on the riverbank and they reclined.

"I am sure by now you have heard why I am here. I wanted to know if you have had any inkling of my arrival."

"I have had a few dreams foretelling me of your arrival. The moment I saw you on the river there was a strong attraction. I sensed you have been on a quest and desired to understand the mysteries of life."

"I have had the attraction to you since I first dreamed of you over a year ago. Can you help me find the answers I seek?"

She smiled and raised an eyebrow. "I have to know your questions first."

In the face of her request, he forgot all of them and spoke from the vast emotional reservoir of his heart. "Yes, yes. I have this great yearning. . . It is as if I feel unfulfilled?"

"Do you have a name for God?"

"Yes, it is Beloved."

"What a beautiful name. Do you mind if I use it as well in place of Creator?"

"Of course not."

"Thank you. Now let us get to your yearning. It is similar to someone yet to meet the love of his life. In your case the one you yearn for is the Beloved."

"I have never seen my Beloved. Will I ever?"

"I am certain you shall. I am uncertain of the way or how Beloved will present Herself to you. Some of us see a symbolic representation of the Beloved, the rest of us sense the Beloved as a presence, as love, as energy, as stillness, as the person we are talking to, a smell, a tingling or a peace enveloping us."

"Your words intrigue me. I thought by being a hermit I would find Beloved. I did not. Can you help me?"

"It will be my pleasure. When you were alone did you quiet your mind?"

"No it was filled with questions and thoughts."

"I believe it is your problem. You were speaking to your Beloved. Now you must listen to Beloved and open your heart. I want you to come to the healer's hut before sunrise. The Talker Healers, High Priests and Warrior Hunters sit in silence every day as the sun rises and sets."

Moshe eagerly nodded his head. "Is there anything else I have to do?"

"Yes. I want you to attend every Relationship Session and Spiritual Awareness Service we conduct. In addition, every moment of the day you are not interacting with someone, I want you to say this little prayer over and over from sunrise to sunset: Beloved, I love you. And you need to say it with affection and passion."

"How long will it take before I am united with my Beloved?"

"I do not know. Perhaps before you leave or during the next blue sky season or the next or the next. It all depends on how much you love the Beloved. I do sense you are earnest in your desire, so it will happen."

He took her hand and kissed it time and time again. He finally felt as if he was home. He felt cradled in love. Her tenderness brought tears to his eyes.

"Thank you."

She wrapped him in her arms. "I love you."

Moshe returned the gesture and love.

Moshe arrived before the sun crested. He sat on the bench and waited for the others. They arrived in small groups and everyone embraced everyone else. The walk to Taja's meditation site was done in silence. Moshe was used to silence after living alone for three years. Trying to control his mind was far more difficult than he had imagined. His mind kept fluttering from one thing to the other like a butterfly. The meditation ended and the group walked back to the village in silence. The first opportunity he got he asked Kaathi for help to control his racing thoughts.

"It is difficult to control the mind," she acknowledged. "I would like you to pay attention to your breath. You could do it by feeling your in breath and out breath as air passes through your nostrils. If it does not seem to be working you could try paying attention to the movement of your stomach as you breathe in and out. If those are not working well for you could silently say the prayer: Beloved, I love You."

"Thank you."

CHAPTER SEVENTY-SIX

Moshe had made Kahali his home for two years. During those years, he had faithfully attended every Relationship Session, Spiritual Awakening Service and meditation meeting he could. Moshe was seated at Batu's tree together with Kaathi, Ashlee, Scarlet, Marie, Mara, Kacy, Janos, Sharika and Jacob. They had finished their sunrise meditation and waited for someone to share.

Jacob broke the silence, looked at Moshe and said, "I am glad you left your home and found your way here."

"It was indeed my good fortune. The fact is I could not stay; wanderlust had captured my heart and I had to find Kaathi. When I return, I am hoping I can impart to my people all I have learned from all of you."

"It is a noble venture, Moshe," exclaimed Marie.

"I need to thank all of you for the kindness and love you have given me. The only consolation I have for leaving you will be the pleasure of thinking of all of you, while waiting to fall asleep. I especially need to thank you, Kaathi. You have patiently answered every question I have thrown your way and have been a magnificent example of whom I want to become. Through your guidance, I have experienced my Beloved. I cannot express my gratitude enough to you."

Kaathi smiled. "You are almost as inquisitive as Ashlee." The remark brought laughter from the group. "I am so pleased you spent so much time and energy finding how to improve the culture and spiritual nature of your village. I sensed your desire from the start and was blessed to have you so driven to understand how to cause as little harm as possible in life.

"I know people will oppose you and what you want to share. Do not get discouraged if they do not converge on your sessions in droves. There will be times they will set upon you in anger and violent remarks. Take heart. Your village will eventually be transformed by what you have learned here. It would be wise to ingratiate yourselves to the leaders of your village and let them see the wisdom of what you have learned.

"Trust yourself. What you have to offer them is going to improve their relationships with others and with Beloved. At one time or another, all of us have told you stories of the difficulties Taja, Batu and we have had changing the attitude of people. Our persistence and patience reaped progress. And remember to love your detractors.

"The hope of those sitting here is everyone on Mother Earth becomes instruments of peace. It is what we are striving for in our instructions. You have accepted what we shared and have become a shining example of what it means to be an instrument of peace. Bless you and your endeavor."

CHAPTER SEVENTY-SEVEN

Moshe and Kaathi finished their meditation at his favorite site, which had been Taja's as well. He sat across from his beloved teacher and was happy to have her all to himself. He preferred it. When others were present the conversation was not as intimate and revealing.

Moshe's eyes settled on Kaathi. "How would you describe yourself?"

The mystic smiled at his question. "Loving, humble and free of desire and will."

"You have left out forgiving and kind," he pointed out.

"If you are truly filled with love, you are always kind and forgiving," she sweetly replied.

"You have told me the twelve Ancients are all likely enlightened. Is there a percentage of people attaining enlightenment in every village or nation?"

"As far as knowing the number enlightened, I honestly do not know. I would have to be in their presence or know of their experiences. In my travels I have noticed spiritual people can come in many guises. They do not have to be pious. Spirituality has to do with every aspect of life. There is nothing that is not spiritual. How can it be otherwise, if Beloved created everyone and everything?

"Those actively pursuing to be spiritual tend to gravitate to each other. I felt unconditional love from the Ancients something rarely found on Mother Earth. The enlightened have no ego, desires or will of their own. Enlightenment comes from the depths of their consciousness.

Love is the foundation of Beloved. Beloved is all you see and do not see in the universe. Beloved is the fabric of consciousness and existence.

"An enlightened person discovers all creation is in a state of perfection."

"I would hardly consider myself perfect," Moshe responded.

"It is due to your state of awareness or consciousness. Beloved and all of those enlightened see you and everyone else as perfection."

"If the good and bad disappear in enlightenment, what controls the person?"

"In the greater self, her ethical values, spiritual truths and love guide her in all aspects of her life."

"Can you give me other examples of what it is to be enlightened?"

"I will do my best. Sensing love and the energy permeating everything and everyone is an exquisite experience of the enlightened. I sense the Awe, the Beloved, and it brings me to tears. At times it is so strong, it takes my breath away or elicits great sobs from me. During these states thinking ceases. In mystical states of awareness, my vanities and illusions are shattered and disappear and allows the truth of love to shine. My devotion has enabled me to surrender to Beloved. The silent presence of Beloved is constantly with me and keeps me in a perpetual state of love. I sense Beloved's presence, even as I am talking to you. I liken the awareness to be similar to being aware of the breeze caressing my face. If I chose to concentrate on Beloved, I would be swept away to another level of awareness or consciousness. To be one with Beloved you must be graced and the ego must be sacrificed; it must die. Your spiritual experiences can be contained in every event, every experience, every person and everything. All of it can be graced with Beloved's love. In one of my experiences, I recall being present at the moment of creation. The magnificence of it and the energy emitted was beyond expression and comprehension. Another experience with Beloved came about with a hummingbird. You have to open yourself to the sacredness of life."

"Can I live an ordinary life and attain enlightenment?"

"Not ordinarily. Enlightenment takes dedication to the spiritual practices I outlined for you.

"Is enlightenment your goal?"

"I must say no. My goal is to love Creator every moment of the day. Beyond this singular goal I do have others. I sense a need to help people evolve in consciousness and love. I sense this same need in you, Moshe. When you return to your people humbly serve your people. They will notice your growth, love and sensitivity. They shall welcome your new insights. I know you have suffered great losses in the past and it devastated you. I urge you to remember you are not your memories. They are there for you to use as stepping stones to freedom and a new awareness."

"When you sense you are in the Presence, what is going on inside you?

"The moment a benediction envelopes me, I am in a profound peace, a deep stillness and immense love."

"You have mentioned your will and Beloved's is the same. Does it mean you are a co-creator?"

"No. At some levels of consciousness it appears as if it is happening. This is because your mind activates consciousness into creation and consciousness is Beloved. In enlightenment you know you are doing nothing and Beloved is doing everything. Everything is Beloved's play. Everything is Beloved."

"With everything you have shared with me about enlightenment, it seems you are."

Kaathi's eyes twinkled. "You are gracious to include me as an enlightened person. I chose not to judge, if I am or am not. I have had moments of exalted bliss, where all body functions ceased. It was in these states the breadth and depth of Beloved's love was beyond any other experience I ever had. Time as we know it was also suspended."

"Are you saying you did not breathe and your heart did not beat?"

"Yes."

"It is incredible. You broke so many of man's concepts of how we are able to stay alive. Is your mind or intelligence expanded?"

"It appears everything is available with the proper focus."

"Can you give me an example of how a person would go about attaining enlightenment in non-spiritual terms?"

"I believe I can. First you need to understand everything you do is spiritual. We cannot escape being spiritual beings. It is from spirit we have our expression and existence.

"I will answer you in societal terms. I will use a theoretical woman in my examples. There are usually three areas a woman needs to attain before she can enfold enlightenment. The first area concerns a sense of security, comfort and having her basic needs provided such as food and shelter. The villages have ratified the peace treaty thus providing her with a secure future free from the devastation of war. She and other people have gathered together for security since beginning of recorded history. There is strength and security in numbers. It is a basic need of the first area. So long as there is sufficient rain, the river provides water to drink for her and her livestock and to use in the irrigation of crops. She can also eat the fish in the river. In this area she and others must feel comfortable about their environment and be protected from predators.

"With those stipulations from the first area taken care of, she can proceed to the second area of need. It is based upon emotional and psychological stability and is a major step toward the peace of mind needed to move to the next area. By introducing the Relationship Sessions to her, she will come to understand how important her relationships are with friends, family and spouse. Learning ways and techniques to promote well rounded relationships presents a sense of accomplishment. She no longer needs to lash out in anger at a friend's response. Instead she can breathe deeply and endeavor to understand the underlying reason for her reaction. Was it her friend's words or something said by someone in her past brought forth her reaction? Once she acquires the exact knowledge, she can act with the appropriate sensitivity to defuse the situation within herself or her friend. Such emotional and psychological stability in relationships is as necessary as breathing. Loving and caring relationships relieve stress and provide a nurturing atmosphere for her and everyone involved. Woven into this fabric of awareness is the ability to forgive past and current offenses.

"Securing her emotional stability she can move to the third and most crucial area of development. It is her ability to reach her potential in relation to herself and others in her society. The Spiritual Awakening Services are especially helpful to those arriving at this plateau of consciousness. This includes utilizing and satisfying her creative nature. By reaching her potential, she can achieve a sense of accomplishment through helpfulness and volunteering on a personal or a societal level. At this level of consciousness, she is confident in herself and is closely aligned with the purpose of life and Beloved. It is at this point in her progression she is able to love fully, freely and confidently, knowing it is the purpose of life. At this point, even if she is an atheist, she will evolve and realize there is a Divine Power giving substance to creation.

"I believe all of the tribes, villages, kingdoms and nations I know of are psychologically and spiritually emerging and are providing the fertile landscape for our hypothetical woman to attain enlightenment."

Moshe tucked the information away in his memory and continued his inquiry. "When Mother Earth was populated by millions or billions of people was there a corresponding number of enlightened souls?"

Kaathi minutely nodded her head. "I believe so. I think they were scattered around the world and present in all capacities of governing bodies, education, the arts, religion and philosophy. After attaining enlightenment, they may abandon what they were doing and seek a solitary life or they may continue in some way to help humanity in a variety of ways outside of their original chosen endeavor."

"Were I alive during those times, how would I know them? What would be the indicators I would look for?"

"Hmm, they would be accomplishing great tasks using wisdom and example and not by coercion. They would not control people they would accept criticism and allow you freedom of thought, and would abandon their idea in favor of yours, if yours had more merit. An enlightened person would respect you not demean or belittle you. He or she would be an example of inclusiveness and not be divisive or exclusive and would work to expand your knowledge not hinder it. The person would be tolerant and understanding as he or she guided you along your determined path of fulfillment in the areas of justice, equality, freedom and spirituality."

"I would like to get off the subject of enlightenment, if you do not mind."

"I do not."

"Why did you take all those dangerous trips?"

"Love motivated me in taking the trips. I sensed some people needed to make the trips with me. I knew I would meet people in need of growing spiritually and help them."

"Would you have made the trips for your own benefit?"

"No. What I am searching for is within me and to answer your next question, yes it is Beloved."

Moshe grinned.

"Everyone I have spoken to says you are the best healer the village has ever had. Is it because you are enlightened?"

"I do believe the more spiritual and devoted to healing you are the better healer you will be."

"Have you ever been sick?"

"No."

"Will you die from an illness?"

"Of course. This physical body will have served its usefulness and it will cease functioning, afterwards I will exist in a non-physical form and continue to learn about love, consciousness and creation, while experiencing Beloved."

"Are there precepts you have urged your apprentices to follow I can follow?"

"Indeed, I have. It has guided me on my journey of discovery. Many great mystics have shared this wisdom in the past. Keep these thoughts in your heart. Forgive everyone who has injured you, so you can help others to forgive. Where people find doubt, show the strength of your faith. Wherever others find falsehood, reveal the truth. Whoever is in pain, give them comfort. If anyone has lived in silence, sing them Beloved's praise. Where people live in despair, give them hope. If anyone has lived in darkness, bring them light. If they profess hatred, shower them with your love. Above all, always be an instrument of peace."

CHAPTER SEVENTY-EIGHT

Moshe sat across from Kaathi at Batu's meditation tree. It had been days since he had her all to himself. For many cycles of the moon, he had affectionately called her Dear One. It was in response to all the love and attention she had showered on him. They had finished meditating and he needed to share what was in his heart before he left for his home village.

"The time has come for me to return home. I want to thank you for accepting me without hesitation into your inner circle. Thank you for helping me achieve union with my Beloved. Our friendship and what I have learned has been rewarding beyond my wildest expectations. I owe you so much Dear One. I would love to spend the rest of my life with you. Alas I am driven to return to my home to share what I have learned. I hope you are not disappointed with me leaving."

Kaathi reached out and laid her hands on Moshe's, while sending him love. "How could I ever be disappointed with you? You have loved me and blessed me with your presence and yearning to understand your connection to Beloved. By telling me you want to share what we have discussed in private and what you have learned at the Relationship Sessions and the Spiritual Awakening Services, I know you shall be a powerful instrument of peace in your village.

"I have encouraged others to share what they have learned, but you, Moshe, are the first to set out to be the instrument of peace without my asking. Changing the viewpoint and attitude of people is why we created the Relationship Sessions and the Spiritual Awakening Services. You have seen how the sessions and services impact people's lives. You are going to be a marvelous representative in your mission to help your people understand the goodness of the sessions and the sacredness of the services. Through those gatherings and the witness of your experiences with Beloved, they will reap the benefits of you being an instrument of peace."

Moshe nodded moved by her praise. "If I am a worthy instrument of peace, it is because of you Dear One. You have opened your heart and soul to me. You have not held back your wealth of spiritual knowledge and experiences. Doing it has meant the world to me. It showed me I cannot hold back anything to those in my village with a desire to know the truth and know Beloved."

"As you share your understanding, Moshe, be aware there might be one or a few with a deeper desire to know the truth and driven to be in union with Beloved. Take them under your wing and guide them more intimately, for they will be the ones to help you teach others longing for the truth."

"I will Dear One."

"Do not be surprised if women will accept your understanding of the truth quicker than men. Women are heart oriented and men are head oriented. Men will readily change, if they have had military experiences similar to yours."

Moshe knew a few of his soldiers who exhibited signs they had enough of the terrors of war. He made a mental note to contact them upon his return.

"I wanted to tell you of my intention to leave before I said anything to the others."

"I appreciate it. I think the next time we gather as a group it would be appropriate to let them know."

He looked at the mystic. "Are you ever going to journey to Delta Nation?"

Kaathi smiled. "The future unveils in surprising ways."

"Yes it does. Whichever way it unfolds, I wanted to tell you how much I appreciated your love and friendship. I was pleasantly surprised and thankful at how generously you shared your knowledge and experiences."

The next morning Kaathi, Ashlee, Scarlet, Jacob, Keri, Janos, Sharika, Marie, Mara, Kacy and Moshe assembled at Taja's meditation site. The Great Sun was warming the air. A gentle breeze moved over the distinguished group, providing them with an assortment of scents from blooming flowers and decaying plants and leaves. They concluded their meditation, and Moshe cleared his throat to get the attention of everyone.

"I spoke to Kaathi yesterday and let her know I am going to return home. Most likely it will be tomorrow. I have been blessed to have Kaathi and you as my teachers. I am grateful for your patience. I know I have asked a great deal of questions." He paused, looked at Ashlee and smiled. "Not as many as Ashlee, but her circumstance dictated most of them.

"Since I mentioned Ashlee let me start with you and express some of the things I have noticed about you. Almost any woman appreciates being told she is lovely and you my dear are lovely of face. Having had a few chances to talk with you, I found you also have a lovely personality and a great love for Beloved. After all you have suffered at the hands of the mutants, you are a perfect example of forgiveness for people to follow, and I shall endeavor to be as forgiving.

"Scarlet, we have gypsies living in my village. You, my dear, have their free spirit. It is easy to see you as part of the King Edmund's Armada. In my estimation, you would have done anything to have a chance to see Jacob. You have a tenacity about you few others have. An outstanding characteristic about you is your bewitching eyes. I have often succumb to them, and were you not married, I would pursue you until you were mine."

Moshe looked at Jacob. "I apologize if I offended you."

"You have not." Jacob smiled at Scarlet. "Her eyes bewitched me the moment I first saw her in Homar."

"Jacob, it would have been an honor to serve at your side in any military engagement. Kahali is in your hands and they are secure. Over the two years I have lived here, I saw you serve admirably on the council with integrity and intelligence. There is no finer example of a man being strong when needed and gentle when needed. I fully understand why Kaathi selected you to be by her side on the adventures she has taken.

"I want to give praise to you, Keri. You are a ground breaker in Kahali society. You may not have been as driven spiritually but you have all the magnificent qualities of the spiritually driven. You may not have been as vocal and persistent as Batu, but you are a ground breaker. You took two women into your home and it speaks profoundly of your character, strength, love and confidence. The few times I had the privilege of talking with you, it reinforced my opinion of you. You proved to me that you do not have to be spiritually driven to be a wonderful person.

"The quality and intelligence of healers determines the physical health of a community. Kahali is blessed by three such healers. The all-encompassing body-mind-soul approach to helping sick people is proving to be the best approach. The body-mind-soul method is an outstanding one, and Marie, you are an outstanding healer. Marie, I have seen you exhibit confidence time and again in your dealing with the sick. The Kahali are fortunate they have you as their healer.

"Mara, you have gone to the Land of No Shadows for me on two occasions. On the second one, I forgot to inform you that you might encounter individuals still at odds with me. You met them and defused the situation without any problem. I apologize again for having forgotten to tell you about the men.

"I was always interested in your lack of hair and small stature. To your credit you answered all my questions about yourself with dignity and calm. It is a shame your village was not led by you so they could evolve. I am happy you found Coloma to fall in love with. He is a fortunate man to have you bestow your love on him.

"Janos, it has been my pleasure to be your friend. I have enjoyed our hunts and talks. I have never known anyone to turn my sour disposition into a sweet one in the span of a few breaths. I shall remember our easy banter and jokes and smile with their recollection. In chatting with your children, I have noticed they have your gift for making people smile. It is a marvelous trait and rarely passed down from parent to child. Of course in getting along with people, it helps a great deal that your daughter is as beautiful as her mother.

"Sharika, there are two stories in my village relating tales of women from the land of the Amazon River. This race of women were the warriors and the men were the child caretakers. If the tales are true, you are the perfect representation of the Amazonians. You are strong physically and mentally and possess a set of ethics few others can claim. I am proud the Kahali people have recognized your qualities and created stories recounting your prowess. Janos told me you turned down a marriage proposal from Prince Zach. I think you would have been a marvelous asset as a princess.

"Kacy, Kacy, Kacy. Your ability to read energy lights around us is legendary. You also have stories about you as has everyone here. None of us can hide anything from you and yet you love us. You have learned a great deal from Kaathi and the others. You have been very patient with me and all the questions I put to you about what you see represented in the lights around us. I have tried to keep things hidden from you and they proved unsuccessful. You have made me better because I could not hide anything from you. It is a good thing all of us do not have this capability, otherwise we would be at one another's throats.

"I saved you for last Kaathi. I am certain everyone here knows what I am going to say, but I shall say it anyway. I nearly lost my mind along with my arm and life on a battlefield. As I lie recuperating, I knew I survived because there was something I needed to do. During my time alone, I often prayed I would meet someone like you. My prayers manifested dreams about you time and again. Meeting you has tremendously enriched my life. You guided me to experience my Beloved. I never dreamed I would be graced and have a spiritual experience with my Beloved. When I am back in my village, and I am under starry skies, awaiting sleep, I shall tremble and weep, remembering my experiences with you and wish with all my heart I could have stayed to have more."

Moshe bowed his head. "It has been a blessing to love all of you."

Kaathi responded, "I know I speak for all of us when I say it has been a pleasure to share our lives with you and receive your love. You have learned how important it is to have a sense of expectancy and anticipation, so expect the people of your village to accept your good news and brave new thoughts about love and Beloved, and you will succeed. You have cultivated the correct attitude and walked the path of love during your stay with us. Rest assured your loving countenance shall draw people to you and they shall feel your goodness. And remember Beloved is always with you."

Moshe rose and hugged everyone. He had become even more sensitive to energies and now enjoyed the love each one of them bestowed on him. Kaathi was the last to embrace him. Tears had accumulated in his eyes and spilled over as he clung to her.

"Oh my goodness I shall miss you."

"I love you, Moshe, and I shall miss you."

"How am I ever going to describe the essence of who you are to people back home?"

Kaathi smiled. "Do not tell them complicated stories of me. My life and love are simple. If they ask of my relationship with Beloved, tell them I am in love with Beloved, and Beloved is in love with me."

He smiled. It was so like her to downplay who she was. "I am certain there will be resistance to the spiritual message I share with people back home. How can I to convince them I am sharing the truth?"

Kaathi leaned forward and placed her hand over Moshe's heart. He felt the love emanating from her hand and eyes. "Share sincerely and lovingly of your experiences with Beloved. Tell them not to trust what you say. If they are truth-seekers, let them know they have to discover the truth themselves. They have to put forth the effort necessary to discover God for themselves. For it to happen, they must love and seek God and the truth with all of their minds, hearts and souls. Upon uncovering the Source of Love, they will believe everything you have shared."

"Why did you seek Beloved?"

Kaathi looked aside for a moment to collect her thoughts and feelings. "Ever since I can remember, I sensed something, some energy, within me. At the time, I was too young to fully understand the sensation. At nine years of age, I committed myself to discover the truth of who I was. In the same year I made the discovery. I felt immersed in Beloved and Beloved was immersed in me. I knew, at the deepest level of my existence, Beloved's exquisite love always enveloped me, protected me and nurtured me and shall throughout eternity. One day you shall make the same discovery and know it is the same for everyone and all of creation."

The End